Murder At Maple Springs

A
Colin O'Brien
Maple Springs Mystery

Robert John Terreberry

NFB
Buffalo, New York

Murder at Maple Springs: A Colin O'Brien Maple Springs Mystery/
Terreberry- 1st Edition

ISBN: 978-0692738191

1. Murder at Maple Springs. 2. Crime Fiction. 3. Detective. 4. Noir.
5. Mystery. 6. Terreberry.

Author photograph by David Cox
Maps designed by Kathy Cherry
Cover image © 2016 Kathy Cherry

NFB
<<<>>>
No Frills Buffalo/Amelia Press
119 Dorchester Road
Buffalo, New York 14213

For more information visit

nofrillsbuffalo.com

I wrote . . .
You read . . .
win win situation

Hope you enjoy . . .

Goss Terreberry

MURDER AT MAPLE SPRINGS

Lake Erie

I-90 to Buffalo ➢

◄ I-90 to Cleveland

Mayville

Chautauqua Belle

Route 430

CHAUTAUQUA LAKE

Dewittville

Chautauqua Institution

For Roligt

★ Maple Springs

Route 394

Bemus Point

Stow

I-86 to Salamanca →

←I-86 to Erie

Route 430

Lakewood

Celoron

Jamestown

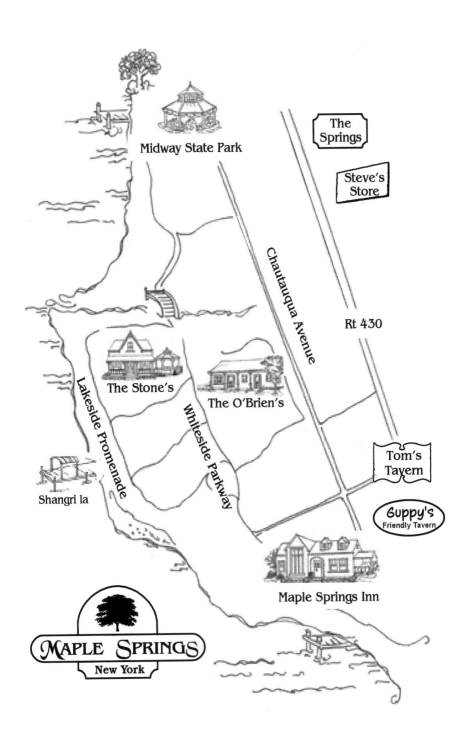

Midway State Park

The Springs

Steve's Store

Chautauqua Avenue

Rt 430

Lakeside Promenade

The Stone's

The O'Brien's

Whiteside Parkway

Tom's Tavern

Guppy's
Friendly Tavern

Shangri la

Maple Springs Inn

MAPLE SPRINGS
New York

CHAPTER 1

Colin loved these days at the lake cottage. Days that start when the sun filters through the pines leaving lacy shadows, and the lake is like a mirror, not even an early morning fisherman. Dew sparkling. Silence. Days that end with a huge red sun sinking down behind the lake horizon and leaving a glowing red sky.

Now every day was a lake day at the lake cottage. Colin would have to stop calling it "the cottage." It was a cottage, but now, it is a house, a home. Funny what a huge chunk of money and great patience can do to make a dinky, rundown summer cottage into a cozy retirement home. Funny what a day in a place like this, a June day at the lake, can do for the soul of a man.

Colin O'Brien had only lived in Maple Springs, on Chautauqua Lake in south western New York State for a few weeks now. He and the Mrs., Vonny, had moved in just as the workmen were finished sanding the last of the spackle. This remake of the cottage into a winterized, livable, year-round home had taken longer than they thought it would. Who would have dreamed that a trucker's boycott, a strike at a window factory in Michigan and excessive rain could slow up a project so much? Actually, the time from the day that the sale had closed until "move in" had stretched into just a little over two years. The big stumbling block in the process had been the sale of the O'Brien's previous home in order to get the money to redo the cottage. That beautiful, three-story house with all hardwood floors, pocket doors, eleven leaded windows and a large fireplace had been a bear to sell. Just the right person had to come along and fall in love with it and have to have it. It took a long time for that person to show up.

Colin and Vonny had loved that house, raised three kids there, called it home for close to thirty years, but it was time to get out of it, out of the city and out of all those organizations that took so much time, energy and patience. They loved living in Jamestown where they could walk to stores and the library and the civic center, and the kids could walk to school. Not that all this walking actually took place, but it was nice to be near places and people, to feel that everything was accessible.

Colin had taught school for 40 years and retired when the school board made teachers offers that they couldn't resist. Actually, Colin was ready to retire, to move on to something different. Colin had taught what was referred to as Special Education. There were great kids over the years and really terrific times, wonderful teaching moments that made it all worth-while, but Colin felt that he was aging, gracefully of course. The students were getting bigger and tougher and he wanted to retire feeling good about kids and teaching and not leaving when he felt bitter or was counting the days until retirement.

Actually, the retirement decision was made on a Thursday, and Friday, the last day of the school year, was the last day of that cumbersome teaching career. No one at school believed him when he told them that he was leaving and that they could have any of his teaching materials that they could use. The administration was sorry to see him go, but knew that they could save a lot of money by hiring a first year teacher to take his place. Fellow teachers, and the students, even the ones that gave Mr. O., as he was affectionately known, a hard time, were stunned. Classroom materials disappeared into drawers and cabinets of other teachers, four boxes of personal things went home and the rest remained for that first year teacher that would work to fill the shoes of Mr. O.

Colin was sure that his retirement would sink in and he would find this new phase of his life rewarding and exciting. This was the long awaited retirement opportunity. The big house was sold, he and Vonny had rid themselves of a lot of stuff and the kids were, more than likely, permanently gone. A move into a small house without room for the kids and their junk would help to make this retirement stick. Oh sure, the kids could visit and would be welcomed and maybe someday there would even be grandchildren, but there would be no thirty-something living with Mom and Dad if Colin could help it. Their stuff? Oh, that was all in a self-storage unit waiting to be claimed and enshrined in the home of its rightful owner. Yeah, right.

Vonny was having trouble with Colin's retirement. She had reduced her work schedule to part-time when Colin retired, but because she was ten years Colin's junior, their dual retirement was a few years off. For Colin, retirement brought with it some free time. Free time was not something that the O'Briens had enjoyed during their years of marriage. They had met backstage at a community theater and then remained part of the theater community for the next thirty years. Free time does not exist when one is involved in a season of five or six theatrical productions. For Vonny and Colin, and soon all three kids, theater was their recreation, their social life and sometimes there was even a monetary profit in the picture, but theater had to be one of those past endeavors surrendered for free time, for retirement time. So, it looked as though the stars had aligned and Colin and Vonny were in the right place at the right time, and all was well with the world.

CHAPTER 2

A walk around Maple Springs was always a treat. There were birds flying and tweeting and there were lots of trees, flowers and bushes in various incarnations. Colin decided to purchase Roger Tory Peterson bird and wildflower guides so that he could identify all those lovely creature and plant neighbors of his. Peterson was an area native and in nearby Jamestown there was a nature institute bearing his name that was inspired by his work. Perhaps Colin would visit, maybe even volunteer there. Probably not right away. Possibly not at all.

It was fun to be a lakeside resident. It was fun to keep track of the neighborhood painting, planting and fixing up that seemed to be endlessly going on. Little men in trucks (as Colin called contractors) showed up each day and did work for someone in one of those more elaborate cottages. Colin and Vonny were the newest residents of Maple Springs, and probably the poorest. Not that they were poor in any sense of the word, but in comparison to the doctors, lawyers and professors from Pittsburgh, Cleveland, Buffalo, etc. that owned 90% of the cottages, the O'Briens were definitely the downtrodden.

Some people were yearrounders, not a lot of them according to the postmaster, Art. There were only three year-round families near Colin and Vonny, but there were others too. Art said there were 45 people in all. He should know. Art was an interesting guy. He and his wife were also relatively new to The

Springs and had reopened a long-closed antique shop. Soon after they opened the shop, when the former postmaster was tired of running a money-losing post office, the post office became part of the antique shop and the newcomers became the postmaster and postmistress, or is it PC to use the term postperson? Either way they were permanent residents with four feet solidly stuck in the community. Silly as it may sound, Colin and Vonny, and other Springers, enjoyed walking over to get their mail and they also enjoyed the pleasant postpersons.

When comparing Colin and Vonny to other Springers, it was obvious that the O'Briens had the least "stuff". No jet skis or boats, no wicker, no stained glass windows and no MGs, Saabs, or BMWs. And the O'Briens didn't compare to the winter weekenders who had all those snow toys and winter paraphernalia. The Springers were mostly those weekenders or summer folk who lived in Cleveland, Pittsburgh, Buffalo or some other distant city (Savannah, Denver, Cincinnati, Baltimore) who needed a retreat from their stress filled lives and who came to Maple Springs for R & R, peace and quiet, escape. Colin and Vonny were yearrounders and newcomers. In fact they were the first new folks to settle in a long, long time, if you didn't count postpersons Art and the Mrs. The weekenders were glad to welcome Colin and Vonny because now that dump of a rental cottage they bought would be fixed up, there would be fewer itinerants (summer, weekly renters) and the O'Briens were a very nice twosome.

Vonny still worked, part-time, but then there is no such thing as a part-time job in social work. She received an hourly rate of pay as a part-time employee, but she worked just about 40 hours a week. Although it was never really computed, she probably earned more as an hourly, part-timer often working 40 hours a week than she earned as a full-time salaried employee working 70 or more hours a week.

The O'Briens had lived just up the road (as Springers said) in Jamestown and had been looking for a place on the lake. This new home was actually just eleven miles from their old home. This move allowed the O'Briens to retain their life in town and to live down the road and enjoy the lake. Their friends from Jamestown loved the fact that they now had access to the lake and they didn't lose the O'Briens to a town in Florida or North Carolina.

Most Springers were pleasant, but were busy with houseguests or children or grandchildren and kept mostly to themselves on their porches, boats and docks. No one seemed mean or snobbish or rude, but then Colin and Vonny hadn't been around long enough for folks to feel comfortable enough to confide in them about the behaviors, manners and the tactics of others. Sure the O'Briens heard about arguments over dock rights and property lines and puppy poop on lawns, but then too those squabbles were easily and amicably settled. No doubt the time would come when the O'Briens would be privy to the details of family squabbles, ancient, of the recent past, present, and even future. Surely at some point, Vonny and Colin would be able to put name and face and cottage and squabble together.

It was impossible to remember cars. It seemed that each weekend brought a new field of motor vehicles. Weekenders must each have four or five at home and drive a different one each weekend, or they are borrowing from neighbors back home in order to impress the other Springers. One set of weekend neighbors arrived in an SUV one weekend and the next, it was that racy MG and then the Volvo with the sun roof. Who could keep track, Colin couldn't. He had no head for cars. They were all the same to him; Coronet, BMW, Volare, he neither knew nor cared.

When Colin and Vonny took evening walks, they tried to learn names from those cute little plaques on the cottages announcing the owners, often their home city or, hopefully, a cute little summer home, lakey name...Week's End, Lazy Akers (guess who lives there?), Serenity Lodge. Many of the cottages had a large stone on the lawn with the occupant's name lasered into the surface. One home, where there obviously lived someone with a great sense of humor, had a stone that said "Our Name". The lady of the house had probably said that she would like a stone with "our name" on it, and that is exactly what she got.

Vonny liked to take a walk in the late evening so that she could see into lighted windows. She made no qualms about her reason for these walks and Colin, just to be sociable, would walk with her. Colin had a better way to see what a cottage looked like. He would, when he knew the owner was back in wherever they lived full time, walk right up on the porch and look in the windows. A much more direct method of solving the curiosity problem, Colin never denied it or made excuses. He one time told Vonny that he was just being neighborly by looking after neigh-

bors' homes when they were out of town and Vonny laughed so
hard that he never tried that lame excuse for nosiness again.

Each home had its own charm and the right stuff to make
it unique and unlike any other cottage in Maple Springs. Vonny
liked to try to guess something about the owners by the way they
decorated their houses. Were they in the arts? Did they have lots
of people to visit them? Were they new rich or old rich? And so
forth. Sometimes she told Colin her assumption and he would
give one of his cute answers (he was full of cute answers)…for
example, "never assume, because when you do, you make an ass
out of u and me."

One Vonny assumption Colin had to agree with. It had
to do with the little white and pink cottage on Lake View Avenue with pink geraniums in the flower boxes and lacy curtains
in the windows. There were also sweet little statues of cats on
most every window sill, all looking out at the passersby who
often returned the curious stares of the cats. Vonny thought the
cottage looked like one of those gingerbread houses that pop up
every Christmas. She called it "confection cottage" for just that
reason. That sweet little place looked good enough to eat. Vonny
was sure that the place belonged to an older couple, she assumed
from the south (definitely not Cleveland or Pittsburgh or Buffalo)
who had money. The place was strictly a bit of fluff in the owner's
lives, not a necessary retreat. It was cute in a sort of old-fash-
ioned way, but there were a few bucks invested in the place
too. One could see the outdoor lights edging the sidewalks, the
satellite dish carefully hidden by the rhododendron, the slivers of

silver tape on the windows that foretold a burglar system guarding the place, and the massive chimney that informed careful observers that a huge fireplace covered most of one wall in the living room. Often men in trucks came to keep the place ship-shape; lawn care folks or a crew from Jamestown Awning. The place was ship shape, but seemed habitually empty.

It was early one Tuesday morning in early June, Colin and Vonny had only been full time Maple Springs inhabitants for a few weeks and Vonny noticed the occupants of "confection cottage" coming out of the front door. She immediately realized that "confection" was an appropriate descriptor for the owners too... there they were dressed in pink and white striped shirts, white shorts and hightop walking shoes, and she had hair like cotton candy, even with a pink rinse, sort of spun up on top of her head. Of course there was a bow on the side of the teased, sprayed confection. Pink. He had on a Captain's hat complete with scrambled eggs on the brim, but the most commanding observation was the identical shapes of the twosome. Except for the hair and hat, they looked like Tweedle-Dum and Tweedle-Dee, or were they Weebles, possibly a set of salt and pepper shakers. Squat was the descriptor that immediately came to mind. It was a much kinder term than what most people might have used.

"Colin, Colin, come quick. You won't believe," Vonny called in a stage whisper to Colin who was in the kitchen scrapping burned omelet from what was once an expensive Teflon pan. He never could quite get the hang of making a decent omelet.

"Won't believe what?" he said as he came into the living

room drying his hands on a dish towel. He stopped, looked out the window with Vonny and made strange hurrumphing sounds.

"That's all you can say?" she asked and Colin wolf-whistled through pursed lips.

"I'm too stunned to talk. I just gotta gawk for a bit," he finally got out.

They both gawked, but then decided that the confectionery couple looked cute and wasn't it great that they were going for a walk around The Springs. Soon the walkers were out of sight and Colin went back to that omelet pan and Vonny finished getting ready for work. Vonny knew the walking route through The Springs and that within about twenty minutes the tacky twosome would be right in front of their house, probably tired by then, and walking slowly. Vonny and Colin could get a really good look.

Sure enough, in just over twenty minutes, there they were right outside the O'Brien's window. In a flash, Vonny grabbed a tin, toll-painted, watering can and yanked out the silk violets "growing" in it and scurried out onto the front porch pretending to use it to water a real geranium. Isn't she bold, thought Colin? Then he heard, "Mornin' folks. Lovely day for a walk." Bolder still. The walkers dueted back, "Howdy", and kept on walking, probably anxious to sit on their porch, get off their feet and out of the early morning sun.

"My, you're a one person welcome wagon," said Colin as Vonny came in proud of herself for getting a better look and in the process being, or at least appearing to be, neighborly.

Before Colin had a chance to make a crass remark, as was

his style, Vonny said, "Gotta go, Hon. Meeting at ten. Lunch with Mom and mammogram at 2:00. See ya for supper. What are we having?" and she was gone. During that one minute recitation of her schedule, she managed to grab her briefcase, a pair of shoes, a purse and a bottle of water. The she was out the door. No love ya or see ya. On the road.

Colin went back to the kitchen, opened the refrigerator to see what supper might be, if he felt like making her supper, and then he heard a car horn honk. He stepped to the door, pushed open the screen just in time to see and hear Vonny roar down the street throwing kisses like Baby June and Rose Louise. Folks in The Springs are gonna get her number, she'll be pegged as old lead foot, thought Colin. He better talk to her about that. How sweet of her to head off in a cloud of kisses. She was a cutie. Looks, brains and personality, and she loves me. In truth, Vonny looked very much as she did when Colin first met her thirty-five years ago: short, or as she says vertically challenged, with short blond hair, an athletes body and eyes and a smile that told you there was a terrific person in there. Okay, he thought, supper will be a priority: grilled portabella mushrooms just as she likes and maybe even vegetable shish-ka-bobs as long as he had the grill going.

Colin quickly put on sneakers and his jaunty little safari hat and off he went to the market. It was exactly an eleven minute walk from the cottage. There were a lot of routes to get there. Today, Colin decided to take the road closest to the lake and check on some of the cottages where there were little men in trucks. It was fun to keep track of these construction projects and to see progress. And progress was being made because "the season" was starting and the owners wanted their retreats ready to occupy. They didn't want to live in sawdust or plaster or with paint fumes. The little men in trucks knew that and valued these wealthy customers and did their best to complete the projects. Colin was so glad that he and Vonny had done everything in one fell, but expensive, swoop. They had done the final interior painting themselves and had been ruthless with the contractor when they had their final walk-through so all the details were attended to; the cottage was completed in every way and Colin would not have to spend his days repairing, repainting or fixing anything. At least that was the theory.

CHAPTER 3

The eleven-minute walk to the market took a bit longer because Colin had to slow down to get a good look and see if the various construction sites showed progress that was noteworthy. He had meant to bring a pad and pen and to write down the name of these little men with trucks so he could call them if, just if, he might need a little repair here or there. He forgot that pad again, but told himself to bring one on his next walk. One truck simply said "The Handy Man" and listed a phone number. How bold, thought Colin, to proclaim yourself "The Handy Man". What were the rest of us? He knew what he was, "The Unhandy Man". He knew too that he had better get that number. He wanted someone with that confidence whenever he had repairs to make. He'd bring that pad and pen for sure next time he headed to the market, Steve's Store.

Steve's wasn't really a super market, but it surely had the stuff the O'Briens liked. Vonny and Colin had been vegetarians for about 25 years and it had taken them a long time to settle into some really good eating habits. When the kids were young, Colin and Vonny had fed them well, no junk, lots of variety, healthy snacks. As the kids got older, it became difficult to keep meals simple, nutritious and affordable, but Vonny and Colin had tried. Now that the kids were gone and living away with "significant others", they had become health nuts and ate using specific diets and only certain products, usually organic, packaged in exotic places like Vermont. Vonny and Colin continued to eat healthy foods and were glad to be out of the short order food business. Meals were simple and predictable. Then too they were not getting any younger and the doctor's warnings kept them away from fried foods, red meats, salt, carbs, etc.

Steve's Store was a funny building that looked like it had grown incrementally over the years. One section had at one time been the post office, there was a deli with questionable looking meats like olive loaf and then a walk-in cooler (mainly for beer), a section with cards and magazines, an area with fisherman supplies including worms by the dozen in styrofoam cups with lids and then the shelves of packaged and canned goods. The market was also a gas station and sold ice and tanks of propane for all those picnicers out there. In the summer, several nearby farmers brought in their wares and Steve offered fresh vegetables and fruits. One farmer, who probably had a consultant in Pittsburgh, even had items obviously not grown locally, but which suited the summer folks and the weekenders. Portobello mushrooms, eggplant, cherry tomatoes, Brussel sprouts, red potatoes and the like were abundant and Colin and Vonny were enjoying having them regularly. Colin was there early in the day and enjoyed picking out the really good stuff.

After he paid for his treasures, he walked to the post office and checked the mailbox and sorted junk from good stuff, although it was hard to call bills good stuff. Outside, he set his bags on a bench to look through the good stuff. There were a couple utility bills, they were smaller now that they were out of that three story mausoleum that gobbled up gas and electricity, and there were also credit card and insurance "reminders". One letter in the bunch was addressed to The Stones, P O Box 133. Colin's box number was 113, so he knew it was just a sorting mistake. He noted that the return address was G.E.M. Stone Jewelry, Inc., Savannah, GA. He immediately thought of the Weebles although the thought had no basis except he wished it was their letter and they did have a bit of an accent when they said 'Howdy'. So Colin decided to take the letter home and try to deliver it himself rather than give it to Postperson Art to be put in the correct mailbox.

Colin put his mail in with his veggies and distributed the weight evenly in his recyclable bags and started home. Along the way he created little scenarios depicting his arrival at the "confection cottage". The flashing scenes ranged from moments of wild thanks and an invitation to enter and eat, to a grumble and a door slammed in his face. He'd risk it in the hopes of having a chance to see the house and get some information on his look-a-like neighbors.

It took exactly seven minutes from the combination post office and antique store to his door and by that time Colin's arms and legs were a bit tingly. That was okay, he was going to continue walking, he would not resort to one of those three wheel bicycles (it's a tricycle no matter how you cut it) in which he saw so many retirees tooling around. Several Springers piloted around in golf carts, but these carts were never going to see a golf course. Colin wasn't resorting to a battery propelled, wheeled conveyance. Not yet. Not ever hopefully.

He quickly put the groceries away and left the fresh vegetables in the sink for washing and was out the door, letter in hand, on his way to "confection cottage".

Colin noticed that there was no nameplate or sign on the cottage as he walked up the brick walk that went from the road to the front steps. The three stairs went to a porch that spread along the front of the cottage and around the corner where the porch became rounded and morphed into a gazebo. It was all furnished in, what else, wicker with cushions in a pink, tea rose pattern, very lovely, very inviting. No sooner had Colin reached the top step when appearing in the doorway was the male weeble, without the scrambled egg hat, in khaki shorts and a pale orange t-shirt. Colin must have registered surprise on his face.

"Howdy, young feller. D'I startle ya?" asked the cottage occupant.

"Why, no, not at all," said Colin not too convincingly. "I just stopped by to…"

"Doesn't matter why you're here. Come on in, sit. We'll get to the why later," said Mr. Weeble and Colin was in, seated in a sunny breakfast nook and drinking coffee before he knew it.

"Gorgeous day here at The Springs. Selma and I don't get much of a chance to get here and 'njoy the lake. We're gonna try to reside here all summer this year. Maybe after our trip, we'll stay a spell and maybe even into the winter months. We're 'nsullated, y'know. You?" the Mr. proceeded.

"Why yes, we are," started Colin. "That was one of our priorities when Vonny and I redid the cottage into our home. Oh, I should really introduce myself."

"We know who ya are," added Mrs. Weeble from the counter where she was arranging almond squares onto a plate. "This is a small community, ya know. And what do you know about us?"

Colin hated to admit that he didn't know anything and was here enjoying their hospitality with one real thought in mind; he wanted more information on these folks.

"Well, I don't know anything really," said Colin. "We are so new here that we don't really have any sources of information. I brought this letter," he said extending it to the Mr. "I'm guessing that it's yours, it was left in my mailbox, and I thought that maybe my bringing it to you would give us the opportunity to get acquainted."

There, he had been honest in telling them why he was there and he didn't have to resort to words like nosy, prying, snooping or gossip.

"Well shoot, you can come anytime you want, ask all the questions you want and ya know what, we'll welcome ya and never invoke that fifth amendment," said the Mr. as he and the Mrs., who was just serving the squares, refilling coffee and getting seated, both laughed a hearty, but gracious, laugh. And the Mr. started in.

"This here is Mrs. Selma Stone," he said and gave Selma a gentle pat on the hand as he spoke. "I call her Cookie sometimes. I'm G.E.M. George…Elliot…Martin Stone. Get it? Here, I'll write it for you," he said as he took a pen out of a cup full of pens on the counter next to his chair, turned over the envelope that Colin had brought and said, "George," then he wrote G., the letter and then a period. "Elliot," he said and he wrote E., the letter and a period. "Martin," he said and he wrote M., the letter and a period. "G.E.M. Stone. My last name is Stone. I'm G.E.M. Stone. Gemstone. That was my Mama's little joke. Daddy, who was a jeweler, never got the joke till after I was born and the birth certificate was printed. Soon the initials were monogrammed and engraved on things and it all said GEMS. Free advertising mother called it. I was never George or Elliot or Martin. The name G.E.M. and I got to be a source of pride for Daddy, so I guess it was a joke gone right."

"I love my G.E.M.," said Selma, and then added, "and my little gems," as she waved two hands loaded with diamond rings, some with emeralds and some with sapphires, "and these are our precious gems too," she said as she pointed to three ornate frames on a kitchen hutch shelf each holding an oil-painted photograph of a beautiful young woman.

G.E.M beamed, the diamonds sparkled in his eyes and his hand walked, just like a hand did in the vintage Yellow Pages advertisement on television, up Selma's ample arm to her shoulder.

"And to me, my Selma is the most rare and treasured jewel in the world," said G.E.M.

There was silence as all three enjoyed the moment and then Colin said, "May I call you G.E.M. and Selma?"

"You sure can, Colin," said G.E.M. "See we know who you are and we've seen that lovely little thing of a wife you have. Her name's Vonny, right?"

Colin only had time to nod before G.E.M. went on. "Our three daughters have appropriate names. What do you think we named these lovely daughters of ours?"

Again, Colin had no time to answer.

"The oldest one is Ruby. A lovely child, so expressive, so bent on helpin' others. Hates jewelry. Sold every piece we ever gave her to help those less fortunate. She's workin' in some mission in Oklahoma or is it New Mexico? In the middle is Opal. Opal is a dancer. Well actually she is a dance teacher at a lovely conservatory in Savannah. We're from down there. And the baby is our Pearl and she is a cultured beauty. She was Miss Peach Pit at age ten and went on winnin' contest after contest till she was Miss Georgia, somewhere in the early 2000's, can't recall the exact year. She was a Miss America runner up too. She's now a contestant adviser and pageant consultant and tours around the US. We love 'em all. None of 'em have an intended that I know of. All livin' on their own, sort of."

Selma made a harrumph sound and Colin knew just what she meant. "Livin' on their own", Colin was sure that it meant living away from home, but tied by the purse strings. He could just see G.E.M. being generous upon many occasions. Generous to a fault.

"My precious girls used to come here ev'ry summer. The Stones have been comin' here since the mid-1940s, three generations, but once the girls started lessons and wanted to go to camp and had boyfriends, they only came for a few days durin' summer. Then they just moaned about how borin' it was and they made our stay miserable, so we hired our own "summer playground director" to stay with the girls in Savannah and Lula and I came here. This is the fifth wonderful summer for me and Miss Selma here and we probably won't see the girls. They say they're comin', but we shall see."

"I'm Mrs. Stone number two," said Selma. "G.E.M. and I married only five years ago after the girl's mama, Lula, passed away. She was a wonderful woman. I was G.E.M.'s secretary for 27 years. No hanky-panky in those 27 years, but with Lula gone, I chased G.E.M., sometimes I slip and call him Mr. Stone even now, and he caught me." This brought on more finger walking, from the shoulder to the ear, and a hearty laugh from G.E.M.

At one point Selma took Colin by the arm and walked him through the small rooms on the first floor of the cottage. Each room was "countrified" (to use Selma's word for Lula's decoratin') and Selma pointed out collectible dishes and nature photographs and small paintings and sculptures, most reflecting scenes of the old west. There were also several small shelves with bric-a-brac that depicted small children or dogs in cute poses. Colors and fabrics were dated and it looked as though not much had changed in those rooms for many years. Pink, green and cobalt blue glassware, visible through the glass doors of the kitchen cabinets, abounded. Dancing Dutch boys and girls were clogging on the mantle and ballerinas on music boxes covered the built-in shelves on each side of the fireplace. Lovely crystal serving pieces, vases and wine and water glasses shone in the built-in china cabinet in the cramped dining room. A tiger maple buffet that matched the dining room table and chairs had a surface covered with a huge silver tea set and matching trays and a cream and sugar set. Probably the buffet drawers were filled with silver flatware. Shades of Grandma O'Brien's house, thought Colin.

Colin felt very comfortable and stayed for a couple hours only excusing himself to hurry home to get the vegetables washed and dinner started. They had to eat early because Vonny had Yoga tonight and hated to go right after she ate.

Colin had learned all about the three generations of Stones that had been in the jewelry business and of the chain of jewelry stores in the greater Savannah area and beyond; G.E.M. said that he "served the jewelry needs of the south." Colin had shared with them about the O'Brien children, his retirement and his plans for the future. Selma and G.E.M. were great fun to be with.

As Colin was leaving, Selma took his arm and said, "Now you and that bride of yours come by for some expresso tonight. We won't take no for an answer. Come to our dock about nine o'clock. We'll be waitin'. We're right off the Promenade, just got the dock functioning today. We'll have candles out. Ya can't miss us."

Colin said yes, was on his way, got busy with supper, and Vonny came home.

CHAPTER 4

Vonny changed into her yoga gear and helped finish dinner preparations. They sat down on the front porch and ate their dinner consisting of fresh vegetables lightly cooked in a wok served over some microwaved rice that Colin always had on hand. Colin decided to save the portobellos for the next day. He told Vonny all about his gaining entrance into the Stone household and all the information he had acquired. Again, he just reported on his adventure and never used words such as nosey, prying, snooping or gossip.

"I don't think I want to go for expresso at 9:00," Vonny said when Colin told her about Selma's invitation.

"You, rather we, have to. Selma wasn't taking no for an answer. You can take a nap when you get home tomorrow. No work on Wednesday afternoons, remember. I'll be off to Rotary and you can get up and have your coffee without me hanging around. It's all planned. Go to Yoga. Get right home and we have a date with Selma and G.E.M," said Colin as he moved in on Vonny and hugged her tightly.

"G.E.M., what kind of a name is that? Okay, okay, I'll get right home and we'll have that coffee. See ya," said Vonny and she was out the door with her Yoga mat and a towel. As usual, roaring away, she honked and was gone. He'd have to talk to her about that lead foot.

Colin had cleaned up the kitchen and himself, e-mailed

the kids, same message to all three, and was sitting on the porch reading when Vonny, home from yoga, slowly drove around the corner and parked on the lawn by the hedge in the back yard. She headed in the back door, surely to quickly change. They were still parking on the lawn because they hadn't figured out where to put a driveway, but that decision would come soon enough, hopefully before winter. Who ever knew there were so many decisions to make when rehabbing a house? The kitchen cabinets alone called for at least a dozen decisions…color, size, material for the counter top, design on the door front, type of handle, width, height, placement, etc. The parking decision would have to wait for some future date and future money.

Colin thought for sure that Vonny would be out on the porch soon, but she didn't appear. He went inside to hurry her along and found her rummaging in a metal safety box where she stored important papers.

"Checking the IRA's to see if you can get it all in a lump sum if I drop dead, or if I'm helped quickly through the dying process?" inquired Colin.

"Cute. If you must know, I am looking for my current driver's license. I thought I had it in my purse. Do you know where it is?" sputtered Vonny.

Colin sensed a problem and was in the midst of vowing to himself that he would not dig for a cute answer when she asked again.

"No, dear," Colin ventured. "Unless you left it in the glove compartment with the insurance card."

She left the room and Colin returned to the porch. She was soon sitting next to him.

"I got a ticket and the jerk got me for every violation he could think of. No license, no seat belt, no signal when I pulled off the road to give him the opportunity to humiliate me, going a little too fast and a piece of a tail light missing. I have to be at the fire hall, I guess that's where they hold traffic court, next Tuesday evening," said Vonny.

Colin, playing the wise man, did not say a word.

"I guess I deserve it," she went on. "I guess that I need a makeover with regard to driving. The license was with the insurance card. I showed him the insurance card, it's the only thing I had going in my favor, but didn't know the license was there. I must have left it there the last time I had to show them both, when there was that insurance mix up last year. Anyway, I will go to the fire hall and not be petulant and pay the fine and call it a lesson learned."

There was a long pause. What could Colin possibly say that would be accepted? He would have opted for "nah, nah, I told you so", but he was far too wise to go there.

"Let's go gab with Selma and G.E.M., you'll find them delightful," said Colin as he stood up and pulled Vonny up from her chair and hugged her gently.

"Where is their dock?" asked Vonny.

"They said it was right off the Promenade and that we should look for candles," answered Colin.

CHAPTER 5

And, oh boy, were there candles. The dock was white and seemed very long with a platform at the end of the dock that seemed to float over the water. A green and white striped tent covered the platform. It wasn't one shade of green and one shade of white, it was many shades of green, variations of white, with differing stripe widths, all intermixed. At each station that held up the walkway of dock pieces, and there seemed to be two dozen, there was a candle in a wrought iron holder that hung from a pole. It was like the scene from *The Phantom of the Opera* where the Phantom floats away with Christine through a forest of candles in the labyrinth of streams under the Paris Opera House. Colin and Vonny didn't say a word, but just looked at each other and walked side by side, for the dock pieces were that wide, out to the tent at the end of the dock. If they thought it was lovely getting there, they were even more awestruck when they walked onto the platform under the tent.

The platform was covered by green carpeting that looked just like grass and not that bright, green, fake astro-turf that one sees at every miniature golf course in the country. No, this looked just like grass, real grass, with variations in color and size of blades. Colin wanted to kneel down and touch it, make sure it wasn't real, but he resisted the temptation.

"Sit down, let us get you a drink, we got everything you could want," said G.E.M. as he opened the double doors of a

stainless steel, compact, waist-high refrigerator that held everything from wine coolers to splits of champagne.

Vonny sat quickly before she collapsed in awe and Selma
sat right next to her and said, "Hi, Vonny. I am Selma Stone and
this is my little man, G.E.M. We are so glad to meet you. Your
sweetheart was at our little cottage today and we just felt we have
been his friends for years. We're sure we'll feel that way 'bout you
too. G.E.M., get the lovely lady a drink or maybe you'd like that
cappuccino I promised your guy?"

Vonny asked for hard lemonade and as G.E.M. poured it
into a frosted glass, she managed to get a good look at the dock
platform. It was wonderful. Besides the stainless steel refrigerator, there was a small sink and a grill with a little warming plate
on the side. In a tall, thin, glass-doored cabinet next to the sink
there was a full set of pink carnival dishes with glasses to match,
stemmed glasses. The furniture looked like wicker and the pillows looked like leather, but in reality it was probably a mixture
of plastic and synthetics, but either way it looked lovely and was
very comfortable. Selma had never been to Wal-Mart.

"We call this little bit of heaven 'Shangri La,'" said Selma.
"You remember that movie, don't you? *Lost Horizons.* Ronald
Coleman and Margo were the stars, I think. There was this lost
city up in some mountains somewheres and there everything was
perfect and no one ever aged. That city was named Shangri La
and this here is our Shangri La. Although we haven't figured out
that non-aging trick just yet." Selma said this as she pointed to a
lovely hanging sign that looked like jewels glued to a long piece of

mirror that spelled out the dock platform name.

As G.E.M. handed Vonny her lemonade, he pushed into place in front of her a footstool that was part table. Before it could catch her legs in between the footstool and her chair, Vonny whipped her legs in place, onto the footstool, took the drink from G.E.M., went limp in the comfortable furniture and uncontrollably let out a loud sigh.

"Now that's a satisfied guest," laughed Selma as she lifted her glass in a salute to Vonny.

Colin asked for a beer, his only vice in the alcohol family, and he too melted into the furniture. Candles on the tables and on hooks hanging from the canopy let off a lovely smell. Small bouquets of wild flowers added just the right accent colors and the company was divine. Life in Maple Springs was getting greater all the time, thought Colin.

CHAPTER 6

The first meeting of the O'Briens and the Stones went by swiftly. The O'Briens enjoyed drinks, nibblies, laughter and later a walk home and a collapse into bed.

The alarm buzzed Colin awake and he was off to the shower and quickly on the road for his Rotary meeting. Colin had belonged to Rotary for over twenty years and loved the meetings, his fellow Rotarians and the projects they completed to help improve the community. He proudly wore his perfect attendance pin, but didn't have it or the standard Rotary International pin on today. That surely would earn him a fine, but if he had looked for it, he would have been late for the meeting and that would be a fine too. He'd take his chances that no one would notice his lack of appropriate Rotary jewelry.

As he drove along Route 86 to town, Colin thought about the socializing that had occurred last night, about the charming Stones and the plans the four had made for an antiquing trip on the weekend. G.E.M. and Selma were a hoot. They knew how to include you in conversations, how to make you forget cares and pains and to enjoy yourself. Surely there were a lot of things they could all enjoy this summer. The Stones have been coming to the cottage for three generations, well four actually counting the precious Stone daughters, and even though stays weren't generally long, G.E.M. knew the area well. The three precious girls hadn't spent the summer at The Springs for many years, but apparently that hadn't stopped Lula and G.E.M. or Selma and G.E.M. from enjoying the lake, the glorious summer and the magic of Maple Springs.

The Rotary meeting was terrific. The fact that Colin was out of Rotary uniform had gone undetected, a great breakfast of French toast with pure, local maple syrup and a talk by an exchange student from Brazil had all contributed to his enjoyment. The fact that he left the meeting without a task to complete was great too. That was Colin's current goal for every meeting he went to, get out unscathed, no fund raising duties to perform, no committee to serve on or job to complete. After many years of activity for the benefit of his community, Colin not only retired from his job, but retired from the offices, boards and committees he served on. Time for a break. Maybe he'd serve again. Maybe. Probably not.

Colin liked Wednesdays because he had Rotary and Vonny only worked a half day. They usually tried to plan something special even if it was just a trip to the outdoor market or to Amish country for fresh eggs and baked goods. A leisurely cup of coffee and a bagel on the lakeside deck of the Italian Fisherman in Bemus Point was usually part of their day, even into the fall months when they were the only ones on the deck. Once the owner, Don, had even swept off snow and had a chiminea on the deck by their table so they could be out there on the Wednesday before Thanksgiving. If Vonny got home early enough today, maybe they could just hang out on their dock for a while. After all of the work and money put into that dock, it was only the right thing to do, to lounge there, savor the sturdiness of the structure, be enveloped by the sun.

Colin decided to pack some sandwiches and press their mini-cooler into service and leave a note telling Vonny where he was. By 11:00 he had completed a few chores, made sandwiches and was lounging on the dock in a folding canvas chair reading his favorite magazine, *The Week*. He woke up when something got between him and the sun. It was Vonny trying gently to wake him. She had a bag of apple fritters from Jones Tastey Baking, his favorite, and she was looking great in a floral two-piece bathing suit she just bought at Skillman's in Bemus Point. It looked very expensive, but he was sure that she'd say that she got it off a reduced rack. Right.

"Hi Hon. Enjoying the solitude?" she asked.

"Not now," was his, he thought, cute answer. "I brought lunch and am not leaving until it's dark and swooping bats drive me homeward."

By 3:00 they were home, kneeling on thick foam mats trying to sculpt the flowers, rocks and statuary in the garden that ran along their front porch and under the trees at each end. Late last summer before they had even moved in, they had planted perennials, lots of irises, hosta, ground sedum and little purple flowers that were also guaranteed to spread out. They were sure that their work last year would be evident in this year's garden. This year too, they would buy some colorful annuals to insure that the garden was full, maybe even crowded. As they worked the earth and carefully planned their garden so that it would be spectacular, they hardly spoke, but were still enjoying the task, each other and the lovely day.

"Looks like too much work to me," said G.E.M jumping up and then balancing on a big flat rock in the middle of the garden.

"Hello, loves," said Selma.

"Well, hello. Out for a walk?" asked Colin as he unsuccessfully endeavored to stand with some grace.

"Just that," said G.E.M stepping onto the small patch of lawn between the garden and the road. "Enjoyin' the sun and that breeze offa the lake. Portends rain ta me. If ya get done there and can hobble to the cottage, we are having a Summer Wine Festival, local stuff, and a spread of dippin' breads, cheeses and that hummus I know you vegetarians will love. Payne's Pantry's caterin', we're invitin' and hope you'll be eatin' and drinkin' with us...5:00, our back deck. Rain or shine. Right Selma?"

"We should have mentioned our annual Summer Wine Festival when we were with ya last night, but we got so relaxed and I just plum forgot. We'd love to have you join us, meet some new folks, but if you have other plans, we understand. Oh, and don't forget Saturday, breakfast at The Springs Restaurant at 7:00 and off to Salamanca. That casino is open 24 hours a day you know," said Selma excitedly.

"I've had enough of this forced labor," said Vonny and she stood more successfully and gracefully than Colin. "We will be along as soon as we get cleaned up and I plaster Colin with Bengay. You two get going, you'll have guests soon."

The four parted, each headed to tasks needing to get done and with an excitement for the upcoming Summer Wine Festival.

CHAPTER 7

Who knew there was a back deck at the "confection cottage"? Who knew it was so large, built around a tree and could easily hold thirty-plus people? Again, the Stones had furnished an area so that it looked incredibly expensive, invitingly comfortable and easily cared for. The deck was painted high gloss white and trimmed with shades of yellow and orange as was the trim on the back of the house. The other three sides of the house were white and trimmed in pink, so this back area looked like it didn't even belong as part of the cottage. Having a party "rain or shine" was possible because of the two huge Mexican print roll-up-awnings that were, so far, only partially unfurled. The deck-o-rations, as Selma later called them, had been inspired by a tour of Mexico that she and G.E.M. had taken, and obviously a designer had been used, no expense had been spared and the end result was enfolding all the guests as they arrived.

Colin and Vonny, it appeared, were some of the final arrivees. Selma greeted them, separated Vonny from Colin and whisked her off to meet some of her local lady friends. Colin went to the bar area under one of the awnings and joined G.E.M. and some other men pontificating over the caliber, smell, bouquet, etc. of local wines.

"Colin, glad you made it. Everyone! This here is Colin O'Brien. Colin and the lovely Mrs. O'Brien just reconstructed the old Whitbeck cottage and are gonna be yearrounders. Colin, this

is Bernie King, sounds like he's a bandleader doesn't it? He's just
four doors down facing the lake. This here's Tim McMillan. He's
a vet, but I'd trust him with my medical care in a second. He and
Cindy live in the cottage that backs up to our yard here. We share
the croquette court you see spread out there. You play croquette,
Colin? Course you do. You'll have to join us some time. We play
for money. You game? Course you are. One summer, hot as hell,
we had a few Tanguary and Tonics and we played strip croquette.
Not a pretty sight. 'nough said. Welcome Colin. Beer's your
drink and I got local stuff from the Southern Tier Brewing Company. Help yourself."

And with that G.E.M. rolled to Colin a huge, round cooler
on wheels filled with ice and a wide variety of beers. Colin took
one that had a label promising a wheaty flavor and he shook a
couple hands and easily fell into the conversation which turned
from wine to fishing.

Vonny had a similar experience meeting folks as Selma
guided her around the deck and introduced her lady friends.
Each time she met someone new, Selma also pointed across the
deck indicating Colin and his role of husband. Vonny thought
that the ladies looked too long at Colin, but then Colin was a
handsome man, solid, still with lots of hair, over six feet tall with
almost a pretty-boy face. She had to admit that, but then too
these were not "desperate housewives" so she could readily go to
work each day and not have to worry about her house-husband
being compromised on the homefront.

Vonny met Binky King, wife of Bernie, and her pursedog,

not unlike a lapdog, Elgin. The humans were retired interior designers. It seems as though Elgin was a perfect guest and was never left alone or in the care of other family members or, heaven forbid, strangers.

Cindy McMillan introduced herself as the wife of "dog boy over there" and indicated Tim standing next to Colin.

"But seriously, Vonny," said Cindy, "he is a vet and a darned good one. He specializes in caring for fancy dogs owned by rich folks back home. Some of his clients have been to the Westminster Kennel Club shows in New York City. He's very much in demand in doggie circles in Cleveland. Before we go any farther, Vonny, that's a different name. Where'd that come from?"

"Oh, it's not so strange in my family," said Vonny as she started an oft repeated story. "My real name is Veronica, and somehow, back a generation or two, it got shortened to Vonny. My mother and grandmother are both Veronicas and both got stuck with Vonny too. The Bible tells the story of Veronica who was the woman who stepped forward and wiped Jesus' brow as He carried the cross to Calvary. Though stories conflict regarding Veronica's true identity, she was at one point declared a Saint and my great-grandmother claimed that she was visited by Saint Veronica when she was pregnant with my grandmother. Saint Veronica identified herself and told my great-grandmother that for generations her offspring would only work in the healing professions. Saint Veronica also told great-grandma that she was a blessed woman, the descendent of ancient healers and leaders and entreated her to encourage others to serve their fellow man.

My great-grandmother was very devout, and even more devout after that visit. In fact, after my great-grandfather died, she became a nun, at age 73. Oh, I am sorry, it got a little heavy there. But that is the story of how the name Veronica got into generations of my family and yes, before you ask, I have a daughter, Ronny, short for Veronica."

"I think that is a lovely story and I love the name Vonny," said Selma as she worked to be the perfect hostess and moved Vonny along to meet others.

"Now Selma, don't you whisk Vonny away. Go get her a Tanguary and Tonic and let us ask her more about this saint sighting four generations ago," said Cindy McMillian.

Selma hurried away and Vonny spoke right up. "Sorry ladies, but that is it. Great-grandma Ruth took it all very seriously and named her unborn child, thank heavens it was a girl, Veronica and encouraged her to go into nursing. My mother was also a nurse and mid-wife and I work as a social worker in a nursing home. There are lots of health care practitioners on both sides of my family and in Colin's family too."

Vonny was glad to see nods of heads and smiles and then the conversation moved to other topics, but Vonny knew the ladies would all be repeating that story to their husbands when they got home later. She didn't care, it was true and she felt that it gave her a certain cache so that folks would remember her. Vonny didn't have to worry, she was lovely, exotic even, and always remembered, especially by the men.

"I bet you're wondering where the name Binky came from,

aren't you Vonny?" said Binky as she grabbed Vonny by the elbow and steered her to a small swing next to a huge planter at the end of the deck. Although Vonny wasn't really curious about knowing where Binky, the name or the person, came from, she was sure that she would find out that and a lot more. True, Binky was a talker and the three of them, Binky, Vonny and Elgin, the pursedog, did spend a lot of time on that swing, but it was quite enjoyable and Vonny and Binky had a lot in common and Vonny was glad to meet her and all the other ladies at the party.

Colin also enjoyed himself and had lots of laughs with "the boys" as G.E.M. call the assembled men from The Springs. He learned that this Summer Wine Festival was considered to be the opening social event of the summer social season in Maple Springs. G.E.M. and Lula had initiated the party years ago and it continued even during the last two, unhealthy years of Lula's life. G.E.M. and Selma re-deck-o-rated and eagerly continued the tradition. Colin spent a lot of time trying to put names, faces, cottages, cars and home towns together, but he quickly realized that this was going to be a sharp learning curve for him. By the time he figured them all out and got them sorted and categorized, summer would be over, they'd be gone, and he'd have to start all over again next summer. He also learned that many of these folks were third and even fourth generation Springers. They willingly came all that way, from wherever, for a few weeks in a small summer community on a small almost unknown lake. The O'Briens were soon to learn how special, how inviting and, even, how exciting Maple Springs could be.

CHAPTER 8

Colin should have realized when the Summer Wine Festival started at 5:00 that it wasn't going to be in motion once the sun set (8:47 on this particular day). A great time was had by all, food and conversation were great and Vonny and Colin were home and in bed reading by 9:15. The O'Briens were now confident that Maple Springs was a great place to live. Colin really liked the fact that the Springers had this unwritten law concerning the length and depth of their party making. Folks weren't party poopers, they just had a great time wherever it was that they were partying and then they called it a day. Actually Colin admired the skill, and it was a skill, of knowing when to go home. He equated it with a habit demonstrated by most dogs; they played hard, swam in the lake, chased squirrels or whatever and then once they had enough, they just found a comfortable spot, flopped themselves down, did some meaningful stretching and went to sleep. Springers showed up, were polite and, in most cases charming, and then they easily walked home and rested for another lovely day in lovely Maple Springs. Oh, there might be a few people sitting on their porch, sometimes as late as eleven o'clock, but they were quiet in deference to those at home re-charging for the next day. Early rising was also a feature of the inhabitants of this sleepy, lakeside community. Up early, but quiet for the other locals still sleeping. What a civilized place to live.

And this was how the summer was going; lovely and

charming and ever so civilized. Colin and Vonny soon were swept up in the social swirl that engulfed The Springs: wine on a cozy porch, homemade brownies on a Saran wrapped plate left on your porch by a kind neighbor, a honk as a neighbor drove by, a neighborly offer to share iris bulbs, invitations for boat rides, to join a book discussion group or for an early evening pot luck dinner were just some of the pieces of the summer that were so welcomed and enjoyed by Vonny and Colin.

But, it was the almost daily contact with Selma and G.E.M. that made this first summer in Maple Springs so enjoyable for the O'Briens. They shared past experiences that brought them close: cancer scares, caring for disabled parents, religious conversions, tragic losses of siblings.

It didn't take long for this foursome to synchronize their free time and to hit the road visiting local attractions. Their first trek was to neighboring Salamanca. They hit the road east, Route 86, right after the "farmers breakfast" served up at The Springs Restaurant. In reality, no farmer could eat all that and then get themselves up on a tractor for a day's work. Salamanca held many enticing attractions, but it was the Seneca Casino that lured them at first and it was the Seneca Indian Nation Museum, the Railroad Museum and the Antique Mall that were in reality more exciting. At the Casino, they all agreed to only play twenty dollars each and to share their winnings. G.E.M. was the only winner and he generously treated everyone to lunch at the Casino' smorgasbord (the Native-Americans didn't use that word) and he bought museum tickets for everyone. They were all dazzled by the antique mall with its dealer-defined areas filled with all types of antiques and collectibles. Shopping there was like traipsing through a museum of middle-America from the '50s with Coca Cola memorabilia and all types of hats, toys and books to the great antique furniture, jewelry and statuary. Each couple bought a couple treasures, ostensibly for an unnamed friend, and a good time was had by all.

The Stones planned what they called a "mystery trip" and had the O'Briens meet them at "Shangri La" early one Wednesday evening.

"Wear something warm, but comfortable," was Selma's directive when she invited them on Tuesday.

When they got there, a wonderful, obviously antique, wooden boat was tied up at the end of the dock. On board were G.E.M. and Selma dressed alike in white pants and navy blazers with red polo shirts and, thank goodness, no hats. Bernie and Binky King were also aboard, dressed more sedately in khaki and navy blue. Vonny thought that she and Colin were properly attired in their black jeans, white t-shirts and lime green, zip-up hoodies.

"Get yerselves aboard. Cap'n Tommy is anxious to get underway and Mate Jeanmarie is tellin' us that dinner is about to be served," said G.E.M.

Colin and Vonny boarded with help from another mate, Alex, who appeared and offered assistance, and off they shoved. The boat turned out to be the "For Roligt", Swedish for "for fun". The boat, a 43 foot 1903 Mathews Day Cruiser, had originally been owned by the Packard Family, of Packard car fame, and was now available on the lake for what G.E.M. called lolling. The Packards had built several homes on the lake shore and were, in past generations, regular visitors to the area. Later when Colin talked with Captain Tommy for a minute, he learned that Henry Ford, Thomas Edison and Harvey Firestone had all been passengers at one time.

After their lovely, light vegetarian dinner, with fruity local wine, they made it to the Chautauqua Institution on the other side of Chautauqua Lake where a golf-cart-like vehicle met them and whisked them from the dock to the 3000 seat amphitheater where they enjoyed the "Boys of Summer". Those boys, hardly still in the boy category, were Fabian, Bobby Rydell and Frankie Avalon, singing those same, great '50s songs with lyrics still familiar to the six friends. It turned out that Binky and Bernie were personal friends of Frankie Avalon and at the box office waiting for all six of them, there were front row tickets and a pass for backstage afterward. Binky and Bernie had redecorated the Avalon's house in Beverly Hills a total of three times over the course of the King's twenty five years of operating a home décor business in the LA area and the Kings and the Avalons had formed a mutual admiration society.

The show was great and afterward all "the boys" were very charming and Binky was the center of attention. Bernie, and of course Elgin was along for the evening, hovered and beamed as Binky made introductions. The backstage time was short because "the boys" soon boarded a customized travel bus and had to hit the road to Cleveland where they were appearing at the Rock and Roll Hall of Fame and at a political fundraiser the next day.

The Springers made their way back across the lake enjoying espresso and canolis, served by the lovely Jeanmarie, which capped off the evening. Once the O'Briens were in their own bed, sleep appeared before their heads hit the pillows.

Colin and Vonny also planned a "mystery trip", this time to Amish country and both the Stones and the O'Briens bought toys and quilts and maple syrup. They resisted hooked rugs, pastry and baskets. G.E.M. and Selma bought quilts to take back to Atlanta as gifts for the friends who were watching their cats. Colin and Vonny bought a baby quilt for that first grandchild they were sure would be part of their family at some point.

Summer proved to be incredibly short. Never was so much food, friends and fun crammed into what Vonny and Colin thought would be their lazy season. Wine and beer were consumed. Colin even rented a jet-ski for a weekend of roaring up and down the lake. Walks were enjoyed after dark to see all the people sitting on their porches with candles glowing and white wine flowing.

G.E.M., Selma, Colin and Vonny got to be great friends. Vonny thought the age difference would prevent them from seeing much of each other, but the mathematical difference proved to be smaller than Vonny liked to admit and to not be a problem at all. In reality, they were all in the same generation and all young at heart. The foursome browsed, ate and shopped at The Viking Trader gift shop, lolled again, this time on the Chautauqua

Belle steamship and they enjoyed the 4th of July fireworks and a great parade and an afternoon of games at The Springs with all the Springers and their extended families visiting for the holiday.

During all this togetherness, the Stones told the O'Briens about their upcoming trip to Italy, or as G.E.M. called it, It'ly. And the inhabitants of that far away country were, of course, Eye-talions. G.E.M. gave Colin his travel agent's e-mail address and Colin, with G.E.M.'s permission, requested a copy of the trip itinerary and a map of Italy highlighting their stops up and down Italy's western coast.

As scheduled, in late August, the Stones headed to Toronto and took an over the top of the world air flight to Rome. Colin and Vonny thought that things would settle down for the end of summer, but it was during late August that all three O'Brien children came home to visit. It was great fun to have the kids around. Actually it was a flurry of meals and friends from Jamestown coming to see the kids and a lot of late nights. And with the kids, came dogs. Colin loved the dogs, but two, big, shedding, slobbering canines have a way of taking over. Luckily it was great weather and everyone, dogs included, was on the porch, on the dock and in the lake. The best part of the visit was the excursions to Midway State Park which was an historic trolley park that was part of Maple Springs. When the O'Brien kids were young, the family had spent many summer afternoons on the giant slide, the Hershel Carousel and the dodge 'em cars. These latest trips to the park were really trips down memory lane for the kids. Skeeball and frozen custard were the lures this time around.

Vonny took a couple days of vacation and spent most of it cooking. But she loved that Harriet Nelson role and the kids helped prepare, not clean up, and so all went well for the six days the kids and their mates and dogs were home. Actually, it wasn't home to the kids. They still loved that big, old house in Jamestown. They never lived in Maple Springs and if the truth be told, they probably thought the move was silly, the house too small and the Springers a bit stuffy. But they lived away, had lives of their own, friends and jobs, and Colin and Vonny were blissfully happy in The Springs. They had actually made a great investment in real estate and were trying to stay healthy and out of the kid's hair. The kids were out of their parent's hair and it was only fair to return the favor.

Ronny, their eldest, and her fiancé Dan, both teachers, drove in from West Virginia. Jack and his long term girlfriend flew in from Vermont. Colin loved Lindy, the girlfriend, but never quite knew what to call her: the significant other, the partner, the life partner, the squeeze. She was great, like a daughter, and a good influence on Jack. Erin and her long-time partner, Carrie, could only stay for a long weekend, had to get back to work and their two dogs which they had thoughtfully left home. The eight people crowded into the small cottage had a great six days, although it seemed longer, and when the six adult children and two dogs were gone, it was very quiet. Very quiet.

CHAPTER 9

Colin had promised to water the perennial garden at the Stone's cottage and G.E.M. gave him a key and showed him the list of emergency telephone numbers that were magneted to the refrigerator. Colin made a copy at Quick Solutions Copiers so that if he were to have to make an emergency call for the Stones or to the Stones, he could make it from home. After their Italian trip, Selma and G.E.M. planned to be back in Maple Springs for a few days in September before heading to sunny Savannah thus avoiding the sure to be rugged Western New York winter.

As yearrounders, Colin and Vonny were finding that they were being asked by some absentee owners to look in on a house or to check a particular door after a storm, a sump pump after a heavy rain. Summer residents battened down the hatches before leaving The Springs for the winter. Boats were stored, docks and boat hoists brought ashore, porch furniture covered or even brought inside. Maple Springs got very secured and deserted. Often during winter, summer residents kept their furnaces on low heat and had lamps in their windows with red light bulbs in them which turned on when the indoor temperature dipped below what the residents had it set at, usually 55. If yearrounders noticed a light on as they were out walking their dogs, cross country skiing or snowshoeing, they were to call a local plumber for a quick boiler check. Most Springers drained their water pipes for the winter.

Colin was glad to oblige his neighbors and even had a special key rack by his back door that contained labeled cottage keys proffered by many of the summer folks. It was the O'Briens' first year as solid, permanent residents and yet folks trusted them with keys. As Colin eyed the keys, he couldn't help but feel accepted.

Colin carefully plotted the Eye-talian tour of the Stones on his map. He highlighted all of the stops on the Eye-talian eye-tinerary and waited for promised post cards to arrive from each destination.

Three cards came at once. The earliest postmark was on a card that gave a great view of their five-star hotel in Rome, the Palazio de Roma. The second card was a depiction of the Coliseum with half of the card "before" and the other half "after", then and now. The last card was a pen and ink drawing of a narrow, meandering street in the little village of Avitzia which was a two hour drive south of Rome. It was a village inhabited mostly by artists and G.E.M. and Selma had been there before, had a favorite pension, enjoyed several local restaurants and knew some Americans who had retired there whom they were anxious to visit again. The Stones were sure that the Avitizia stop would be the highlight of their tour. To make this tour stress-free, G.E.M. had rented a car and hired a driver to whisk them from place to place. Colin and Vonny thought that was a great idea. Selma and G.E.M. were not in the best of health and not a couple of kids backpacking through Italy, so a driver would facilitate matters and help the Stones to safely keep to their itinerary.

Regular post cards were going to help the O'Briens travel vicariously throughout Italy. Both G.E.M. and Selma signed their name on each of the three cards and a heart was drawn around the names ala high school romances. G.E.M.'s signature was all fancy capitals with a bold dot after each letter. Selma provided the short commentary on each card and after a couple of Xs and Os there was her name and that cute little heart; "Weather is great, we're having fun, food to die for." After reading the cards, Colin drew a line with a hot pink hi-liter from Rome to Avitzia. He then tacked the cards on the perimeter of the map that he had attached to his small bulletin board covering all his reminder notes, some of which had been there for months. It was to be a five week tour with five stops, the first and last being Rome. This would bring G.E.M. and Selma back to The Springs for a few days to close up for the winter, with help of course, and maybe they'd even get a good glimpse of the fabulous fall foliage that was the habit of Western New York State. Vonny and Colin missed their new-found friends, but were happy that they got to take this long awaited, planned and deserved vacation. A reunion in September was sure to be a joy.

It was three weeks into the tour and there were no more postcards since the first cluster of three. Vonny was concerned that things abroad weren't going smoothly for the Stones. Colin told Vonny not to be a worry-wart, but if they didn't receive a postcard in a day or two, he promised Vonny that he would use one of those emergency telephone numbers and make sure that all was well. That evening as he checked his e-mail, hoping to get messages from a kid or two or three, he received a message from the Stone's travel agent in Savannah asking Colin to call the agency first thing in the morning. The agent provided an eight hundred number and signed the message Kyle. Now, Colin too became a worry-wart.

At 8:59 the next morning, Colin took the telephone, a cup of decaf, his map, pencil and paper, and went out onto the porch to call Savannah. Vonny had gone off to work in her worry-wart mode and Colin had promised to call her as soon as he talked to the travel agent.

When the receptionist at the Peach State Travel Bureau answered all southern and business-like, Colin asked for Kyle.

"Whom shall I tell Kyle is calling?" she cooed.

"Just tell Kyle that I am a friend of Selma and G.E.M. Stone and I am calling from Maple Springs, New York. I am calling in response to her yesterday's e-mail," explained Colin.

The receptionist, maintaining a syrupy demeanor that Colin thought she couldn't possibly continue throughout the day, said, "Just one moment, sir. Kyle will presently be joining you on the line."

Telephone elevator music played for about twenty seconds and then a low, female voice said, "Hello, Mr. O'Brien. This is Kyle Kennedy speaking. Thank you for calling."

"Hello, Kyle. Kyle, you're a surprise. I thought Kyle would be a guy," said Colin fumbling so as not to be rude or sexist.

"I get that all the time. Actually, I think it has helped people to remember me. I get a lot of return customers. Mr.

O'Brien, I remember sending you the itinerary and the map of Italy so that you could track the Stones on their trip. I am so sorry to have to be the one to call you and tell you the sad news from the Stones in Italy."

Kyle stopped talking and Colin quickly asked, "Are they OK? We haven't heard from them for a few days. Actually, I was going to call you, or someone, in a day or so, but then your e-mail came and I called. Go ahead, tell me, I'll shut up."

"Well, it is so sad, sad," she said, her voice getting lower, quieter and a bit of a drawl slipping in. "Selma passed away two days ago. They were in Avitzia. In a lovely pension with a charming Italian couple hosting them. Apparently Selma wasn't feeling well. They thought she had too much sun, she went to the room to lie down before dinner and when Mr. Stone went to check on her, she was dead. He said she was just lying there looking so peaceful that he thought she was asleep. He tried to wake her, but she was gone."

"Gone," repeated Colin. "Just like that. Gone."

"Yes, sir. The host called a doctor that lived nearby, but Selma was gone."

There was silence on the line as both Kyle and Colin digested the ramifications of the word gone. Neither wanted to hear the word again.

"Well, Kyle, thank you for calling and for breaking the bad news so gently. I'll bet that this conversation isn't like one you have ever had before as part of your work day," said Colin.

"I have never lost a traveler before. I've arranged huge

spring break tours, weddings in Cancun, even Himalayan tours and always brought them back alive. And I loved Selma and G.E.M. They helped me to get through travel school and even put up my share of the money to go into this business with two friends from down home. I will really miss Selma. They promised to bring me to Maple Springs some time. Not sure that that will happen now," Kyle said, her voice starting to show the stress of having to break the sad news and to recall the kindness of the Stones.

"Kyle," said Colin, "I have a few questions. How is G.E.M.? Where is he now? Is the body being sent home, to Savannah? What can we do to help?"

"I received a very long e-mail from G.E.M. this morning. I will forward it on to you and then you can see what is to happen. Apparently he and Selma had discussed what to do if there was some sort of emergency. I don't know if death was discussed, but they did have contingency plans and G.E.M. outlines what he'll be doing. You read it and then please call me because he's asked that you and I, and of course your wife, and Scarlet his secretary, to be the only ones involved in his planning. I want to do what he wants, but I feel burdened with this knowledge and no one to share it with."

"Kyle, send me the e-mail and I will get right back to you. I am sure that G.E.M. is being rational and I bet we can help him out. There has to be a ton of things to do. Just the business of dealing with a body and then there is the trip itself, tickets to change, etc. We'll talk, I promise. Send me that e-mail. Okay?"

Kyle said that she was forwarding the e-mail as she spoke and she repeated her request that Colin get back to her as soon as possible.

They both hung up, shook-up, but eager to help G.E.M.

By the time Colin got into the house and booted up his computer, the e-mail from Kyle Kennedy in Savannah was in his in-box. He didn't even read it on screen. Instead, he clicked on print and went for his car keys and sun glasses. He had to go see Vonny at work. This wasn't news to share over the telephone as poor Kyle had had to do.

CHAPTER 10

"What are you doing here?" said Vonny as she looked up from her desk to see Colin standing in her office doorway. He didn't answer. He shut the door and sat down in the chair next to the desk.

"Oh no. It's news from Italy, isn't it?" said Vonny.

"It is. It isn't good," he replied.

Colin took Vonny's hand and proceeded to give her a shortened version of his conversation with Kyle Kennedy. He kept talking because he knew that once he stopped, tears would fall. He stopped. No tears.

"I'm stunned," Vonny said. "I had a bad feeling when there was no post card for so long. Oh, poor G.E.M.. Poor Selma, she waited so long for this trip to Europe. Oh, poor me."

There was a short pause and then Vonny went into her social worker mode and started asking questions about plans, the family, legal items, insurance, etc.

"Hang on, Honey. Let's read the e-mail that G.E.M. sent Kyle and then we will both be up on all the facts as we know them at this particular time. OK?"

"You read, I'll absorb," was her reply.

Colin read the e-mail aloud. Vonny took notes.

Dear Kyle,

I hope that you are reading this alone at your

desk at the end of the day. *You once told us that that
was your way of dealing with e-mail. I am in the office
at the pension in Avitzia. Most of Italy is on the net.*
    *I have sad news…Selma has passed away. It
was very peaceful and that makes me peaceful, now
that I have gotten over the huge shock of her passing.
She was feeling woopsie (as we always say when someone is getting ready to upchuck). I thought she had
too much sun. Marguerite, our hostess, took her to
our room and helped her to get settled in bed. Selma
thanked her for her help and they exchanged those
cheek kisses that these Italians are so fond of. When
I went to check on her, after about thirty minutes, it
looked like she was still sleeping. We needed to get
ready for dinner, so I tried to rouse her. She wasn't
breathing. Carlo, our host, called a doctor in the
neighborhood and he came immediately and told us
what we already knew. Poor Selma went to sleep, the
sleep with no dreams. We all just sat there, then Carlo
brought wine and we drank, cried and toasted my
wonderful Selma.*
    *Selma and I had agreed on a lot of things before
we left to come to Italy. We agreed that you made
wonderful plans for us and that we loved you. We
agreed that if one of us wanted to call a halt to the trip,
that the other could go on if he/she wanted to. We
agreed that if this was to be our last trip together, that*

*we wanted it to be fantastic. Well, it's been fantastic
up until the last two days. We had a wonderful time in
Rome (the hotel is great) and Avitzia is more wonderful than we remembered. Marguerite and Carlo have
been like angels to us.*

*I have decided to have Nicholas drive me north
to Pisa and Florence as was our plan and then to take
me back to the Palazio in Rome where I will stay for a
couple days before heading home as we had planned.
Selma is being cremated and Carlo will take care of all
that and he will bring Selma to Rome when I return
there. I will bring Selma home with me. Carlo will
call the concierge at the Palazio (who happens to be his
cousin) and have him change my plane reservations.*

*I will be sending the girls e-mails giving them
"just some" of these details and I am e-mailing Scarlet
and swearing her to secrecy. She will be very helpful.
I'll send you a copy of the e-mail that I sent to the girls.
I'll do this today. Scarlet will NOT place an obituary
in the Savannah Morning News; we wrote each other's
some time back and Scarlet will complete Selma's, but
won't provide it to the newspaper until my return. If
anyone should make an inquiry, please don't offer any
information. You know nothing. I will deal with them
(everyone) when I get back to Savannah. I will spend
a few days in NY at the lake and then will go home
and confront life there as a single person. And speak-*

ing of the lake, please call or e-mail Colin and Vonny
O'Brien in Maple Springs and tell them about our loss
and that I will be there in a couple weeks. Please tell
them too that I'd like some privacy while I am there.
I will get in touch with them when the time is right.
Maple Springs will be deserted right after Labor Day
when the summer folks head home, but Colin and
Vonny can run interference for me with those few folks
that are still there. I trust them. I'm sure that I gave
you their e-mail address (but I don't have it with me).

I am well and will enjoy the rest of the tour for
myself and Selma. We had five short years together,
but what a half decade it was. I miss my Cookie.

Bye for now, we will talk soon, lots to talk to you
about, love you,

G.E.M.

Colin finished reading and sat there, numb.

Vonny, ever the social worker, was silent for a moment, then, "I didn't miss Selma until now. She was gone, but not *gone*, you know? I'm at a loss here. Let's see," she checked her notes. "I know who Carlo and Marguerite are, but who are Nicholas and Scarlet? I'd guess that Nicholas is the driver and Scarlet, oh my, is she southern, she's is G.E.M.'s secretary in Savannah. Right? Did Kyle also send you the e-mail message that G.E.M. sent the girls?"

"No, but I will remind her to send it. Right. Her telephone number is on the emergency list that G.E.M. gave us," said

Colin, still virtually trapped in silence.

"Well, what do we do now?" said Vonny. "Seems as though they had things all worked out and had Kyle, Scarlet, their driver and the two angels in Avitzia to help. I'm sure all will go well. What we need to do is to sit and wait for G.E.M. to come back to the lake and be there for him."

Colin got back in gear. "I think I need to call Kyle, get her calmed down and let her know that we are planning on being involved when we next see G.E.M.," he said. "I will wait a couple hours and then call Scarlet also. Her telephone number is on that emergency list too. Did I already say that?"

Colin stood up and Vonny went right into his arms. They just hugged and stood there.

"I can't believe she's gone," Colin said. Gone, there was that word again. Another tight hug, a kiss on the cheek and he was out the office door, out the lobby door and headed home, not feeling great, not woopsie, but sick to his stomach nonetheless.

CHAPTER 11

Colin was glad that the telephone number for the Peach State Travel Bureau was an eight-hundred-number because Kyle and he talked for about forty-five minutes. Before Kyle had talked to Colin, she had talked at length with Scarlet and that had settled Kyle down a bit. Scarlet had received a similar e-mail from G.E.M. and she knew that G.E.M. had things in order. The jewelry stores were packaged into a small corporation with G.E.M as CEO, so there would be no business upheaval if he decided to stay away longer or absent himself from the company as he dealt with Selma's passing. Selma had no legal or managerial ties to the corporation. She was still Selma to everyone who worked there. Actually, Scarlet had been G.E.M.'s secretary since Selma moved up into the role of Mrs. Stone and Scarlet spent equal amounts of time on company and personal business for the Stone family. Scarlet assured Kyle that things would go as G.E.M. planned and not to worry and to just be the good and confidential travel agent and to wait for him to return to Savannah.

Colin too helped Kyle to realize that all was well, except for the fact that Selma was gone, and that she should just do as G.E.M, and Scarlet, wished. He promised to call her immediately if he learned anything new or if he had a thought on how she, we, could help G.E.M. He reminded her to forward a copy of the e-mail that G.E.M. had sent his daughters. Kyle apologized for not having sent it and promised to do so right away.

Just as Colin was ending the conversation, Kyle threw him for a loop when she said, "I am worried about the girls calling. They were never sweet young things, they don't, ah didn't, like Selma at all, probably don't care much for me, and I think that they have very much so taken advantage of and hurt their father over the years. I know they will badger me. I am no pushover, but if they triple team me, I regret to say that I may falter."

"Kyle," Colin was processing this information as he spoke, "G.E.M. is your boss, he writes the checks for your travel expertise. The girls won't be using your agency. Right? Respect your customer and the heck with the girls. I probably won't ever meet them, so it's easy for me to give advice, but I'm sure that you, Ms.-big-time-businesswoman, can handle those belles."

Kyle thanked Colin for his advice and hung up. Colin was proud of his fatherly, yet business-like advice and he hung up feeling quite proud of himself.

Vonny would be home soon and so Colin began washing and drying some home grown lettuce he had bought at Steve's Store. He mixed it with other fresh veggies and looked for craisins and some walnuts and sunflower seeds and mandarin oranges to make a cool, summer salad. Most of the vegetables were from local farm stands and Colin bought them with the idea that they were the first steps of his and Vonny's becoming locavores.

He checked his e-mail for G.E.M.'s letter to his daughters and it had arrived. He printed it to read later with Vonny.

Colin moved the bistro table into the shade in the back

yard so they could have dinner there and then he made a pitcher of iced tea and lemonade mixed together and put it in the fridge with the salad. He took his folding lounge chair, the cordless telephone, G.E.M.'s e-mail to his daughters and a book and sat under a tree on his next door neighbor's lawn. He often did that, even sat on the porch, with the neighbor's approval. The seldom-there-neighbor, Mitch, liked the idea of people seeing someone around his house; keeps away robbers he thought. Colin just liked the view and obliged.

Before he headed next door, Colin did some figuring after checking the original Eye-talian eye-tinery and the details from G.E.M. in the e-mail. He revamped the time line and predicted G.E.M.'s arrival in Maple Springs. The Pisa and Florence part of the trip was actually a three day guided tour of the famous buildings and art work of those two cities. The original plan called for another week in Rome, but that had been shortened to two days and then the flight home, probably Rome to Toronto, maybe an overnight in Toronto. Colin was sure that G.E.M. would have Bill Morris, who owned the only local limousine service, pick him up in Toronto and deliver him to The Springs. Bill had taken Selma and G.E.M. to the airport when they left for Italy, surely he was lined up for the Stone's return trip to Maple Springs. Colin figured that G.E.M. would be there in about eight days. He decided to call Bill Morris and see if his thinking was correct. Bill's answering machine asked Colin to leave a message, but he only left his name and number preferring to give and get details from a person as opposed to a machine. Colin and Bill were longtime friends. They had taught school together – Colin in Special Ed and Bill as the beloved Drivers Ed teacher – and had kept in touch and Bill stopped, or at least honked, whenever he delivered or picked up folks in The Springs.

About twenty minutes later Bill called.

"Hi Colin," he said. "What's up? Haven't seen you in some time. Must be quiet at your place with all the summer folk decamped."

"Quiet it is, but there is a bit of confusion that I bet you're not aware of," replied Colin.

Bill was quick to reply, "If you're talking about the passing of Selma in Italy, you're wrong. Remember, I took them up to Toronto and I had a standing date to pick them up. G.E.M. e-mailed me and I will be picking him up on Friday of next week, but at the International Airport in Niagara Falls."

With that statement, Colin knew that his calculations had been correct and that G.E.M. would indeed be here for the final days of summer as planned, but Selma was no longer part of the plan.

Bill had no details except that Selma was gone, he used that word too, and G.E.M. would travel a bit more and then head back to Maple Springs before heading south for the winter. Colin gave him as little information as he could, but just enough to help Bill to understand the situation and to be aware of the privacy that G.E.M. was looking for. Bill, as a limo driver, knew the meaning of discrete. Movie stars, rock musicians and politicians had enjoyed a ride in Bill's back seat and Bill told no tales. The two friends hung up agreeing to keep each other informed and promising to get to the local tavern, Guppy's, for a beer ASAP.

Vonny was home by about 3:00. Colin waved as she pulled into the on-lawn parking out back and decided not to go over to the house; let her get settled and changed. She had just had to sublimate all the G.E.M. and Selma information and continue social working. She needed some alone time.

In less than five minutes though, Vonny, looking fetching in shorts and a tank top, barefooted, was headed across the street with her lounge chair and it looked like two Corona and a bag of corn chips. She easily unfolded the chair with one hand and plunked herself into it as she simultaneously handed Colin a beer.

"Damn it," she said. "I always forget that you need an opener for Corona. Why can't these Mexicans realize how lazy we Gringos are?"

"Sit! I got it," said Colin as he jumped up and hot-footed it across the street. He was back in a flash with two more beer, an opener and a tub of hummus and a hidden baggie of lime slices that Vonny had neglected to bring along. He opened them each a beer with a flourish and sat, rather sunk, into his chair and the two of them sat in silence ready to enjoy the wonderful handiwork of the south-of-the-border brewers.

"No lime?" said Vonny. "Selma would never serve a Corona without that neat little slice of lime sticking out the top. No glass to be sure, but lime was a must and maybe a paper napkin wrapped around the bottle and salsa not hummus with the corn chips, served in authentic Mexican bowls. God, I miss that woman."

Colin took Vonny's hand, slipped her a lime slice, and then they sat in silence, enjoying the beer and each silently remembering and toasting Selma.

Soon, Colin started telling Vonny about his latest conversation with Kyle. He didn't expound upon his skillful, fatherly advice to Kyle, he just relayed information.

"So, Kyle doesn't agree that the three jewels of the next generation of Stones are as sparkling as some others might think?" said Vonny.

"Right. They've no doubt been a bit spoiled. G.E.M. probably didn't deny them much over the years. If they were not fond of Selma," and then Colin demonstrated his best deep-south accent, "Ah'm downrat sho that they nevah demonstrated that in frunt of theh daddy.

"Also," said Colin, "let me read the copy Kyle sent me of G.E.M.'s e-mail to his daughters."

Dear Precious Daughters,

All is not well on our trip in Italy. Italy is wonderful, our health and well-being are not. Upon our return to Savannah, we must meet and conduct serious family business. Do not be forlorn, as we are each where God wants us to be at this present time. We will contact you upon our return.

Daddy and Selma

Wow," said Vonny, "talk about skirting an issue, but he knows those girls best. In-person discussion will probably be more productive."

"It's just enough information to warn the girls that something is up, but no specifics," said Colin. "I imagine that there are wills to be found, etc. The e-mail will probably get the girls on the telephone to Scarlet and maybe even Kyle, but they can handle those three. I'm sure that G.E.M. knows what he is doing."

Colin told Vonny about his conversation with Bill Morris and G.E.M.s arrival date at The Springs. Vonny sat quietly processing all the information thrown at them during the last few hours.

Finally Vonny said, "I think I'll make a couple pies and freeze them and make sure that I have all the ingredients for some fancy meals so that we can keep G.E.M. fed and distracted once he gets here. I wonder how much of Selma's personal items are in the cottage. Most of the décor," and Vonny air quoted as she said décor, "was compliments of Lula, but there are still enough memories to keep Selma foremost in G.E.M.'s mind. Poor guy."

"I wouldn't worry about G.E.M. I'm sure he'll enjoy those memories," said Colin. "Remember, they talked this all out, had things in writing, planned contingencies. He's still out there enjoying It'ly for the two of them."

Two beers each, lounge chairs, a sunny late afternoon and the one you love did their work and Vonny and Colin dallied, supper was late, bedtime was early.

CHAPTER 12

It was September, but summer still had a grip on Maple Springs and no one was complaining. Late summer blackeyed susans and vivid impatiens continued to offer color as did the bright green lawns. The sun was a willing accomplice and those who hadn't shrink-wrapped their boats continued to enjoy the lake. Ah, Maple Springs.

Colin kept busy with small repairs and some calking as he tried to prepare for winter without snow actually being on the ground. In the past, his winter preparations were all too often accomplished in late November, usually in the midst of a storm. One year, when the kids were small, Colin was hanging Christmas lights around the porch of that monstrous home in Jamestown and was lying on the porch roof, reaching under the eaves and wrapping light cords around hooks and his clothing actually froze to the roof. He was stunned for a minute and then began rolling left and right trying to break the hold of the ice. He broke the hold and gave up the get-those-lights-up-today-or-else order he had given himself and climbed back in through a bedroom window, shut and locked it and got into the shower to thaw. He told himself that he would try putting up lights again next year, earlier.

Things were a little different these days. Colin had lots of time to work around the house. All vertical surfaces outside and inside of the house, except the roof, were accessible by step ladder and since the major remodeling was just completed, all winterizing was on a small scale and quickly accomplished. Colin, not exactly handy around the house, was loving this new house in this lovely, lakeside community.

Over the weekend, Vonny did large scale grocery shopping and made three pies and a veggie lasagna that she immediately froze. She planned to work just four days the next week so that she could take Friday off and be home when G.E.M. arrived. Colin had reread Vonny parts of G.E.M.'s e-mail about his desire for some privacy and she promised to comply. She also visited Binky and couple of the other year-round residents to "run interference" as G.E.M. had also asked. She planned on keeping an eye out for any weekenders arriving on Friday, as G.E.M. would be, to be sure that they knew about Selma's passing and that they would refrain from dropping by until G.E.M. was ready for visitors.

Dave, G.E.M.'s lawn guy, had kept the cottage lawn, gardens and bushes mowed, trimmed and watered, but Colin decided to hose off the porch and back deck and wash down the outside furniture. Soon the furniture would all be placed in G.E.M.'s storage shed, along with the dock furniture and trappings, when the cottage was closed up for the winter, but when G.E.M. arrived, he might still be able to enjoy The Springs.

It was only Monday and G.E.M. wasn't expected until Friday, so Colin was going to wait until Thursday, probably, to do any work at the Stones, but meanwhile he'd still keep an eye on the place and even give Dave a call and make sure that the lawn was cut by tomorrow or Wednesday.

Colin was just finishing his Monday morning ritual of sorting recyclables and getting them and the garbage to the curb for pickup when he heard a lawnmower in the neighborhood. He looked over the hedge in front of the house and saw Dave at G.E.M.'s. There was also a white van backed up to the front steps and a ramp of some sort connecting the porch to the van. There was a sign on the door of the van, but Colin couldn't read it. Colin, already wearing his hat, sunglasses and sneakers, was ready for a walk and so he headed down the street.

"Brad's Carpentry...the one to call for the best in craftsmanship" read the sign on the van. As Colin read this, it was immediately obvious that there was no telephone number provided for callers. That's either one big mistake, or one shrewd advertising coup, Colin thought. The reader, the potential customer, had only to remember the name of this great craftsman, not a telephone number and surely if the reader went to "carpentry" in the yellow pages, there would be a large, paid advertisement and all the information any potential customer would need in order to contact Brad. Colin would remember to check for that advertisement when he got home.

As Colin slowly passed the Stone's, Dave waved from the seat on his riding lawnmower as he carefully circled a tree on G.E.M.'s side lawn. Colin signaled for Dave to turn off the mower. Colin told him about Selma's passing, but was short on details in the telling. Dave said that he hadn't heard the news about Selma. He said too that he was surprised to see workmen in the house. Dave told Colin that G.E.M. had paid him for the summer and he would keep things mowed and pruned, but he would not bother G.E.M. when he arrived in Maple Springs. Colin didn't see any action in the house, neither carpenters nor painters were looking busy. He continued his walk and made mental notes of menu items to be sure to have on hand once G.E.M. returned home and joined him and Vonny for dinner. Vonny had given the menu some thought, but Colin would be sure to have G.E.M.'s favorite ice cream, beer and coffee on hand too. Chocolate chip mint. Labatts' Blue Light. Eight O'clock.

After an early, light lunch and an impromptu nap from which he awoke when his book hit the floor startling him, Colin again looked over the hedge and checked out the "confection cottage" and saw Brad or his subordinate loading a couple of cardboard boxes into the van. He hadn't heard any power tools at work, no buzzing and no grinding so he was curious as to what repairs were in progress. He thought that it was probably tile work or planing of drawers and doors or other small problems requiring repair that most other people just learned to live with. He decided to walk over and introduce himself, not being nosy, just a congenial neighbor. Before he could set off down the street, Brad, Colin guessed, and another man, both in khaki shorts and shirts and baseball caps shoved the ramp into the back doors of the van, slammed the doors, climbed in the front doors, two more slams, and they were off down the street. As they passed him, Colin waved, but got no response from either of the van's passengers. Good thing he didn't go visiting, he thought. Maybe I'll venture over earlier tomorrow. Perhaps. Perhaps not.

CHAPTER 13

Brad did not appear on Tuesday, but on Wednesday morning when Colin returned from Rotary, the white van was again pulled up to the front steps. There were boxes on the porch and someone was taking boxes from the van into the house. Probably new light fixtures, faucets or electrical or plumbing supplies thought Colin. There'd be a busy crew over there today. He decided to wait until after noon to stop by to chat, but by noon, the boxes were gone from the porch and so was the van. Colin decided that he was no longer Mr. Nice guy and he'd storm, or at least walk quickly, over there the next time he saw the van. He then remembered to look up "Brad's Carpentry" in the local yellow pages. He didn't find him there or in the white pages. Colin Googled "Brad's Carpentry", but only found a place in Williamsville up near Buffalo. Could be him; often specialty craftsmen find work in a wider area than generalists. If that's him, Colin thought, then he really needs a telephone number on that van, or maybe not. Colin found him, so could others.

On Thursday, Colin got busy hosing off the Stone's porch and deck and their respective furniture and took the tea rose cushions from the shed out back and made the porch presentable. By 10:30 he was finished and he headed home to hose off his own porch, change and get to Steve's Store before all the really fresh produce was gone. He lucked out with some local peaches and what he thought would be the last of this summer's corn. Grilled corn and mushroom turkey burgers sounded like a great dinner for tonight. Vonny had the rest of the week's meals under control with her list of things she could prepare or thaw for G.E.M. once they had the go ahead to visit, hopefully during this coming weekend.

Brad's van never reappeared at "confection cottage", so, thought Colin, the work must be done. Colin thought it odd that he never heard a power tool, not even a shop vac, but he wasn't the nosy sort, so he didn't worry about what got done or didn't get done. Maybe he should check the house, after all he had a key, and make sure it was ready for G.E.M. No he better not. Brad was "the best of craftsmen". Brad knew how to please his customers. Clean up was an important part of any project.

At supper that evening Colin and Vonny reviewed the plans for ignoring and then pampering G.E.M. Vonny was sure that she had spoken to all of the Springers present for the weekend, there weren't many, and they all understood G.E.M.'s wishes and would comply. Bill Morris had called just as they were doing the dishes, just as they had done dishes together for the thirty six years that they had been married, and said that G.E.M.'s Maple Springs arrival time was about 6:00 in the evening. Steve was delivering a cooler of food at about 5:30, so all was in order.

Friday seemed to creep by at a very slow pace. Vonny had taken the day off, but had wisely scheduled a haircut, took her mom to visit her sister who had recently moved into a senior citizen apartment building and had coffee with a group of her knitting friends. Colin on the other hand had paced, gawked periodically at the Stone's cottage, tried to read, rearranged the furniture on his porch, carefully fluffing pillows. Vonny was home by late afternoon, they just snacked for an early dinner, and they waited for 6:00. A big white Styrofoam cooler appeared on the Stone's porch at 5:30, but Colin hadn't seen Steve deliver it. Colin had missed the food delivery, but he was sure that he wouldn't miss Bill Morris as he drove his sleek black limo by their house with the long- awaited passenger up front. G.E.M. didn't like to ride in the back seat. He said that it made him sick to his stomach to ride back there, but he probably just liked to be up front to get a good look at where he was headed and to give backseat driver help in spite of his up front position. About 6:30 the telephone rang, it was Bill.

"Hi Colin, I just dropped off Mr. Stone and I am driving around the Springs waiting for you to get your shoes on and to get out front of your house so that I can pick you up and take you to Guppy's for a beer. Don't dally, my meter is running," said Bill and with that he hung up.

"Vonny! That was Bill Morris. He's picking me up as I speak. G.E.M. is home. I'm headed to Guppy's. Beer. Bill must have news. I'll be back ASAP. Call Bill's cell if you can't wait for my return," said Colin as he scooped up his crocs and headed out the kitchen door to the front porch. He could see the limo down a couple houses and before he knew it, the limo slowed, he opened the door, fell in, and they were off on the half mile ride to Guppy's.

Guppy's Friendly Tavern was one of those places that the

locals would not let fall completely into the hands of the summer folks and tourists. Good food and prices, a great staff and just enough ambiance to insure a positive eating experience. Danny and Krissy who ran the place had their act together and Bill and Colin could see that the joint was jumpin' as they parked out back where there was just enough room for the limo to squeeze behind Danny's truck. They lucked out with seats too as they settled on two high chairs at one of those high tables for two, close to the bar, that are popular in a lot of restaurants.

"Two Labatts," called Bill to Krissy who was behind the bar and before they even got settled, the beer and a basket of parmesan popcorn arrived at the table. They sent the waitress away without even taking menus.

"So just let me talk for a couple minutes, then you can ask questions. OK?" said Bill. Colin nodded yes and Bill was off.

"The plane was on time in Niagara Falls and just for fun I had made one of those cardboard signs that limo drivers often flash in airports to insure that they get the right customer. I know G.E.M and he knows me, but I thought he'd get a laugh out of the sign. Well across the terminal he comes with a porter behind him pulling a cart with four big suitcases on it. Wonder what they paid extra for those bags. Believe me they were heavy; I loaded them in the trunk. Well, he is all business; moving along quickly, wearing sun glasses and a dorky hat probably from Italy, and a strange beltless, knee length raincoat. A quick tip to the porter, he climbs in the back. THE BACK. Didn't even respond to my sign. I was sure he'd sit up front. Anyway, he's sounding all gravely and he says hi, he's tired, get me home and he cozies up on the chaise end of the back seat. He closes the window between us and that's all I hear till we get here. Traffic's a mess and we had lots of pelting rain up in the Buffalo area, but I made pretty good time. G.E.M. usually has me stop somewhere along the way for ice cream, but not this time. Weird, that's all I can say, but then he's been through a lot, Selma and travel and all, and he probably has some jet lag and who knows what intestinal germs traveled home with him.

"When we got to Dewittville, I lowered the window and told him that he'd be home in five minutes. He grunted something and I closed the window. Altogether, it took almost two hours to get here and I was really surprised how aloof he was. I don't think that he was sleeping. I think he was just avoiding.

"Anyway, we got right in front of his house and he is out and starting up the steps before I even have the car in park. 'Bill me,' he yells as he turns when he gets to the top of the porch stairs. By this time I'm out of the car and standing by my door. 'Just leave the suitcases on the porch,' he yells and he and the cooler are inside and the door is closed. So that is all I know. Your turn. Questions?" asked Bill.

Colin didn't have any questions after Bill's detailed recitation. So they just talked for a while and Bill elaborated on the weather, G.E.M.'s pseudo-sleeping and the weight of those four suitcases, very heavy. They shot the bull some more, had a second Labatts and Colin was carried home, in style, in the back of the limo. He explained everything to Vonny. She too had no questions and they decided that what was, was. Tomorrow'd be another day and they would probably learn firsthand details from G.E.M. of It'ly, the Eye-talian eye-tinerary, and the trip home.

CHAPTER 14

A ccording to the *Jamestown Post-Journal* there was a chance of rain for Saturday, and as usual, the weather prognostication was less than accurate, just plain wrong. The sun was hot, not fall warm, and it was up, bright, early and much welcomed. Colin got out the knee pads and he and Vonny gleaned the garden of the remainder of those withered stems and blossoms and even cut back the irises, the day lilies and the lamb's ear. Cut back, hell; they hacked them off within an inch of the ground. Colin trimmed the hedges for what he hoped was the last time before winter's arrival and he raked the scraggly bishops weed out from the base of his undulating green hedges. Lookin' good, thought Colin as he stepped back to admire his sweat equity in the yard.

"Lunch is served, M'Lord," said Vonny as she carried a large tray featuring hummus pita sandwiches and a large, pink Fiesta Ware bowl filled with cut up fresh fruit; the blueberries, strawberries, kiwi, mango and honeydew looked great and tasted even better.

Colin had positioned his chair on the front porch so that he could see the front of G.E.M.'s cottage.

"I really want him to step onto the porch and motion us over for iced tea," said Colin after a couple minutes of silent eating.

"Patience, M'Lord. He'll be out in his own good time.

Meanwhile just sit there and pretend that you are enjoying lunch with your gorgeous wife, and don't plan on putting away those garden tools just yet."

Colin didn't have to pretend that he was enjoying being with Vonny. He always enjoyed being in her presence, in her arms, having her in his thoughts.

After lunch there was a half-hearted attempt at more fall garden clean-up, but by two o'clock the tools were stowed, they had taken showers and Colin, in that same chair facing G.E.M.'s cottage, was prepared to begin the latest Archer Mayor mystery. Mayor's crime solver, Joe Gunther, was part of the Vermont Bureau of Investigation and since two O'Brien children lived in Vermont, Jack and Erin, the stories always had a special interest for Colin. Often locations familiar to him were used as part of the stories. Colin and Vonny loved Vermont, the natural elements in all seasons and the inhabitants in all their laid-back splendor.

Before he even reread the jacket cover and author profile, as he often did each time he picked up a book, any book, Colin saw Binky, with a large purse slung over her left shoulder, coming down the street. Binky was willowy. Colin never knew anyone who actually could be described with that word. It was often used to describe super-models or those painfully skinny ingénues in the tabloids in the racks at Marsh's Supermarket, but only Binky seemed to be tall enough, graceful enough and to glide and flow enough to actually carry off willowy.

Before he thought it through, Colin jumped to the conclusion that Binky was headed to G.E.M.'s and he got up and headed quickly down the street to head her off at the pass. She was probably just strolling, but Colin did not want to take the chance that she would stop at "Confection Cottage" and disturb G.E.M. Anyway, he wanted to be the first one to console G.E.M. and to play personal assistant and run interference to make G.E.M.'s few days in Maple Springs quiet and restful. He faked walking in a nonchalant manner as he neared Binky and the two, three if you count Elgin, Binky's pursedog, met in front of G.E.M.'s cottage.

"Colin, sweetheart. I was just enroute to your digs to steal one of your yummy tofu recipes. Bernie invited a boater he met in Bemus Point to lunch and he, the boater, not Bernie, Bernie would never dare tell me, told me that he is a vegan. Vegan! I thaw Stauffer's, that's it… 'I don't know nothin' 'bout cookin' no tofu," laughed Binky.

"No problemo," said Colin as he placed himself between Binky and the sequestered G.E.M. who was probably lounging behind the pink and white facade of "Confection Cottage".

"We just had a baked tofu casserole the other night and there is tofu scramble with eggs and peppers and mushrooms. The boater, and you and Bernie, would probably enjoy either one of them, with a nice little salad and some cantaloupe. Yummy. Vonny is home. I never get into her recipes. She has them all organized and I know where I am not wanted."

Just then there were rumblings in the Laura Ashley purse hanging from Binky's willowy frame. Indeed, she was willowy. Elgin's adorable face popped out and Colin could sense that his little body secure in the bag was flopping around, wanting out.

Colin rethought that thought because in reality he had never seen Elgin out of the bag, on the earth, touching dirt, never even knew if the dog had legs. Perhaps he was a quadriplegic, canine, Army Corp pursedog nursed back to health by the willowy Binky after a tour in the Middle East. Binky sensed Elgin's agitation and scooped him out of the purse and set him on the ground while trying to clip the matching Laura Ashley leash onto the matching Laura Ashley collar. Evading the leash, Elgin was off in a flash, up the steps and scratching at the door of "Confection Cottage". He got a paw between the screen door and the door jam and slipped into the house barking all the time. Suddenly, the barking stopped. Colin, off like a shot after Elgin, up the three steps in one leap, threw the screen door open, he stopped dead in his tracks.

Elgin sat next to the body that was on the floor partly in the living room, face down with its feet pointed into the small hallway one entered once through the screen door. The upper half of the body was in a pool of red, of course it was blood, and there was no sound in the house, no movement, not a fan, not a dishwasher in cycle, just panting. Colin scooped up Elgin, turned and was out the door, one leap down the three steps.

Colin plopped the dog in the purse that was on the ground, said "Go home Binky, you're not gonna like this," and he was off to home, dialing 911, giving specifics, and frantically looking for Vonny. Where the hell was she? "Vonny. Vonny."

Almost immediately, Colin heard a far-away siren. He ran around the house, where was Vonny? He ran back to G.E.M.'s.

The siren sound was no longer audible. Binky was standing exactly where she was before Colin had headed home, but now she was clutching the purse. No sign of Elgin, no head out, no rumbling sounds.

"Binky go home, honest, you should."

Binky did move when she heard and saw a sheriff car coming down the street. She was on a neighboring lawn now and Colin was beside her, not holding on but ready to hold or catch or be leaned against.

"Inside Joe, on the floor right as you get in, lots of blood, it's G.E.M., I'm sure, he's dead," yelled Colin to Sheriff Joe Green as he exited his car and did the three-steps-at-one-time that had just gotten Colin up and down the Stone porch steps. The Sheriff went right in, the door flapped shut and there was no sound coming through the screen. Binky was making low, moaning sounds, Elgin was silent, Colin was in one place, but bouncing in place. Not big bouncing, but subdued, on-the-balls-of the-feet bouncing to expend pent-up anxiety.

Sheriff Green came out of the house, walked across the porch and down the three stairs up to Colin and Binky and Elgin still standing on the neighbor's lawn.

"You're right Colin," the Sheriff said, "there's no life in that body, but it's not G.E.M. It's Selma."

CHAPTER 15

Selma?" said Colin.

"Selma?" said Binky.

"Selma?" said Vonny approaching the threesome as she was power-walking down the street.

"Vonny, I couldn't find you. There's a dead body in the cottage, but it's not G.E.M., it's really Selma. You and I thought it was G.E.M. here, back from Italy, but no, he's Selma. I'm flummoxed, stunned. Can't be. Can't," Colin fumbled as he tried to talk.

"Vonny, would you walk Binky home," said Joe, getting all official, "and both of you please keep this quiet. I'd like to get some investigating done before we have gawkers. I know there aren't many folks here, but for some reason, crowds seem to form where they are least wanted. That's why I turned off the siren when I started down into The Springs. Binky, I will come visit and get your story of this event here. How long are you going to be staying?"

Binky assured the Sheriff that she would be around for a few more days and she gladly let Vonny take her by the arm and lead her, and Elgin, home. Vonny eyed Colin before she headed down the street with Binky and he knew that she would be right back as fast as her new power-walkers would carry her.

"Joe, how could that be Selma in there? She died last week in Italy. Everyone here knew that. Help me with this," Colin sputtered.

"To quote you, I too am flummoxed, stunned. I'd heard about Selma from Connie at The Springs Restaurant. How'd she know? I gotta get a coroner here and some crime scene guys. I was at Guppy's Tavern trying to sell them an ad for our Sheriff's Department Charity Golf Tourney booklet when your 911 call came in, that's how I got here so fast. Yikes! Flummoxed, I never heard that word before," said the sheriff as he pulled out his cell phone and flipped it open. It rang, he punched the answer button and before he could talk, he got pale and stood there with wide opened mouth and eyes.

"I'm on my way... gotta go Colin. Shannon is being taken to Hamot in Erie. The baby is early and I gotta be in Jamestown in ten minutes to take StarFlight with her. Guard the house. Don't leave until the coroner gets here. I'll call him from the car. I'm deputizing you, right, guard the place," said Joe as he got in his cruiser, cranked the siren, and was off. He sort of invited a crowd with that siren, but then Deputy O'Brien would have to take care of the hordes. Colin looked down the street and saw Vonny hightailing it back from Binky's. He decided that he wouldn't mention the deputy thing to Vonny, she would probably just call him Deputy Dog and laugh a lot.

"Colin, Binky is a mess, Elgin is shivering and won't come out of the purse and Bernie isn't too sympathetic toward Binky in her time of trauma. I told him that I would come back and try to answer his questions. Tell me, what is going on here," said Vonny and she kept quiet waiting for Colin's response. Colin told her everything he knew, it wasn't much, but he did include the reason and circumstances for Joe's quick departure. Vonny asked no questions, gave Colin a big hug, he could feel her shaking, and she was off, rapidly, to the King's to settle down the three of them. Colin wasn't sure about his deputy status; he was just standing there and fifteen feet away a good friend was dead in a puddle of blood, bludgeoned to death and probably robbed or so Colin surmised given what he saw during his brief ten seconds in the house chasing Elgin to retrieve him for storage in Binky's purse.

He just stood there for the longest time, probably five minutes.

Given his role in this situation (he did make the initial 911 call, although it was actually Elgin that discovered the body) and his elevated status of deputy (bestowed upon him in this emergency situation by a duly sworn sheriff needing to absent himself from the crime scene, yes crime scene, to attend to a family emergency) Colin felt that he had the right, nay the duty, to secure the area and examine the crime scene. One is not nosy if he is investigating a crime, he is fulfilling a civic responsibility. Colin was sure of all this as he climbed the Stone's porch steps, one at a time, and crossed the porch prepared to examine and secure the crime scene.

"Colin, you shouldn't go in there. You crazy?" shouted Vonny from the street. "Don't touch that door handle. Prints, remember?"

Fortunately, Colin had not actually put his hand out to grab the door handle. He was just looking in and contemplating entry. And, yes, he did remember prints. He recalled too that the sheriff had opened the door at the top, avoiding the handle although when Colin went to retrieve Elgin he had used that same handle.

"I know, I know. Joe is sending the coroner. I am to stay till he gets here," Colin replied to Vonny as he moved to the top step and sat down on it. "I will head home as soon as the coroner comes. I'll pump him for information and blab it all to you. OK?"

Vonny needed another hug, Colin complied and then Vonny went home. Colin stayed on guard. He knew that Vonny would get busy in the kitchen. That was how she dealt with things. She'd chop a lot of vegetables and make a lovely salad, maybe soup, and soon she would be settled down.

As soon as he saw Vonny enter their kitchen door, Colin was at the Stone's door again and opening it, much as Joe did, without handling the door knob. He looked up and down the street, no one in view, and then he slipped inside. He was pleased that there was no smell and as he stepped closer and looked at the body on the floor, it was just a body, not Selma. He could see the back of the head battered quite badly, but there weren't any brains or anything else oozing anywhere. This didn't seem real. It was as though it was a scene fabricated and staged for an audience touring a fright house at Halloween.

Everything within the cottage was in order, or so it seemed. Colin progressed further into the house to the kitchen. Selma's purse was on the table and its contents spread out. It didn't look like it was looted, more like she was in the middle of cleaning it

out or changing purses when she was interrupted, and killed. The
back door leading to the Mexican deck was open and the screen
door closed, but not hooked. Colin was so pleased that he was
noticing the details of the crime scene...there'll be no laughing at
Deputy O'Brien. The sink was clean, dishes on the drain board.
He went into the living room. The four, heavy suitcases were
there. One was opened on the couch, its contents partially removed and spread on the back of the couch and onto a side chair.
It looked like Selma had decided not to unpack, but to instead
live out of a suitcase for a few days. Nothing was disturbed, but
yet the place looked different to Colin, not as cluttered, unbalanced he thought, but then he couldn't decide what unbalanced
meant. Different was a better word. There was still a lot of "stuff"
but it wasn't as "big". He didn't know what that meant either. It
was different stuff he finally decided. There were still glassware
and knick-knacks and statues and pictures on the wall and everything was okay but it wasn't the lovely things, quality things,
expensive things that he had seen when Selma gave him a tour
early in the summer, on the day he first poked his nose into their
lives. There was a lack of Dutch skaters and cowboys on bucking
broncos and pastel stemware. It was Dollar General merchan-
dise, not collectibles and real art.

He looked at the body again. The red terrycloth bathrobe
was probably G.E.M.'s and the fluffy slippers were Selma's. The
hair, caked in red, was Selma's too. What happened here? Colin
had seen enough of *NCIS, Law and Order,* and *Criminal Minds,*
he could reconstruct the crime, he was pretty sure about that.

Deputies do that sort of thing. Back in the kitchen, he looked around, was sure not to touch things, looked out the back door. He actually clasped his hands behind his back as he walked around, reminding himself that he didn't want to, what's the word, corrupt, yea that's it, corrupt the scene. He also didn't want the authorities, one of which he was now, to think that he was nosing around.

At the sink, looking out of the window to the back yard, he saw an envelope on the windowsill propped up between two mugs with cats on them. He craned to read the front of the envelope which was partly obscured by the mugs. All he could read was "Col"; it most probably said "Colin" or "Colin & Vonny". It was his, he should have it, he wanted it. Was it Selma talking to him from the grave? Was he losing it? He was positive that "Col" was three-fifths of his name and he should have it, the envelope, it's his legacy, inheritance.

He heard a car door slam shut out front, he unclasped his hands, snatched that envelope, folded it, put it in his back pocket and went to the front door, hands re-clasped just over the letter sequestered safely in his slim-cut jeans patch pocket on his butt.

"You must be Conan O'Brien," said a large, tanned, casually dressed, buzz-cut man somewhere in his mid-forties. "Funny, you don't look like him. Bet you get a lot of kidding." He came right in. He had a large black bag slung over his shoulder. Must be the coroner Colin thought.

Colin had suffered the "Conan" barb a lot, though not lately, and he gave his rehearsed answer, "I wish I had his money, but

I will settle for being more intelligent, funnier and better looking." The newcomer didn't respond to Colin. Didn't laugh. Did he even hear Colin?

"I'm Glenn Fourtney, your friendly, neighborhood coroner. I'm new to the county, new to this job and love this little community of yours. What have we here?"

Colin never got a chance to say anything. He heard a beep, saw the coroner put on a headset with a thin microphone wand bent across his right cheek ending in front of his mouth.

"The body is prone, face down, a few steps inside the front door of the house. The upper half of the body is in a pool of blood, dark red, assumed to be the victim's," said the coroner as he put on latex gloves taken from his shoulder medical bag which he had places about six feet from the body. He knelt carefully and worked, handled and poked, and spoke into the microphone. Colin stepped back and watched and listened.

"The victim appears to be female, estimated age is seventy, weight 160-175 pounds, five foot two and yes the eyes are blue, hair is white and yet pinky and without style. The victim is in a man's bathrobe, and fluffy slippers. There is no other clothing on the victim. There are no visible marks on the arms or face or legs. There is major force trauma to the back of the skull. There appears to have been several strokes to the head with a weapon with a flat surface (a frying pan vs a baseball bat), not a sharp weapon (shovel), a large weapon as opposed to a small weapon. The skin is bruised, indented, has great discoloration, but the skin is not torn nor are body fluids or the brain leaking out, excepting the blood of course. The victim is neither cold nor warm. Death occurred approximately one to two hours ago and it is currently 1515. Oops, and it's September 9, Saturday."

Another beep and the coroner removed the gloves and stowed them in a zip-lock baggie that he put in a side pocket of his medical bag. He removed the headset and stowed it too.

"Oh, Mr. O'Brien. I forgot you were even here. You didn't hear all that. I gotta get a handle on all this HIPPA stuff. Anyway, using the recorder built into the headset is easier than taking notes and I type from that recording, fixing it up of course, into my computer when I get back to the office."

"It's okay that I heard. Sheriff Green left me in charge, I guess that he deputized me, and anyway, I am not a blabber," replied Colin.

"Can he do that, deputize I mean? Well I guess he can. He did. So, I'm gonna get a few pictures. I don't have to do that, but I always do. Pictures were required where I used to work."

"Where did you use to work?" asked Colin.

"Olan Mills," said Coroner Fourtney laughing. "Just a little humor. I try to keep things light. Of course, if family was close by, I would keep the yuks to a minimum." Then almost as an afterthought or as an attempt at good manners, he added, "Do you have any questions?"

Colin jumped at the opportunity to get more information. "Have you given any thought to what actually happened here? I know you are the corner, you pronounce deadness and perform autopsies, and I know you probably didn't see much of this type of circumstances at Olan Mills, but care to venture a guess as to what happened here?"

"Very funny, Mr. O'Brien. I probably shouldn't hazard a guess, but there is just the two of us here. I will tell you what I think. Keep it to yourself and then we will see what the crime scene team thinks. They should be along any minute. I have to stay until they arrive."

Fourtney walked toward the front screen door, turned and walked to the body, looking around. He walked into the living room and to the kitchen and then went to the back screen door and looked out. He noted the hook and eye that would have secured the back screen door and looked from there to the front door, probably checking to see if a hook and eye existed there. He then went and stood near the head of the body avoiding the red circle staining the floor. Colin continued standing to one side in the entry hall almost leaning against the light summer jackets that were hanging there. He remained in that spot, not frozen to it, but unsure of where else he could go and not wanting to be in the coroner's way.

"I think," said Fourtney too loudly and succeeding in startling Colin, "that the victim, I hope that you will be able to make a positive identification for me, damn I near forgot that part of this procedure, was hit from behind as she ran from the door when the perpetrator of this crime surprised her when said perpetrator came to the door, then entered and accosted her. Looks like she had just showered and was unpacking, or was she packing, and she was maybe even relaxing. Doors were not secured, she wasn't fearful. I suppose there is little or no crime in this community. There is no sign of a robbery or a struggle, the rooms aren't tossed, there is money on the kitchen table. Perhaps she knew the perp, not sure. Do you think I'm on track?"

Colin stepped further into the house and was about to add his two cents to Fourtney's story when a car came to a quick stop out front and two men came quickly onto the porch.

"Fourtney, you in there?" said the first man in the door as Fourtney moved quickly towards the front hall. All Colin could do was to step back into his spot in the front hall and let the three men meet, exchange handshakes and move into the edge of the living room to get a better look at the body. It was as if Colin wasn't there. That didn't last long.

"Hey you, you there in the hall. What are you doing hiding there?" said that same first man in the door.

"He's okay," said Fourtney. "He's a neighbor that Sheriff Green pressed into service when he had to whirlybird it to Hamot with his wife. Colin O'Brien, this is Sgt. Pete Gianna and Sgt. Steve Johnson of the crime scene team for the county. The other team members will be along soon."

There were hellos and how are yous, but then Gianna and Johnson sent Colin from the house. The word contamination was not mentioned. Fourtney asked Colin to wait for him on the porch. Colin did go to the porch, very close to the front door, but he could not hear the men talking inside.

Fourtney came out onto the porch and asked Colin questions regarding the identification of the victim. Colin responded:

Selma Stone, Savannah, GA, late sixties, just returned to Maple Springs for a few days, from Italy. This information Fourtney wrote on a three by five card that he then slipped into his shirt pocket.

There was a lot more information regarding Selma, and G.E.M. and It'ly, but Colin shared none of that. The coroner had a specific job, deadness, and Colin and his boss, Sheriff Green, would put all the other information together when the two of them had the chance to next meet. The crime scene team had their specific tasks to complete so Colin didn't think they'd be sharing much with him.

Colin pointed out his house to Fourtney and left for there agreeing to return if assigned or needed. Fourtney thanked Colin for his help and went back into the house.

CHAPTER 16

As Colin reached his front porch, he heard the harp music and sounds of waves hitting the shore that told him that Vonny had a relaxation CD playing and was in the middle of the living room rug in some contorted yoga position that she would insist was very relaxing. He entered quietly, peeked into the living room and his presumptions were validated. He quietly walked to the kitchen to see what Vonny had chopped and diced to fruition; vegetarian vegetable soup with lentils, smelled great, thick.

He got a soup spoon from the silverware drawer and was returning to the stove to sample the soup when Vonny padded into the kitchen wearing little cloth shoes with rubbery bottoms that gave her traction on her yoga mat. They also allowed her to silently sneak up on Colin.

"You aren't going to eat right out of that pot, are you?" she asked, humor in her tone.

"No dear," he replied and he hid the spoon behind him, she probably saw it, and then slipped it into his back pocket. Oh yes, he realized, there was an envelope there too.

They stood together for a while in the center of the kitchen, it wasn't really a hug, and then sat down at the round kitchen table and Colin told her everything, well almost everything, that had happened on his watch at the Stone's cottage. He told her about the coroners method of taking notes, had to so that she knew how he had gotten all the details. They heard a vehicle of some sort loudly pass their house and Colin and Vonny went to the window. It was a green van with an official looking seal on the side. It stopped at the Stone's behind the coroner's car and two men exited from the driver's and passenger's doors and were quickly up the stairs and into the house in a blur.

The sad O'Briens stood there looking out of the window, out there where there was no movement from humans, vehicles or nature and then the ring of the telephone broke their pose. Colin went to get the telephone and Vonny returned to the living room.

"Colin, it's me, Sheriff Joe. I'm in the waiting room at Hamot, in my scrubs and waiting to be let into the birth theatre, that's what they call it here. They said I can't go in. They said I'm not sterile. I said you're not telling me anything I don't know. I got five kids, soon to have six. Sorry to have left you holding the bag there at Stone's. Did Fourtney show yet? How about the crime scene team?"

"Hey Joe. We are all here, on duty, following procedure. You just take care of that wife of yours. We got things under control in The Springs. You and I have a lot to talk about, sort out. When do you think you'll be back?" asked Colin.

"Things are moving quickly, probably tomorrow. I hate to add to your duties Colin, but if you know any next of kin, could you call them?"

Yikes thought Colin. More duties, I love it. "I have numbers. I can call. How do I explain what has happened? I know what happened, but explaining it is going to be tricky."

"Colin, you can do it. It's not my favorite thing to do, but I have four rules for giving bad news. Write some of this down: #1. Tell whoever it is you are calling, right off, that you have unpleasant news, I always call it unpleasant. #2. Say that you are sorry to be the one to have to call, sorta gets them feeling sorry for you. #3. Tell them the unpleasant news, in this case death, very few details, we are investigating, blah, blah, blah. #4. Give your sympathy and tell them that you are available for them to call later if they have questions, you are going to be there for them at this difficult time, I always call it a difficult time." There was silence on both ends of the telephone line for a few seconds, then, "Colin, you there, you get that?"

"Yes," said Colin who always had a pad and pen at the telephone. "I got that Joe. I can do this. Hope I see you tomorrow."

"Gotta go. There is a nurse in a mask calling me, unsterile me, into the birth theatre, curtain going up. See ya," and there was a click and Joe was headed to meet his newest kid.

Colin went back to his front window. The county van and another vehicle were still parked at Stone's, but the coroner's car was gone. Vonny was prone in the living room. Proneness was also an instant relaxer for Vonny. Her eyes were closed, but she was just yoga zoned out and not asleep. He'd await her return to Earth and have some soup with her. The soup was simmering on the stove, smelling great, over a burner on the gas stove with one of those burn guards placed between the bottom of the soup pot and the grate over the flame.

Colin got the list of telephone numbers that G.E.M. had provided before the Stone's trip to the Eye'talian Peninsula. All the numbers he'd need were there, mostly cell phone numbers, all with the same area code, 912, Savannah. He made a calling order list, rewrote and then reviewed the four rules that Joe had provided including things to be sure to tell or ask, like the script one might use when making charity solicitation phone calls:

#1   *Introduce self, friend of Selma and G.E.M., location
"I have some UNPLEASANT news that I must convey to you"
#2   *Sheriff asked me to call, county law enforcement are involved…me too
"I AM SORRY to have to be the one to tell you" (foul play)
#3   *Many questions are still unanswered, I'm sure you are confused…me too
"The body found in your Maple Springs cottage is Mrs. Selma Stone…DEAD
#4   *If you have questions, call & I will call as info surfaces (give phone #)
"Please accept my sincere SYMPATHY during this DIFFI-CULT time.

Goodbye.

Kyle and Scarlet would be called before the precious daughters. Colin kept his telephone list, Joe's four rules and his script handy, but he was pretty sure that he would not need them during his first two calls.

It was still bright sunlight outside, but the sky was pinking up and the sun was off to visit the horizon as Colin sat with his cordless telephone and his lists and script in an Adirondack chair near the flagpole in his backyard. He settled himself, but then decided to get a pen and a can of iced tea. He settled again and looked to the base of the flagpole and saw the stone that was settled there. There was a plaque on the stone, "In Memory of the Awesome Giftgiver, Mary Jane Gerstel". It was a stone commemorating the flagpole that was a gift one Christmas from Vonny's sister. How many people have a stone commemorating a gift of a flagpole? Mary Jane, Vonny's only and older sister, had died young of cancer. She took great pride in her shopping, bargains and in picking just the right gift for everyone. As the gift recipient opened the package, be it a birthday or a holiday, when the delight appeared upon the recipient's face, Mary Jane would shout "Awesome Giftgiver" and do the arm pump usually reserved for football cheering. She was an awesome giftgiver, a generous giftgiver and a terrific person. The O'Briens all missed Mary Jane, MJ, Aunt Mary Jane.

Colin took a drink of the iced tea, underlined Kyle's cell phone number on his calling list, dialed it and waited, dreading, for her to answer. She answered, damn.

"Hi Kyle. It's Colin O'Brien from Maple Springs. How are you this evening?" So far so good thought Colin. "I wasn't sure I'd catch you at work late on a Saturday afternoon."

"Well hello Mr. O'Brien. Nice to hear your voice. Yes, I'm

usually here until at least six most days. I suppose you're calling to tell me that Mr. Stone made it safely to Maple Springs," said Kyle in her best business voice with just a slight southern coating.

"Kyle, I am afraid that I have some upsetting news to convey to you. I am so sorry that I have to be the one to do so." There was silence in the Peach State Travel Agency in Savannah, GA. Colin continued, "A body was discovered in G.E.M. and Selma's cottage here at The Springs." There was a gasp from the Peach State Travel Agency in Savannah, GA.

"Kyle, are you OK?"

"Yes, Ah am. Ah am alone, so glad to be, and am stunned. Was it G.E.M.? Are you beating around the bush on me?" this time more drawl was evident.

"Kyle, it was Selma." Silence. "She returned to Maple Springs dressed as G.E.M. Vonny and I didn't know this until the sheriff examined the body." Silence. "We were giving G.E.M. time to settle down, do some private grieving and then just this afternoon the body was discovered. We all thought it was G.E.M. Why not? But, it's Selma, honest, I saw her. Just let that sink in a minute." Silence in both GA and NY.

Colin waited an appropriate amount of time, then said, "Kyle, you are the first person that I have called. I am going to call Scarlet next and then the girls. You knew Selma's and G.E.M.'s health problems and you even helped them with emergency plans, but I'm pretty sure that this has ended much differently than you ever thought it would end. There's not much else to tell you. I was there when the coroner arrived, the sheriff has me helping out, deputized sort of, and so I know that they are sure that she was murdered." Gasp. "You OK? I know it's a lot to take in."

"Thank you so much for calling me." Back to the non-accented businesswoman. "I loved those two. I can't believe the way their lives are playing out. So it was G.E.M. who really died in Italy, right? And Selma continued the trip. Those details were not part of their emergency plan that I was privy to. I am stunned, flummoxed. How are you Mr. O'Brien, you're right there, you must be very upset."

Colin admitted to Kyle that he too was confused, flummoxed. In his best fatherly mode he assured Kyle that he was fine, he would be part of the investigation and he would keep her apprised of progress made in the case, new information. He told her that he was going to call Scarlet next and that he would have Scarlet call her. The two of them needed to keep anything he told them under wraps until the sheriff released information to the media. Colin also told Kyle that he would work with Scarlet on obituaries.

"Bye Colin and I thank you for your kindness in calling me. I do not envy you having to try to explain this to the Stone girls, but I'm sure that you can handle them. You are a little over 800 miles away. You can always blame your cell phone for a bad connection and hang up. Bye," said Kyle, a flicker of defeat in her voice.

Colin wasn't scared to call the three Stone sisters, but he was glad to be able to talk to Scarlet first. Fortunately G.E.M. had provided her personal cell phone number. She would probably not be in the office on Saturday. He took another drink of the iced tea and connected again in the 912 area code.

"Hello. This is Scarlet. I am unable to come to the telephone just now. Leave a name and number and I will return your call as soon as possible." Beep.

"Hi Scarlet. This is Colin O'Brien calling from Maple Springs in NY. I am sorry to bother you, but I have some…" he didn't get unpleasant out.

"Hello Mr. O'Brien. Sorry that I did not answer right away. I screen my calls because I have an ex-boyfriend that I am trying to discourage. So glad that you called. I assume that Mr. Stone has arrived. Are you calling for him? What does he need? I can go into the office tomorrow if need be. I'm sure…."

Colin interrupted her, "Scarlet, let me stop you. I am afraid that I have some unpleasant news for you. Just let me get it all out. Are you sitting?" Colin continued to talk and using his cheat sheet repeated the facts much the same way that he had done for Kyle. Scarlet too was flummoxed, although she did not use that word, and she was the stoic, big-lady professional that Kyle had been. She asked a couple of questions and then told Colin that she had some things that she could share with him that might help with the investigation. Her mind was racing, but she spoke slowly and clearly.

"I can't believe that someone could have murdered either one of them. What really happened in Italy? Oh my, oh my." Silence. "You know that this trip was really important to Selma and G.E.M. They really had it planned, no details were omitted. They visited twenty or more places in the past five years and were always very quick to plan, go and return and always with stories, pictures and gifts. They were Kyle's best customers. Also, your sheriff might want to contact their lawyer, but first let me tell you that before the Stones left for Italy, they updated, or I should say changed, their wills. They used a lawyer up there in Jamestown. Their lawyer here is Savannah, Carlton Chase, had a college fraternity brother practicing law in Jamestown and several years ago Mr. Chase matched G.E.M. and Lula with him. G.E.M. and Selma wanted to get some changes made before they left for Europe, so they used the Jamestown lawyer. His name is Neil Robertson of the law firm Robertson and Johnson," said Scarlet.

"I know him," said Colin. "Neil and his wife go to our church. He coached one of our kids in a church basketball league, but I don't think he'd tell me anything, lawyer's oath and all that."

"Mr. Robertson can at least verify that he is their lawyer. You will probably need him, he has all the details, cremation, the cottage, etc. I will call him first thing Monday morning. Do you think he will know about the....," here Scarlet stumbled, "...problem...situation in Maple Springs by then?"

"I think that the sheriff, who by the way is in Erie, PA having a baby, would like to keep this quiet for a while to get some investigating accomplished," said Colin. "Actually, his wife is having the baby, their sixth. I'm not sure how long he can keep the crime hushed up. It's always a slow news day around here.

The newspapers would love this story. I tell you what, let me call Neil and fill him in a bit and I will tell him that you will contact him on Monday. OK?"

"That's probably best," said Scarlet trying to stay composed and business-like. "Well, here is some information that might help you with the investigation. G.E.M. named me as the executrix of their estate, so I pretty much know the focus of their wills, no particulars, but a general view. Oh, Mr. O'Brien, I just realized that I can't do all the executrix things I have to do with me here and Selma and I guess G.E.M. too, you know, there in New York State. This could get very confusing. I hope that you, and Mr. Robertson and probably the sheriff can help me in this difficult time"

Colin had to smile when Scarlet said that this was a difficult time. She too knew Joe Green's four steps for breaking sad news. She probably learned them on the same web site that Joe Green had learned them. Colin assured Scarlet that he would be her man up north. He also asked her to call him Colin.

"Oh, thank you Colin. I am relieved. Back to the wills: everything in Savannah involved in the business is tied up corporation-wise and has its own lawyers and accountants to count on; G.E.M. was the CEO and salaried so nothing should halt the business from going forth; their house here in Savannah is held in a trust for the Historical Society of Greater Savannah, all part of a foundation that they had created. The house and everything in it stays. A few years ago G.E.M. and Selma had a dinner party for some of their friends and relatives. At the party, they gifted all of us. Yes, I had been invited, Kyle too and of course the girls and other friends and some long time business associates and servant. G.E.M. hated the word servant. He called the cook and gardener and cleaning lady property managers. We were all presented with wonderful antiques and art and jewelry. It was very sweet and that night the Stones announced that the trust had been set up with the Historical Society. They also left enough money to take the property managers into retirement. He and Selma did not want these wonderful, longtime friend and managers to suffer any loss of income until they reached Social Security age. They are all close, I can assure you."

"G.E.M. and Selma were something. I bet they got great joy out of that evening. Probably prevented a lot of future problems and arguments too," said Colin.

"They were very gracious and generous," answered Scarlet. "Actually, each of their wills expresses unique bequeaths depending upon which one should pass away first. A lot of points were the same in each will. The big, recent change was the ownership of the cottage in Maple Springs. In G.E.M's previous will, the cottage went to the girls probably because Selma and G.E.M thought they had more interest in it than Selma did because she hadn't spent as many summers there as the girls had. Over the last five years Selma grew to love the place, I think lately you and Vonny had something to do with that, and the girls haven't even been there in the last few years. So with this will change effected with Mr. Robertson, if G.E.M. were to pass on first, the cottage was to go to Selma and then upon her death, Mr. Robertson was to sell the cottage and the money was to go to Selma's church. The Stone girls all have their own homes and income mostly as a result of investments that G.E.M. initiated for them, so there was no need to worry about them, financially. There may have been other changes or additions, but none of which I am aware. G.E.M. told me one time that he felt that his will was quite fair and he wasn't going to be mean or vengeful. I told him that I didn't think he had a mean or vengeful bone in his body. I don't think I told you anything that is a deep secret, you can share all this with the sheriff."

"Scarlet, that's all news to me. In all the time we spent with Selma and G.E.M we never talked wills, finances, even health concerns. Oh, we laughed about aches and pains and meds, but never talked about disabilities or death. It looks like it was a good thing that they made their updates. Do you think that you are the only one in Savannah that knows all this?" asked Colin.

"I am confident that I am. G.E.M. told me about the changes on the telephone. He said that he didn't want to put it in a letter or e-mail. I am a confidential secretary. He was a wonderful boss, very generous. I respected him and any information that he shared with me. So I'd say that it was Selma, G.E.M, Mr. Robertson and I that knew there were will changes," said Scarlet and it appeared that she completed what it was that she wanted to share with Colin, what she thought might be an important part of any investigation that would surely be undertaken regarding the deaths of G.E.M. and Selma Stone.

"My, my," said Scarlet. "I did talk a lot. I think that I was talkin' so that I wasn't thinkin.'"

"Scarlet, you have been very helpful. This crime is only a couple hours old, so there is lots to do. We will get to the bottom of this. I will keep in touch. I told Kyle that I would have you call her. She's still in her office. You two need to support each other."

"I will call her right now. There is a cute little café and bar that just opened right next door to her agency. I'll see if we can meet there and toast Selma and G.E.M. Goodbye Mr. O'Brien and good luck talking with the precious Stone girls," said Scarlet.

Colin hung up and just sat there for a moment. He was contemplating postponing calls to the Stone girls until the next morning. The telephone rang. The sound of the ring seemed to be really loud. He quickly punched the talk button so that the ringing wouldn't wake, Vonny.

"Hello," he said.

"Mr. O'Brien, Colin, it's Scarlet again. I just thought that you might have a difficult time connecting with the girls, so I called to share a code word with you that will almost guarantee your connection with them. Mr. Stone got angry because not one of the daughters would answer her telephone. They never called back even though their answering machine said that they would. He made them all promise to answer immediately when he called and left the code word 'Peaches'. Peaches was the name of the Corgi dog that the Stones had when the girls were growing up. When G.E.M. said that word, he would hang on and they were to answer the telephone. He knew that all three girls screened calls, but when he wanted to talk with them, he wanted to talk with them. He only used the code word a couple times, but this system worked. Try it. Also, I neglected to tell you that all funeral arrangements have been made for both G.E.M. and Selma. They made their wishes known a couple years ago. The girls know the wishes. G.E.M. entrusted me to make sure that all was accomplished according to his, and Selma's desires. I will be ready to act when you tell me to go ahead. I have obituaries too. There are blanks in them for me to fill in, but I won't do that until your sheriff gives me the right words and the go ahead. I'm going to call Kyle now. Hope to talk to you soon. Bye."

Colin said goodbye and the connection was broken. The ice tea wasn't the quencher that Colin needed, so he went inside to make a gin and tonic, a favorite Maple Springs summer drink second only to white wine. He checked and Vonny was in the same position she was in before he spoke to Joe, Kyle and Scarlet. It was sleep, she was in in-the-arms-of-Morpheus variety of sleep and not a yoga zone.

Gin and tonic in hand, he returned to the Adirondack chair geared up to call the Ruby, the Pearl and the Opal. Kyle and Scarlet said that the experience wouldn't be too bad, but Colin wasn't so sure about that. The fact was that he had to tell the girls that their stepmother had been found murdered in Maple Springs and that their father had, apparently, passed away in Italy. It was sparse information that he had to relay to the three Stone daughters, but he had to call nonetheless. He really did not have a solid plan when he dialed again into the 912 area code.

"Ah am so sorry that Ah am unable to answer your call jest now. Call another tom. Ah hope that we get to talk real soon," said a voice, probably Ruby's, on Ruby's answering machine.

"Peaches," said Colin feeling a little foolish. Then he reminded himself that he was on official business, following orders given by Sheriff Joe Green. Colin waited.

"Daddy, it's Ruby here, but then you know that, you called me. Back from It'ly? Tell me ahl about it," this time it was the real Ruby talking. "Where is this number that is appearin' on my phone's caller ID screen?"

"Ms. Stone, my name is Colin O'Brien and I live in Maple Springs, on Lake Chautauqua."

"How did you get my number and the code word? Are you selling somethin'?" Ruby hissed.

"Ms. Stone, your father gave me your number and the pass word," answered Colin. He decided not to involve Scarlet. "I have been delegated by the local sheriff to call you and your sisters. You are the first that I have called. I'm afraid that I have some unpleasant news for you," Colin said as he started through the four steps for breaking bad news as prescribed by Sheriff Green.

"Mr. O'Conner, Ah do not like the tenor of your voice. Sounds like you are nervous or about to tell lies or both," said Ruby.

"My name is O'Brien and I am not nervous nor am I lying. Please allow me to speak uninterrupted for just a moment."

There was no response from Ruby, so Colin proceeded,

starting again with step #1 of the breaking bad news instructions. "As I said, I have some unpleasant news to convey to you. I am sorry to have to do this, but it is important that I give you this information in a timely manner." Still no response from Miss Ruby. "Just two hours ago a body was discovered in your family's cottage which is just down the street from my house. It was not your father. It was Mrs. Stone, Selma." As he had requested, Colin was not being interrupted. "We think, at this time, that your father died in Italy and Selma completed the tour and returned here to Maple Springs. Also, it is apparent that there is foul play involved in the death of Selma Stone, Mrs. Stone, your stepmother," said Colin. He decided to stop here. He realized that he was getting carried away and he didn't want to become melodramatic.

"May I speak now Mr. O'Brien?" asked Ruby.

Colin told her that she could and that he would be glad to try, he emphasized try, to answer any questions she might have.

"That certainly is unpleasant news, like a bolt of lightnin' come from outa nowhere. Ah assure you that Ah do understand all that you said. Ah am deeply saddened hearin' this information, but, too, Ah do not know the reasons for some of the actions that you have relayed. Surely you must know more than what you have just conveyed to me. I received an e-mail statin' that both Daddy and Miss Selma would be returnin' home and needin' to talk to my sisters and myself. Your news belays all of that."

Colin wasn't about to give Ruby, or her two sisters, any more information than the steps called for.

"That is all that we can share with you at this point. Please accept my sincere sympathy. There is, as we speak, an ongoing investigation taking place. I will give you my telephone number, I have yours, and I will call, or the sheriff will call, to update you. We may have questions for you too, so please be available to take calls from area code 716 without the caller having to say 'Peaches." Enough, thought Colin and he stopped talking, proud of himself because he had hit all four points of his giving sad news patter.

"Ah certainly wasn't accusin' you of keepin' me, us, in the dark and Ah do so appreciate you being ever so kind in callin' me, Deputy O'Brien," said Ruby. Colin decided that there was no need to explain anything to Ruby with regard to his deputy status.

"Ah will call my sisters and give them your telephone number just in case they have any questions," added Ruby.

"No," said Colin, his voice too loud he thought. "I will be calling your sisters right now. Sheriff department protocol requires that each next of kin be informed by personnel from our department. There can be no second-hand or worse yet telephone-tree or answering machine calls regarding news of a death. I hope that you will comply in this matter. You may want to call your sisters later this evening. I am sure that you will be needing support in this difficult time," said Colin glad that he had had a chance to include the word difficult, and pleased that he had concocted a sheriff's department rule regarding making contact with next of kin.

Colin again offered his sympathy, gave Ruby his telephone number and said goodbye. He waited for a goodbye, didn't get one, and he pushed the disconnect button on the telephone.

Phew, that was tough thought Colin. He wondered where

Ruby was. He knew that she was the only sister that did not live in Savannah. She could be anywhere and still maintain a cell phone number that originated in the 912 area. She maintained her 912 accent, why not her 912 cell phone number. G.E.M. had said at some point that she was helping the less fortunate in the southwest of the United States.

Colin immediately continued his duties and placed the call to Opal.

"You have reached the Savannah Academy for the Dance Arts. We cannot attend to this call at the moment. We are in the studio and all else stops when we dance. Our receptionist monitors this telephone from nine to five, Monday through Friday. For more information, please check our website at www.savannahcandance.com."

Even though there were no instructions about leaving a message and no beep, Colin said "Peaches."

"Daddy, Daddy, Daddy. I am so glad that you are heah. Forgive the message, Ah gotta do business ya know. Are you OK?" said Opal.

"Ms. Stone," Colin started right in, "my name is Colin O'Brien and I am a neighbor and friend of your Father. I live in Maple Springs on Lake Chautauqua. I am afraid that I have some unhappy, rather unpleasant, information to pass along to you."

"It's Daddy, isn't it? He musta got somethin' in It'ly. Nevah shoulda gone on that trip. Nevah. Sick as a dog Ah bet." Opal rattled off her opinions in rapid succession.

"Ms. Stone, I am sorry that I have to give you the news that a body was found in your family's cottage here at Maple Springs.

The body was that of Selma Stone, your stepmother," said Colin in a soft voice hoping to help Opal stay calm.

"What? You have got to be kiddin'. What kind of sick joke is this? Daddy would have called, not asked you to call." Opals rapid fire talk came to a halt.

Colin jumped right in adding his half of the dialogue. "The sheriff here is investigating all aspects of this situation. Miss Selma returned to Maple Springs alone and we assume that your Daddy, I mean your father, died in Italy. I cannot say for sure that that is what happened, but the facts of the death in Italy will surely be a part of our investigation."

Colin paused to let Opal take in what he had just told her. He was sure that her mind, and not at this time her mouth, was racing.

"Also, there was criminal intent involved in the death here on Lake View Avenue. I assure you that the situation is being taken very seriously. I will give you my telephone number in case you need to call for clarification and I assure you that we will keep you informed of our findings during this difficult time," Colin concluded, but he was not happy with his use of the four rules from the sheriff. He had done better with Ruby. Hopefully he would get back on his game for Pearl.

"Well Mr. O'Brien, you certainly took me by surprise. Ah have been overtaken by deep and serious sadness. Mah Daddy gone, it is too much. And Miss Selma involved in a crime at my cottage," said Opal.

"Ms. Stone, please. Selma's only involvement in a crime is to be the victim of some cruel person's violence. Miss Selma was a lovely person and she made your father a very happy man. I have a great deal of respect for both Mr. and Mrs. Stone." Colin had to speak before Opal rushed to erroneous conclusions.

"Oh my, oh my. Mr. O'Brien, you must think I am awful. I am not. I am heartbroken and in a serious quandary over the details of this crime. Can I call it a crime?" asked Opal.

Colin could just see this call going on for some time, so he took this opportunity to get in his final salvo of information and to get on to his call to Pearl: yes, it is a crime; do not call your sisters now, I will, you can call them later; here's my telephone number; the sheriff or I will call you; goodbye.

It was now almost seven o'clock and Colin wanted to call Pearl, wake up Vonny and get to the soup. He could now, out in the back yard, smell the soup.

Just as he dialed Pearl in Savannah, Vonny came out of the back door and sat in the Adirondack chair next to him. He realized that she had no idea what he was doing, who he was calling, why. He put his finger to his lips in a shush signal and turned to his list and got serious concerning his duties as prescribed by the sheriff.

"Good evening, this is Pearl Stone speaking. How may I help you?" said a very smooth, even voice without any trace of an accent at the 912 end of the telephone line.

"Peaches," said Colin.

"I beg your pardon. Perhaps you have the wrong number," said that same lovely voice, no accent.

"Oh, I am so sorry," said Colin realizing that he had reached a real person and not a machine. "Ms. Stone, my name is Colin

O'Brien and I am calling you from Maple Springs on Chautauqua Lake."

"Yes, what is it?" asked Pearl Stone.

Colin could hear the concern in her voice and when he turned to look at Vonny, he could see the incredulity in her face. Again he shushed her with his finger and he jumped right into his unpleasant message.

"I am sorry that I have to be the one to share some very unpleasant news with you this evening," said Colin mixing two steps into one. Vonny's presence was throwing off his game.

"Yes," again from Pearl, still concerned.

Colin charged ahead. "Just a few hours ago, a body was discovered in your family's cottage on Lake View Avenue. Our preliminary investigation suggests foul play. The body has been identified as Mrs. Selma Stone," said Colin and he waited for a response from the other end. He got one.

"Mr. O'Brien, a week or more ago, Mrs. Selma Stone and my father, G.E.M. Stone, e-mailed from Italy, where they are touring, that they would be contacting us upon their return to Savannah. I think they are still enjoying that tour. Surely you, someone, must have made a faulty identification," Pearl intoned in her lovely voice.

Colin wasn't sure where to go with this back and forth, and Vonny was all ears and he was getting the idea that she thought that he was treading where he shouldn't have dared to tread. Vonny was on the edge of her chair, all ears.

"We are very sure that the body is that of Selma Stone. Both the sheriff and I have positively identified it, her. We have just begun our investigation and will be sure to keep you apprised of new information as we move through this investigative process," said Colin. Now Vonny was up, hands on hips.

"This is extraordinary news. And my father is where? Miss Selma appears to be in a situation that she needs to explain, but at the same time, she will be unable to explain her actions. May I speak with my father? He wasn't well. I tried to persuade him not to go abroad. Miss Selma was insistent and things are now a mess and there is no one to untangle this mess," said Pearl obviously trying to make sense out of a situation that was both confusing and contradictory.

Colin could not let Pearl's questions go unanswered. He felt that he was making a mess of this phone call to Pearl.

"Ms. Stone, it is also apparent that your father passed away in Italy. Miss Selma returned to Maple Springs alone, but was dead before we could learn from her about your father. This situation is a tangle, to be sure, but there is someone to untangle it; Sheriff Joe Green and his crime scene team will be investigating and I am confident, solving this case. Remember too, your father was also very insistent upon making the trip to Italy. My wife and I spent many wonderful days with Selma and G.E.M. and both were eager to tour Italy. They had both made the plans with Kyle Kennedy and both had prepared in many ways for the trip; physically, logistically and legally," Colin said this casually, but immediately realized that he said too much and he hurried to end the call.

"I have spoken with your sisters and I gave them my

telephone number in case any of the three of you need to call for more information. I assure you that Sheriff Green will be calling you. You have my sincere sympathy. Good night Ms. Stone."

Colin didn't get in difficult, but that was OK, he was just glad to get off the phone, but he wasn't glad to have to face Vonny.

"What the hey? I can't believe that you took it upon yourself to call G.E.M.'s daughters. Are you bonkers?" Vonny's arms were going, she was pacing, but her voice was not neighbor-hearing loud.

"Wait, wait, wait," said Colin. "I was following orders from Joe Green. It was Joe that called right after I came home from G.E.M.'s. He called from Erie. Remember, a baby entering the world?"

Colin was going to continue explaining, but just then two crime scene vehicles came to a stop in the road in front of the O'Brien's house. Pete Gianna stuck head and shoulders out of the passenger window of the police car. The van idled right behind the cruiser.

"Hey Mr. O'Brien, we're just checking so we know where you live. We are headed outa here now. The Sheriff called, told us you were gonna call nexta kin for him. Man, we really appreciate that. We hate those calls and then on top of it, Joe makes us use his four points for breaking bad news," said Pete, doing air quotes and simultaneously screwing his face into a sneer.

Colin had actually liked using the four points and wanted to defend Joe, his friend, but thought this a bad time to express that opinion.

Vonny sidled up to Colin as Pete spoke and so Colin introduced her to Pete and then Steve Johnson. After polite hellos, Pete told them that the body was being removed to the county morgue and that a guard was posted at the Stone's for overnight and that they, the sheriff or possibly the DA would be around tomorrow and then, they were gone.

Colin and Vonny looked towards the Stones in time to see two men dressed in light blue uniforms climbing into the driver and passenger doors of a county vehicle that looked like a cross between a panel truck and a hearse. Then that vehicle was out of sight, it took another route and did not go by the O'Brien's house. The only vehicle left on the street at Stone's was a small blue, hatch-back car of some sort, perhaps a Honda, the overnight guard.

"Oops," was all Vonny could say.

"That's it, oops? You actually believed that I would interfere that much, that I'd want to spread the bad news, what, for kicks?" Colin said laying on the guilt, enjoying laying on the guilt. He returned to his Adirondack chair and Vonny found her way back to her chair too.

"Sorry," Vonny said. "I came in at the end of a series of conversations and had no idea about you helping Joe. I should have known that you wouldn't take matters into your own hands. Come on, accept my apology. Please."

"Soup's on," said Colin bounding out of his chair and going in the back door. He'd let her stew for a few minutes more, it wasn't quite time to forgive her. It also wasn't time to tell her about his deputization. It may never be time for that.

CHAPTER 17

The soup was great. Vonny had also made cornbread muffins. Healthy, comfort food…what a treat. Before Colin sat down to eat the soup, as he went into the silverware drawer for spoons, he remembered the spoon in his back pocket and, oh yes, the letter. He put the hidden spoon nonchalantly in the sink, he and Vonny ate, he washed the dishes, all the time ignoring the letter afraid that its revelation during the meal might give Vonny the chance to review the interference charge and to renege on her oops and sorry.

Vonny and Colin sat on the porch after their soupper, that's what the O'Briens called supper that was primarily soup, and they tried to sort out the Selma and G.E.M. scenario. Much of the story was pretty clear, but confusion set in quickly. Perhaps it was time to whip out the letter, it might give some clarity to the situation.

"Vonny, I have to admit that I was in the Stone's house before the coroner came." He couldn't lie. "I thought that I heard a timer go off on a dryer, coffeepot, something. And I went in to check." Alright, he did lie. "As I looked around, I found an envelope with our name on it and decided that it belonged to us. I took it. Want to read it?" Colin blurted out. He took it from his pocket and placed it on the table between them. It just sat there reeling them into the mystery and murder.

The look on Vonny's face showed her pique, but she was

excited to think that only they would be privy to the envelope's contents. Was it a letter, coupons, something from Italy?

"Well it is addressed to us. It says 'Colin & Vonny' on the front. I took it. I'll open it," he said.

Colin lost no time. The envelope was not sealed, the flap was merely tucked in, but Colin very quickly and carefully extracted the sheet of paper that had been neatly folded and placed in the envelope.

"It's a letter. I'll read it," said Colin not wasting any time scanning it first.

My Dear Colin and Vonny,

I'm home, but I am not who you think I am… the person currently residing in the Stone's cottage is me…Selma Stone.

Bill Morris brought me here from the Niagara Falls Airport. I pretended that I was G.E.M., had to, I'm dead you know…I'm pretty sure that I did not fool Bill.

Yes, you're right if you are now thinking that it was my wonderful G.E.M. who died in Italy. I finished the tour as myself, but then I traveled home as G.E.M. I had good reason.

I thought that I had this rouse all figured out, but now that I am here, I'm confused. I know that I can count on you two to help me sort this out, deal with reality and, hopefully, mend any breaches I may have caused.

Come for coffee and almond squares after church tomorrow. While you are at church, say a prayer for me...I am going to need your help and your prayers.

You must be confused. I am.

See you soon, Selma

PS Someone has been here and cleaned, Eileen I presume, but also, lots of things have been removed, replaced...Eileen, one of G.E.M'sdaughters, local bad boys, you two? All is neat, no damage, I'm sure there is a logical answer?

"She's right, I am confused," said Vonny. "She didn't want anyone to know that G.E.M. was dead, she said that she had good reason, but she can't explain it to us now. And, things taken from the house, oh and let's not forget her murder. Colin, I don't like this," Vonny was becoming distraught.

"Come on, Hon," said Colin as he moved his chair away from the table and reached over and pulled Vonny on to his lap.

"It's OK, we have a security officer at Stones, the sheriff has the investigation underway, I promised the sheriff that I would help him, so we'll know what's happening. Relax. OK?"

Without Selma there to explain things, Colin and Vonny decided that Sheriff Joe would have to make some official calls to Italy in order to make sense of the situation. Then there was the murder and the murderer to ponder. Vonny was tired and had to admit that she was even scared. Colin agreed to lock the doors, something they almost never did, and he would come to bed early. Vonny just wanted to be prone; proneness always led to sleep, Vonny wasn't fooling anybody.

CHAPTER 18

Vonny was prone and asleep before Colin had a chance to roll up the car windows, rain predicted, and stack the porch cushions so that they wouldn't get wet. As he completed the stacking, each pile consisting of a particular size and color, Colin looked down the street and saw the security guard sitting on the Stone's steps just in front of the yellow police crime scene tape, talking on a cell phone. Colin decided to take him some coffee and a couple corn bread muffins to help him get through the night.

When Colin arrived at the Stones with a six cup coffee carafe, a cup and cornbread muffins on a small tray, the security guard was not in sight. It was quickly getting dark and Colin wanted to get home and lock up. He too was tired. Colin set the thermos and tray on the porch steps and called not too loudly, "Hello, anybody here?"

"Mr. O. is that you?" said a tall, very slim, young man as he stepped from behind the rhododendron at the end of the porch.

"Billy, Bill Korbin, is that you?" said Colin as the two met on the sidewalk and shook hands.

"What are you doing here?" asked Billy. "I'm working, so I got a reason to be here."

"I live down the street. I was the first person to see the body," said Colin carefully choosing his words. Everyone would agree that Elgin is not a person. "I brought you some coffee.

There's no Tim Horton's in this neighborhood and I thought you might need something to keep you awake."

"I was just on the phone with my girlfriend. She works at Tim Horton's, but can't get out here. I told her that I'd be OK. It is going to be a long shift. I worked all day as security at the mall in Lakewood and came right here when the sheriff's office called. I figure that I'll be up over twenty-four hours when I get relieved in the morning. I never turn down Sheriff Joe when he calls. I wanna make points with him, be part of his department someday. This coffee, yikes, and my favorite, cornbread, will help me get through the night. Thanks."

"Glad to help. Glad that you're working. Are you allowed in the house or are you just supposed to patrol outside?" asked Colin.

"I can't go inside. That was a problem, but I solved that problem in the rhododendrons just now."

Colin laughed. He vividly remembered Bill, he was Billy then, and all the problems that Billy had. But he remembered too that Billy had an older sister that was tough, determined, and she was keeping the family together and making sure that Billy towed the line, got to school, etc. Looks like her persistence paid off.

For the last few years of his teaching career, Colin had taught Alternative Education. Alt Ed was defined as educational programming for students, bright though they might be, but who were failing because they couldn't deal with the structured setting of regular school. Billy and all the other students in the program made progress, most actually graduated from high school once some of those bothersome school restrictions upon their personal expression were lifted, bent, forgotten.

"Hey, Bill. I can relieve you for a couple hours if you want to get some sleep. Sheriff Green enlisted my help, actually he deputized me, because he had to go by chopper to Erie with his wife. Kid number six joined the Green household within the last few hours."

"Mr. O., it would be great if you could give me a break. Not just now though. Can you come back later? Whenever you show, I'll catch some zzzzs in my car. That'd be great."

Colin and Bill caught up on life's twists and turns since they had shed their teacher/student roles a few years earlier. Each seemed genuinely interested in the other and they were glad to be working together again albeit with a different set of roles and rules.

Plans were made for Colin's return. It wasn't ideal for Colin to return at midnight, but he was anxious to help Bill and he was willing to sacrifice some sleep time for the good of the department. He headed home. Her Proneness was asleep, an inevitability. Colin locked the doors and doused the lights before he slipped out of his crocs and got comfortable on the couch. He set the small travel alarm that he kept in the coffee table drawer for 11:45 and that was all she wrote.

CHAPTER 19

Colin actually awoke before the alarm chimed his wake up time. He quickly got himself together, checked on Her Proneness, sleeping, and left the house quietly headed to take up the post of security guard on Lake View Avenue.

As Colin approached the Stone's cottage, he saw Bill Korbin pacing on the sidewalk and humming to himself. Then Colin noticed the earphones and realized that Bill was listening to music and probably pacing in an effort to keep himself awake. Bill noticed Colin and removed the headphones and put them in his shirt pocket.

"Glad to see you Mr. O. My eyelids are like lead and I am sort of tingling head to toe, don't think I have ever been this tired. Thanks. I am going to put my passenger seat back and stretch out. I'll set the alarm on my cell phone and be perky when I return. Shake me if you need me," and with that Bill was in his little blue hatch-back, it was a Honda, and was probably asleep as his head settled back on the headrest.

Once Bill stopped talking and his car door shut, The Springs was silent, dark and for the first time since Colin had settled there, a little scary. Two hours Colin thought, I should have offered one. Nah, two would be just fine he easily convinced himself. The crime scene guys had left a couple lights on inside the house and the front porch and a back deck light were also on, but the light didn't spread anywhere, it just wrapped the cottage in soft glow like a lit snow globe set in the sea of darkness that was Maple Springs in the middle of the night.

Colin took his first walk around the house, nice and slow, not really looking for anything or anyone, just walking and looking. He made a couple turns around and then seriously did notice where things were placed as he walked slowly around for the fourth and fifth time: deck furniture was huddled close to the house, the front porch was still all set up looking inviting, the garden hose was coiled near the deck out back and a stack of clay pots of varying sizes was hidden under an exposed end of the deck near the back door. No junk, no disarray and no clutter; just a summer cottage ready to be bundled up for the winter. Colin wasn't sure how that was to happen this year. He'd have to call Eileen, the Stone's cleaning lady, and see if she had a bundle up plan in place. Eileen cleaned for a lot of the Springers, but was more like a personal assistant because she also coordinated lawn care, dock placements, painting and even did some cooking and she often chauffeured Amish craftsmen, house cleaners and child care workers for families in The Springs and in the immediate area. She'd surely know the Stone's routine. He also needed a call to inform her about Selma's demise. She might be very helpful to the sheriff in determining if anything was missing from the house. In her letter, Selma had said that things were shuffled around, replaced. And why was that? Who did that? Eileen had been there to clean and Brad, "…the one to call for the best in craftsmanship"… had done his thing, whatever that was. Who else had crossed the Stone's threshold recently?

Colin also thought of the Stone's carpet stained with Selma's blood that would have to be taken care of. Eileen would probably come through and have this job accomplished as soon as the yellow crime scene tape came down.

Colin enjoyed his turn as a security guard at a crime scene, for about thirty minutes. He was enjoying the quiet, the dark and all the subtle night sounds and smells of Maple Springs. He hadn't been up this late since he and Vonny had settled in their new home, but it was okay to be up and out tonight, he had duties to perform.

Not a car went by, not a person. A couple dogs sniffed their way down the street, ignoring him, and he heard owners too tired to walk their dogs one last time of the day whistle for their errant pets' return. That was about it for activity, domesticated activity anyway. Colin had a sighting or two of woodchucks, called ground hogs in these parts, as they scurried under a porch, into a dense patch of bushes, or once, boldly, right across the Stone's sidewalk. The local cadre of squirrels must have had the day off, Colin didn't see one. He also experienced a bat or two as he circled the house. All in all, it was another quiet night in Maple Springs.

An hour and a half into his tour of duty, Colin, tired of the outside of the house, slipped under the yellow police tape and approached the front, screen door. He looked in and saw that there was no longer a body in the front hall, the spot where the body had laid was covered with a square of blue tarp that looked like it was specifically cut to cover that area. He could see through the

house and out the back screen door. He moved into the center of
the porch and squeezed between the back of the wicker settee and
the front wall of the house in order to look into the living room
windows. The four very heavy suitcases were still where he had
last seen them and the one that Selma was living out of was still
opened on the couch. Colin was pleased to see that the cottage
looked orderly. On most television police shows and in mystery
novels, when the crime scene team, in their efforts to be thor-
ough, searched a crime scene, they virtually trashed the place.
Colin was sure that the crime scene team had searched the place,
but this team was considerate and neat.

Colin moved from behind the settee and slipped back under the yellow police crime scene tape and went down the stairs
and off the porch. He crossed the street and turned and looked
at the Stone's cottage. He stood there for a few minutes and all
kinds of questions, memories and emotions bombarded him. He
shook them off and headed back to the Stone property and to
the back of the house. Again, he slipped under the yellow police
crime scene tape and this time he boldly entered the house. He
didn't worry about fingerprints, the sheriff knew he was there, he
was in the commission of his duties, he was hardly a suspect.

Colin thought it strange to be in the house, a human piece
of a crime scene, neither victim nor perpetrator, just an interested
neighbor, friend and deputy. He took two steps into the kitchen
and stood very still and looked around. Now he could see the
work of the crime scene team; drawers were not quite closed,
items on the counter were askew, the contents of Selma's purse
that had been spread out on the kitchen table were now all placed

in a plastic evidence bag in the center of the table alongside of the purse yawning open. The light coats from the hooks in the front hall were now piled on a seat for boot-putting-on that was in the hall close to the front door. The spot on the floor where earlier Selma had laid was now completely covered with a piece of blue tarp. With no body and no view of the stained floor, it was easy for Colin to be more at ease. He wondered if there was a chalk outline of Selma under the blue tarp, but he did not lift it to look. He went into the living room, skirting the blue tarp on his way, and again noticed the handy work of the crime scene team. It didn't look like the three unopened suitcases had been disturbed, but the fourth that was opened on the couch had obviously been ransacked. Several items from the suitcase had been placed on a dish towel spread on the buffet in the adjoining dining room. Serving items that had been displayed on the buffet were now all pushed to one end and even piled one on the other. The items that had been taken from the suitcase and were now placed on a towel were the items that would hold a fingerprint; shoes, plastic bottles, a cosmetic bag, a small hair dryer. The assemblage of silver and ceramic serving items stood sparkling at one end of the buffet. Colin thought, and was sure that his crime scene team also thought, that the perpetrator or perpetrators had not han-dled them.

Colin didn't touch a thing, he looked at everything. It looked as though the crime scene team hadn't completed their work. They said that they would be back tomorrow and Colin hoped that he could be incorporated into their investigations. He took a last walk around the downstairs, through the living room, then the hall, the kitchen and back into the dining room. His eyes were drawn again to the clutter on the buffet top. Selma's items were in a single layer, nestled close to each other and held no surprises. At first, Colin thought it odd that there was no jewelry among Selma's effects; G.E.M. Stone's wife traveling the world without a piece of jewelry? The jeweler to the best families in the south hadn't adorned his beloved wife with the best of jewels? Probably, Colin then thought, Selma didn't like to travel and be a walking invitation to thieves. She had jewelry, lots of good stuff, Colin knew that, he'd seen it, but he also knew that Selma wasn't one to flaunt her wealth.

"Pssssst...you in there?" It was Bill's voice calling from the front porch.

Colin slipped through the dining room into the kitchen and soundlessly out the back door and stepped off the deck and onto the ground as he said in a stage whisper, "I'm out back, comin' your way."

Bill and Colin met by the rhododendrons.

"Thanks Mr. O, I really needed that sleep. I'm good till morning now. Everything quiet?"

Colin filled Bill in on his totally uneventful tour of duty. He mentioned animal visitors and his circumnavigation of the house, but made no mention of his interior house tour and then he headed home. He thought he might see Bill in the morning and was anxious to meet with Sheriff Joe, the crime scene team and maybe the DA. Varying scenarios of those meetings played in Colin's head, briefly, as he fell asleep.

CHAPTER 20

"Colin, Colin, wake up. Lots to do today." Colin opened his eyes expecting to see Vonny on the other end of that deep voice. Deep voice?

"I made coffee, get up," said Sheriff Joe.

"You got a warrant to be in here, disturbing my sleep, frisking Mr. Coffee?" Colin asked. Even lack of sleep could not dull Colin's strong comedic bent. He thought it was a strong comedic bent, his family thought he was comically challenged.

When Colin joined the sheriff on the porch, there was coffee and gigantic cinnamon rolls from the Bemus Point Inn. Joe let Colin have a sip and bite before he started in.

"First, here's a note from Vonny," said Joe and then he let Colin continue sipping and commence reading.

Hi Hon, (aka Lazybones)
Went to Stash Busters in Kennedy with Barb.
(I had to "get out of town" during all that CSI stuff…
don't think me a chicken)
Would you wear alpaca sox?
I talked to Joe…it's a(nother) boy. Antony,
Tone for short…love it.
We should be home by noon (?).
Might stop at the Amish quilters. Might stop
for lunch.

We should be home by 3:00 (?)

Dinner at Guppy's, my treat.

XOXO, V

"Okay, Joe, I'm sufficiently awake. You talk first. Tell me about the baby, anything new regarding Selma and what's in store for today? I'm free all day and reporting for duty," said Colin and he was going to stand up and salute, just to be funny, but he demurred.

"The kid is great," said Joe. "We're calling him Antony, Tone for short. Shannon is excellent, should be home late tomorrow, not exactly eager to get home. My folks are at our house with the horde and Shannon's folks are at Hamot with her. They're gonna switch places around noon and I'm going to the hospital this evening. Obviously we made great plans beforehand. The only glitch was the trip to Erie. Tone should have arrived in the Westfield Hospital. Any questions?"

Colin didn't have any questions about the baby, but he did congratulate Joe on boy number six. That earned Colin a cigar with a blue band.

Joe continued, "Not much new regarding the Stone case, in fact nothing. The coroner did his work, but the crime scene boys will be back before noon. We usually don't do this sort of work on a Sunday, but we gotta hop on evidence ASAP and I'm anxious to keep this from the media till we have something to report, or at least we are well into an investigation."

Sunday, Colin hadn't even thought about day or time. Must

have missed church too. Vonny had let him sleep in. Sunday, there'd be no Amish business being conducted on Sunday, he thought. Sorry Vonny.

Colin was eager to report to Joe regarding his telephone calls to Savannah, his late night tour of duty and his take on the crime. He quickly changed his mind and decided not to mention that he got a lot of crime scene details when he was "shadowing" the coroner and then on second thought he also decided not to mention his spelling of Bill during the wee hours of the morning. Colin thought that he might get coroner Fourtney and/or Bill Korbin in trouble for letting down their guards with regard to securing the crime scene using only the professionals. He thought too that he should get some clarification on his status as a member of this murder investigation team. Joe had said that he was deputizing him. Why would Joe joke about that? Colin knew that he had skills as a team player, smart too. The team needed him.

Colin was just getting ready to report to Joe when Joe withdrew a narrow, thick notebook from a pocket on his right thigh, flipped it open and got right down to business.

"Colin, I have a few questions; clarify a few things for me, will ya?" said Joe.

"Yes Sir," said Colin perhaps a little too loudly, "but first I need to make a pit stop. Be right back," and he was gone.

When he returned to the porch, Eileen Miller was seated across from Sheriff Joe and she had a cup of coffee that Joe and Mr. Coffee had supplied. She was in the middle of an explanation of what she did for the Stones.

"I'm their point man here in The Springs. I open the place up in the spring and I get closing-up plans in the works in the fall. I was also in there on Thursday of this week cleaning up for G.E.M.'s return, or rather Selma's return from what you're saying. I hope you and your men aren't as confused as I am about this whole mess. I loved Miss Selma, reminded me of my momma, and G.E.M. has been a Godsend to me for over twenty-five years," said Eileen.

"I am not proud of my youth," Eileen continued. "Actually I don't remember much of said youth, my remote youth. But I do remember the day that I was in Jamestown and decided to hitch-hike to Midway Park and get me a summer job, doing anything. G.E.M. and Lula, the first Mrs. Stone, picked me up; told me they got nervous when they saw 'ladies hitchin'. They could see that I was hurtin', hurtin' in lots of ways. I never made it to Midway. They took me home and I lived with them, for two years actually, taking care of them when they was here and taking care of the house in the off season. I could have cleaned them out rather than cleaning up, but they trusted me, trusted me when I didn't even trust myself. They got me work with lots of folks they knew and bought me a used car and I was in business. Business is good. My life is good, but when you think of G.E.M. and Selma, life is pretty cruel too."

Eileen stopped talking and the three of them just sat there each wrapped in their own thoughts. Joe sat tall, ahemed and referred to his notebook and then got the conversation back on track.

"So when you cleaned this week was everything in order? Any breakage, signs of vandalism?" said Joe.

Eileen thought for a moment. "No vandalism, nothing damaged, but lots of stuff traded out."

Joe asked, "Traded out?"

"You know, new essentials and decorative stuff in place of the good old stuff that was there. One item, really lots of items, replaced for another of the same type but for sure cheaper. F'rinstance, some of the paintings on the walls have been replaced with prints; a signed Roger Tory Peterson replaced with a print of a Paris street scene. Dishes replaced, servin' pieces, especially, replaced with cheap stuff. Stuff like I have at home, dollar store stuff. Fiesta Ware replaced by Melmack, that sorta trading out," Eileen explained. Then she added, "I thought that Selma might have wanted to take some stuff home, but shoot, they got lots of stuff in Savannah, I visited them there couple times, and if she was needing trading out, she'da called me. Now, I'm not trying to do any detecting here, but it looks like an antique or art dealer was told to help themselves to the Stone's stuff, but to be sure replacements were supplied. Lots of beautiful stuff gone, junk arrived. Quality, expensive stuff gone. Collectibles. I was gonna ask G.E.M. about the trading out, I noticed it when I cleaned on Thursday, can't do that now. Whatd'ya say sheriff?"

Colin didn't give Joe a chance to answer. He jumped to his feet and blurted out, "Brad, that's who it was, Brad, the best in craftsmanship."

To say that both Joe and Eileen were startled would be to

say the obvious. Colin gave them a few seconds to settle and then, creating a scenario as he spoke, he gave them a running account of Brad's visits and what he thought took place inside the Stone's cottage during those visits. All those boxes going in and out was really a trading out caper. Colin didn't use the word caper. Joe and Eileen listened intently and in fact, Joe took some notes on his thigh pad. Eileen nodded a lot. Colin finished and they all sat there quietly for a second chewing on the information presented.

"Colin," Joe said, "I'd say you are on to something." Colin glowed with pride; newest member of the crime scene team and he had valuable input.

"Eileen," Joe turned to her and asked, "is there an inventory of the Stone's belongings? Sometimes insurance companies require them especially on buildings that are only inhabited for a few weeks a year. Who is their insurance carrier? Do they have a local agent, or is the home covered on a rider with a Savannah policy?"

"Hold on Joe, too many questions smushed together and no room in between for answerin'. I know the Anderson Agency in Jamestown has their homeowner's policy, we had to put in a claim once for ice damage. Lula was the collector. I'm sure she had a list. No, no, now I remember. One day Lula had me follow her around the house with a video camera and she talked and pointed at things and I videoed. You can hear G.E.M. in the background laughing and teasing her about being Jackie Kennedy and taking us on a tour of the house like Jackie did with the

White House. That tape must be somewhere in the house, with the insurance company or in a safety deposit box somewheres."

Again the three of them sat for a few seconds in silence each processing the new information Eileen had provided.

"OK," said Joe, "looks like we have a possible motive here, but I think we hang onto this info so it doesn't spook the perps. I'll share a lot of this with the crime scene team, but let's keep quiet about the 'trade out.'"

There was no moment of silence for the three of them to ponder. Colin just couldn't help but get back in on the conversation.

"I bet the perps thought that by trading out that no one would notice the missing items, or it might buy them some time or help shift blame to someone else. Wasn't locals, I bet. No other break-ins I know of. They knew what to take. Took the good stuff. Who breaks in and trades out?" Again, Colin noticed that Joe was valuing his input.

Joe turned to Eileen. "Eileen, we should be finishing up today with the Stone's cottage. Any chance of you getting in there and cleaning up some of the...mess?"

"I can do that Sheriff," she answered. "I have cleaned up after lots of gruesome stuff and I have the supplies, chemicals actually, to do a good job. Monday mornin', first thing. You'll be able to get back in, it'll be dried up, come Tuesday. I'll set up a fan."

Joe agreed with Eileen's plan and she left Colin and Joe alone to discuss other aspects of the situation. Colin refilled coffee cups and launched into a recounting of his telephone calls to Savannah. First he reported on the calls to the Stone jewels and he told Joe about the code word to break through the caller ID barrier, but he also said that he had asked the girls to readily accept telephone calls from the 716 area code without the caller having to say peaches.

Joe listened intently, took no notes and then asked Colin, "Any info from them that might have bearing on this case? Doesn't sound like they asked you any questions, had any interest."

"Well, I used your four point plan to talk to them and I told them we didn't know much yet and that we, actually you, would be calling them today or Monday. They were going to talk among themselves and I bet that they called Scarlet and maybe even Kyle. There was a lot more input from Kyle and, especially, Scarlet," said Colin.

"And who might Kyle and Scarlet be?" asked Joe.

Colin, feeling like a real fountain of information, told Joe about Kyle and Scarlet, including the information regarding the new Stone wills, and he opined that he was sure that these two ladies would be very helpful during the forthcoming investigation. He provided their numbers to Joe who quickly copied them into his official notebook.

"Also," said Colin almost as an afterthought, "the Stones had local legal and insurance connections. You know them both; Rhoe Anderson for insurance, like Eileen said; Neil Robertson for legal. He's with the firm of Robertson and Johnson in Jamestown.

When we need funeral home help, I know we can count on Jeff Carson at Lander's Funeral Home for good service. Speaking of that, Scarlet mentioned cremation and I think that G.E.M.'s ashes must be there somewhere in their cottage, in one of the unopened suitcases maybe. If you want, I'll care for them and get them to Lander's. What about Selma's body? When can that go to Lander's? And should we get permission from Scarlet for that, she is the executor of the will, but then, I guess that the will and the funeral specifics don't have much to do with each other. Am I right?" Colin finally finished talking and noticed that Joe was just sitting there looking at him. Silence.

"You know Colin, this is not my first murder case and currently it's slow in the office, so I think we can jump on all this stuff in an official capacity. I like the fact that you have been thinking about this and everything you said is good information that I am duly noting. And, yes, get those ashes and keep them safe," said Joe in an official but kind, appreciative voice.

Just then two cars passed the O'Brien house and turned down Lake View and stopped in front of the Stone's Cottage.

"Looks like the team is here to complete their work. I let the overnight guard go home before I woke you," said Joe as he got to his feet. "He said to thank you again for the coffee and corn muffins and I brought home your tray and carafe."

Joe didn't mention Colin's turn as the night watchman. Colin didn't mention his turn as the night watchman. Obviously, Bill hadn't mentioned Colin's turn as the night watchman.

"I better get over there and support my guys. Come on

over when you feel like it. Doc Fourtney, the coroner, is coming too. It's almost eleven, he should be here soon."

CHAPTER 21

Joe headed to the Stone's cottage and Colin was up, into and out of the bathroom in five minutes, changed his clothes and on his way to join up with his fellow crime scene team members. He grabbed Selma's letter from Vonny's dresser, just in case. He arrived just as the Coroner made his arrival known driving a little yellow sports car with the convertible top down and the radio blaring Donna Summer. The crime scene team was checking in the bushes around the cottage and they all came to the front lawn looking like a hastily arranged welcoming party.

"You're all probably wondering why I called us all together," said Joe obviously trying to be funny. Colin was the only one who laughed, probably the only one who got the joke. But then too, perhaps the crime scene team was in the work zone and wanting to be, or at least wanting to appear to be, on task, or they had heard that comment from Joe upon other occasions.

After giving due appreciation to the yellow sports car, the team moved up the steps and took seats on the flowered cushions in the genuine, wicker chairs that filled the porch. There was no wicker at Colin's house, but he appreciated its look, utility and longevity and he jealousy counted that eight people could sit, in wicker, comfortably on the porch. The fact that the color of the flowers in the floral print matched the geraniums in the eight flower boxes lounging on the wide railings surrounding the porch was not lost on Colin.

"OK," said Joe. "Let's get started. I asked Colin to join us because he was the one who first discovered the body and he can most likely give us the best background information regarding the Stone family. I also asked him, as I am sure you all know and appreciate, to call the next-of-kin and he can tell us about that too."

Colin was pleased to be a getting support and acceptance and credibility from Sheriff Joe. Colin didn't respond to Joe, he'd wait for a go-ahead. He still didn't think that he needed to credit Elgin with discovery of the body and he would continue to postpone telling Joe that he had drawn a shift of night patrol, but he knew at this point that he had to share the letter from Selma in fairness to his teammates. He'd hang onto that letter for a few minutes more.

"Can I talk first?" asked the coroner.

"That's fine by me," said Joe. "We need to all be succinct. I appreciate you all being here on a Sunday and I know that there is a Buffalo Bills kick-off time of one o'clock that we'd all like to make. Glenn, you're up."

Glenn, Dr. Glenn Fourtney, coroner, lost no time, had no intro. "The victim succumbed here on these premises at approximately two o'clock yesterday afternoon as a result of forced trauma to the back of the head probably suffered as she turned to get away from her assailant. She may indeed never have seen it coming and probably suffered very little from successive blows, probably four or five. I saw no instrument of administration of those blows, you might have found something since I was here yesterday, but I would say that from the structure of the wounds, that the weapon was flat, like a frying pan, that shape, and not a round club, like a baseball bat, and nothing with a point." He paused here, everyone was still, probably replaying that attack in their mind. "The victim is a white, female, in her mid-seventies and weighing 170 pounds. Two positive identifications, Mr. O'Brien and Sheriff Green, name the victim as Mrs. Selma Stone a resident of this house in the summer and a resident of Savannah, GA during the rest of the year. Mrs. Stone's death can most assuredly be categorized as a homicide." Dr. Fourtney stopped talking. The entire team gave his report great thought and there was a general nodding of heads.

"Thank you, Glenn," said Joe. More silence. Then, "I'd say that you can guess from the round of head movements that you just received that we all think that you are right on with your findings. Questions?"

"If the murder instrument didn't have a point, then the skin wasn't broken, so why was there so much blood?" This question just fell right out of Colin's mouth.

Glenn gave the question credence and said, "There was certainly lots of internal damage in the head and with the face down on the floor, blood from that internal wound came out of the mouth, not a lot because the body was horizontal on the floor and so there wasn't a lot of flow."

Colin was sorry he asked, probably more information than he needed. But, it wasn't a stupid question, others probably had the same thought. No wait, they all had probably experienced this scenario many times before so they knew the answer. Maybe. There are no stupid questions. There were no other questions.

The Sergeants Gianna and Johnson stood and started talking, tag-team-like, giving their report. It was cut and dry, no surprises and all the facts, just the facts ma'am. The murder, they agreed on that too, was just that. It was a murder, not a break-in and a robbery, or the work of a crazed perp, but a homicide probably conducted by someone that Mrs. Stone knew, maybe even knew well. No sign of robbery or even of rifling drawers or a purse. The contents of the purse were displayed, but the sergeants thought that Mrs. Stone was cleaning out her purse just prior to her being attacked. The place was immaculate. Appliance and fixtures shone. Windows too. There were very few fingerprints and the sergeants were pretty sure that all prints would be Mrs. Stone's. The coroner and the sergeants concurred. More head nodding.

"Thanks Pete, Steve," said Joe. "Looks like we are all in agreement and the only pieces of information that we are lacking are the identity of the perp and the motive for the murder," was Joe's summation of the two reports.

"We're moving right along here. I'd like to ask Colin to give us a quick review of what he's found out. You've all met him. He's retired, lives just down the street, was friends with the Stone family and he jumped right in to help when Shannon and Tone got their schedule screwed up. He was good enough to call next-of-kin and I know you all appreciate the fact that he accomplished this chore for you. Colin, your turn."

Joe indicated that Colin was to begin, the others gave Colin thumbs-up and big smiles of thanks-we-hate-those-next-of-kin-calls.

Colin felt all at once that he had been validated and ensconced as a team member and a valued source of information. He started his report to his fellow team members out of chronological order, but decided to continue and to be sure to backtrack and to leave nothing, well almost nothing, out. As he began, he took the letter out of his pocket so that he would not forget it at the end of his recitation.

"The Stone next-of-kin consists of three daughters all who live in the Savannah, GA area. Well, one may live elsewhere, but she has a Savannah telephone area code. I talked with all three and they were shocked, frankly confused, just as we are about motive, etc. These calls were complicated by the fact that I had to tell the girls, too, that their father was dead, had apparently died in Italy," began Colin. He noticed confused looks on the faces of Glenn, Pete and Steve and he realized that these three team members didn't know the back story leading up to the discovery of Selma's body in the Stone's cottage; didn't know about the Italian trip, the return, etc.

"I guess I better back up and make better sense of what we are in the middle of here. It all began in late August when Mr. and Mrs. Stone left for a tour of the western coast of Italy," began Colin. He narrated the story of the trip, the e-mails, the death in Italy, the discovery of Selma's body, the telephone calls and ended with the meeting they were actually in the middle of. He didn't provide all of the details that he had previously given to Sheriff Joe, didn't mention Kyle or Scarlet, but he didn't skirt any issue and he was ready to answer questions, honestly and in detail, if asked.

When he stopped talking, it was quiet for a minute. It all made sense and Colin felt that he had laid it out in good order. Lots of thinking, no questions.

"What is that envelope that you've been fingering for the last few minutes?" asked Joe breaking the silence.

"Oh," said Colin. "This is the last contact that we, my wife and I, had with Selma before her death." Okay, so far. "I think she meant it to draw us into helping her, which of course we would have done, to unravel the intrigue that she had orchestrated and now was trying to weasel out of, or correct, or at least face. We can't do that now, but I think we can sort things out and find Selma's murderer." Colin read the letter to the assembled team. No questions, but lots of confused looks on everyone's faces.

"Hello. Can I interrupt for a minute?" It was Vonny coming up the stair of the Stone's porch. All five of the men on the porch rose to greet Vonny. She beamed and it was obvious that she was both surprised and flattered by their display of manners.

"When I got home," said Vonny, "there were four messages on the answering machine and they were all for Colin, but I was sure that they all had to do with this situation regarding Selma, so I brought over the messages and the telephone list from the refrigerator. That's all. I'll go. I'm not part of this official crime scene team. I watch *NCIS*, I know my place. Bye."

The quintet of men laughed and said goodbye to Vonny. She was gone as quickly and as quietly as she had arrived.

Colin looked at the messages and immediately read the list to the others and added more information as he spoke. "Scarlet, she's Mr. Stone's private, confidential secretary called; call ASAP, I have news. Also Kyle called, same message. She runs a travel agency in Savannah and she made all travel arrangements for the Stones, for years. Ruby Stone, eldest daughter of G.E.M. Stone and step-daughter of the deceased, says that it is imperative that she speak to me. And Bill Morris called. You all know him. His message is to the point. Three Stones to arrive on Tuesday. Call if you like."

"I'd say," said Joe as he let fly with his rapid-fire translation of the messages, "that it looks like Miss Ruby Stone is calling to inform you that she and her sisters will be arriving, Scarlet and Kyle are calling to warn you that the three Stone girls will be arriving and Bill Morris is facilitating their arrival by picking them up in his limo and shuttling them here on Tuesday. D'I get that right?" Heads nodded.

"OK. We are all up to speed on what has happened here. Colin gave us the background, he's our color-man here, so now we can all understand what has transpired and our work is set for this coming Tuesday. Past. Present. Future. Thanks for coming here today. I will probably talk to Scott at the *Post-Journal* so don't be surprised if they jump on this. All inquiries come to me. Got that?" said Joe. He waited a minute, got eye contact and nods from everyone. "Now go home, don't speed, you can still make kick-off."

Everyone got up and moved off the porch.

"Here Colin," said Steve Johnson. "We found these packages in one of Mrs. Stone's suitcases. Looks like gifts, probably from Italy. Can you get these to the daughters? There's also one with your wife's name on it and now I know who gets the other two, Scarlet and Kyle." Steve handed Colin a silver plastic bag with small velvet boxes inside.

"Thanks Sgt. Johnson. I will get these to the ladies," said Colin. "The Sheriff said that I could also take charge of Mr. Stone's ashes. Did you by any chance find them?"

"I think we got 'em," said Pete Giana as he quickly stepped inside the front door and came right back out and walked to Steve and Colin. "We were wondering what this box contained. It says G.E.M. Stone on the top and it's sealed with some waxy substance all around the lid. Now we know what's in there."

He gave Colin a silver box, square with rounded corners, about the size of a one pound can of coffee, that looked like it was made of bright tin and which was tied with a burgundy cord.

"I'll take good care of these items," said Colin as he accepted them from two of his team members. "Feel free to call me if you think of something that you'd like to know more about. I'll be around."

Glenn, Pete and Steve were gone within the next couple of minutes, not slowly or quietly, and Joe and Colin locked the doors of the Stone's home, removed the crime scene tape and started walking back to Colin's house.

"I don't think we'll need to secure this place for another day. We've got lots of pictures and Steve and Pete say they have all they need. Eileen will be cleaning it tomorrow and I am sure that the daughters will want to be in here on Tuesday or Wednesday. I'd hate to have them stay here though, a bit gory, and I don't want them stripping the place before the will is read," said Joe and then he stopped walking and stood silently.

"Colin, what would be your call regarding the girls if you were in charge?" asked Joe.

Yikes thought Colin and then he spoke and ideas he hadn't really thought through came out quite decisively.

"I think the daughters should stay at the B & B and we, Vonny and I, can make arrangements. The Stone's sent a lot of business in the B & B's direction over the years. I'm sure Will and Elizabeth will be gracious to the daughters once they know about the situation here, maybe even throw them a freebee, it's a slow season, right? And I'd be glad to call Rhoe, Jeff and Neil and have them available for the girls to talk to about their folks' wishes. And, I'll call the ladies in Savannah and Bill Morris if you'd like." Did I really offer all that? thought Colin.

"Great," said Joe. "I really need to get home to the wife, kids and Bills. Call me later, after the game, dinner, baths and bed time, and update me. Really, I appreciate this, you're the right guy in the right place at the right time. You're sure that you're cool with this?"

Colin assured Joe that he was cool with all this and he sent Joe on his way. There was no argument on Joe's part.

CHAPTER 22

When Colin entered the house, Vonny was in the process of making pies and she had two pans of sweet rolls cooling on the kitchen table.

"I'm on a roll here," she said. "No pun intended. Let me finish and clean up and then we can catch up. I was going to buy Amish pies, but I decided to make my own. I was helped with that decision when I realized that the Amish bakery and all the other Amish stores aren't open on Sunday."

"Take your time. Once again, honest, I have some calls to make for Sheriff Joe. We're still headed to Guppy's for dinner, right?"

Guppy's was a go and Vonny didn't falter in her charge into baking, nor did she make a face at Colin when he emphasized the word honest. Colin carefully, for he didn't really know their contents, placed the gift boxes he carried home from the Stones on an empty shelf in the bookcase on his side of the bed. He placed G.E.M.'s ashes there too. Vonny didn't know about the gifts, he'd give her her's at dinner.

Colin took the cordless telephone and headed to his chair in the living room. He also took the local telephone book, his calendar, a pen and the list of telephone numbers that G.E.M. had provided. He loved this chair. It had been his fathers and it held lumps, smells and memories that made Colin think of his childhood whenever he saw it, sat in it or vacuumed anywhere near it. His father had been an avid sports fan, something that did not rub off on Colin, and the chair was his father's official reserved set for most televised baseball, football and basketball contests. More than one Coke, his dad's drink of choice, had been spilled in a moment of exuberance and surely corn kernels and the dregs of bowls of chips were down there way beneath the cushions, resting on that mysterious piece of black cloth that is stretched on the bottom of most furniture, probably only old pieces of furniture, to hide the springs. Colin couldn't help but sigh as he sat down and allowed himself a couple minutes of real, total relaxation before he got on the telephone. He decided to call Bill Morris first.

"Hey Bill," said Colin before Bill could spout off the name of his company and ask how Colin's call may be directed. "Got your call and pretty much figured out what you were calling about. I got three other calls regarding the same topic, I guess, but I thought that I best call you first. I don't know what you know. And I was pretty sure that all this couldn't wait until Monday, so here I am calling on a Sunday afternoon. Speak, oh wise one."

"You through? Can I get a word in?" Silence. "Hello, Bill Morris and Associates, we can take you anywhere, anytime and in your choice of vehicles. Bill Morris speaking. How may I direct your call?" Colin was silent. "Hi Colin. I got a telephone call from Kyle Kennedy in Savannah requesting a pick up at the Buffalo Airport and I wasn't sure if she would be calling you and I knew it was information that you'd appreciate knowing. She told me about the situation at the Stone's cottage. I'm in shock. Why didn't you call me? Your turn."

"Hi Bill. Sorry for the mini-rant there, I was just trying to set up my reason for calling, getting right to the topic. Sorry too that I didn't get to you with the ugly details, you know at the Stone's. Got a little nervous, I didn't know what you knew and I was probably going to have to give you some of that ugly news. I have seven calls to make for Joe Green, my sheriff, and I was waxing efficient. Why so businesslike on your part? You have office hours on Sunday?"

"Colin, old boy, this is a very slow season for us and the office is in my kitchen and we are always open."

"What about all those associates you have? Can't they be manning the phone on weekends?" said Colin knowing full well that Bill and his wife, and sometimes during the Chautauqua Institution season, a teacher-brother-in-law, were the only three that formed the company. "Alright Bill, give me details. I have my calendar and a pen. Shoot."

"Well, Kyle called and she said that she made reservations for two of the girls, Hope and Diamond I think, to fly from Savannah to Buffalo on Tuesday afternoon and would I, as she said, 'be agreeable to fetching them for transporting to Maple Springs'. I assured her that fetching was my specialty. I'm to be at arrivals at 3:30. All three sisters will be there, one's coming on her own from somewhere else, arriving about that time or earlier. That's all I know. Kyle wasn't sure where they would be staying. She was working on that. She did tell me about Selma's demise and I didn't ask her any questions because I knew that I had to call you and that you'd probably had more information."

Colin gave Bill a quick overview of the situation in Maple Springs, what had happened in Italy, and mentioned that he was part of the crime scene team, although he did not use the word deputy. He asked Bill to keep this all to himself. Joe was going to talk to someone at the *Post-Journal* and Joe wanted to keep it all on the QT for now. Bill understood and was eager to help and glad that he had all the information prior to meeting the bereaved Stone sisters in Buffalo.

"Thanks for calling me earlier. I will get back to you later today. I best call Kyle right away and I can let you know what she's planned for lodgings," said Colin. "Anything else?"

Bill assured Colin that that was all he knew and after a reminder from Bill about the Buffalo Bill's kick off, Bill and associates were gone to watch the game.

Colin, thinking one down, six to go, dialed Kyle's business number. If he knew Kyle, she probably had her business phone number patched into her home on weekends, or worse yet he thought, she's working.

"Hello Mr. O'Brien. So glad you called. I was nervous that I wouldn't get to warn you of the south arising in the form of the Stone sisters who will descend on Maple Springs come Tuesday. I scheduled their arrival as late as I could to give you a couple days to prepare for their invasion," said Kyle. Colin could hear what sounded like a boat whistle in the background.

"Thanks for thinking of my welfare. I'll circle the troops

and lay in waiting for their arrival. Where are you? Do I hear a ship in the background?" asked Colin.

"Well Mr. O'Brien, Scarlet and I are on a singles cruise that I won in a cruise line contest to name the cruise. It was just for travel agents, but I won passage for two and Scarlet and I needed to get a way for a bit. It's just a three day cruise to Bermuda and we are setting sail, actually there are no sails, as we speak. I called Bill Morris and Associates and they will fetch the girls from Buffalo and then I have to tell you that I have a regret of mine to pass along. I regret so much that I have no lodgings for the ladies. They were sure that they could stay at the cottage even though I tried to tell them that it might still be considered a crime scene and did they really want to stay in a house where a family member had been murdered and a possible murderer could be prowling around, but they were nonplussed so I did what I could for them and then got Scarlet and myself on this boat and I refuse to worry about them. They all travel, although I have never before had the privilege of making any arrangements for them, they know the rules. Scarlet is right here. I'll put her on the phone, bah," said Kyle. That last word was the first hint of an accent that Colin had noticed.

Colin was sure that he learned all that Kyle had to say and he was glad to be able to talk to Scarlet and not have to worry that he might not be able to get her at home; three calls down, four to go.

"Scarlet, my dear. So glad that you and Kyle are getting away. You deserve it. Quickly tell me why you called and then get back to your cruise ship cavorting," said Colin.

"Hello Colin, see I remembered to call you Colin. I noticed that Kyle did not. Before I give you my news, what's new with the investigation at Maple Springs?" said Scarlet with no trace of accent.

Colin told her that things were pretty much the same, no new insights, no questions from the crime scene team. The team members were all in sync with their view of the murder, now they were looking for a motive and hoping that it would lead them to the murderer.

"Oh Colin. It's all so ugly," said Scarlet. "We, Kyle and I, are so glad that you are helping the sheriff, so sad that we are so far away, so ready to help as best we can. I called to tell you that I personally spoke with Neil Robertson in Jamestown, NY. I got his number from Mr. Chase who is the Stone's lawyer here in Savannah and Mr. Robertson was most agreeable. I told him what little I knew about the situation at the Stone's cottage and said that I would have you call him, you two know each other, and as the executor or trix whichever you prefer, I gave my permission to move things along especially with the daughters being north. They, the girls, somehow know that there are changes to the wills of G.E.M. and Selma and they are probably wanting to know the specifics. I also called Eileen who has been so helpful to the Stones in the past and she will be making herself available to help both the lawyer and the insurance man. You know cleaning the house, closing it up for the winter, appraising it for sale, etc. She is very competent and I am sure that she will keep you informed.

I have a favor to ask of you. May I?"

With no hesitation, Colin said yes and Scarlet asked the cremation question. "Yes, Scarlet, I can take care of that. I have a friend, Jeff, he knows the sheriff, Neil and Rhoe at the insurance agency and he can take care of things and we will have the ashes sent to you. I secured G.E.M. ashes, Selma brought them home from Italy, and once Selma's body is released by the coroner, Jeff can accomplish all the burial specifics."

On that sad note Scarlet and Colin ended their conversation with Scarlet promising to call Colin when they returned CONUS, her words not Colin's. Before Colin could hang up, Kyle was back on the telephone.

"Oh, Colin, I neglected to tell you my winning name for this cruise. I won't ask you to guess. I called it 'High Seas Single Mingle'. The cruise line loved it and we are off to Bermuda. The ship is the High Seas. We are the mingling singles. We'll talk soon. Bye."

Colin had to digest all of this new information before he could call number one daughter, Ruby. She'd be call number four. Now why was it Ruby that had called here? She wasn't in Savannah anymore, he guessed, although she still had that accent, and the area code. She could hardly run rough shot over her two younger, professional, high power sisters. Then he harkened back to the rules of primogeniture; the eldest child inherits the fortunes, titles and lands with the passing of the father. In Medieval days, it was the eldest son who inherited all of the family assets and the rest of the siblings had to hope that he would be gener-

172- Murder at Maple Springs

ous. In the case of the Stone family, it was probably always the
case that the eldest daughter, the first jewel, was the top kid and
Ruby was hardly ready to abdicate that role at this point. She
might have been the one to institute gifts for the parents, or to
be sure that G.E.M. and Selma had their paperwork in order and
she probably worked toward this day and would hardly step aside
now, but the three sisters knew the terms of the original will, they
were already enjoying their inheritance. The changes that G.E.M.
and Neil wrote were surely the hooks that had snagged the Stone
trio of siblings and enticed them to venture north. It's best to
call her right now, thought Colin, and act dumb regarding some
of the facts in this case especially regarding the information just
passed on by Kyle and Scarlet.

"Yes, Mr. O'Brien, it's me Ruby Stone and Ah do so appreciate your quick response. Ah see your name and telephone number on my caller ID screen and Ah am reminded of ahl the times
my father called from the lake and Ah saw 716 on the screen.
Poor daddy. And Selma too, of course. Let us move quickly to
business. Ah am sure you have plans for your Sunday afternoon
and won't be wanting me to usurp your time," Ruby said, all business and speaking with an effort to be the leader.

"Hello Ms. Stone. What is it you called about? How can I
help you?' said Colin matching businesslike with businesslike.

"My sisters and Ah have determined to visit Maple Springs
within the near fucha and Ah took on the task of calling you so
that possibly you could give us assistance as we endeavor to deal
with a lawyer and an insurance man and the sad reality of losing

two members of our already small family. It is our understandin'
that Daddy and Miss Selma made alterations to their wills prior
to their trip to It'ly. Scarlet, Ah don't even know her last name,
Daddy's secretary, said that she would e-mail you the name of the
lawyer up there that assisted Daddy in what was probably his last
legal business. Miss Eileen, Ah don't recall her surname either,
who was so kind to daddy and Miss Selma and, of course our
dear mother, for so many years can, I am sure, can be of assistance also. Miss Kennedy from a local travel agency has secured
reservations for our travel to Maple Springs so we will not need
your assistance in travel matters." Ruby stopped speaking and
Colin was quick to jump in.

"Miss Stone, I can probably offer some assistance. You did
not mention accommodations so I feel that I must try to offer assistance in securing lodgings for your stay here in Maple Springs.
The Stone cottage is in fact a crime scene and it should retain that
status for a few days yet. I will find rooms down here in Maple
Springs that I am sure you will find comfortable. Your father was
very generous toward the proprietors of the Maple Springs Inn
and I am sure that all three of you would be very welcomed and
comfortable there. It's just a short walk to the family cottage from
the Inn which functions as a bed and breakfast," Colin reported.
"Do you think I should make those arrangements?"

There was a long pause and then Ruby spoke slowly and
deliberately. "It is incomprehensible that we cannot stay in our
own home during this visit, but Ah am sure that the sheriff has
his reasons for keeping us from the premises. We will yield to

his authority. You may make those reservations. Ah would hope that we could each have our own room and I will require my own, private bath."

"Yes, Miss Ruby," said Colin. "I will see to your accommodations and I too must comply with the sheriff's authority and I will be arranging for meetings, hopefully at the Inn, for you and your sisters to meet with Neil Robertson, the lawyer that assisted your father with updating his will, and Miss Selma's also, and with Rhoe Anderson, the insurance agent that your father engaged."

Enough said, Colin thought. I will mention the ashes after the meeting with Neil. This should work. Joe will be wanting to speak personally to the girls regarding his findings and the ongoing investigations. The Inn is the perfect place.

"I look forward to meeting you and your sisters on Tuesday," Colin said hoping that the conversation was at its end.

"Yes. See you on Tuesday," said Ruby. Click.

Colin quickly dialed the Inn.

Those other calls would have to wait.

"Hello Elizabeth. It's Colin O'Brien of the red shingled house two blocks down on Whiteside. How are you today?"

Elizabeth, affable and lovely in equal portions, said, "Well hello Colin. Of course I know who you are and where you live. How is Vonny? We missed her at Study Club last week."

"She's fine, but we are feeling low around here because of the situation at the Stone's cottage. That's why I am calling," said Colin and he proceeded to give Elizabeth the sad news regarding

Selma. He didn't follow Sheriff Joe's four step plan for giving sad news, but he did use a few key words. Elizabeth was shocked and saddened. She offered to help in any way she could once she had digested the sad news. Colin and Elizabeth proceeded to make arrangements for the accommodations of the three Stone daughters and to clear the way for meetings in the Inn library that Colin knew to be both large enough and yet lovely, offering a splendid view of the lake. Elizabeth reminded Colin just how generous and charming that G.E.M and Selma and Lula were to both her and Will and she casually mentioned that the Stone daughters would be their guests, non-paying guests. Before they hung up, they had also agreed upon specifics for a dinner on Tuesday with Sheriff Green, and Vonny and Colin included. Colin offered to bring sorbet for dessert, bread to go with the agreed upon meal of vegetable quiche and fruit salad. And he offered sweet rolls, cinnamon, for breakfast on Wednesday. Surely Vonny would agree with his generous offerings.

Five calls down, four to go; this calling assignment was proving to be time consuming. Colin made a list of names: Neil, Rhoe, Jeff, Joe. He consulted the telephone directory for the correct telephone number for each individual, he already knew Joe's, wrote them next to the proper name and then he proceeded to complete, hopefully, his calling assignment. He was sure that these four would be home, enjoying, possibly, a Buffalo Bills football game.

Neil was home, not anxious to talk long and miss game time. He quickly told Colin that he had talked with Scarlet and that he could and would be pleased to accommodate the Stone daughters while they were in Maple Springs. Scarlet had made him aware of Selma's death and yet, lawyerly in his thinking, he did not ask any questions regarding the investigation. A meeting for Wednesday morning at nine o'clock at the Inn was set.

Rhoe, also home watching the game, said that Eileen had called regarding Selma's death and had asked if he had any knowledge of the video tape taken for insurance purposes of the interior of the Stone's cottage that Lula and Eileen had made several years ago. He had the tape and would bring it and a small, portable projector to the meeting.

Jeff too had to be told about the death and investigation. He was not invited to the meeting, but told Colin that he stood ready to comply with any requests made by the sheriff, Neil or the Stone daughters. He said too that he hoped that all those desiring his services were in sync with regard to their desires. He told Colin that his was a calm business and that he really didn't relish any familial or legal squabbling. Colin assured him that Joe and Neil would be making decisions based upon the wills of G.E.M. and Selma Stone. The daughters would not be interfering. Colin also gave him Scarlet's name and number, told him that she was the executrix for the Stones and that she was also charged with making all funeral arrangements.

Finally Colin was ready to make the last call, but it was too early. Joe had hardly accomplished Bills watching, family dinner time and baths. Colin would call when he and Vonny got home after dinner at Guppy's.

CHAPTER 23

How about the salmon special for Vonny and I'll have the veggie lasagne, as usual," was Colin's reply when Tessa, their favorite waitstaff, came to their table to take their dinner order. The restaurant was full, it almost always was, and yet the O'Briens were able to have a conversation and not be worried that neighboring patrons were listening in. Colin told Vonny about the team meeting on the Stone's porch and when he got to the part about having G.E.M.'s ashes and the gifts from Italy, he whipped out the gift with Vonny's name on it. Excitement and sadness washed over Vonny. She took the gift and held it carefully and just stared at the black, velvet box, tied with a silver, string-like ribbon that Europeans seem to use a lot. A small, off-white card with Vonny written on it was under the string. Vonny slipped the card out and held it looking at it as though it was pages of something that she needed to carefully read. She turned the card toward Colin so that he could read her name and she handed it to him. He took the card, read it and placed it on the table between them. Vonny untied the silver string-like ribbon and handed that to Colin. He placed it on the table with the name card. The box lay before Vonny and she carefully opened it, it was hinged, and when it was opened she let it sit right there in front of her and she leaned forward to stare down at the contents almost like it was not permissible to hold the box while it was opened. She closed the box and pushed it to the middle of the table with the silver, string-like ribbon and the off-white name card. "You can look at it," she said. "I'll take it out at home. I can't do that now."

Colin opened the box and he too leaned forward and stared at the contents. It was a cross, a silver cross. A cross that Colin thought to be an Irish cross. Was it actually a gift from Italy? An Irish cross from Italy? No, thought Colin, it's an Irish cross for an Irish lady. Inside the box, printed on the silk lining in the top half of the box, it said Giancarlo, Avitzia, Italia. Would they ever know the story behind this gift? Did the other five black, velvet hinged boxes all contain the same silver cross, the Irish cross? Colin took the box, the off-white name card and the silver, string-like ribbon and put it into the sport coat pocket from which it had come.

The salmon special and the veggie lasagna were delicious, as usual. Colin and Vonny sat and slowly ate and savored and enjoyed spirits and Colin explained to Vonny about the success of his latest telephoning efforts. Vonny agreed to donate her cinnamon rolls and offered to bake bread and to make some chocolate biscotti cookies to go with the sorbet that Colin would be purchasing for the dinner.

Vonny wasn't sure that she should be included in the Tuesday night dinner, but she did want to get to meet the Stone sisters and this might be her only chance. She said that she would call Elizabeth and offer to go early to help with the table setting, etc.

"You're a peach my dahlin', not a Joja peach, but a peach jest the same. Ah sure do 'preciate your willin'ness to assist with this most impotant dinnah," said Colin using his best, but not accurate, southern accent.

It was after eight o'clock when Vonny and Colin arrived home. They had walked to Guppy's and on their walk home, they took the long way along the Lakeside Promenade. They passed the succession of docks that were now jutting into the lake but that would soon be piled high on the shore, actually back from the shore so that the tide and winds did not launch them across the lake on a blustery winter day like discarded sticks. They came to "Shangri La" and just stood there each remembering the great times with G.E.M. and Selma, both gone now, that they had shared this summer. They walked on silently avoiding Lake View Avenue and the scene of the crime, the murder scene.

Once home, Vonny took the silver string-like ribbon, small off-white card with her name on it and the black, velvet hinged box and went into her room and sat on the edge of the bed. Colin moved into the living room and gave Vonny the privacy that he was sure that she needed.

Colin got the cordless telephone from its cradle and moved to the porch dialing Sheriff Joe's number as he walked.

"Joe Green, the people's representative in the Chautauqua County Sheriff's Department. How can I help you?" was Joe's pat response to every telephone call. He appreciated the voters, he was eager to serve the voters and he wasn't about to forget who had for four consecutive terms elected him to the office of sheriff.

"Joe, Colin here. I just wanted to tell you about the nine, this being the ninth, calls that I made this evening."

"Shoot," said Joe. Colin thought that that might not be the best expression for a sheriff to use.

So Colin shot and Joe got it all, agreed with all the plans, was available for the Tuesday dinner and the Wednesday meeting.

"How long are the Stone sisters staying?" asked Joe.

"Oops, I never asked that question. I can call Kyle or even Bill Morris. Those two should know," said Colin. "I'm sure that the ladies have return trip tickets, but possibly the information that is presented at the Wednesday meeting could have an impact upon their plans for departing, you know skedaddling."

Joe gave Colin kudos and thanks for his efficient telephoning and promised to call Colin on Monday with new information should some arise and to reconfirm the plans for Tuesday. He said too that he was sending Sergeants Gianna and Johnson to talk to Binky and he repeated his intent to talk to Scott at the *P-J*, and mentioned that Johnson was also investigating craftsman Brad in the white van.

"Also Colin," Joe continued. "I had Pete Giana call the Chief of Police and the hotel owners in Avitzia, Italy. Pete speaks Italian and Spanish. He also talked with the coroner, I forget the Italian word for coroner, and it looks like G.E.M.'s death was of natural causes. The hotel owners, very reputable people, took care of all the details for Selma and she finished the trip and then returned to the US, but as we know, she returned as G.E.M. and sent word ahead that it was Selma that had died. I think if we can figure out why she did that, it may lead us to the murderer. There was something or someone that she feared; it seemed to her that her death would be easier on her than G.E.M.'s. Does that make sense?"

"Yes...I think," said Colin. "With G.E.M. gone, there was no one to protect Selma from the girls, the Stone daughters. Selma had no family, it was just her and G.E.M. Selma stalled for time and needed to get home and get her ducks in a row. Remember the note that she sent Vonny and me? It said that she needed our help to untangle the rouse, I think that's what she called it, that she had initiated. She said that she had good reason to be impersonating G.E.M. I'm just guessing here, but maybe there is something in that new will that Neil has that Selma was thinking might come back to haunt her. Sorry, poor word choice there."

"Colin, I gotta go. I gotta think. I also have three kids in diapers so you know what else I gotta do. Did you see that game? Pathetic. Call ya tomorrow."

No, Colin hadn't seen the game. It was on the many televisions at Guppy's, but, as usual, Colin tuned it out. He enjoyed Vonny so much more than the Buffalo Bills.

Colin hung up the telephone determined to call someone and find out if he or she knew of any return-to-Savannah plans that the Stone daughters might have so that he could give that information to Joe in the morning. But he didn't want to call Kyle and Scarlet and interject murder questions into their high seas single mingling. He thought too that it was too late to call Bill Morris. Colin was tired and he decided, as Scarlet had, O'Hara not Ames, that 'tomorrow was another day'.

It was starting to get dark earlier these days and Colin

didn't like that. He loved those long, hot summer days, but he knew they were giving way to fall, winter, snow and soon early bird dinners and sunsets would be showing up at the same time. He went in the house and found Vonny asleep wearing her new, silver, Irish cross. He covered her with her favorite quilt, made for her as a Mother's Day present by their daughters Ronny and Erin when the two sisters were in middle school. Lots of jolts had been absorbed by the O'Briens in the last couple days and although chopping vegetable for soup, yoga poses and pie making were initiated by Vonny to ease her through the turmoil, Colin knew that what she needed was a good night's sleep and perhaps happy dreams of Selma and G.E.M. in a little jewelry shop on a crooked side street in Avitzia buying lovely silver, Irish crosses for the women in their lives. Colin, not immune to trauma, would sleep too.

CHAPTER 24

When Colin woke up on Monday, he experienced the same scenario as his Sunday early morning wake-up with Sheriff Joe Green being the waker and Colin the wakee, but this time Joe was on the telephone.

"Hello," was all Colin could muster as he grabbed and punched the cordless telephone that he fumbled for and found on the nightstand on his side of the bed.

"Colin, it's 8:30, time to rock and roll, heave out and trice up, hit the deck, etc. Any of those orders sound familiar?" Joe was sounding much too energetic.

With feet on the floor, "Hello Joe. Yes, I am up, sparkling. Reporting for duty," Colin answered, glad that "face time" was not a feature on his cordless, land line phone.

"Colin, I am on Route 430 headed to Maple Springs. I've got breakfast burritos and coffee. You got about four minutes to pee, comb and brush. Over."

Within the allotted time, Colin was on the front porch casually looking at the *Post-Journal* seemingly oblivious of Joe even as he placed the food and coffee on the table and sat down.

"Oh, hi Joe. I didn't hear you coming."

"You're all right Colin. I figured you'd be up and moving. Guess I was wrong. Sorry I woke you up. Again," said Joe.

"No problem, Joe," said Colin. "Vonny let me sleep in. Again. That's two days in a row. My plan was to call you after

I spoke to Bill Morris or Kyle in Savannah about any plans for the girls for a return trip to Savannah via the Buffalo Airport. I haven't talked to anyone yet."

"Let's just review what we're gonna do for the next couple of days. I don't want to be unprepared when we meet the Stone sisters," said Joe as he took out his handy dandy note pad prepared to tick off as done the 'to do' items on his list. The two men ate and drank the coffee as they organized their next steps.

"You sure you don't mind taking on some local organizing, Colin? I don't want to put you on the spot, but you're sort of embroiled now, part of our team."

You can't possibly do this without me, I know too much, who's gonna be your 'color man', thought Colin.

"No problem. I got lots of time. That is if you think I can be helpful," said Colin.

"Thanks Colin. You can handle it. I'd like to see us proceed as we are rather than get cops down here to set up the accommodations and then try to deal with the Stone sisters. I'd say that you already have things lined up. Right? We gotta handle this just right.

"Moving on. Binky called me last night and I don't think she can shed any light on the situation. She and Bernie are headed to California tomorrow and she didn't want to "skip town if she was a suspect". Yea, that's what she said. I told her that she wasn't any kind of a suspect, but I've got Steve and Pete visiting her today and taking a deposition. I am also on my way to see Scott at the *P-J*. He knows something. He called the office this morning trolling for info. I'm gonna give him the basic story, but no details. Vagueness is good. I might want to use those details to trip up the perp. Also, I don't want this situation to be portrayed in a salacious way at all. No need to even mention about Selma impersonating G.E.M. or the trade out, or lots of stuff. I'm sure that Scott will be helpful. I think too that I will call Rhoe Anderson, Neil Robertson, and Jeff at Landers' Funeral Home just to keep them in the fold. Whatd'ya think?"

Colin thought it wise to get Scott on board, but he didn't think much of the idea of Joe repeating the three calls that he had already, so carefully, made.

"I'm sure that Rhoe, Neil and Jeff are okay with our plans," said Colin. "But if you want to call them, that's your call, or calls I should say."

"Well, if I get a chance to call them, I will, but Monday is always a busy day in the Sheriff's Office. All those weekend DUIs stir up a lot of lawyer, political and family interventions and everyone always wants to talk to the Sheriff privately."

After Joe and Colin agreed on the main events for the next two days - the 6:00 Tuesday dinner and some Q & A with the Stone sisters and the 9:00 Wednesday morning meeting with Rhoe and Neil - Joe left for Jamestown and the *P-J* and Colin finished scanning the newspaper, cleared the wrappings from the boring breakfast burritos that Joe had brought and called Vonny at work, something he didn't like to do, and thanked her for letting him sleep in. She assured him that she was in good form, she was wearing her new, lovely Irish cross, and then she proceeded to give him a list of baking supplies that she'd need to make the biscotti and cinnamon rolls for the upcoming events at the B & B. It was a short list, but Colin also needed a few items for the week's meals at the O'Briens. Vonny had a lasagna, a turkey roast and salmon steaks, plus pies, in the freezer, they'd been made for G.E.M., but Colin wanted to get yogurt, cottage cheese, fresh fruit and vegetables, plus milk and juice so that there'd be no need for multiple trips to the grocery store. It wasn't nine o'clock yet, but Colin knew that Bill Morris would be awake, so he called him.

This time, Colin let Bill exercise his First Amendment rights.

"Good morning. Bill Morris and Associates, we can take you anywhere, anytime and in your choice of vehicles. Bill Morris speaking. How may I direct your call?"

"Good mornin' Mr. Morris, Colin O'Brien here. Just calling to set up a pro-active plan for the Stone sisters' arrival tomorrow in Maple Springs."

"I been thinking and as a matter of fact, I was going to call you shortly about just that. I have a gig from the Buffalo Airport into Buffalo tomorrow and so I will be up there for the ladies' arrivals in the afternoon. At 10:00 tomorrow, it's Hillary Rodham Clinton to UB for a speech. You know she makes $200,000 a speech. Then I wait, listen, have lunch and have her back to the airport for a 2:30 departure. I think the Clinton people called for an out of town limo so there would be no haggling with Republican and Democratic limos in Buffalo. Not a bad gig, AND I have a secret service guy, could be a gal, hope it's a gal, riding shotgun all the time, *and* I will conveniently be up there for the 3:30 customers headed to La Springs. How 'bout that?"

Colin agreed that was a fine piece of business for Bill, but Colin was most concerned with the afternoon customers, not that he wasn't a Hillary fan, in fact he had voted for her for senator a few years ago.

After a quick discussion, Bill and Colin agreed that Bill would call once he had the three Stone daughters riding comfortably in the back seat and that ninety minutes from then, Bill would be depositing them at the Maple Springs Inn. Bill couldn't talk long. He was scheduled to deliver a human heart for transplant and he and his helicopter were headed to Erie, PA for a pickup. He wasn't sure where he was delivering, but he had all day free and a $300 an hour helicopter rate so the farther away, the better.

Colin had a lot to do, so after a quick shower and the performance of his Monday morning ritual of sorting recyclables and putting out his garbage, not to be confused with his trash, Colin quickly made a list of things to accomplish on this fine day and then he prioritized them with stars, asterisks and underlinings. He was headed to the grocery store, but at the last minute stopped at the B & B to see if there was anything that Elizabeth needed. He knew that Will was in San Antonio, Texas, at an entrepreneur convention, so Colin thought that Elizabeth might need some help or an item or two from the store.

When Colin pulled up the driveway and into a space designated for "Our Honored Guests", he saw Elizabeth on a ski lift seat that had been rigged as a swing-for-two in a big maple next to the three car garage that served as a greenhouse, kayak loft, canning cellar, pool hall and ping pong parlor and, of course, tool repository.

"Hi Elizabeth. I'm on my way to Tops. Need anything?" Colin called out after only a couple steps from the car.

"Come sit. I've got my planner and I was just reviewing what had to be accomplished today," responded Elizabeth.

The planner was not the ringed, paper calendar type that Colin had used habitually prior to his retirement. This planner was one of those electronic Books or Nooks or Kindles that was the size of a small magazine. It took Colin a couple tries to get himself up into the ski lift seat just as getting into the ski lift had caused him problems when he skied years ago. Once seated, with just a little pumping on Elizabeth's part, they were gently swinging and Elizabeth was demonstrating the joys of technology as she quickly accessed more information in a minute that Colin had extracted from his computer in the last six months. She had a complete inventory of all foodstuffs on the premises, including the contents of freezers in the garage. She had schematics of the house and of all the rooms individually. There was a list of local tourist attractions and a complete listing of all local craftsmen and artists, churches and home repairmen. Colin noticed that Brad was not on Elizabeth's all-inclusive list. She even listed a stained glass repairman, but Colin didn't recall there being stained glass anywhere in the B & B. One file provided menus. There was a gardening file complete with a schematic of the grounds and all of the plants on the premises.

"I love this thing," gushed Elizabeth. "I save so much time and paperwork with this. I do all my banking with this thing too and of course take reservation in my availability file. I don't need much of an office now, so we turned the office we had into another guest room. Love my technology. And, finally, to your question, no I don't need anything at the store. Thanks."

Colin and Elizabeth swung and talked for a few minutes more and got in synch regarding the arrival of the Stone sisters and the dinner meal, Tuesday night, and the meeting on Wednesday morning. Colin reminded her that Vonny would be over about 1:30 on Tuesday, she was only working half of the day, and that she would be bringing bread and biscotti. All was at the ready.

CHAPTER 25

When Colin arrived home from the grocery store, the flashing light on his answering machine told him that he had missed three calls:

"Hi Colin. Rhoe Anderson here. I was hoping that I could tour the Stone Cottage before the meeting on Wednesday. I reviewed the inventory video. I'd like to see how the place changed over the last few years. The video is dated July 7, 2006. Give me a call."

"Hey Colin. Eileen speaking. I hate these machines. I got the job done at Stones. Meet me there at noon. Bye."

"Hey, it's your boss. Kidding. So, Scott at the *P-J* is cool. He wants background info regarding Maple Springs. He'll call ya. At ease, deputy."

I'm official, thought Colin. Joe said deputy again.

Colin didn't erase the messages. He was hoping that Vonny would listen to the recorded messages and hear in the Sheriff's own voice the use of the title of deputy as it applied to her husband.

Colin looked at the clock, 11:52. He decided to call Rhoe and Scott when he got back from meeting Eileen at the Stone's cottage. They were both busy men and they both would probably be out to lunch, or they might not answer the phone if they spent their lunch hour at their desks, but he would at least leave a message.

Eileen was sitting on the top step of the Stone porch steps when Colin walked up to the Stone Cottage.

"This type of cleanup is not a favorite with me and it is even worser when it, you know the mess, belongs to a dear friend. You know what I mean, don't ya? No need to answer. Come on, let's go in," spouted Eileen as she quickly stood and got to the front door before Colin was even up the first step to the porch.

"No smell, no stain, all dried. I'd hate for those delicate southern bells to have to deal with the harsh reality of reality," said Eileen. "When they arriving?"

Truly there was no smell or stain and when Colin felt where the blood spot had been, the rug was dry.

"Nice work Eileen," said Colin. "The contingent from Savannah arrives at the Inn sometime after 4:30 tomorrow. Bill's fetching them. No need for them to stay here and Will and Elizabeth are being very hospitable. I don't know when they, the girls, will tour here. Do you want to see them? I can let you know when we will tour here, or for sure you can just drop in at the Inn."

"I have no need to see them. They were never warm to me and I haven't much respect for them after I saw them be rude to Miss Selma, of course when their daddy wasn't around; ignoring her, calling her Velma or Thelma, never offering to help with nothin'. Don't never need to see those folks again."

Colin promised to keep Eileen informed concerning what was happening with the investigation. He reminded her that Rhoe Anderson had the video of the inventorying of the house and he would show it to the sisters on Wednesday. It got awkward standing in the hall talking, so Colin and Eileen finished talking while on the porch. Eileen locked the front door using a key that she isolated from the, at least, fifty keys that she had on a snap clip that she had attached to a belt loop on her pants. They said quick goodbyes and she was in her Toyota truck and out of sight before Colin even started down the steps and headed for home. The number five was flashing and the new messages were from Rhoe and Scott asking for return calls ASAP. Colin obliged.

Colin called Scott at the *P-J* first and begged off providing information regarding Maple Springs. He told Scott that in reality he was a newcomer to The Springs and he was unsure, actually confused, about what was fact and what was lore with regard to the 'legend of Maple Springs'. Colin directed Scott to a web-site created by one of the long-time Springers, www.maplesprings.com, that could accurately provide him with any information he might need to provide color for the article that he was preparing that would inform locals about the murder at Maple Springs.

Scott very expertly foraged for information, but Colin remembered his bosses' admonition that no one was to speak to the press except the sheriff himself. Colin was proud that he hadn't blabbed and he got off the line by telling Scott that he had an incoming call that he needed to take; he lied to the newspaper. Not exactly perjury, but it was a lie, a white lie brought into play for good reason.

Colin called Rhoe. "Hi Rhoe. Colin here. I can meet you at the Stone cottage whenever it is convenient for you."

"I'm headed to Mayville in about ten minutes. I pass right by The Springs. I can be there at 1:00. How's that?" was Rhoe's reply.

Colin agreed on the time and then he got busy with putting away the groceries that he had bought at Tops and stowing his recyclable grocery bags for future use. He then took a book and a can of iced tea and went to sit on the Stone's porch to wait for Rhoe. Rhoe arrived before Colin even got to open his book.

As they toured the cottage, Rhoe had a clipboard upon which he took many notes. The two men didn't really tour together, they roamed independently throughout the down stairs' rooms. Rhoe went upstairs alone and stayed there a few minutes. He came downstairs and went right to a comfortable wicker rocker on the front porch and worked on his clipboard. Colin gave him about five minutes of alone time then went out onto the porch.

"So whatd'ya think about the 'trade out'?" said Colin.

"Trade out?" was Rhoe's response.

Colin explained the concept of a 'trade out' to Rhoe just as it was relayed to him by Eileen only yesterday. Even though Rhoe had never heard the term 'trade out', he personally thought that he might have experienced one or two in the past. He understood the process and told Colin that indeed it looked as if a 'trade out' had taken place with the Stone's possessions.

"Whoever did the trading," said Rhoe using air quotes when saying the word trading, "knew what they were doing. I was looking for particular objects, you know paintings, dishes,

silver, books that I had just seen on the tape and they weren't in
the house here. I made a list on this clipboard of the items that
I know to be missing and I decided that I am taking this list and
the tape to a friend of mine who has an antique store and I will
ask him to put dollar value on the missing items."

"There's a lot of items traded out," said Colin. "I've only
been in the house six or eight times and I even know that. Why
would someone go to all the trouble to do that? They couldn't
possibly think that no one would notice...Fiesta or Melmac, oil
paintings or cheap prints, fabulous quilts or cheap cotton blankets. In this case, is the missing stuff insured? Does replacement
money go to the estate? Now with both Selma and G.E.M. gone,
this cottage belongs to Selma's church. Oops, I probably shouldn't
have told you that. I'd appreciate it if you would keep that information to yourself," said Colin.

Rhoe thought for a couple minutes. "I'm not sure what to
do," he said. "I am taking this one step at a time. Okay, I got the
tape, well actually I had the tape made into a DVD, and will be
at the Wednesday morning meeting. Nine o'clock, right? And
I am taking the list I just made and the DVD to my friend, Ron
Hughes, at his antique shop in Ellington. I'm sure that he can
provide replacement dollar amounts for the missing items. I'm
also going to go to my List-Serve page for insurance brokers and
see if any of my fellow subscribers can fill me in on motive and
other details regarding any 'trade outs' they might have had to
deal with."

Rhoe quickly got up, shook Colin's hand and was down the

porch stairs and headed quickly to his car.

Colin called out after him, "Meeting's at nine. See you there. Let's not talk about this 'trade out' to anyone and don't forget, no mention of the disposition of this cottage."

Rhoe acknowledged Colin with a thumbs up, then he slid into his little, black, expensive looking, two-door and was gone from sight in a flash.

CHAPTER 26

When Colin returned home from his tour of the cottage and his meeting with Rhoe, there was a seven flashing on his telephone answering machine:

"Hi Mr. O. It's Bill Korbin. Just called to thank you for the spelling last night, helped a lot. I'm back at the mall, but ready to help you and the sheriff anytime you guys need me. Thanks again. Here's my cell number just in case."

"Hello Mr. O'Brien. My name is Sara Marsh and I am calling for Neil Robertson. He asked me to tell you that he received a call from a Scarlet Ames in Savannah, Georgia. She identified herself as the executor of the Selma and G.E.M. Stone estate and she gave Neil permission to provide you and Sheriff Green with any information regarding their estate that we may be privy to. Please do not hesitate to call should you have questions or concerns. Neil also asked me to tell you that he will be at the 9:00 meeting at the Maple Springs Inn on Wednesday. I e-mailed Sheriff Green with this information also. Have a nice day. Goodbye." After her goodbye, Ms. Marsh left Mr. Robertson's cell phone number. Colin made note of both Bill Korbin's and Neil Robertson's cell phone numbers.

The rest of Colin's afternoon was very uneventful. After lunch he went outside and collected all of the porch chair cushions and put them in plastic bags that he secured with twist 'ems. He would stow these bags along with other summer items in a storage unit that he maintained in Jamestown. The unit was originally rented to store his children's childhood belongings until they had houses to which they could take all those treasures; Barbie dolls and Barbie's Dream House and car, baby doll cribs, G.I. Joe and Star Wars men, Pretty Little Ponies, Cabbage Patch Dolls, Pound Puppies and lots of books, games and big wheeled items helped to keep the unit filled. He put the cushions in the trunk of the car so he could drop them off at the unit the next time he went up the road to Jamestown.

Colin worked at cutting down plants in the garden, Vonny called this giving the garden a brush cut, and he pruned bushes and took down a few of the screens. By three o'clock he was beat and needed a shower. He also wanted to get supper started and to get out baking paraphernalia for Vonny. She had biscotti and cinnamon rolls to make for the meals at the B & B for the Stone sisters. Vonny said that she would be home early to get to baking and indeed she was home by 3:30. Colin had finished all that he wanted to accomplish and he helped Vonny by staying out of her way, in fact, out of her kitchen.

By 7:00 all the baking, cleanup, supper and more cleanup was completed and Colin and Vonny sat out on the porch and watched the sun set over Lake Chautauqua. The sunset was a great perk of living in Maple Springs. Every night the sun was a red ball sinking into the lake and coloring the sky and the surface of the lake with seemingly hundreds of shades of red and orange. Colin was sure that the telephone would ring and spoil all this calm, all this nature showing off, but it remained silent. Colin

recapped his day for Vonny and she asked questions to be sure
she knew the plans for the next two days. She went inside to get
ready for bed and Colin lingered on the porch taking in the last
of the bright orange and red streaks across the horizon. He heard
the telephone answering machine beep and knew that Vonny was
listening to the seven messages that he had saved. A minute later
he heard a series of three beeps and knew that Vonny had erased
the messages. He knew too that she heard the word that he wanted her to hear. He remained on the porch for a minute more until the top rim of the sun slipped below the horizon. Humming
a favorite song of his, *"Orange Colored Sky"*, Colin went into the
house to get ready for bed. He locked the door, brushed his teeth,
turned on the light in the hood over the stove as he did every
night and then went to the bedroom. He was surprised that the
room was already dark. Vonny couldn't have gone to sleep this
quickly. He moved into the room silently and reached behind his
closet door for his summer pajamas.

"Is that my little deputy coming to search the room for
clues? I'm not on your list of suspects, am I?" said Vonny in the
dark, almost in a whisper. "Ya gonna frisk me?"

Right there and then, Colin knew that this new, crime
fighting career of his was going to work out just fine.

CHAPTER 27

"Colin, you best wake up. The *Post Journal* has a front page story about Selma and G.E.M. and it says that you figure prominently in the investigation down here. You best be up and ready for your public. I think you may hear from a lot of people. I called the kids and warned them about the article so that when they read the *P-J* on-line that they don't panic," was Vonny's wake up call. He would have preferred the irritating bell from their alarm clock.

"I'm up," and he was, pulling on shorts, headed to the kitchen, then seated at the table, to see that article for himself. He was a quick read artiste, a skill that he had acquired in high school many years ago.

RESIDENTS DEMISE UNDER INVESTIGATION
Scott Sterns

MAPLE SPRINGS— Investigators have flocked to sunny, quiet, usually peaceful Maple Springs in their efforts to determine the cause of death of a veteran summer resident. The body of Salma Stone was discovered yesterday in her summer cottage on the lake just a five minute walk from all the fun offered at Midway StatePark which is also located in Maple Springs.

Mrs. Stone, a legal resident of Savanna, Georgia was a long-time summer resident and a reserved lady not known to have any enemies.

Cause of death is suspicious and the sheriffs office is leading the investigation to determine the cause of death and the possible motive for anyone to do bodily harm to Mrs. Stone.

"We have a wonderful crime scene invetigative team and they have been on the scene and are currently following leads, and cataloging evidence," said Sheriff Joe Green.

"A Maple Springs resident found the body and has been very helpful in keeping a lid on this case. As sheriff I fully indorse any assistance that the citizenry can contribute."

The victum recently returned from touring in Italy with her husband, G.E.M. Stone. During the course of that visit to Italy, Mr. Stone died. Mrs. Stone returned to Maple Springs prior to her return to Savanah for the winter. The sheriff is confident that the two deaths are unrelated although the deceased individuals were related. Mr. Stone was the President/CEO of G.E.M. Stone Jewelry, Inc., a three generation business which "Serves the jewelry needs of the south".

Maple Springs calls itself "a shining resort on Lake Chautauqua". It was home to the White Side Inn which was demolished in 1988 after offering hospitality to the county rairoad and steamship passengers for over 100 years.

Maple Spring residents enjoy leisurly summer residence, many homes there house third and fourth generations of vacationers. Some residence are year round residents.

The investigation into the death of Mrs. Stone continues.

"If anyone has any information that may shed light on the situation, our office would welcome your call," said Sheriff Green.

"I'm not mentioned in this story," said Colin loudly so that Vonny could hear him regardless where she was in the house. He got orange juice from the fridge, a glass from the cupboard and sat again to give the story a second read. The teacher in him loved reading the *Post-Journal* and counting the mistakes. He counted fourteen errors in this one article alone. There could be hundreds in the entire edition.

"I know you're not mentioned," said Vonny entering the kitchen with shoes in her hand and looking ready to head off to work, "but you have to admit that you did get out of bed in record time. I did call the kids so that they weren't shocked when they read the paper on-line. I think they all read it each day. They never read it when they lived here, but now it's a must read."

"Joe said that the article would be generic, not a lot of details, not prurient at all. That's good. I'd hate to see a bunch of gawkers cruising around The Springs," said Colin.

"Oh, we'll get a few anyway and friends in Jamestown will

surely call looking for juicy tidbits. I gotta go. I am headed right to the B & B after work and then I will come home and change for dinner. Please take the cinnamon rolls and the biscotti to Elizabeth. You did remember the sherbet, didn't you?" said Vonny as she slipped into her shoes and headed out the back door. Colin followed, managed to sneak up behind her and give her a kiss on the back of the neck.

"Looks like Deputy O'Brien best keep his eye on you. You're lookin' mighty suspicious, ma'am. Foxy and suspicious. You best not be holdin' out on me," said Colin in his best, but pretty poor, John Wayne imitation.

Vonny give Colin her best pouty face, slid in the driver's seat, clicked her seat belt, started the car and was gone. Colin could hear her laughing over the very loud radio. She always played the radio loudly and most times sang along, loudly. Colin waved goodbye until the car was out of sight. God, I love that woman he thought.

CHAPTER 28

Colin read the rest of the newspaper, finished his juice and had coffee. Vonny always made coffee. It was the first thing she did each morning. Often in a fog and with slits for eyes, she still made good coffee. Colin needed to get a lot of things done today. It was 9:00 when he began making a list of those things. He couldn't call Bill Morris because right about now he'd be headed to Buffalo to collect Hillary Rodham Clinton and squire her on her appointed rounds. Colin would wait for Bill to call him. He needed to stay close to home to take calls and to be Sheriff Green's point man on duty in The Springs. He quickly shaved and showered, taking the telephone into the bathroom with him. Then he made a dash to the B & B and delivered the baked goods to Elizabeth explaining that he couldn't stay, duties to perform, but telling her too that he'd be home if she needed him for anything. When he got home there was no flashing action on his answering machine, so he hadn't missed any calls. Ten minutes later the first of fifteen calls came in. Concerned friends from Jamestown, son Jack from Vermont, a stringer from a Buffalo weekly newspaper, Binky from the west coast and a couple Springers comfortably installed in their winter residences all called in response to the front page article. Colin was matter of fact with everyone, telling them that the newspaper article told all that he knew. He did not mention his deputization, although Jack knew, nor did he mention the upcoming visits by the Stone sisters. Each call was brief and a couple he even ended when he took beeps supplied by the call-waiting feature on his phone.

Colin also made a couple calls. He called Scarlet and Kyle. They were both at work, recovering from their terrific, three day cruise and glad to talk to Colin and to be in the investigation loop again. Colin brought them up to speed, though there really wasn't much to tell, and he promised to e-mail them both later in the evening after his first meeting with the sisters and their dinner at the B & B.

"Colin, I Googled the Maple Springs Inn and I am sure that the precious Stones will be very happy there." said Kyle. She also gave Colin her cell phone number and told him to call any time.

"I spoke with Neil Robertson and he seems very nice," said Scarlet. "I also faxed him information that explains the disposition of the Stone estate in the Savannah area now that both Selma and G.E.M. are gone. He can share all that and he can call me too or he can call his friend, the Stone's lawyer here in Savannah. None of this is a secret. G.E.M. and Selma gave an interview to the *Savannah Morning News* when they donated their house to the Greater Savannah Historical Society. All that will be new to the girls is the information regarding the disposition of the cottage, the changes made with Neil before the trip to Italy."

It was mid-morning and Colin gathered his garden tools and got busy in the yard. All the planting in the spring had been worthwhile, the gardens had been beautiful all summer and now Colin was determined to recycle as much as possible from the garden and to be ready, to be planned for the garden come May of next year. He took the telephone outside with him, but thankfully there were no calls. He got the annuals and all the plants that he had potted into the compost pile and he managed to save most of the potting soil and the stones that he had placed in the pots to help with drainage. He collected the garden furniture, that's what he called the decorative items that stood sentinel in the garden, and would store them away in plastic totes tomorrow. He cleaned up his mess, dirt, leaves, and himself, had a quick lunch of yogurt and a bagel, and by 3:00 he was relaxing on the porch confident that he could finish his Archer Mayor mystery.

The phone rang, it was about 4:15 and Colin had to hot foot it inside to grab it. Should have taken the phone to the porch with him.

"Hello, Mr. O'Brien. This is Bill Morris from Bill Morris and Associates. I have been asked to call you and to tell you that I am currently transporting three ladies from Savannah, Georgia for whom you have made lodging arrangements at the Maple Springs Inn. The ladies will be viewing their family home before they settle in at the Inn. I will deliver them to the Stone cottage and then will take their luggage to the Inn. They are requesting that Sheriff Green meet them at the cottage. We should arrive there at approximately 5:00. Could you possibly inform the Sheriff of their planned stop prior to their arrival at the Inn?"

"Good afternoon, Bill," said Colin knowing that somehow, someone was monitoring Bill's message to Colin. Bill had a telephone headpiece that he used while on the road. Bill knew the law with regards to cell phone use while driving.

"I will make every effort to inform the sheriff. I am sure that he was planning on being at the bed and breakfast, but he may not be available to be at the Stone cottage. You may plan on the stop. I will do my best to have the cottage available. Goodbye Bill."

Colin didn't want to ask a bunch of questions and put Bill on the spot, so he quickly signed off. He had a key, was part of the sheriff's investigation team, a deputy to be exact, and he knew that he could facilitate the cottage visit. He made efforts to call Sheriff Joe on his cell phone, but all he got was an opportunity to leave a message; "Hi Joe. The Stone ladies want to visit the cottage, you know, their cottage, before they go to the Inn. Bill will have them there about 5:00. I can be there. Hope you can too. If not, we will see you at the Inn. Looks like dinner will be later than we thought."

Colin then called the Inn. "Hello Elizabeth. I just heard from Bill Morris and the Stone sisters will be touring the family cottage prior to their arrival at your place. Bill will drop their suitcases off at the Inn after he drops the ladies at the cottage, so I guess that means that we will be walking to the Inn after their tour."

Elizabeth, totally used to being flexible with her guests, said that was fine. She would wait for the ladies to arrive at the Inn before she put the quiche in the oven. She also mentioned that Vonny was on her way home to change.

Vonny arrived home, changed, sipped some Chardonnay and filled Colin in on the preparations at the Inn (gorgeous, comfortable, heavenly). Colin caught her up on his day (phone calls, garden, Bill's call from the limo). Vonny decided that she'd meet the sisters at the Inn.

"Now my dear Deputy," said Vonny turning to face Colin just as she started out the door. "I hope y'all will be most hospitable to these ladies who have ventured all the way no'th, enemy territory you know. They deserve your assistance at this difficult time." And she was gone.

Colin downed his glass of wine and went to the Stone cottage to meet and greet the ladies. He talked to himself all the while he waited to see Bill's limo drive down the street; I shouldn't prejudge these ladies by what Scarlet, Kyle and Eileen said about them. They are probably charmin', genteel, southern bells. Vonny's right, they have had to deal with several losses in a short period of time.

At 4:50 Bill's limo, he had the white one today, turned the corner and came down the street. Bill flicked his headlights on and off, a signal of some sort, but Colin wasn't exactly sure what Bill was trying to tell him. He'd find out soon enough about the flicking of headlights and a whole lot of other things too.

Joe hadn't appeared. Deputy O'Brien would be in charge. Perhaps deputization just got sticky, thought Colin.

CHAPTER 29

No sooner had the limo come to a stop and all four doors opened and out they all came, a limo driver and three ladies of the south. Colin was sure that Bill was expecting to open the doors for the ladies, but he never got a chance. The ladies were up onto the porch and at the door in a flash. Colin had wisely stepped aside as they rushed up the stairs.

"The doah's locked," said one sister.

"I've got my key," said another.

Bill moved to Colin and said softly, "All I can say is that I am glad that I will be leaving these lovely ladies in your care. One of them, the one in the peasant skirt, was sitting up front so I couldn't actually talk when I called you. The stop here at this cottage is their idea. None of them talked all the way here, to me or to each other. Well, maybe the two in the back did a bit."

"This lock has been changed," bellowed someone from the porch. "Someone get up here and unlock this doah."

"I'm headed to the B & B with the luggage," said Bill and he did so.

"Did I make myself heard?" said the bellower.

Because I heard her does not mean that I need to obey her, thought Colin.

"Good afternoon ladies," said Colin brightly as he headed up the porch stairs. "I am Colin O'Brien and I spoke with each of you on the telephone a couple days ago. I am pleased that you are visiting our community and I am glad to be able to facilitate your stay here".

Someone started to talk, but Colin pressed on. "First, allow me to offer my condolences once more at the loss of your father and Miss Selma. They were both gracious and sincere. They both spoke highly of their lovely daughters. They were very proud of you all. And you are?"

In turn each daughter spoke her name and Colin forced a handshake with each of them; two wet fish and a professional shake.

"I must remind you that this cottage continues to be considered a crime scene and Sheriff Joe Green has asked me to facilitate this tour, but to also remind you that nothing can be touched, drawers cannot be opened, etc.," said Colin laying his authority right out there for the ladies to ponder.

"Will you by any chance be openin' the doah soon?" inquired Pearl. Pearl, as Colin recalled, was the youngest and was a former beauty pageant participant and current beauty pageant consultant. She was indeed lovely and every detail of her being was in sync: perfectly fit and styled clothing, a hairstyle both casual and structured and make-up that Colin thought was there, but was so naturally applied that he doubted its existence.

Colin paused, crossed to the door and unlocked it. Without opening it, he said, "If you don't comply with the restrictions placed upon this visit, I will remove you from the house."

Colin stepped aside and two of the ladies, Pearl and Opal, entered. Ruby sat on the front porch swing.

Colin entered and observed the two sisters moving through the house. He wanted to hear their comments regarding the 'trade out'. Did they know there was a 'trade out'? Did they know what a 'trade out' was? They hadn't been to Maple Springs in over five years, surely they didn't retain a mental inventory of the Stone cottage furnishings, decorations and bric-a-brack. Or did they?

"The Remington is gone," said Pearl aloud, to no one in particular.

From the kitchen Opal said, "I see no Fiesta Ware, none, there's none."

Colin knew that she must have opened a cupboard or two, but he let that go. He wanted to hear their comments.

"Mr. O'Brien, would you kindly join me in the dinnin' room?" asked Opal. Colin did join her and she said, "There are awl paintin's and several crystal vahses missin' from this room. I suppose you know nothing about the obvious lootin' of our cottage?"

By this time, Ruby had come into the house and she and Pearl joined Colin and Opal in the dining room. Colin spoke, "Ladies, yes our investigation team noticed that items had been removed from the house. We noticed too that they were replaced with items of the same sort, but of obviously lesser value and in most cases with no attempt to fool anyone regarding their value. We have an old video tape of all of the belongings which we will show you and we can discuss the 'trade out' with the sheriff at the Inn later today if you'd like. We though that you ladies might be able to help explain how this 'trade out' occurred."

"Trade out?" said a trio of voices.

Colin defined the term 'trade out'. He then gave the ladies just ten minutes more to tour the house, same rules still applied, before he would have to lock up and send them on their way to the Maple Springs Inn. This did not settle well with the ladies, but ten minutes later they quit the cottage and were headed down the porch stairs and to the Inn just two blocks away.

"I surely was uninformed that we would be walkin' through the streets and avenues of Maple Springs," said Pearl. "My footwear is totally inappropriate." Her six inch, black pumps surely fit into the inappropriate footwear category.

"Those shoes are a poor excuse for footwear," said Ruby who was wearing plastic flip-flops. "Our driver told us that this stop was not on his itinerary, he had other customers needin' tending to and he said that if we stopped, we would be required to walk to the Inn on our own. He did agree to drop our suitcases at the Inn, so I would say that we have been well served by Mr. Morris."

Opal, in low, sneaker-like shoes, went walking toward the lake. "I'll find my way to the Inn," she said. "I prefer to, right now, have a few moments of quiet time and a snappy walk along Lakeside Promenade. Don't be worryin' 'bout me at awl."

"You go ahead too Pearl," said Ruby. "I shall sit here on the porch for a spell and will join you at the Inn presently. Mr. O'Brien, would you see that Pearl finds her way to our place of lodging?"

"I need no help. I have spent more tahm in Maple Springs than you evah did, sistah dear. I am quite capable of...nevah mind," sputtered Pearl and she was off down the street, unsteady, but moving quickly.

Colin locked the cottage door, told Ruby that he'd see her at dinner and he went home, passing Pearl on his way.

"I will see you soon Miss Stone. Enjoy your walk to the Inn."

In reality, Colin wanted to get home to make some quick telephone calls; he called Elizabeth and warned her that the ladies, none too happy, were on their way. He also called Bill, but he had to leave a message; "I'll call you later, after dinner with the ladies of Savannah."

Then he called Joe. Joe answered. "Hi Colin. I saw your name on my caller I.D. I am at the B & B, just got here. You have been touring longer than I thought you would. I just couldn't make it there on time. How'd the tour go?"

Colin filled Joe in on what transpired with the Stone sisters starting with the phone call from the limo up until the ladies headed out, singularly, for the B & B. He explained in a purposeful but not bragging way about how he took control and did not let the ladies walk all over him.

"I am not going to prejudice your view of the ladies, so I won't give you my first impressions. You greet them there. I'll be along," said Colin.

"Thank you Deputy. You're on the ball," said Joe as he hung up.

Colin sat in his chair for a moment and charted some notes on the Stone sisters much as he had done with students during his teaching days. There was too much information to commit to memory. He might even share these notes later with the sheriff;

<u>Pearl</u>

Pageant Consultant
Fashion Plate
Knew value of traded stuff
Helpless?
A force
A belle (think Susanne Sugarbaker)

<u>Opal</u>

Dancer
Casual/cool
Aware of family belongings
Independent
A force
A modern belle

<u>Ruby</u>

Social Worker?
Hippie? Mousey?
Unaware of household stuff
Aloof
Hard to peg
Not a belle

Once he finished making notes on the Stone ladies, Colin headed to the Maple Springs Inn.

"Hello Mr. O'Brien. I was waiting for you." Colin was greatly startled when Pearl spoke to him from a chair on his front porch. "I was waiting here for you thinking that you might be driving to the Inn and I could tag along. These shoes originally screamed 'buy me, wear me', but today my piggies are screaming back and it isn't a pretty sound."

Colin laughed to himself, but he avoided smiling. "I intend to walk," he said. "I can offer you a pair of my wife's flip-flops, do you call them flip-flops in the south? and we can be there in just a couple minutes."

Pearl was thrilled to trade the pumps for some comfort and their walk to the B & B was indeed brief. Colin was glad to have this alone time with Pearl. Always the deputy, recently anyway, he thought that he might get some insight into Pearl, the youngest Stone sister, that might help to explain the sister's northerly visit.

No such luck. Pearl talked continuously enroute to the Inn, but it was talk of how much Maple Springs had changed since she last visited the community over five years ago, actually it was more like eight years ago. She thought it now looked more prosperous.

"I remember," she began, "that many of the houses had lovaly porches, but they were in poor repair and a great deal of paintin' was called for. I love that people have actually taken efforts to have colorful houses, with awnin's that add so much to

218- Murder at Maple Springs

the design aspect of these really nondescript little cottages. They were always plain ol' whaht and needin' paint. It's quite lovaly now. I recognize that."

As they approached the Inn, Pearl talked of the size, colors, landscaping, roofing, etc. of the Inn. She must have said the word 'lovaly' ten times. Elizabeth and Vonny met Pearl and Colin at the door and introduced themselves. Pearl was very southern in her greeting and she then excused herself so that she could go to her room and freshen up in order to be ready for dinner. Elizabeth showed her to her room.

"Vonny, my love. Is all in readiness here?" said Colin as he grabbed Vonny and took her into the library. "Are Opal or Ruby here yet? They must be. When's dinner? Where's Joe? I talked to him on the telephone and he was here. Well?"

"Are you through? That was a string of five questions. Hush and I'll tell you what's going on." Vonny paused and Colin, wisely hushed, sat and waited for Vonny to speak. "Opal is in her room. Joe is outside, on the front porch, on his cell. All is ready here. The quiche is in the oven and in about twenty minutes, we eat."

"Where's Ruby? Shouldn't she be here? Do you think she got lost? Should I go look for her? Should I tell Joe that she is missing? You're sure that she isn't in her room?"

"Colin, you managed to get six questions out that time. I love you, you are driving me crazy. Yes, go look for Ruby and bring her back alive. Take my car, it's behind the garage. Go!"

Colin went directly to the Stone cottage. Ruby was not

seated on the porch as she had been twenty minutes earlier. Colin drove to the waterfront, no Ruby. Colin saw no one walking, no cars. He worried that Ruby had somehow gotten into the house, but upon returning to the Stone's and walking the perimeter of the cottage, it was clear no one was there. As he stood on the Stone's porch surveying the area, down the road came three teenagers on bikes, a white van followed them, but at the corner nearest the cottage, the teenagers came flying low by the house and the van turned and went another way. The kids waved. They were the grandchildren of the postpersons. They were regular visitors to The Springs. Colin stood for a few minutes and then got back into Vonny's car and cruised slowly, making his way to the Inn. As he approached the stone pillars that set off the entrance to the Inn, he saw Ruby headed up the driveway. He couldn't figure out how he had missed her, but he had. Okay, everyone is accounted for.

He parked and went into the Inn meeting Ruby as she too entered. He held the door for her and then had the chance to introduce Elizabeth and Vonny. They both were, again, waiting just inside the door to meet and welcome their quest.

Elizabeth escorted Ruby to her room. Colin heard Elizabeth telling Ruby that dinner would be ready in ten to fifteen minutes. The quiche was settling before she would cut and serve it. It's best eaten hot.

CHAPTER 30

When the Stone sisters reappeared in the living room of the Inn, they were each wearing a version of their travel clothes. Pearl, now sporting stylish glasses, had her hair pinned back with a series of combs and she wore a filmy white tunic over her dark travel skirt and blouse. She had wisely exchanged her six inch heels for comfortable flats. Opal replaced her white sweater for a pink cardigan set and wore a matching bow tying back her long dark hair. Ruby hadn't had time to change, but had removed her knit poncho revealing a turtleneck blouse and a bright green vest. She remained unstyled.

Vonny, Joe and Colin greeted them and led them to the dinner table.

Dinner was an example of the gracious demeanor that Elizabeth possessed. Will too was gracious, by association. The round dining table was placed in the middle of the sun porch which extended the length of the southern side of the Inn. A profusion of plants, all on deep plates or in fancy planters, covered every available flat surface. Low bookcases, topped with plants of course, lined the outside wall below a bank of tinted, wide, uncurtained windows and small areas with chairs, sometimes footstools, lamps and small tables dotted the room. This was an obvious place to read, or perchance to snooze and relax on your day(s) at the B & B.

On the dinner table each place setting of dishes and silverware was of a different pattern, but they all had a flower motif. The napkins, all different in color and style, echoed the color of one of the flowers on the varied dinner plates. Water was poured and pitchers of iced tea and lemonade were on a sideboard that also held a perked pot of coffee on a warmer with delicate cups and saucers and coffee fixin's next to it.

Elizabeth served quickly by placing a smaller, white luncheon plate directly on the dinner plate in front of each guest. On that luncheon plate was a generous portion of quiche, it turned out to be a vegetable quiche, and a small silver dish of fruit salad. Two freshly made, warm bread sticks completed the plated meal.

A conversation regarding the sisters' journey north helped everyone to settle into casual conviviality. Pearl ask questions about the Inn. She hadn't remembered its existence when she was a child and young lady summering in Maple Springs. Joe explained the evolution of the Inn and mentioned that there were also several new houses and rehabs of existing cottages. Colin told a bit about the rehabilitation of their cottage. Opal seemed to have the best recollection of the changes to the Stone cottage. She remembered the year that Daddy added the deck on the rear of the house. She remembered having summer boyfriends to dinner at 'Shangri La'. Pearl remembered a photo shoot at 'Shangri La'. It was just after she was crowned Miss Georgia, she neglected to give the year, and the Georgia Miss America Committee wanted lots of pictures to use in their campaign to insure that Miss Georgia would become Miss America. There had only been one Miss Georgia to be elevated to the status of Miss America. That was in 1953 and the Georgia Miss America Committee was determined that the lovely and charming and talented Miss Pearl Lucille Stone would once again bring that honor home to Georgia.

A local photographer, Jon somebody, had taken the pictures, but regardless of that effort, and many others within Georgia and across the nation, Miss Stone was merely a Miss America runner up.

Pearl and Opal were forthcoming with information regarding their careers when Colin had switched the topic to their lives in Savannah. Ruby showed little interest in conversation. Instead she ate slowly, methodically cutting everything into small bites including the warm, fresh bread sticks.

"I am very pleased to be able to tell you that the Savannah Academy of Dance Arts is doing very well down home," said Opal. "We have classes from acrobatics to Zumba including classical ballet. We employ ten full time dance and exercise instructors. I'm a wreck when I think of all that we do; classes, tours, school residencies, choreography consults for local musical theater companies. If I didn't have Owen, I would never keep it all straight."

"Owen! Owen Adams! My Owen Adams? He works for you? Opal, my dear sistah, tell me this isn't so," said Pearl right on the heels of Opal's statement about her dance academy.

"It's so," Opal replied quickly. "He isn't yours. He was yours. Now, recently, he's become mine, or more politely and politically correctly, he is VP in charge of all things computer, financial and marketing. I maintain artistic and personnel control. I assumed that you knew Owen was on top of the business end of things at the Academy," said Opal and it was pretty obvious that she was through with this topic.

"I bet that Owen is on top of more things than what transpires at that Academy," came out of Pearl's mouth possibly before she thought. "I was under the impression that he had returned to Mobile to facilitate the closure of a family business. Since when does herding moppets through shuffle-ball change and pas de baret dressed as poodles and flowers necessitate the talents of Mr. Adams?" Pearl was working real hard at demonstrating civility.

"The Savannah Academy of Dance Arts is the only professional dance company in Savannah and but one of three in the whole state, and Mr. Adams spirits us forward through these lean financial times in splendid form. We at the academy are fortunate to have him as part of our team."

"Ladies, please, I have a few questions that need answering," said Sheriff Green obviously redirecting the conversation away from Owen Adams. "Perhaps you three could continue the Owen saga later."

"I resent that Sheriff," said Ruby incredulously. "I do not live in Savannah so I know nothing of their squabble or Mr. Adams and if I did live there, I would hope that I would still know nothing of this petty problem."

Ruby's comment brought responses from Opal and Pearl, not real words, but sounds, word-like, that surely were understood by all three sisters. Joe was anxious to move to a new topic. Colin's curiosity was up. He wanted to know how this Owen Adams fit into the dynamic competition that Colin felt existed between Pearl and Opal. He made a note of the name and would be sure to get Scarlet or Kyle's take on Adams.

"Ladies, I see that everyone has finished eating. I am off duty as sheriff, but on duty as a new dad. Before I leave, I want to make sure that we are all in synch for tomorrow. I want to answer any questions you might have regarding the investigation into Selma Stone's death and I want to show you cute pictures of son number six," said Joe.

Joe sure knows how to defuse a sticky situation, thought Colin. I'm proud that he thought me worthy of deputization.

The Stone sisters agreed that Tone was an adorable child and, strangely, they had no questions regarding the investigation into Selma Stone's demise.

"Looks like you're reticent to ask specific questions," said the Sheriff, "so let me summarize the situation in a couple sentences. Selma Stone was found dead in her home, her body was discovered by Mr. O'Brien here, and we are using every investigative tool available to us to find the perpetrator of this crime. You have the condolences of the Chautauqua County Sheriff's Department on the death of your father and your stepmother. We are certain that the perpetrator of this crime will be apprehended in the very near future."

"Sheriff, perpetrators come in many forms and act out for many different reasons. Surely your department hasn't, in the three days since the enactment of the crime, been able to take into account all the variables that converge to enact a crime," said Ruby almost as a rebuke to the confidence expressed by the sheriff.

"Miss Stone, it is Miss Stone isn't it?" asked the sheriff of Ruby.

"It is," said Ruby followed by more of those sisterly, word-like sounds from Opal and Pearl. This time the sounds obviously expressed disbelief.

Joe took in the sister sounds, but went right on with his efforts to bring the group together and to get home to Antony.

"Our sheriff's office probably has more, and higher tech equipment than the metropolitan police department in Savannah, GA," said Joe. "And we have an expert forensic team and access to laboratories and experts in Albany, that is our state capital, and even connections with the FBI if we need their assistance.

"The piece of the investigation that is causing us consternation revolves around the 'trade out' that has taken place at your cottage. Colin has told me that he has explained the concept of a 'trade out' and you have seen for yourself how deeply traded out the cottage is," said Joe.

"I do not think many items have been removed, sheriff. Over the years many household items have come and gone from that cottage. I am sure that Miss Selma replaced items that she knew were treasured by my mother," said Ruby.

"You barely looked through the cottage when we stopped there this afternoon, Ruby. You haven't been in that cottage in years. I dare say your memory isn't able to bring forth remote recollections of summers here when you were more interested in summer romancin' than summer cottage furnishin's," said Pearl while glaring at her sister.

"Enough!" began Opal. "It is so obvious that there was as you call it, a trading out, a large scale trading out. I know Miss Selma, and of course Daddy, loved that cottage and everything in it. Crass as she was, Daddy had Miss Selma under control and would never have allowed her to dispense with items that he, and Momma, treasured. Sheriff, it is obvious that this depletion of items at the cottage is a part and parcel to the demise of Miss Selma. Have you, or your many experts, been able to correlate the two events?"

Joe took a deep breath. It was obvious that he wanted to correct the Stone sister's misguided view of Miss Selma and to take them down a peg or two.

Colin jumped in and started to speak and Joe was relieved.

"Tomorrow, Mr. Rhoe Anderson, who has acted as an insurance agent for your father for many years, will show us all a video tape that your mother made with Eileen Miller in 2006. I have not seen the tape, but Mr. Anderson says that it will show us a 'then' vision of the cottage and you can see for yourselves the many items traded out. On your tour of the cottage earlier you experienced the 'now.'" Colin barely took a breath before he continued. He didn't want to hear anything more from the southern ladies who were trampling on the long admired southern tradition of grace and charm. "Mr. Anderson made a list of the traded items once he had viewed the tape and then toured the cottage. He has asked a local antique and fine arts dealer to place a dollar value on the missing items. He will speak to us first in the morning and then Neil Robertson, a local lawyer who was engaged by your father, will explain changes to your father's will and will discuss further provisions to be enacted now that Miss Selma has also passed away."

A few family, sisterly, private language sounds were emitted. They were similar to the sounds of disbelief heard earlier

"Is it possible that you plan on attendin' our private, family meetin' in the mornin' Mr. O'Brien?" asked Ruby.

Silence followed. Lots of thinking took place. Joe spoke.

"Deputy O'Brien's presence is required. The gathering in the morning should be considered a phase of the investigation rather than a family meeting." Joe was on a roll. "The executor of your father's and stepmother's estate has provided information that we will all hear from Lawyer Robertson at the same time."

A brief silence followed.

"It was truly a lapse in good judgment when my father named that woman the executor of his will," said Ruby

"I shall be retiring for the evening," announced Pearl. "I have many things to take care of prior to bed time. Good night." With that, Pearl was gone from the room.

Opal was the next to arise. "I too must retire. It has been a long day and there is much to mull. Pearl has a suitcase of goos and gobbs to knead into that face, and probably other regions. I have my lap top and Academy details to attend to. I shall be happy to see you all in the mornin', you too Mr. O'Brien." With that Opal was gone from the room.

Following suit, Ruby stood and said, "Sheriff, I assume that it is safe for me to take a walk in Maple Springs just as night is about to fall. I am a serious walker and have miles to log. Good night." With that, Ruby was gone through the door that lead to the outside from the sun room.

Vonny, Joe and Colin sat in silence for a moment, each dealing with the first impressions they had just formed of the Stone sisters.

CHAPTER 31

"Oh dear," said Elizabeth as she came into the room with a tray of short, crystal bowls filled with lime sherbet and each having two chocolate covered biscotti sticking out of the top. "I misjudged how long it would take to eat dinner and I am late with the dessert."

Having extra desserts did not prove to be a problem. Elizabeth sat and had dessert with her guests and Joe and Colin each had two. No sense in good desserts going to waste. As the four enjoyed the sherbet and the delicious biscotti that Vonny had made especially for the occasion, they spoke quietly. They agreed that the Stone girls were each living in a world unto herself.

Vonny was the first to speak. "I purposely didn't say anything tonight. I thought that the ladies might have concerns, questions, but they never even asked about their father's death in Italy or asked about a funeral. I can't say as I am inclined to offer them much sympathy. I can't even figure out why they are here. You'd hardly know that they are sisters." Vonny paused for a minute, then said, "I have gifts for the girls, from Italy, from Selma and G.E.M., but couldn't give them to them after the things they said about Selma. Perhaps tomorrow at the 'investigation meeting' the gifts can be given out. Or better yet, Elizabeth could place these gift boxes in the girl's rooms at some point in the morning." Vonny then passed to Elizabeth the three black, velvet boxes, tied with silver string-like ribbon that Europeans seemed to use a lot.

"You're right, those ladies are strange ducks," said Joe. "I will see that the gifts are handed out tomorrow." Elizabeth passed the boxes to Joe. Joe continued, "I also think that I can shed some light on why they are here. I meant to tell you this earlier Colin. I called Scarlet Ames today to make sure that she was clear on us talking about the changes to the Stone wills and she told me that she got a long e-mail from the Chief of Police in the town in Italy where G.E.M. died, can't remember its name, and he wanted to be sure that G.E.M.'s next of kin had all the details surrounding his death. Miss Ames offered to talk to the girls and to give them the information. She called each one and offered to meet with them, individually, and they all declined her offer. They each just wanted the e-mail forwarded. So that is exactly what Scarlet did. The girls have all the information that we have. The information rightfully so provides the details surrounding G.E.M.'s death. And the funeral...well Scarlet has that all under control. G.E.M. and Selma made all the plans and they asked Scarlet to make it happen according to plan. Jeff, at Lander's Funeral Home, will take care of things at this end. Once Selma's body can be released to Jeff, he will take it from there. At one time, the girls probably knew the disposition of the cottage, now they are unsure. Scarlet thinks that maybe they know something, not sure what. They need firsthand, current information...so here they are."

"When I called them right after we found Selma's body, I gave them all the information that we had about that 'difficult situation," said Colin. "They are not concerned with Selma's passing. I also think they are here to hear the specifics of the will and of course they all had to come, couldn't let their sibling, or siblings, get an upper hand. I'd say too that they all knew what items were in the cottage, knew there was some valuable stuff. They may have even come to do some trading out. The fact that the locks are changed and that the cottage is still a crime scene must really be grating on them."

"They must be angry too that the good stuff is traded out," added Joe. "Trading out, by the way, is usually performed by family members. I can't wait to mention that at the meeting tomorrow. Usually one family member thinks that he or she is being treated unfairly and so they even out the playing field by getting what they think should be rightfully theirs."

"They all saw the depth of the trading out, even Ruby who hardly spent any time in the cottage knows, and it will be a blow to them tomorrow when Rhoe puts a price tag on the traded items," said Colin. "A few years ago they each were given money, art, help with careers and starting businesses, homes too I think. The disbursal of other items in their parent's estate was announced at that time too. The cottage, I think it is all that G.E.M owned outside of Savannah, is the only thing whose disposition is unknown. This is the girls' last chance to get something from their daddy. He would have had a fit if he ever heard them talk about Selma the way that they have been doing."

"If they have money, art, houses and had help getting established in business, where does Ruby fit in this mix?" added

234- Murder at Maple Springs

Elizabeth. "She doesn't look like money at all. Mousey. Am I being cruel? Pearl and Opal have nice luggage and clothing, carry themselves like they are used to money, or privilege anyhow."

"I agree," said Vonny. "I think Ruby is wanting to play the first born and to be the family spokesperson, but she can't play that role with those two sisters that she's stuck with. We know something about Pearl and Opal and can even Google them. I know, I did at work today. But Ruby! No citations on the computer and she's told us nothing."

"She just said that she was a serious walker and she went walking, but she only had on flip-flops. That's what she was wearing when she went walking earlier. She's weird. Am I being cruel?" said Colin.

"I'm outa here," said Joe. "I'm on call, always on call, and I gotta get home. I'm on call there too. Colin, let's meet in the morning before we come here. I want to make sure that we are in charge of the meeting and that 'the girls' don't squabble among themselves or stonewall us when we ask questions."

"Good thinking. Come to the house and we will come here together for the 9:00 meeting," said Colin.

"I'll have it all set up in the library with coffee, juice, Vonny's cinnamon rolls and some fresh fruit," said Elizabeth.

"Say Elizabeth. Do you know when the ladies are leaving for home?" asked Joe.

"They said that they would be appreciatin' my hospitality for just two nots," replied Elizabeth. "Am I being cruel?"

Joe and Vonny talked kids on the porch for a few minutes

and both headed home. Colin helped Elizabeth to clear the table and to put the dishes in the dishwasher. They left the table set up in the sun porch in case it was needed for a meeting or Joe needed to spread out papers or evidence or crime photographs.

Colin walked home using a very circuitous route to see if Ruby was indeed out there somewhere walking. The usual five minute walk took him almost twenty minutes and he never saw Ruby. He saw someone walking a dog. A small red convertible with the top down passed by, he thought much too quickly. A light colored van was parked at the far end of Lakeside Promenade; probably neckers, as Colin called young folk kissing and probably doing other things.

When Colin got home, Vonny was in the bathroom. He called Elizabeth and asked if Ruby had come home yet. She hadn't, but Elizabeth said that she would wait for Ruby's return and then lock up and so he could rest assured that the ladies were all safe and sound.

Colin took the cordless phone with him to the computer. He wrote a quick e-mail to Scarlet and Kyle and in a couple sentences told them about the tour, the dinner and the sort of abrupt ending to the evening when the Stone sisters each excused herself and was off to her own little world. He also mentioned that Opal and Pearl had discussed one Mr. Owen Adams. Did they know him? Feel free to dish some dirt. Colin promised that he'd call after the Wednesday meeting. He was sure that there would be lots to report on.

Colin got ready for bed and closed down the house for the

night; shut doors, closed windows to slits in case of rain, turned on a light over the stove, a general walk-through.

The telephone rang and it was Bill Morris. Colin forgot that he was to call him.

"Hey Colin. How was your dinner? Aren't they, G.E.M.'s gems, something?" said Bill. "When I fetched them in Buffalo, they were standing on the arrival level and not happy campers. Their plane, or is it planes, arrived early and they had waited for about five minutes. AND, horrors of horrors, as one of them said, 'I retrieved my own bag. I have never had the occasion to do that. Yes sir, I retrieved it and it was frightening'. I think it was the one with the big hair."

"Sounds like Pearl to me. She had on six inch heels and couldn't even walk, yes sir, I said walk, to the Inn. I had to loan her Vonny's flip flops," said Colin.

"Two of them sat in the back after I opened the doors for them. Whenever I looked in the review mirror, they were on opposite sides of the car. One, skinny and short, had a lap top out and fussed with that from Buffalo to Maple Springs. The other one tweezed eyebrows and then put polish on her toenails and her fingernails. I don't think they spoke although I did see them talking as I drove up to them on the arrivals level. Maybe they were agreeing to not talk all the way home. The other sister, hippie-like, is that cruel?, sat up front and did not talk to me or ask me questions until she spoke to tell me that they would be going to the cottage first and not the Inn and could I make arrangements for that tour. So when I called you, she was 'rot nexta me list'nin' ta ever'thin' Ah sade'. There is oddness here, Colin," said Bill.

Colin took a few notes as Bill talked so that he could report to Joe in the morning.

"They demonstrated that oddness at dinner, but you never know how grief approaches people. They just lost two family members, they could be having ambivalent feeling and it's throwing them," said Colin.

"You're being too kind," said Bill.

"Bill, did they make plans with you for a return trip? I understand that it will be Thursday. They told Elizabeth that they'd be 'appreciatin' Elizabeth's hospitality for just two nots.'"

"The two in the back each took one of my cards and said that they would call me," said Bill. "The one in the front, Miss Woodstock, said that she'd be making alternative plans. And speaking of alternative travel, I know I picked her up at the airport, but it seemed that she got there by some other means of transportation than an airplane. I been picking up folks for years and she didn't have that I-just-sat-in-a-stuffy-airplane-for-the-last-five-or-six-hours-look. Something was off. I didn't stow her luggage in the trunk, she kept her bag with her, it was on the floor in the front seat and I couldn't see tags. The other two had tags, fancy luggage too. They must have talked at some point and decided to stop at the cottage or the one riding shotgun made the decision to stop and didn't tell the others. I didn't have any other fares after I left them, as I told them I did, but I was damned if I was going to sit around and wait for them when the Inn was just two blocks away. That's all I got Colin," said Bill and he let out an audible, huge sigh.

Colin thanked Bill for his input. Colin said too that he'd call him if he or Joe had any further questions.

"Good luck, Colin. Those ladies are gonna piss you off a lot. Mark my words," said Bill and he hung up.

No sooner had Colin pushed the off button on the cordless phone when it rang while still in his hand. The area code registered 912 on the small telephone receiver screen and Colin immediately pushed the on button.

"Hello, Colin O'Brien here," he said.

"Colin, see I remembered, it's Kyle Kennedy in Savannah. I hope I am not callin' too late. I received your e-mail and we, Scarlet and I, are on the case. She's headin' over here and we will commence prowlin' for Owen Adams," she said with laughter in her voice.

"Oh Kyle, thank you so much for getting back to me. I certainly didn't expect you two to prowl the streets. You know this guy?" said Colin.

"Yes we do. If you are under thirty and wear a skirt and live in Chatham County, Georgia, Mr. Owen Adams has in some way entered your life. I am sure that Scarlet won't mind me telling you, it's no secret, but she and Owen did date for a while. He moved on, with her insistence, and she is careful to avoid him, like the plague. But tonight we are trackin' that varmint down. What specifically are you lookin' for?"

"Oh, Kyle, you are a riot," said Colin and then he proceeded to tell Kyle the basics of the squabble between Opal and Pearl. "I'm assuming that Owen is still with Miss Opal, and that relationship probably has nothing to do with this case, but the sisters are not forthcoming with personal information unless we prod. Joe is agreeable to tricking them into some divulging of information, so maybe we can use Owen info as a crow bar to get sister info. So, let's see: what's his role with Opal's Dance Academy? What's he up to down there with Opal up here, you know north? I don't know, you know, the dirt," said Colin.

"Will do, Colin. Also, if the Sheriff wants police information, he can call Sergeant Jimmie Lee Sands with the Savannah police. He helped Scarlet rid herself of the big O. I graduated from high school with Jimmie Lee. He's very much the gentleman and the professional. I really don't have any facts regarding Owen's skirmishes with the police or in bars or with women, but if anyone does, it's Jimmie Lee. I hear Scarlet beepin' out front. Gotta go. Look for an e-mail in the mornin'," and Kyle was off the line.

Colin pushed the off button on the cordless phone and looked at it as he held it in his hand. It did not ring. He put the phone in the cradle on the kitchen counter, laughed at the thought of Kyle and Scarlet prowlin' Savannah, and went to bed.

It was only 9:30, but Colin had had a busy day and the continuous talk and tension had exhausted him. Vonny was asleep. Joe turned on his reading light and found his book of choice and within three minutes the book and his glasses were on the night stand and Colin was asleep.

CHAPTER 32

By 8:15 on Wednesday morning, Vonny was off to work and Colin and Joe were on the porch formulating a series of questions and a loose agenda for their upcoming meeting making sure that they did not forget any topics.

"I'm surprised that you didn't go to your Rotary meeting," said Joe. "I thought that your attendance was required or you lost a digit."

"Attendance is very important. We are fined for lateness or absenteeism, but we can retain digits. We get a lot done, just because we are all always there. I am in a special class of Rotarians, so my attendance isn't required. It's encouraged, but not required. I figured that the meeting at the Inn took precedence."

"I really haven't got all morning, so we gotta streamline this get together," said Joe, "but I think there is a shady deal going on with these ladies. They are not suspects, but their being here and their interest in the will, given what they already have, is creepy. They didn't express any love loss with Selma and there was only one mention of the perpetrator and the crime itself and you'd think that the loss of their father and the murder of their stepmother would affect them somewhat."

"Oh, almost forgot. Bill Morris called when I got home last night. He had some insight into the ladies too," said Colin and he proceeded to tell Joe about the Stone sisters' behavior enroute from Buffalo to Maple Springs. "Bill also said that only two of

them, Opal and Pearl, asked for his card so they could call him
for a return trip to Buffalo. Ruby said that she had 'alternative
plans', whatever that is. Elizabeth said that the sisters will just be
there two nights. And, before I forget this too, I e-mailed Savannah last night to see if Scarlet could give us any information on
Owen Adams. Kyle, I copied her with the e-mail, called and told
me that she and Scarlet were going out on the town, actually she
said prowlin', looking for Adams and would be getting the scoop
on him and the Stone sisters. She was going to e-mail me when
she got home. Let me go check my computer."

Sure enough the e-mail was there. Without reading it, Colin printed it and took it to the porch and read it aloud.

Dear Colin,

Scarlet and I, looking good if I say so myself, went
to The High Life and sure enough, there was the big O, as
he likes to call himself. He was not alone, surprise, but
he was still working the room right from the stool that he
occupied at the serving end of the bar. His woman was
into him and into looking at herself in the mirror behind
the bar, so his prowling the room with his eyes wasn't
a problem for her. Gloria, a friend of mine who works
there as a cocktail waitress, said that they had come in
separately, but had been together since arriving. She had
never seen the two of them together before. The girl's
name is Audra Somerville and Gloria thinks she is a
graphic artist, works for some local PR agency. Just for

fun, Gloria counted the women in the room whom she
had seen the big O with in the past. Counting Scarlet,
the total was seven. It wasn't a busy night, it's Tuesday
after all, but there were lots of singles. Scarlet, pushy
lady that she is, went right up to the big O and started to
have a conversation. She didn't wait for Owen to introduce her to his woman, but introduced herself and the
two of them got to laughing. Lots of hands flying, hair
tossing, smiles. I was back at a table and could only see
them shaking hands and then laughing. Next thing you
know, the two of them head to the lady's room. The big
O did not like that at all. Owen looked around to see
where Scarlet had come from, but he doesn't know me so
I checked my cell phone and ignored him. It seemed as
though Scarlet and her new BFF Audra were gone a long
time and when they came back, they buzz-kissed, Scarlet
ignoring O. She walked right by me and out the front
door. I waited a minute and got up, talked to Gloria for a
minute and then headed out the front door too. I didn't
have the nerve to look at Owen and Audra. I found Scarlet in the driver's seat of her car and she was very, very
proud of herself.

Here's what she learned:

*Audra and Owen are "very serious, involved
    personally and professionally"

*Owen has a MBA, but doesn't like to flaunt it
    (doubtful)

*Owen is fresh off a relationship, "so
vulnerable"
*Audra works for Georgia Grafix, Gloria is
right, as an artist
*Owen is currently semi-unemployed(?) – may
be at Georgia Grafix soon
*Audra's daddy is the (only) BMW dealer in
the greater Savannah area
    Are you sensing a pattern here? It looks like none
of what Owen does is illegal, he's just sleazy. I think
we did well for our first caper (did I use the word caper
properly here?) Scarlet gets the credit, she was the shill
(I'm sure I used shill incorrectly). That's all from here.
For police information, you'll need to call Jimmie Lee
Sands at the Savannah PD. Hope we helped...can't wait to
hear back from you.

                  Kyle (and Scarlet)
                  (your own private Cagney & Lacey)

    Just then the telephone rang. Colin had brought the cord-
less out onto the porch earlier.
    "O'Briens," he answered.
    "Colin, it's me. What are you doing?" said Vonny.
    "Joe and I are on the porch prepping for the meeting at the
Inn. What's up?"
    "Put me on speaker phone. You both gotta hear this," said

Vonny.

Colin did as requested and Vonny got right down to business.

"Hi Joe. Well, I got to my office early so that I could again Google Ruby Stone, I couldn't believe that she was so anonymous that she can't be somewhere on the internet, but then I thought that that might not even be her name any more or might not be the name that she is currently using. I e-mailed G.E.M.'s secretary, I took G.E.M.'s telephone list to use, and asked if there were any other names that I might use to find Ruby. I didn't expect to hear from Scarlet until after 9:00, but she answered right away. Not only did I get a name, but I also got the name of a charity that Ruby was supposedly involved with, even working for, in Arizona."

"You social workers are a clever lot," said Joe. "Go on. I'm sure that you didn't stop there."

"Well, Ruby Ward, Ranch Rio, Arizona, was my first success. There is a picture of her that was taken at a trial where she was acquitted of fraud. It is a younger, healthier Ruby, but it's her. Money was missing from the accounts of Tribal Trailblazers, of which she was the Corporate Manager, but they could not prove that it was her that took the money."

"What is Tribal Trailblazers?" asked Colin.

"It's a sort of prep school for Native American boys, I should say young men, who have the smarts and potential to be tribal leaders. The organization boasted a 97% graduation rate and a 90% on-to-college rate. It subsisted on donations and with the scandal and the loss of the money, Trailblazers was taken over by a council of tribal leaders. That's all it said. No comments from Ruby Ward or the new council. Her name is eliminated from the list of staff on the Trailblazer's web site, but another citation, obviously from an earlier time, shows Ruby Ward attending a governor's conference on non-profit reorganization. She looks put together in this pic. From one picture to the next, there's a decline in Miss Ruby. That's all I have on her. I could delve into her more, but I do have a case load to maintain, ya know."

Joe was about to speak, but Vonny jumped back in, "I re-Googled the others, Opal and Pearl, and at each site, Pearl Stone Associates and the Savannah Academy of Dance Arts, I clicked on "Itinerary"...ya know, their web sites look alike, I think that that Owen guy had something to do with them both. Anyway, when I got to each itinerary, I could see that they have both been north lately and nearby."

"Nearby?" said Joe and Colin.

"Pearl was the Contestant Consultant for the Miss Pittsburgh pageant a few weeks ago. The itinerary section said that she was there for the entire week and that she also served as a judge and did interviews with local media. Interesting, huh? But not as interesting as the northern trek of Miss Opal. Seems as though Miss Opal and her Academy dance teams recently spent three days in Buffalo competing for spots on "America's Got Talent". I couldn't figure out why they came all the way to Buffalo to try out, but the itinerary said that they were also at tryouts in Atlanta and in Cleveland. They must not have succeeded in the

other cities, so Buffalo was another shot at the audition. These
sisters were both right in the neighborhood. I wonder if they will
be forth-coming with that information. I thought that all this
might help you at your investigation meeting in, according to my
watch, ten minutes. If you need more info, you're going to have
to sic someone else on the internet, I gotta go. Be careful at that
meeting. Those ladies are snakes. Love you both, you more so
Colin. Bye."

"Well, that puts a new slant on the investigation aspect of
this meeting. I say we talk in generalities and see if they, all three
of them, are inclined to be forthcoming with any of the info that
Vonny just passed along. How can anyone nowadays not think
that law enforcement can be onto them in depth, although I must
admit that I didn't do any kind of internet search or run their
names by the FBI. But why would I, they were, or we thought
they were, in Savannah, not suspects at all. But then, there is that
pesky murder that we have to deal with. I shoulda been more,
you know, investigatory," said Joe. He seemed down on himself,
down that he hadn't been the detail-minded cop, Vonny was a
better sleuth than he was, Deputy O'Brien was more in tune with
the case than he was.

"Joe, I wouldn't have thought to check out the Stone ladies.
I don't think that Vonny got on the computer thinking she was
being a cop. She was being helpful and wanted to get a handle
on our southern visitors," said Colin. "We gotta get to the Inn. I
think though that someone on the team needs to pick up where
Vonny left off, especially with Miss Ruby Stone, Ward, whatev-

er. And, let's not skip over the Owen Adams information from Savannah. I bet a lot of what Scarlet and Kyle found out will be news to Pearl and especially Opal.

Joe and Colin drove to the Inn in Joe's Sheriff car. During the brief ride, Joe broke the law and used his cell phone to call Pete Gianna and to tell him to run Ruby Stone, Ruby Ward and Tribal Trailblazers through the usual internet sources and to get back to him before noon. Joe also had Pete check to see if either of the other sisters, Pearl and Opal, had any kind of a record. Joe also gave Pete the name of the SPD sergeant so that he could check on the big O. Pete had been working almost full time on the Stone case, so more leads to follow-up on were welcomed.

CHAPTER 33

When Joe and Colin entered the library at the Inn, Rhoe Anderson and Neil Robertson were the only people in the room. After greetings and handshakes all around, Rhoe said, "We haven't seen any sign of the ladies. Elizabeth set up the buffet here and then she said that she would check on the ladies and hurry them along."

"The meeting starts at 9:00. They know that," said Joe as he looked at his watch. "In two minutes, I'd like to hear from you Rhoe." Joe got coffee and a cinnamon roll and sat down close to the large, high definition television set that Rhoe had rigged to show the Lula and Eileen tour of the Stone cottage.

Colin drank some juice, poured coffee and sat near Joe.

At 9:00 Rhoe began, "I am glad to have the opportunity to show you this vintage video of the contents of G.E.M and Lula Stone's cottage that was recorded in 2006. I had the tape from a small '90s camcorder transferred to a DVD and so it is much easier to present for viewing. The first voice you hear is G.E.M. Stone."

The library was on the west side of the Inn and the curtains had been drawn. The room was sufficiently darkened to allow for a bold black and white viewing of the tour.

"This here is the front door of the G.E.M. and Lula Stone cottage at 27 Lake View Avenue in Maple Springs, New York, a lovely vacation hamlet north of the Mason-Dixon Line. As we tour this cottage, Mrs. Lucille Newhouse Stone will be describin' our belongin's. This is all done for insurance purposes for our insurance agency, Anderson Associates. The videographer is Eileen Miller, a dear friend and valued associate of both myself, G.E.M. Stone, and Miss Lula. I leave the videoing and the talkin' to the ladies."

The cottage door was opened and there stood Lula, smiling and walking backward through the small hallway to the living room. She was a lovely lady, in her mid-sixties at this point. She wore a flowered skirt and strappy sandals in a bright green. Her cotton blouse, also a bright green, showed that Lula was slim, not skinny, and that her bearing was that of someone used to standing tall and being respected. Her hair was cut short, but not boyish looking. It was instead trendy, not severe, stylish.

"We are now in the livin' room of our home," began Lula. "On this wall you will see a trio of original oil paintin's painted by Roger Tory Peterson. We so love his work, he's both local and international, and the birds, cardinals and blue jays, are our favorites. On this shelf are twelve Hummel statues that were a wedding present to G.E.M. and myself from my German Aunt Bertha. The bronze sculpture right here is entitled "Wicked Pony" and it is by Fredrick Remington. There are two more small Remingtons in the upstairs hallway. We shall see them shortly. The furniture in this room is from Jamestown Royal in Jamestown. Just down the road. This is the same furniture that Lucille Ball and Ricky Ricardo have in their California home."

"Her husband's name is Desi Arnaz. Ricky Ricardo is the

guy he plays on TV reruns," G.E.M.'s disembodied voice was heard to say. Lula laughed, on camera, and Eileen too can be heard laughing. This is how the entire 20 minute DVD progressed. As Lula moved from room to room and provided a running commentary on the furnishing, Eileen focused on the items that Lula spoke about. In the background, periodically, came G.E.M.'s voice offering anecdotes and humorous, loving comments.

Lula highlighted items of worth and items that were sentimental favorites. She was still in the living room as she pointed out the grade school photographs of her three daughters. She indicated a television and stereo record player components, but Eileen quickly passed over those objects and focused on the book case next to a handsome roll top desk of fumed oak.

"All the books in this bookcase are first editions, most of them signed, by many famous authors," continued Lula. "Mr. Stone has been collecting these books on our trips north from a 'paper dealer' that we met years ago. G.E.M. says that reading a book, holding it and realizin' that its author actually touched that book, maybe even wrote in it, makes it so much more of a great read. The contents of this bookcase and the desk right here are treasures, treasures."

"Hawthorne, Hemingway, Twain, Wordsworth, Miss Emily Dickenson, Keats, Mary Shelley and others, about 20 more, some doubles," again it was the disembodied voice of G.E.M. participating in the tour.

From the living room, Lula moved quickly to the kitchen.

She threw open all the cupboards and Eileen panned the huge set of Fiesta Ware dishes; the set included all sizes of plates (dinner, lunch, dessert) and bowls (cereal, salad, soup, dessert) and all the splendid, beautifully designed, serving pieces (pitchers, platters, vegetable bowls) and, of course, the cups and saucers.

"I love these dishes, the colors," said Lula. "Many happy memories have originally occurred in this house over meals with this Fiesta Ware. How can I not love it. I have never broken a dish. It's all here, every piece that G.E.M. gave me for our tenth weddin' anniversary. The traditional gift for that anniversary is tin or aluminum, but I'd rather have these dishes. I love these dishes."

The video showed many sets of glasses in the cupboards, and pots and pans and drawers of every imaginable cooking tool, a set of three cast iron frying pans nestled together were in the oven of the vintage, kitchen stove. The two benches at each side of the small kitchen table proved to offer storage space for linens, beautiful linens that Lula held aloft as Eileen dutifully captured them on film.

The tour continued to the dining room where silver and crystal items were highlighted.

A small sun porch on the first floor, that was replicated on the second floor, was resplendent with mixy-matchy colors and prints in the furniture, wall paper, curtains and rug; all based on the sunflowers in the framed pictures on the wall.

"I could sit in this room all day and read, write letters or knit," said Lula. "I love this room. Note the many crystals in the windows, catching the sun. They are those Sarwowski crystals. I think that's their name."

The time upstairs was brief. Eileen merely panned each room and Lula gave a general overview; "The pitcher and bowl in each room are just for show, we have indoor plummin', they are very old. The quilts are from local Amish ladies and are all queen size although we have them on double beds. The prints on the wall are signed Norman Rockwell's and bedsteads are all brass. We had them replated and the gentleman at the shop where we had it done, offered us fifteen hundred dollars for each one. No sale."

A quick look into the upstairs sunroom (yes, it exactly matched the first floor sun room) and a close up of the two small Remington sculptures of cowboys on bucking horses that were on a corner table in the upper hall and then a pan of the series of black and white Ansel Adams, numbered and signed photographs which filled the walls in the upstairs hall and then Lula came into view standing at the bottom of the stairs, leaning on the newel post and looking up into the lens of the camera that Eileen continued to hold as she descended the stairs.

"Well, that about completes our tour. We have outdoor furniture, lots of wicker, and some nice outdoor pieces on the back deck, but there is no emotional attachment to any of those items. We love this house and the nice things we have, but our prize possessions are the Ruby, the Opal and the Pearl that make our lives complete. Did I do alright, Honey?"

"You were wonderful, a real Academy Award winnin'

performance," said G.E.M. and then he came on camera, hugged Lula and sang, "*You oughta be in pictures. You're wonderful to see. You oughta be in pictures. Oh want a hit you would be.*" Fade to black.

The sniffling coming from the back of the room told Joe, Colin, Rhoe and Neil that the Stone sisters had joined them.

Without even turning around, Joe said, "Ladies, come on down front and Mr. Anderson here will continue his speechifying."

The three sisters came to the front row and they silently and gracefully settled themselves.

"I hope that you were able to see all of the video. I can show parts again if you would like," said Rhoe.

"Oh no, not now," said Joe. "We have a lot of ground to cover. You can show it again later."

"Actually, I have made copies of this DVD for everyone here. Although the tape was made for insurance purposes, it is a wonderful, positive rendering of your parents and one you will surely view many times," said Rhoe as he passed out DVDs to the Stone sisters while introducing himself and asking each lady's name. The other three people in the room each received a DVD too. Each sister placed the DVD in her purse, Ruby without even looking at it, but Pearl and Opal after examining it and reading the information that Rhoe had written on the paper sleeve that protected each disc.

"Oh Mr. Anderson, it is indeed a treasurer. I was thinking that I had forgotten the voice and the smile and the walk of mama, and now here it is committed to film or video or whatever and we can see her whenever our memory needs a jolt. Thank you oh so much," said Opal.

Opal was in red stretch pants with white shoes and a cropped red and white striped blouse and earrings and a hair flower also in red and white. "And daddy too." She continued. " He was so adorable, so warm and so generous. I miss him. His accident in Italy started this whole upheaval."

Colin couldn't let the word accident settle as part of the conversation.

"Your father died of natural causes. There was no accident. You have information from Italy, we all do, and it is a final determination that there was no accident, no foul play, no covering up of anything. I hope that is clear."

Colin heard stridency in his voice and he even thought that perhaps he had even spoken out of turn.

"Colin is absolutely correct in what he said. Is there anyone who did not receive the official paperwork from Italy?" asked Joe. Rhoe raised his hand and Colin offered to get him a copy for his files. No one else raised a hand.

"Mr. Anderson," said Pearl, "we saw the DVD in its entirety and I think that I speak for my sisters when I say thank you for requesting this video so long ago and now for sharin' it with us. What is your assessment of the 'trade out' that we just learned of yestaday?"

Pearl was in an outfit that would have looked great, and flowed beautifully, on the runway, but that was over-the-top at an investigatory meeting in a library of a B & B in Maple Springs. She wore a flowing skirt and matching tunic in a floral print accented with spherical earrings the size of baseballs and an arm full or noisy tri-metal bracelets. She was barefooted.

At this point, Joe turned his front row chair to face the ladies, Rhoe sat in another chair also facing them and Colin joined the quickly fashioned circle. Neil scooched in at the end of the front row right next to Opal. Rhoe started right in, he was obviously prepared.

"Two days ago, I viewed the DVD in my office. Yesterday, I toured your family cottage and at that time I made a list of the things I remembered from the DVD that I did not find to be in the cottage. I took that list and the DVD to Ron Hughes who runs an antique shop in Ellington, that's about 15 miles from here over country roads. Ron put a value on each item from my prepared list. First, I'd like to ask you to tell me about items that you might think are missing."

The ladies all started talking at once. "Ladies, one at a time. You first. Ruby is it?" said Rhoe.

"Yes, I am Ruby, the eldest of the three of us, and I would rather see your list than have the three of us succumb to pure guesswork." Ruby appeared restless, even tired, irked, hardly emulating the relaxed, with-it styling of her sisters. She wore a man's long sleeved t-shirt, looking more gray than white, and a pair of double knit high-water slacks. The serious walker's choice for footwear, flip flops, completed her ensemble.

"I have lots of items to mention," said Pearl. "The art work:

Adams, Remington, Peterson, those little German statues, crystal, silver and the quilts, those gorgeous quilts that momma had specially made with only the best materials. The Amish ladies might have made them, but the design and the cloth in them is all momma."

"My turn," it was Opal. "The Fiesta Ware...gone. The linens...gone. Thank God, Miss Selma's jewelry is locked up somewhere in Savannah. Ask Missy Executor 'bout that."

"Well, you have mentioned the major items and indeed all of those items are on Ron's list. He also listed stemware from the kitchen. The pink, I think it's called depression glass. And the books. On the video your father only mentioned a few of the authors and we don't know which books were signed, so we found the value of the last first editions sold by each author mentioned and we quadrupled the value because Mr. Stone said there were about 20 more." Rhoe paused for a moment, he had everyone's silent attention.

"The art alone is worth over $100,000. The artists are all dead, the works are signed, American artists are very popular now. But it is the Fiesta Ware that is the surprise item on the list. Given that there is a complete set, it looks like a set for twelve, and all the serving pieces are included, it is probably worth $20,000 to $30,000. Just last week on *Antiques Roadshow* on PBS a Fiesta Ware water pitcher went for almost $500. Whoever did the trading out, knew his or her business."

The library of the Maple Springs Inn was silent. Each person present had their own thoughts about the DVD, the 'trade out', the value of the items, etc. Joe got up, refilled his coffee cup, stood in front of the ladies and said, "It is almost always a family member who does the trading out." He returned to his seat.

Stone family wordless noises erupted. Then came words. "Are you in any way, shape or form accusin' me or either of my sisters of taking our own items?" said Pearl.

"No ma'am." said Joe. "Just a fact that I was throwing out there, you know, like when you fish and cast out that bait and you don't even know what's below the surface of the lake. Interesting, isn't it. A family member. Almost always."

"What makes you so sure that there was a 'trade out'?" It was Ruby talking. "The missin' items could have been sold off by Daddy or Miss Selma. I am sure that she hardly knew the value of those treasures. They could have been gone for weeks, months, even years."

"I was in that house just before the Italian vacation," said Colin. "All the items now gone, or missing, were in place, were present and accounted for." He stopped there. If Joe wanted more info out there regarding the investigation, he'd have to supply that himself.

"Ladies, a 'trade out', accomplished by family or someone else, occurred when the perpetrator heard about Miss Selma's supposed death in Italy. Now there is a topic that none of you have asked about that I think needs to be thrown out for discussion," said Joe. He paused for a moment and then continued. "Why did Miss Selma send word of her own death rather than be truthful and tell us about G.E.M.'s death. After G.E.M.'s death,

she completed the tour of Italy by herself and then came home.
Did you know that she traveled home disguised as your father?"

Holy mackerel, thought Colin, he's letting everything out of
the bag.

"What? You can't be serious? You just made that up.
Loopy as she was Miss Selma, could neva pull that off. I think
you, sheriff, are out of order here," said Ruby.

Pearl and Opal verbally agreed with Ruby, but their body
language bespoke more of a sense of how could that be, why
would she do that?

"Ladies," began Colin not really knowing where he was
going with this, "the sheriff is telling you the truth. I saw her
dressed as G.E.M. and Bill Morris, the limo driver, knew that
the G.E.M. in his back seat was not your father. Selma wrote
Vonny and me a letter saying that she would explain all of her
subterfuge, that's the word that she used, I think, but she was
dead before she had a chance to explain. She asked for our help
in sorting out a situation that she had initiated. So the question
is, why did she come home as G.E.M. after lying about her own
death?"

The silence was deep and long.

Then. "Perhaps I can shed some light on the discussion."
It was Neil Robertson to the rescue. Joe and Colin had brought
tension to the meeting and now a voice of reason would, hopefully, be a calming force.

"I did not know about Mrs. Stone traveling home as her
husband and about her reporting her own death in Italy until just

now, but it all makes sense to me because of the information that I have of which you are unaware. You are unaware of changes made to your father and stepmother's will, aren't you?" Neil spoke directly to the Stone sisters.

"I daresay we had an inkling of some tinkering with the will or wills, but we are not cognizant concerning specifics," said Pearl.

Ruby blurted out, "All daddy said was that..." Ruby chose not to complete her sentence.

"Ruby, please complete that sentence...all that daddy said was," said Joe.

"It was nothing. I guess that I don't remember exactly his words. All he said was that there were changes, small changes, and he would explain them to us when he returned to Savannah," said Ruby.

"Ruby, I find that I must remind you that you told me, and I assume that you told Opal too, that a change in ownership of the cottage was what daddy had indicated when you last spoke to him," interjected Pearl.

"When was it that you last spoke to your father, Miss Stone, Ruby, and what exactly did he say?" said Joe.

"I don't recall," said Ruby. "I resent this line of questioning. I believe that we should consider other topics."

"Let me ask you all that same question that I just asked Ruby, and tell me also, when did you last see your father and Miss Selma?" Joe was asking questions and taking notes.

"Sir, I saw both my father and Miss Selma in late May after

their return from an eco-tour to Brazil and just before they left
to spend the summer here in Maple Springs. I did speak to my
father on the telephone several times since I last saw him, but our
conversation was mainly about the Italian trip and about the new
friends they had made here at the Springs this summer, mainly
Mr. and Mrs. O'Brien," said Pearl.

"I saw daddy, just the two of us had lunch near the Academy, in May also and I too spoke with him by telephone. Daddy
and I had a special bond. His sense of business was something
that he passed on to me," said Opal.

"And your big ass was passed on too," said Pearl. "Sheriff,
daddy made a major production of treating us all equally and we
all know it. He loved no one best, but each one equally."

That statement by Pearl seemed to silence Opal. Ruby
jumped right in and tried for the second time to answers Joe's
question about her contact with parents.

"I have not seen daddy in several years. Of course, we
spoke. Often. I had no accurate or complete knowledge of a
will change. Perhaps Mr. Robertson could continue providing
insights for us."

"I'd be interested in knowing when you each last visited
Maple Springs," said Colin.

"Yes, I'd be interested in that too," said Joe. "When were
you last here, or even north, possibly near here?"

Oh Joe, great segue, you set the trap, thought Colin.

"North is not a place I clamor for," began Pearl, "but when
business calls, I fly north, work, and fly south. I believe that

during this year's pageant season, I have been north, I recall, two times and I have upcoming events to coordinate in Boston, Burlington, Vermont and Lake Placid, New York I believe. I do not commit my itinerary to memory."

"Perhaps your itinerary is on your web site. You could refresh your memory there," said Joe with a broad smile.

"It's all there. The web site is not massive, but it does its job and I get work from it, often. Oh, I just thought of my other northernly visits, Philadelphia and Pittsburgh, both in Pennsylvania," concluded Pearl.

"Pittsburgh is just down the road a couple hours. Were you aware of that Pearl?" asked Joe.

"I was not aware, but then remember, I fly, work and fly. Often pageants are in big hotels near airports. That works splendidly for me. And to your other question, I was last here with Momma, prior to her taking ill. I have not been here for six or seven years at least."

"And you, Opal. When did you last enjoy Maple Springs for a summer?" said Joe, keeping the meeting moving forward.

"Mostly I never enjoyed Maple Springs for a summer," said Opal. "I visited here for many years, with my family, but I was last here when I was fifteen. After that I attended dance camps. Daddy did not approve, but he acquiesced when he realized how important dance was to me. And before you run out and check my web site, I was north, in Buffalo, New York, actually, nearby, recently."

"Next," said Joe with a smile on his face. It was again Ruby's turn.

"I was last here about four years ago and spent time with daddy and Miss Selma. I was between jobs and enjoyed some R & R before heading home, west, and job searching. I am seldom east, almost never north-east and, although you did not ask, I have not been in Savannah for many years. I was there when daddy was so generous to the three of us, the servants and the city of Savannah. You know about all that don't you Mr. Robertson and probably you too sheriff," said Ruby.

"When you flew into Buffalo yesterday," Joe continued his questioning, "where did you come from? Where are you living now, Ruby? Opal and Pearl are in Savannah I presume, but we have no idea where you call home."

"I try not to discuss my personal life because my professional life is so intertwined with my clients and HIPPA regulations are very strict so..." said Ruby.

"I don't want client names, diagnoses, a fee structure, just a state and city," said Joe.

"I live out west, Arizona mostly, Rancho Rio right now, Okay?" said Ruby with finality.

Just then there was a knock on the door and Elizabeth stuck head in.

"Sorry to interrupt. Joe, I have a fax for you and I thought too that I should make sure that the buffet items were in good supply," she said.

Joe took the fax from Elizabeth and exited through glass French doors to a small patio outside off the library.

"Thank you Elizabeth," said Colin. "We are fine. Everyone, we are going to take a five minute break, have something to eat and we will gather again and continue with Neil after Joe has had a chance to read his fax."

CHAPTER 34

The break was of ten minutes duration, not five, and when the meeting commenced, everyone had a plate with fruit, a cinnamon roll, juice and most had coffee. Their plates were those luncheon plates with the place to harbor one's orange juice or coffee in order to prevent it from sliding off the plate. Joe had come back into the library, refilled his coffee cup, black, and rejoined the circle.

"So ladies, thank you for sticking with the process here," said Joe while waving his newly acquired fax in the air. "My investigators have sent me a summary of our to-date findings regarding the murder of Selma Stone and there are some aspects of this that I would like to share with you, but first, I think Lawyer Robertson should address the group by sharing the new specifics of the wills of G.E.M. and Selma Stone. Take it away counselor."

Neil Robertson, very neat, nattily dressed, quite tall and of great speaking voice stood and pressed buttons or moved a mouse on his computer to retrieve his notes and he began.

"Thanks Joe," he said. "I do have appointments from noon on, so I appreciate the chance to discuss with you this morning the update of the Stone wills. First, I hope that you ladies will accept my condolences for the loss of two very important members of your family. Over the years I have helped your father with minor legal matters and I was pleased to continue our business relationship in the recent past. I knew your mother and was just getting to know Selma. Those were two fine ladies.

"Three things I must speak to before we begin. The first is in regards to Selma Stone. She was a wonderful person, a true lady, kind and beloved. There was not an ounce of pretension in the woman's body. And best of all, she was devoted to your father. If you ladies had objections to her, I would have at least hoped that you could have respected her for the sheer joy that she brought to your father. The second item that needs correcting is something that Pearl said earlier. She referred to the items in the cottage as, 'our own items'. All those items in the cottage, and indeed the cottage itself, were to belong to Mrs. Selma Stone upon the death of her husband. Those items probably never were yours and the changes to the wills made sure that they never would be. Let me make that more clear. If Mrs. Stone were to predecease Mr. Stone, then the cottage and all its contents would be solely his and upon his death, the cottage and all its contents would be sold and donated to the Maple Springs Homeowners Association, but, and this is what actually happened, if Mr. Stone were to predecease Mrs. Stone, then the cottage and all its contents were to be inherited by Mrs. Stone. Upon Mrs. Stones death, the cottage and all of its contents were to be sold and the money given to the Everlasting Evangelical Spirit Church of Savannah, Georgia, Mrs. Stone's lifelong church."

Neil stopped at this point. He had everyone's undivided attention. They were all breathing and so he felt it safe to go on.

"The third item to elaborate upon is my thoughts on why Selma Stone reported that Mr. Stone had died in Italy and why she returned to Maple Springs pretending to be Mr. Stone." Neil paused for a minute, he was carefully choosing his words. "With Mr. Stone gone, Selma was virtually alone in this world. She had no close friends, no blood relatives to help her through grief and the restructuring of her life. Selma needed time, needed gentle help, that'd probably be you Colin, and Vonny. G.E.M. was a big presence and now Selma had to fend for herself. She really hadn't thought out what it was that she had to do, to be prepared for, but she knew there could be unfriendly forces that she would have to deal with. She knew that I would help her with the new will and that Carlton Chase could help her in Savannah. She just bought some time. Poor Selma, hobbled by a plan that she couldn't bring to fruition, no family to be trusted, no G.E.M. to lean on."

Neil was caught up in his own words, in the sadness of Selma's last days. He drank from his cup of coffee, probably cold, and continued speaking.

"There are a few small bequests also. These provisions were to be executed after the death of both parties prior to the disposition of the Maple Springs property to either the church or the homeowners' association. I will paraphrase them for your better understanding," said Neil as he picked up his lap top and referred to the screen.

"To Vonny and Colin O'Brien the Stones left the eight piece set of front porch wicker furniture complete with cushions. I remember the Stones saying that they knew how much you two loved those pieces.

"To Eileen Miller, whom the Stones called their fourth

daughter and daughter by choice, they left any and all of the "toys" in the shed behind the cottage...Vespa Motor Scooter, leaf blower, pressure washer, step ladders, generator, tools etc. etc., etc... anything she wants from the shed, she can have.

"This next bequeath I will read. 'To the Maple Springs Homeowners Association, we leave the 20 dock pieces, 14 dock stanchions, lantern system, dock platform carpeting and awning and furniture for the perpetual use of the citizens of Maple Springs. A yearly bequest from the Stone Family Foundation of Savannah, Georgia will insure that the items mentioned in this gift will be annually set-up, managed and repaired, disassembled and stored over the winter, thus allowing for the perpetual use that we envision.' I think that's clear."

Neil looked up from the lap top screen and said, "It looks as though this next bequest will be more difficult to make. The will says that the collection of fifty first editions, some signed by the authors, is to be donated to the James Prendergast Library in Jamestown, NY, to be added to their rare book archives. The collection was valued at $250,000. I have a detailed list sheriff. I will print it off and give it to Rhoe so that Ron Hughes can get us a more current valuation of that collection.

"I have just read all the will changes that we have come here to discuss this morning. Are there any questions? Ladies? Sheriff? Colin?" asked Neil.

"Prior to your recitation of salient parts of the newly revised will," started Pearl, "you took the occasion to chide us regarding our perhaps somewhat thoughtless or even flippant view of Miss Selma and you gave us your unsolicited view of the her character, so I assume that you saw no sign of her willfully making these changes over daddy's objections. Surely this cottage meant nothing to her."

"Miss Stone, these revisions were accomplished after great thought by your father. Miss Selma came to the meetings in my office and I am sure that she was a party to the formulation of these changes, but your father was the spokesperson."

Robertson continued. "If you ladies have traveled north to... I guess that now is a good time to read you something from the original will that was written and filed in Savannah with Mr. Chase, your father's personal and business lawyer. I am assuming that you three sisters were there when that will's contents were made known to virtually everyone in Savannah. The Greater Savannah Historical Preservation Society and others, including you three, were the recipients of the great generosity of your father. There is no need for me to go over the details concerning those gifts, but I think that I should take this opportunity to reread to you the codicil at the end of that multi-paged document. Ms. Scarlet Ames, will executor, very kindly supplied me with a copy of the will so that I had it as background for this presentation. I never assumed that you ladies would decide to venture north for the unveiling of this very small, indeed insignificant, reworking. Originally the cottage and all of its pieces were part of the bequest to the Historical Society. Your father merely carved the cottage out of the bulk of the estate and gifted it in the manner that I just read to you."

At this time, Neil again picked up his lap top, spoke and then read from the screen. "The previous Savanah will says, 'The provisions of this will that pertain to the Misses Stone, Ruby Mae, Opal Jeannette and Pearl Lucille should not be publicly made known. The gifts of cash, stock holdings, homes and funds to initiate a business will be overseen by The Stone Family Foundation and negotiated with final decisions mutually agreed upon between individuals and the Foundation. Once distribution is agreed upon (again, individually) there will be no further inheritance of money, real estate or personal items. You're getting it when I got it and you need it, girls. I love you, enjoy, Daddy.'"

Neil paused for a minute, closed his lap top and replaced it on the table.

"Mr. Robertson, as you carefully exhibited for us, a will can be changed, something can be carved out, someone can be left out, a codicil can be ignored," Ruby said. "I shall only speak for myself. I have ventured here to see if the change in ownership of the cottage would affect me or if possibly we three would share the ownership."

Opal and Pearl were silent. Colin was sure that Ruby was the lamb sent out to appease the wolf and the two remaining sisters wanted to leave this pasture unscathed.

"Miss Stone, had you been mentioned as part of the will change, you would have been contacted, probably by Mr. Chase in Savannah, and there would have been no need for you, or you Opal and Pearl, to travel north. I have just provided this reading of the will because you all are here and Sheriff Green asked for this highly unusual and quickly arranged reading. I think the changes, and indeed the original will itself are very well written, easy to understand and without a legal flaw.

"I have one thing further to relay," Neil continued. "Yesterday, I had a preliminary conversation with Reverend Vernon Love at the Everlasting Evangelical Spirit Church in Savannah. He was saddened to hear of the passing of Mr. and Mrs. Stone and was humbled to hear of their final generous gift. I shall be working with Mr. Chase and Ms. Ames and Reverend Love in Savannah and when appropriate, I will facilitate the decisions of the Church. Reverend Love will not discuss the passing of G.E.M. and Selma or the provisions of the will until obituaries appear in the Savannah newspaper. He also said that if there were any personal, family items in the cottage that you ladies would like to have, I believe he said share, that you could help yourselves to these items. I told him that I would ask the sheriff to assist you in this task. Are there any questions?"

There were plenty of questions, but no one spoke. Neil gave the ladies and gentlemen in the library plenty of time to blurt out a question or to formulate a question or to even write one down and pass it forward to him.

"Okay, no questions, but I have a couple." Said Neil. "May I ask them Sheriff?"

"Absolutely. I'm working on digesting all that you just gave us. Ask away," said Joe while rearranging his long legs, moving his chair, getting comfy.

"Will insurance cover the items, missing items, the traded out items, from the Stone's cottage? Are you looking for that stuff? All that we are doing here is but a small part of the bigger investigation that is going on, right? Will the fax you just received shed any light on anything? I am sorry, that is a lot of questions," concluded Neil and he sat down.

"Let me, Joe," said Rhoe. "Yes, all those items are covered by the homeowner's policy that G.E.M. carried. In fact, I just remembered this, he had burglar strips on the windows, but they were never set off. The thieves must have disarmed them. Is that part of the investigation?"

"Of course it is. It's only one small part. It's my under-standing," Joe went on, "that insurance steps in and pays for sto-len items after we, the sheriff's department, assures the insurance company that the items are indeed gone, can't be found."

Rhoe assured Joe that that indeed was the way insurance companies liked to work. He said too that he would work closely with Joe and if Joe wanted a second opinion regarding the value of the traded out items, that his office would help with that too.

The Stone girls were quiet, not thoughtful, quiet like one is when she is fighting embarrassment. Quiet like one is when she is afraid to say anything more for fear that her words may come back to haunt her. Quiet.

"So, Joe I would like to suggest that we take a quick lunch break, let Neil and Rhoe be on their way and reconvene at 12:30. It's 11:20 right now," said Colin.

There were grumbling from the ladies. Tough.

"Ladies," said Joe. "I am sure that Elizabeth will provide

something light for a lunch if you'd like, we will discuss dinner later. Please meet us here at 12:30. Have questions for us, you know we have them for you."

There was low rumbling, grumbling from the Stone sisters as they quickly exited the room. Joe and Colin moved chairs and helped Rhoe and Neil to get their electronics packed, thanked them and walked them out the French doors to the small patio and a flagstone walkway that would take them to their cars in the small parking lot behind the Inn. Joe and Colin stayed outside. It was a bright, very warm, autumn day. A day that Colin feared looked like it had just begun.

CHAPTER 35

The seventy minutes that had been allotted for lunch passed quickly. At 12:30 the sisters and the investigators were again seated at the round table in the sun room. Colin thought that a change of venue might be good for the five-some and even though they could not enjoy the sun in the outside, they could observe it through the tinted, floor to ceiling windows that the sun room sported.

That seventy minute break gave Colin and Joe a chance to eat and to evaluate how the investigatory meeting was going and to discuss the contents of the fax that Joe had received. They ate peanut butter and banana sandwiches and drank protein milk shakes that Colin made and they sat in the shade at the bistro table under the maple in his back yard.

"They were good. Rhoe had it all together. He got us through that whole trade out business. And Neil was right on task," said Joe.

"I loved how Neil gave the ladies of the south an etiquette lesson regarding Selma. They are snotty, and snooty, people. They got it all, early, from a generous father. They are wrong about Selma," said Colin. "I think too that Neil was on the right track about Selma's need to take on a disguise, to create a diversion, so she'd have time and reinforcements to take on life as the widow of G.E.M. Stone."

"Right you are," said Joe. "But ya know, Neil never did

come right out and say why he thought the girls have deigned to come up north with all of us Yankees. I think that they heard there was a change in the will and as dutiful daughters they are here protectin' daddy's wishes. G.E.M. must have slipped when he was on the telephone with Ruby, she found out there was a change, told her sisters and they assumed that they would be the ones getting the cottage, and believe me they knew the value of the trappings in that cottage. They came all this way for nothing, but if one came, you can see how the others knew that they'd have to be here too... protectin' theh intrest.

"And they're not interested at all in who killed Selma," Joe continued. "Looks like they are satisfied with the explanation of the events in Italy that Scarlet has forwarded to them, but Selma impersonating their father, the trade out and the murder are not priority items for the sisters. Especially now that they know they aren't getting any of the goodies."

"You said they weren't suspects, right Joe?" asked Colin. "Well who is? What is your team investigating? Are they looking for the traded out stuff? What happened when Pete Googled Ruby? Come on Joe, it's been four days. Are you waiting for this thing to solve itself?"

Joe had to laugh. "Colin, this is the first time you've been involved with an investigation. Let me tell you, they poke along. You'll get used to that. Let me run through the info on the fax from Pete and then we best get back to the Inn. First though, I have just reclassified the ladies of Savannah as suspects. In fact, they are the only suspects that we have."

"What? You gotta be kiddin," blurted out Colin.

"Colin, think for a minute," said Joe. "They are refusing to talk about the murder. I think they are afraid of dropping another bomb like Ruby did when she let it escape that she knew about the will change, that they *all* knew about the will change. They have all been in the area recently. We need to check dates. Well, Pearl and Opal anyway. I'm not sure about Ruby, but she doesn't answer directly and I don't want to be accused of badgering her. How did Ruby get to the Buffalo Airport? Did she actually fly in there? I'm not sure. They all accept the trading out scenario, well maybe Ruby isn't sold on it yet, and they are all well aware of the value of the contents of that cottage. It was Neil that asked about insurance procedures, but I don't suppose that the sisters care much about that now that the cottage isn't theirs anyway. Neil would probably advise Pastor Love to sell the contents of the cottage anyway, but I don't want to see someone, some thief, get away with cleaning out the cottage. And there is still our thought that the trader outer and the murderer are the same person. Too many unknowns yet."

"Joe, we only have a few minutes. What info does Pete include in that fax?" asked Colin.

As they walked back to the Maple Springs Inn, Joe methodically mentioned all areas of the fax from Pete Gianna who was hot on the trail of a lot of things involved with the investigation. He had talked to all the Maple Springs summer and year round residents who were in The Springs around the time of Selma's death. He had gotten a list from Binky in California. Binky had been around and she was sure who the others were. Nothing new was learned. Pete was still waiting to hear about some identification of finger prints. There weren't a lot of prints in the house, Eileen had done some cleaning, so the prints were probably all Selma's. Pete had connected with Ron at the antique store and they were sending a list of traded out items to all the local antique buyers. Pete was also on E-Bay looking for those items. The coroner's final report had come to the sheriff's office, but there wasn't anything new to report. Dr. Fourtney was available if Joe had any questions. Fourtney had released Selma's body to Jeff at the funeral home and Pete had contacted Scarlet with that piece of news. The final item that Joe mentioned was information which pertained to Craftsman Brad. Pete had found a Brad that did construction work. He was from Williamsville, near Buffalo, and he had never even been to Chautauqua County, except to fish with his grandfather when he was in his teens. Pete was checking with people that could vouch for Brad's whereabouts during the times that Colin said that the white Brad van was at the Stone's.

Just as Joe and Colin started up the driveway to the Inn, they saw Scott Sterns talking to Elizabeth on the front stairs.

"Jeez Colin. It's the kid from the *P-J*. Let me talk. Let's pry him away from Elizabeth," said Joe. "Scott, Scott what's up? Come 'ere. Talk to me."

Scott left the stairs and hurried right over to Joe. Joe grabbed him by the elbow and ushered him down the driveway, headed to a car parked, illegally, on the street that Joe figured was Scott's. Colin was glad that Joe hadn't taken the time to introduce him to Scott.

"What was he asking you about?" Colin asked Elizabeth. "Did he sound like he knew something or was he just fishing for information?"

"He just got here and he was asking for Joe, said someone in the department said that Joe had business down here today. Had he gone around to the back door, the guest's door, he would have seen the Savannah contingent finishing up their lunch on the back veranda. He rang the front doorbell and when I answered it, I knew who he was and I stepped outside to talk to him. I was glad to see you and Joe come up the drive. He coulda tortured me, but I wouldn'ta ratted on yous guys," said Elizabeth with a huge smile on her face.

When the investigatory meeting resumed, Joe started it out by informing the ladies about the appearance of the press.

"A reporter for the local paper came to the Inn as you ladies were eating on the veranda," said Joe and before he could go on, the three sisters all made it perfectly clear that they did not want any involvement with the media and that they were hoping that the sheriff was insuring that their loses were not a cause celeb in this county or at home in Savannah.

"Ladies, the Sheriff's Department does not operate in a vacuum. There was a small, front page, article printed a couple days ago. I can't keep ignoring the reporter. He told me that he contacted a reporter in Savannah, just this morning, and the two of them are working on a story. The Savannah guy gave Scott, the reporter here, Scarlet Ames' telephone number and so it looks like stories and probably portraits of your parents will appear in both papers. Remember freedom of the press?" explained Joe.

"Oh thank heaven for Scarlet. She is very organized and well spoken. She has all the details about daddy's wishes, etc. and I am sure that she will be expeditious as she makes arrangements," said Ruby seemingly acting as family spokesperson.

Both Joe and Colin noticed how Ruby had mysteriously become a fan of Scarlet Ames.

Colin wanted to conclude this business of the newspaper's role in the affair.

"When I spoke with Ms. Ames a couple days ago," Colin said, "she said that she had obituaries prepared, G.E.M. and Selma wrote each other's, and that she would follow through with all funeral arrangements, but she would be waiting for the go ahead from the Sheriff."

Joe continued with the topic. "Selma's body has been released by the Sheriff's Department to a funeral home and the proprietor, his name is Jeff Carson, and Ms. Ames will see to it that all of Miss Selma's wishes, and of course your father's wishes, are complied with. I daresay that she will check with you daughters before funeral or memorial services are scheduled."

Colin neglected, on purpose, to tell the Stone daughters that he had their father's ashes on his bookcase. He decided that if any of the sisters asked about those fatherly ashes that he would fess up, but he did not anticipate that question. He would be sure to get those ashes to Jeff so that G.E.M. and Selma could journey together as they had so many times before, home to Savannah.

"Sheriff Green, may I speak with you for a moment?" It was Elizabeth at the sun room door.

"Excuse me ladies. Colin would you look in my documents on the lap top and pull up the article that was in the *Post-Journal*, recently, about Selma, for the ladies to read?"

Deputy O'Brien did as asked and by the time the three sisters had read the article, individually from the computer screen, Joe was back. As he sat next to Colin, Joe passed him a message on a flowered sticky note...*I saw Ruby speaking to a man when she went for her WALK. The other two sisters did not leave the Inn. Elizabeth...*Colin couldn't stop himself from checking Ruby's footwear. Flip-Flops.

"So ladies, questions?" said Joe as a starter to the discussion.

Silence from the ladies.

Joe was just about to start asking questions when Opal said, "If this is an investigatory meetin', I would appreciate you taking your role of questioneer more seriously."

"You got it and boy do I have questions. I'm expecting answers. A questioneer always need answerees to keep the process in motion.

"What is it you ladies had against Miss Selma?" Joe didn't waste any time getting to the point.

It took a few seconds and then Miss Pearl got brave.

"Miss Selma took our daddy away from us. She was his secretary. She wasn't to daddy's level. She spirited him on vacation afta vacation. Spent, spent, spent. Yes, I am sure that daddy cared for her, probably felt sorry for her, but she frittered his time away, his time away from us."

The gates were open. "I appreciated the earthy charm that Miss Selma possessed, but it was uniquely obvious that she was not one of us, couldn't possibly be a Stone. She tried," explained Miss Opal.

Joe waited for Ruby, but Ruby chose not to speak.

Colin couldn't stand it another minute.

"Neil Robertson was right, you ladies are very poor judges of character. Maybe you think you are top drawer Stones, but you totally misunderstood Miss Selma and you lost the opportunity to know and be around and learn from a great lady. You haven't said nice things about Selma, but she always said nice things about you. Your rudeness hurt her I'm sure, but I'm sure that she never complained to your father, she never said it's those girls or me, she was always a lady."

Noises, low grumbles, shifting in seats. Was someone sniffling, crying?

"Next question. Who possibly could have traded out your family cottage?" said Joe. He wasn't beating around any kind of a bush. "Remember who it is that almost always initiates a 'trade out.'"

"Local folk, I believe," said Pearl. "Anyone who had ever been in the cottage, who saw those lovely things, those rare items that Mr. Anderson had valued for us, for Rev. Love I mean. If I had to name one person, I would start with that Eileen, you know, little-miss-she-does-it-all. She knew that house, its furnishin's, she had access to the house, and motive. Let's not forget motive. Money."

Joe said, "And don't forget, she's just about family and it is family that trades out. OK, any other thoughts?"

What are ya sayin' Joe? thought Colin.

Then Joe got back to reality. "I guess we have to connect Selma's impersonating G.E.M. and the 'trade out' and the murder. Now then..."

"Sheriff," it was Ruby sounding meek and mild. "I cannot be a part of this investigatin' or whatever it is you are conductin' at this time. My father is dead, a precious piece of my inheritance, our summer home, has been spirited away from our family to strangers and you are lookin' to me, us, as suspects?"

"Ruby, Ruby, Ruby, my deah big sista. Your inheritance, all of our inheritances, was sealed when daddy gifted us all years ago. I was expectin' nothin' more. Daddy told us there was nothin' more. Did you think we deserved something more, or that you alone were slighted, needed more," suddenly Pearl is thinking and talking more rapidly, "and that more wasn't comin', did you need it, did you participate in tradin' out? You did, didn't you? You did."

"Pearl, relax, that's a big leap you're taking," said Joe.

Ruby was up, but it was as though her feet were glued to the floor in front of her chair. "Pearl, how dare you, how dare you, how dare you. You are soundin' just as you did as a child, blamin', knowin' it all, quick to judge. I know nothin' about disquisin', tradin', murderin'. Damn you! Sheriff, speak to that woman, reprimand her. Is this the way you conduct investigatory activities?"

Pearl was finished with this discussion. She turned sideways in her seat, her back to Ruby. Opal seemed to enjoy her sisters' repartee, didn't join in, she had probably reacted to her sisters like this in the past also. Colin, although he felt like an outsider, neither real cop nor family member, was enjoying himself and carefully taking notes although he wasn't sure why.

Joe fussed with his lap top for a minute.

"Please have a seat Ruby," said Joe. "Ladies, I am sorry if I haven't moved through this investigation as you assumed I would. This is a most unusual case for all the reasons that we have already discussed and here you all are right in the middle of the activity and I don't know what to do with you. I guess that I know why you are here and I guess that you have a right to be here and although I told Colin that none of you are suspects, I am changing my mind. You put yourselves right in the middle of things, you all have motives for the 'trade out' and the murder and you have all been in the area recently according to the research by my office."

He paused momentarily. The sisters hurumphed and sputtered, but no one made a comment or formed human words. Colin watched the sisters without being obvious about his extreme interest in their reactions.

"Ruby," continued Joe. "I need solid answers from you. #1. How did you get to Buffalo? #2. Were you in Western New York in the recent past and #3, exactly where do you live right now?"

"I feel singled out sheriff, but I shall answer as best I can. I was dropped off in Buffalo by a friend. I thought that it would make things easier, that I wouldn't have to answer a lot of questions if we were all just arrivin' together. I currently live with a friend in Cleveland, not exactly in Western New York, but probably in the area according to your criteria. I believe that answers your questions."

"One more," said Joe although Colin was sure that there would be many more for her and then the other two sisters. "Who is Ruby Ward?"

That question was a shocker for Ruby and bewildering for her sisters. Lots of back and forth glances ensued and all eyes ended up on Ruby who sat with her hands in her lap and her head down. There were definitely sniffling sounds. Finally Ruby put her head up, gave Joe direct eye contact and said, "I am, or actually was, Ruby Ward. I have determined to use my real surname as of late, but during an earlier portion of my life and a career, I was known as Ruby Ward."

Everyone in the room had questions, but they all deferred to Joe who recently had been determined to be the questioneer.

"There are many incorrect citings on the internet and a lot of what you read is suspect," said Joe. He then turned his lap top to face Ruby, and Pearl and Opal could see it too. They saw a mug shot, not attractive, but decidedly Ruby's.

Joe gently closed the lap top. Ruby continued to stare at the place where the mug shot had been.

"I was young," she said. "Mr. Ward was younger. I was flattered. He thought I was special. You know how that is. You,

Pearl and Opal, have always been special to someone. I never was. I worked, he was an artist, con artist I learned. We didn't pay bills, moved a lot. It was fun for a while.

"Then daddy asked me to come home, something important he said. Tad Ward and I took a bus to Savannah, actually it was a good time to get out of Arizona. I couldn't work. There was a big deal event hounding me."

"Tribal Trailblazers?" said Joe.

"You are a capable investigator after all, Mr. Green. Yes, Trailblazers finished me with 501c3 work and almost any other kind of public work. I was ready to leave Arizona. I thought that once I introduced them that maybe daddy would take a likin' to Tad, could get or give Tad a job and we could start again in Savannah, but then daddy ruined it all by making me a rich woman. I would have kept all that bequethin' to myself and even would have lied to Tad, but then there it was, all in the paper, all that givin', pictures of the three of us sisters surrounding daddy, all smilin' and an article talking about Savannah's three richest women under thirty. Tad couldn't wait to spend that money."

"And you never did bring Tad home to meet Daddy, or anyone, did you? I'm sure that your father thought that his three daughters would be smart about their future, save, invest, and so forth. Right?" asked Joe.

"Daddy and his banker helped, but there were no strings on the gifts," said Pearl. "Daddy, I guess you could say he was testing us, just gave us the money and inroads to professionals to help us, but we had to coordinate all the particulars for ourselves. The only condition was that we had to have all the paperwork done in order to buy a house and then he paid the lawyer and the lawyer settled with the seller. And we needed a formal business plan to start a business and it had to be approved by daddy's lawyer, you know, that foundation, before we could tap into those funds. Otherwise, we were on our own."

"We bought the house, in Arizona," said Ruby, "because daddy thought I was there working with Native American tribes and two weeks later we sold it, even made a profit. That money took us, in our new SUV, to Las Vegas."

"No Ruby, I can't... it can't be. Is it all gone?" said Opal, not harshly but with sympathy.

"All that's left is the money to start a business, safe somewhere in Savannah. Sold the stocks, sold the Picasso, pawned the jewelry. It took us about three years, but we ran through it all. At first I was dolling it out, trying to get resettled, I worked for a while, Tad ran a gallery, we partnered with a blacksmith making sculpture. It was fun, but actually it was all goin' out, nothing was comin' in and then Tad started investin', in cocaine." That last statement brought the conversation to a halt.

Colin got up and passed around bottles of sparking water that were resting in a large silver punchbowl filled with ice that was on a low table near the windows. He set each frosty bottle on a napkin by each person and then made a second pass to everyone giving each person a container of yogurt and a spoon that he also placed on the napkin. Everyone opened their yogurt, drank the water, fussed with the bottle cap, the spoon, the yogurt container top. It was something to do, a way to avoid eye contact, a way to keep busy.

"I was never legally a Ward," continued Ruby, "so it was easy to leave, Tad probably didn't know I left. We were out of money. He'd find it elsewhere. You all do not have to be avoidin' me or the topic, and I don't want anyone feelin' sorry for me. I was an adult, I made all those decisions, I coulda, shoulda, but I didn't ask for help."

"Then Ruby, you are the obvious family member to pull off the 'trade out'," said Joe.

Joe, come on, how could you? The lady is in great distress, embarrassed, thought Colin.

"Sheriff Green!" said an incredulous Opal, using what could be called a teacher voice.

"You are one crass individual," said Pearl and then she got up and jostled a shaky Ruby out of the sun room and, Colin thought, they probably headed right to Ruby's room.

Opal did not move, or take her eyes off Joe. Joe opened his lap top, ran his fingers over a lot of keys and then turned the lap top screen so that it faced Opal. Opal let out a stifled scream. There was a long pause in the conversation.

"It would have been best if I had exited with my sisters," said Opal. "Are you going to ask questions or should I just ramble on about my personal problems a la Ruby?"

"I prefer the rambling, all-inclusive interview, but I can start you off. Miss Opal, tell us about your escapade on a back road in the middle of the night in Chattam County, Georgia.

What was the year? What in hell were you thinking?" said Joe.

Colin couldn't stand it, he moved so that he could see the screen. Opal shot him a look that registered quickly with Colin, 'don't you dare look at that', and he returned to his seat. He was not successful at getting even a quick look at the screen. He'd have to listen carefully and be sure to have Joe pull up that picture later just for him.

"Obviously, Sheriff Green, I was not thinking. I was at a party and I made decisions that proved to be both embarrasin', rather humiliatin', and downright expensive. The charge was 'using a vehicle for unsafe drivin' without permission from the owner of said vehicle' or somethin' like that. Drag racin'. There I said it. I was not drivin'. I had been drinkin', but I was in that car, lovin' every minute of it. When officers arrived there were just a couple of us girls there, the boys were gone. I do not kiss and tell. I was fined, had to pay for repairs to the 'borrowed' vehicles and believe me, I learned a lot. Money well spent, a lot of money. There. Done."

"Let me guess. You sold stock to cover the lawyer, court costs, fines and automobile repairs. You still have the house, but you've mortgaged that to keep your dancing school afloat. How'm I doin'?" asked Joe.

"Opal, you don't have to answer that." Pearl was back. "Sheriff, is it your desire to make the Stone sisters squirm? I find it difficult to believe that you've pried into our lives via the internet and now, just when we are vulnerably grievin', you attack. Now you know why I fly north, work and fly south."

"Ladies, you misjudge me," said Joe. "I am being ever so professional, but I am also trying to put order to a situation that does not easily fall into order. There is little logic to hang my sheriff's hat on. All the sheriff's horses and all the sheriff's men can't put this case together. Again. I know, it has only been a couple of days since Miss Selma's murder, but the farther you get out from an event, the more murky the evidence is, or it disappears, witnesses forget, or disappear. So here and now is important."

Colin appreciated Joe's expert evaluation of the situation. I'm on your side Joe, Colin thought.

"You're right on the money sheriff," said Opal. "And speaking of money, I have very little left. My academy does well, but anytime money gets tight in a family, dance classes for little Susie are the first thing eliminated. Cash flows very slowly in the dancing school circles, but I am committed to my business plan and I am the businesswoman that daddy said I was and I shall get through the current downturn in the economy."

"So, Miss Opal, would you say that you could be considered a logical family member to enact a 'trade out'?" asked Joe, ever the sensitive sheriff.

"Yes, I would," was Opal's right to the point answer.

"Then there are three candidates for 'trade out' perp," said Joe.

"Three, you are accusing me sheriff? Preposterous," said Pearl.

"No, not you, not yet. I was considering Ruby and Opal

here, and then there's Eileen, we can talk about her in a minute, but let's talk about you right now," Joe said as he made a gesture asking Pearl to sit.

Joe turned the computer screen back so that he could see it head on, but he switched web sites before Colin got to see the Opal picture; could have been a mug shot, a picture of Opal drunk in a smashed up dragster, or just smashed automobiles. He made a note on his pad to remind Joe to show him the Opal pic, whatever it was.

"Pearl, how's business? The pageant business, you know, *Here she comes, Miss America*," Joe sang that last part.

"I find myself to be very busy. There are pageants all over the world, for male and female, toddlers to senior ladies. Everyone loves a pageant," said Pearl.

"I spoke to the former Miss New York City Subway Turnstile of 1975," said Joe. "She lives here in Maple Springs, and she said that she keeps up on the pageants, gets literature in the mail, watches on TV and even gets herself to five or six a year. She said too that attendance has dropped, some cities have eliminated their Miss, Jr. Miss and Mrs. pageants altogether. I asked her if one could make a living being a pageant consultant. I asked her that because she did that for several years, and she said no, not today. No, because more and more the pageants paid less and less, she often had to pick up her own expenses (room, food) and just keeping up with wardrobe was expensive. She's retired, misses the pageant life, sees more strife in pageantdom in the near future."

"I daresay that your Miss Turnstile wasn't motivated to the degree that I am," began Miss Pearl, Miss Georgia 1999. "I have worked continuously as a pageant consultant since 2001 after I had spent two years as a model both in New York City and Milan, Italy. True, some municipalities have eliminated their annual pageants, but with the burgeoning cable networks needin' to fill many hours of air time, pageant related programmin' has proven to be very popular. You know, *Toddlers and Tiaras, Honey Boo-Boo* and others. I have been a contestant consultant for many cable reality programs. In the name of confidentiality agreements, I cannot name those programs or the celebrities that I have worked with. If you check my website, you will see that I have a full and varied schedule. If you check my Wikipedia page, you will be able to appreciate my career."

"Then you can't be considered as a trade out artiste even though you are a relative because you don't need the money, so you don't have a motive," said Joe. "Also, there are locals to consider, and now I should mention that the Sheriff's Department has crossed Eileen Miller off our suspect list. Her whereabouts during what we have calculated as the 'trade out' times have been determined. So we are down to two possible traders. That sound right to you Opal?"

Joe began to utilize his lap top, or did he? Searched web sites, or did he?

Opal began a delicate squirm, but a squirm nonetheless. She avoided looking at Pearl and pulled her feet up into the upholstered chair she had moved to when Ruby left the room.

"Pearl, it's out there, in the cloud, in cyberspace," said Opal. "These gentlemen may be small town folk, but they're experienced investigators. You talkin', or should I?"

Opal took Pearls silence as an affirmative. "Pearl and the Department of Homeland Security have come to a parting of the ways."

"Very funny, missy," said Pearl. "I would consider flying again. It's them that have made a mountain from the tiniest of mole hills."

"Wait one second," said Joe as he searched quickly within the website that he had been perusing for the last couple minutes. "Stone, Stone, Carl Stone, Maureen Stone......Pearl Stone. No Fly List. Care to explain that," said Joe. "Gun in your skivies? Wearing a burka?"

"Toiletries. It all came down to toiletries, sheriff. Too big, too many, unlabeled. Do you have any idea how bitchy those TSA folks can get when you have a carry-on full of powders and unlabeled lotions? Took it all. Took the carry-on too. It was a verah expensive Verah Bradley accessories bag. Lines of people, watchin'. Hundreds of dollars in product tossed. I hope some of those TSA ladies sneaked some of the lotions into their pockets. Believe me they had skin quality equal to the texture of the suitcases they search. It was oppressive, humiliatin', but I stood my ground."

"You mean you were grounded," interjected Joe, smiling.

"I am appealin' that silly and demeanin' determination," said Pearl. "When I said I fly in and fly out, I was speaking metaphorically. A treasured friend has become my driver and I have, luckily, been able to list travel miles as an expense. My flight to Buffalo yestaday was considered a hardship flight, because of the situation here. Kyle at the Peach State Travel Agency made the arrangements. I bought many small, travel size products and put them in my checked luggage. May I be excused, sheriff?"

"Pearl, I would assume that this newly acquired designation has led to other problems for you." said Joe. "Can't have a gun, right? Many agencies check this list, you know? Did it affect you getting a credit card or your credit ratings?"

Again, Pearl's silence had been taken as an affirmative.

Soon Pearl continued her litany. "I got bad press. I daresay some TSA person got a couple bucks and a cheap thrill for discussin' my dilemma with a reporter or two back home. I felt the need to retain a lawyer, he's workin' on my appeal, and I am sure that it has cost me consultin' occasions although no organization has eeked even a suggestion of them knowing the specifics of my, as some have called it, my 'Smackdown in Savannah'," said Pearl. "I'm whittlin' away at my inheritance. Is that what you wanted to hear? Guess that's grounds for being added to the 'trade out' list."

"Yeah, looks like you three amigos are all on that list. Thanks for sharing, Pearl," said Joe as he navigated on his lap top and made lip smacking and clucking noises. "You certainly may be excused. It's just after 2:00. I have other department business to take care of. Colin, would you take the ladies to the Stone cottage and ferret out those picture albums and other family memorabilia that Neil said the Rev. Love authorized them to remove from the cottage?"

Colin agreed to help the sisters at the cottage. He offered to borrow a golf cart from a neighbor and to come back for the three of them by 2:45.

Colin and Joe went to find Elizabeth. The sisters adjourned to their rooms.

Elizabeth explained the contents of the note that she had passed to Joe. "Ruby was talking to a man who was on the side of the road. He was making motions like he was about to commence fishing, but he had on leather boots and just a pole, no bucket, no tackle box. The situation didn't ring true. There was no vehicle around. They didn't talk long. They were just down the road, but I saw them when I was opening some windows in the back to air out rooms for some guests coming tomorrow. You guys remember that Beth Peyton is having her book launch here tomorrow, right? There are only two new guests staying overnight tomorrow. I still have room for the sisters, if they're staying."

"Can you describe the guy?" asked Joe. "Ever seen him before?"

"Tall, skinny, not standing straight, had on a hat and his back to me, jeans, boots, don't think I've ever seen him before," replied Elizabeth.

"Well, thanks for that much anyway. If you see him or the two together again, let us know. Probably you should call Colin and he might be able to be Johnny-on-the-spot and see them too. Pearl and Opal never left the Inn, right?" said Joe.

"No, they ate out back, were happy with just a yogurt and some leftovers from this morning's meeting, were talking like friends. They were distant before, I thought, but were chatting at lunch. Oh they were cell phoning, but talking to each other too."

"I'll be available," said Colin. "Call me if Ruby's male friend shows. Also, I will be back by 2:45 to take the three of them back to the Stone cottage to see if there are personal items they'd like. Neil Robertson said it was okay."

"Joe, you can stop for the book signing party tomorrow if you'd like. It's kind of an open house with Beth reading from the text about 5:00. Have you had a chance to read the book?" asked Elizabeth.

"I've read it, enjoyed it," said Colin. "It's a memoir about life on Lake Chautauqua. Well, not life in general. It's Beth's take on the restorative value of living on the water's edge. It's a very gentle book, Vonny says."

"I haven't read a book since the first kid came along, excepting Dr. Spock, or Suess, or whatever his name is. I'll give it a shot. What's it called?" said Joe.

"*Clear Skies, Deep Water*. I'll loan you mine. I got a few copies. I put one in each room. It's a very positive look at The Springs," said Elizabeth.

CHAPTER 36

Joe and Colin had to walk back to the O'Brien's so Joe could get his car.

"Hey Joe, I got a couple things to ask. I didn't want to ask in front of the sisters," said Colin as they walked along White-side Parkway. "Who is the Miss Turnstyle that lives here in The Springs, the pageant person? And will you pull up on your lap top that picture of Opal that you found, bet it's a mug shot? And what's the web site for the no-fly list?"

"I made up that Miss Turnstyle baloney. It's from a movie that was on television last night. TMC. Frank Sinatra and Gene Kelly as sailors on leave in NYC. Gene, I think it's Gene, could be Frank, falls for Miss Turnstyle, Vera Ellen, I think. But it got Pearl to talk. There's no ex-Miss anything living in these parts that I know of. The no-fly web site was a hoax too. I often get creative as I go along. Opal and Pearl have told their stories many times, I assure you. I just fed the topic sentence and off they went. The Ruby stuff we found on line, Opal too. I still don't think Ruby bared it all. And Miss Opal was upset because of the picture of her was from the front page of the *Savannah Morning News*, passed out, or was she just napping, in the front seat of a car with a headline reading 'Debutant Dragster'. I found it at the newspapers website; go there and just put her name in the subject box. She pops up a lot, troll till you get to the picture, it's huge, front page."

"I'll check out that newspaper website," said Colin.

"I gotta go. Got some motorcycle guys in Sherman causing a ruckus. See if you can help us herd the ladies to Tom's Tavern for wings. We're shooting for 5:00-5:30. The festivities should begin about then. Tell them that we need to talk and determine who will need to remain in Chautauqua County. That ought to help get them there. Thanks Colin, don't know what I'd do without you hanging with our team. Bye," and Joe was in his car and out of sight in a hurry, siren in use.

Colin walked quickly to a neighbor's house about six houses from his, going towards the highway. It was Dianna Warren's house and she was home in Beaver, Pennsylvania. Before she left, a week or so before Selma returned to Maple Springs, she had shown Colin where the key to her shed was hidden on a high window sill and she had asked him to charge her golf cart's batteries during the winter months. Colin hadn't inquired about using it over the winter, surely there would be no need, but as he unlocked the shed and propped open the doors and backed the cart out onto the street, he was sure that Mrs. Warren wouldn't mind, that she would gladly agree to help the investigation team.

Colin arrived back at the Inn on time and the three Stone sisters were all on the front porch waiting for him. Actually, they were preoccupied talking to a hunky man in shorts and a tank top sitting on a riding lawnmower that was at the edge of the lawn where it met the flowerbed in front of the porch. He was obviously entertaining because the girls were laughing and hanging over the railing and vying for his attention. Suddenly he was standing on the lawnmower seat and howling like a wolf. The girls howled back and the four of them were enjoying the moment, the howling and the abandon that had set in. Three of them were enjoying the body of the fourth who was standing on the lawnmower seat.

Colin beeped the cart's horn to get the sister's attention. Had he known it was such a sissy beep, he wouldn't have bothered. The sisters reacted to the horn and started down the stairs to join Colin. They all waved and said goodbye to lawnboy and he in turn threw kisses and howls their way. They were all in jeans; Capri for Pearl, long and baggy for Ruby and Opal's were long and tight. Each had on a light, cotton sweater. Elizabeth must have told them that it would be getting chilly in the late afternoon

Holy cow, thought Colin, that's Pete Giana on that mower; he's a major part of our investigating team, our computer researcher, our Italian speaker. Is he moonlighting, actually on the prowl for these women –couldn't be, they're suspects – or is he under cover?

Just then Pete plopped down into the seat and took off across the lawn and began mowing in earnest, although he was going too fast to make it a proper mowing.

"Where's Tom's Tavern?" asked Pearl as the sisters got settled in the cart with Pearl up front and her two siblings in the back. "Rico, on the mower, invited us for a beer later. He said he wanted to be sure that we saw all the hot spots of Maple Springs. I don't remember any hot spots. So, where's Tom's?"

Smart, thought Colin. How better to get the ladies together and have an informal chance to observe, talk, grill, question. Then he thought, could Rico's invitation and the subsequent rendezvous be considered entrapment? Well, that's the sheriff's problem, he knows what he's doing. The festivities at Tom's should be interesting.

"Now remember ladies, the lawyer, Robertson, said that you can have family items, intimate personal items. He also emphasized sharing. And again, it's a crime scene of a sort, please don't handle items and paw through drawers, etc.," said Colin even before the sisters got out of the golf cart.

"Mr. O'Brien, the good stuff has all been spirited away, remember. We trader outers took care of that," said Opal. "There are picture albums upstairs and mama's sewing box is about I assume. We shall be decorous I assure you." And with that the ladies left the cart and followed Colin to the front door which he unlocked for them. Pearl and Opal entered and went directly upstairs. Ruby sat on the porch. She turned a rocking chair, actually one of Colin's newly bequeathed chairs, so that she could look down the street toward the lake and she rocked slowly with her head back and her eyes closed.

Colin stepped into the house, but then decided that he'd let Pearl and Opal prowl on their own. He returned to the porch hoping to engage Ruby in conversation. He made lots of noise as he exited the door and clunked a chair on the porch floor as he sat down with a deep sigh.

"You certainly have a way of making your presence known, Mr. O'Brien," said Ruby.

"Sorry if I disturbed you," said Colin. "I've been in there enough. I just thought that I'd wait out here for your sisters."

"I too have been in there enough. I don't believe that

there is anything more that I would like out of this cottage. I have memories and a few items that Daddy gave me when I last visited. I am not a collector or a person who has a lot of things. I live simply. Moving a lot, you know, has a way of keeping one devoid of belongin's," said Ruby without changing her position or opening her eyes.

"Miss Ruby. I am not trying to be rude or to pry, but it seems as though you aren't concerned with the huge loss of items that were the property of your parents or, pardon my frankness, the murder of your step-mother," said Colin. He purposely did not include the death of her father as part of his question. He waited for a reply of some kind from Ruby. Ruby said nothing, did not move, but a tear rolled down her cheek and slipped off her jawbone and onto the front of her gray cardigan sweater.

"I'm sure that you have absolutely no idea how grievous I am about both events that you have just mentioned. No idea whatsoever." Ruby still did not move.

After a moment, Colin rose and went into the cottage. Opal and Pearl were at the kitchen table carefully removing photographs from the little black corners that held them fast to the black pages of a large, square photograph album.

"We're sharing, Mr. O'Brien. See, three piles, one for each of us," said Pearl. The two sisters were having fun too, talking about the pictures and mock arguing over some. Also in a neat pile on the kitchen table were the oil painted photographs of the three sisters that had previously been displayed on a shelf of the kitchen hutch.

"We are still looking for Momma's sewing basket and we'd

like to take the wooden, cooking spoons that Daddy had whittled, or is it carved, for Momma. There's not a lot here that is family. The important stuff is in Savannah and we don't have it. It is in an archive room at the corporate offices, generations of belongin's. Most of our family memorabilia will be the property of the Historical Society of Greater Savannah. Probably the most honorable place for it to reside," said Opal.

"You continue your sorting. I'll look for the wooden spoons and I think I know where the sewing basket is," offered Colin. Colin searched the kitchen, opened a cupboard or two, the oven, several drawers and then he found the spoons right where they should have been in a heavy ceramic pot on a shelf over the stove that was just behind the sorting sisters. He found the sewing basket, more like a fold out miniature bookcase, next to a chair in the downstairs sun room.

After a quick second look around the living room, the sisters were satisfied that they had all they wanted. They placed the piles of photographs in three separate brown paper bags that Colin had found tucked on a shelf in the small pantry by the back door, put a couple wooden spoons in each bag, and with Colin carrying the sewing basket, they left the cottage.

"I'm out of here," said Pearl. "Have to admit that I do have some wonderful memories of this place, those down beds upstairs, that leaky canoe, cutthroat monopoly on the living room floor. Let's go. I'm gonna get all goofy."

When Colin, Pearl and Opal walked out onto the front porch, Ruby was nowhere in sight.

CHAPTER 37

Colin drove the girls around The Springs for a few minutes, they never spotted Ruby, and then he showed them a short-cut to Tom's Tavern from the back door of the Inn. He told them about the great chicken wings served at Tom's and informed them that there were twenty-eight beers on tap, but there was no need to sample each. He promised that he and Vonny would meet them there about 5:30.

Again, Colin cruised around The Springs before he returned the golf cart to its cozy winter lodgings in Mrs. Warren's shed. He looked for Ruby, but he still didn't find her. He had cruised or walked The Springs several times looking for Ruby, but had never spotted her. What possible route could she be taking that he'd be unable to see her even off in a distance or sitting way out on a dock somewhere? He determined that he'd ask her about that if she showed up later at Tom's.

When Colin got home, Vonny was there, had been home from work for a while and had managed to have a catnap and to do some prep-work on a vegetarian stew that she had found the recipe for in a *Woman's Day* that Dianne Warren had given her.

"You'll love it, it has five ingredients, no onion and one recipe feeds ten, so we can freeze leftovers," said Vonny.

Without missing a beat, Colin countered her dinner offer, "How about wings at Tom's."

"Sold," and a hug was Vonny's quick response.

Vonny was a connoisseur of the chicken wing and the hotter the better. Way back, when she agreed to "give vegetarianism a try", Vonny carved out chicken wings. It was a comfort food from her youth and she couldn't give them up. She used to make them using a recipe from a friend where the wings were baked. They were great, the kids loved them and there was no deep frying involved. Colin, not a connoisseur of the chicken wing, was glad to avoid the deep frying, his stomach was most grateful. He'd have a few at Tom's or maybe he'd skip them all together and have the great veggie calzone that Tom's featured. Or veggie pizza.

Vonny and Colin sat on the porch and shared a Blue Moon. No orange slice. They'd wait and have another at Tom's. Tom was sure to have the obligatory citrus garnish. Colin started to bring Vonny up to date regarding the day's events, but thought that first he should tell her about the evening's purpose.

"Oh, I should mention too that our southern guests will be at Tom's. I think that Joe finagled it somehow so that the girls would loosen up. Remember Pete Giana, he's on our investigation team, I'm not sure of his job title, but he is now functioning as a lawn boy at the Inn. He got the girls to want to go to Tom's. Pearl called him Rico, so we best not recognize him if he indeed does show up."

"Great. We gotta spend the evening with those brats. Good thing that there are wings involved, or you'd be there all alone with the sisters," said Vonny.

"I'm thinking of them as more regular people since we

had a lot of revelations at our meeting with Neil and Rhoe. Joe's considering them all as suspects, but I think it is just suspects of trading out, not of murder, but then he did say that those two events are probably a cause and effect twosome. Well, I guess that I'm not sure who Joe seriously suspects or what he suspects them of," said Colin with confusion in his voice and on his face.

"One more thing. When Neil was telling us about the disposition of the cottage, he mentioned some small bequests that Selma and G.E.M. had also added to their wills. Eileen gets all, or at any rate all that she wants, of the contents from the Stone's shed. The Homeowners Association gets the dock and all of its parts and," here Colin paused. "And Colin and Vonny O'Brien get the eight piece wicker set from the Stone's front porch, cushions and all."

Vonny appeared stunned, no movement, no words. That lasted for about fifteen seconds and then there were tears. Lots of them along with talking, garbled talking filtered through tears.

The first thing that Colin understood from Vonny was, "Oh that was so sweet, so sweet. I loved those two and I loved that wicker and they knew it. How sweet."

Colin had to keep Vonny from heading out with her wagon to bring home her new wicker set, piece by piece.

"When Neil says it's ok," said Colin, "we'll get the wicker. I should have asked about that. I will call Eileen and Scott, he's the Homeowners Association president, and make sure that we all respond properly."

There were more tears, a hug or two, a lot of "how sweets"

306- Murder at Maple Springs

and then, against Colin's better judgment, he and Vonny walked to the Stone's and sat on the porch in the white, wicker furniture with beautiful flowered cushions on the seats and the backs, O'Brien wicker. Each cushion was tied securely to the chair and each chair also had a small round solid colored throw pillow propped against the back. Vonny sat on the settee and spread her arms across the back. Colin sat in one of the rockers and he rocked. In fifteen to twenty seconds, Vonny too was in a rocker rocking frantically rather than in a relaxed mood as wicker seemed to invite. She moved to a chair with a high back and a rounded seat and solid arm rests. There was another just like it on the porch and Colin moved there.

"Isn't it great Colin? Don't you love it? I think I'll retire tomorrow and just sit in my lovely, white, wicker chairs with floral cushions, maybe read, but mostly just sit." said Vonny. Colin loved it when Vonny was happy, but he knew too that some sadness was part of this elation.

As they were enjoying the simple act of sitting, Colin gave Vonny details about the meeting at the Inn, Rhoe's presentation with the video, the rest of Neil's information about the will and then the information supplied by the Stone sisters under the deft questioning by Sheriff Joe Green. Vonny seriously took her mind off her new, white, wonderful wicker set and paid attention to Colin. She even asked cogent questions.

"Yikes, I can't believe how much those girls blabbed. Joe is really on the ball. This is probably old hat to him," said Vonny.

Colin agreed that Joe was on the ball and Colin admitted

that he was really learning a lot. After a few more minutes in their new, white, wonderful, wicker chairs, Colin persuaded Vonny to head home and get ready for those wings. Once again the term wings was a motivational force dictating Vonny's actions.

Colin quickly washed up and changed into khaki shorts and a polo shirt. As he waited for Vonny, he e-mailed Kyle and Scarlet and gave them a very quick overview of the day. He did mention Ruby's life out west, Pearl's run in with the TSA and Opal's drag race escapade and he also asked them both if they were aware of the sisters' hijinks.

Colin then called Bill Morris. Mrs. Morris answered, "Bill Morris and Associate. Hi Colin. I saw your name on our caller ID screen. Say, how's this deputy role working out for you?"

"Oh fine Michelle, in fact, I'm calling on department business. Is Bill there? I want to keep him up to speed on the investigation and to see if he has any reservations for return trips to the Buffalo Airport for the Stone sisters," said Colin.

"Bill is not here. He's made one of those hurried trips to the Buffalo Airport, but he is with Sheriff Green. He told me not to wait up. Don't know what that's all about. According to our planner for tomorrow and for Friday too, there are no Stone sisters booked," said Michelle.

Colin asked Michelle to leave a note for Bill to call him when he returned home and said, "Nice to talk to you and thanks for the information."

What's that trip to Buffalo all about? wondered Colin. Joe did say that there were lots of phases to an investigation. Maybe

Bill is taking Joe to Buffalo to fly off to somewhere to get information or affidavits, Savannah, Arizona, or who knows what.

CHAPTER 38

In no time at all, Vonny was ready to head to Tom's Tavern, the lure of the wing was still in effect. It was a nice night, no rain expected and Tom's was less than a ten minute walk, so hand-in-hand Colin and Vonny set off, on foot, to dine.

Tom's Tavern, a definite hot spot in Maple Springs, had a special place in each Springer's personal history; first drink, drunken exploits, wing eating contests, etc. There was a pool table, live country music on Friday and Saturday nights, most of Tom's patrons called it shit-kickin' music, a very casual atmosphere, plenty of parking, a covered porch used mainly for smoking, regulation horseshoe pits out back, a huge variety of beers on tap and oh yes, wings. It was really just a bar that offered some food. It wasn't a restaurant, it was as Tom said so eloquently on the sign, a tavern. Safe for families, a favorite in winter time with snowmobilers and home to a huge party every time the Buffalo Bills were playing. Whitey, the regular bartender, kept the food and liquids flowing and kept the place in order too, although his bouncing skills were seldom needed. Tom's was always welcoming, always a fun place to be. Sometime, even Tom himself was in the house.

As Colin and Vonny opened the oversized door that lead right to the table area (no waitresses, no tablecloths, no pretense) several people at the bar turned to gawk at the newcomers, some waved, others returned to their drinks and conversations. A few other patrons were scattered about the room, some on their way home, some come to settle in for the evening. At the far end of the bar sat the three Stone sisters, all in jeans, sensible shoes and bulky sweatshirts that must have been William's and loaned to them by Elizabeth. The sisters were obviously having fun, they were loud teetering toward boisterous, and they all had a sixteen ounce beer sitting in front of them. Colin and Vonny, still hand in hand, walked right up to the sister whose attention was clearly directed to the young good looking bartender, Steve Johnson.

"Evenin' Mr. O'Brien, Mrs. O'Brien. What'll ya have?" asked Steve with a wink. Another moonlighter? Another under cover person? thought Colin. "A coupla Blue Moon, twelve ounce, Sir," said Colin, feeling silly to have used the title Sir, but he didn't dare call the bartender by name.

"Stevie babes, I'll have one of those too. I have twenty six more beers to sample, let's get this show on the road," said Pearl. Behind her head, Opal was signaling Stevie not to fill Pearl's order by drawing her index finger across the front of her own neck, her throat, and screwing up her face.

"Hello Colin, hello Vonny," said Opal. "We followed your quick directions and here we are in the hot spot of Maple Springs, or in reality, just one of the many hot spots that I'm sure are part of the Maple Springs mystique."

"Here's yer Blue Moons," said Stevie. "I'll give you yours, Miss Pearlie Mae, once you guys have your wings. Mr. O'Brien, I understand you are here for wings with these lovely southern ladies, and I do mean lovely. We don't see this exotic species in here often, exceptin' the charming Mrs. O'Brien of course."

"Why thank you, Steven," said Vonny with a bit of a curt-
sey. Then she snagged the enticing beers; just the right amount
of foam, outer surface of the glass pebbled with moisture, that
keg was at the perfect temperature, obviously, and the obligatory
orange slice was perched majestically on the rim of the glass.

"This seem like a hot spot to you, Ruby?" asked Colin trying to draw Ruby into their little conversation circle.

"Enough of a hot spot for me to be sure," replied Ruby and
she returned to her contemplation of the beer right in front of her
settled on a thin, cork beer coaster.

Vonny continued to talk with Opal and Pearl as Colin
moved around the bar area and spoke and shook hands with
some other patrons, familiar to him as Springers. Whitey, usually
behind the bar, was at the pool table. He called Colin over, whispered in his ear and turned back just in time to see his opponent,
Patty, a Tom's frequenter, sink the eight ball at the appropriate
time and win the game.

"You broke my stride here Colin," said Whitey. "Get yourself back to your harem at the bar."

Whitey had told Colin that Stevie, aka Sgt. Steve Johnson,
was on assignment for Sheriff Joe. Whitey would be there to
perform bouncing services should the need arise.

As Colin rejoined the ladies, they were dismounting their
stools and following Vonny to a table for eight near the free popcorn machine.

"We ordered wings, a variety of hotness, and I got you a

veggie calzone. Stevie, he's fairly new here and is he ever cute, is taking care of us." said Vonny with a wink directed to Colin. She had joined in with the festivities. You're all right Miss Vonny, thought Colin.

Just then the door opened and in walked, rather strutted, Rico of lawnmower howling fame.

"Ladies, I'm so glad you came. You southern belles are true to your word," he said. Then he moved to the bar, "Steven, my good man, it'll be a Blue Moon for me. Don't forget the orange slice."

Rico moved back to the table.

"Ladies, have you sampled the Blue Moon beer? My personal favorite." He circled the table kissing hands. When he got to Vonny, he said, "Another sister? Obviously the youngest of the lot." and he kissed her hand too. Vonny introduced herself and Colin as Maple Springers and as she did, she inserted the word husband at least twice.

Rico, in a very tight, bright orange t-shirt and an orange, red and pink stripped bandana around his neck, tight jeans too, plunked himself down between Opal and Ruby.

The police academy sure got their men into great shape. Stevie too, thought Colin.

"Ladies, are we doing wings? Don't tell me you're dieting. We are winging it, dancing, and if we are lucky the band will let us sing with them. Steven, tell me there's music tonight," said Rico.

From the pool table and from behind the bar came the

duet, "No band tonight, Friday and Saturday only."

"We'll have to provide our own music then," said Rico, aka
Sgt. Pete Gianna, as he jumped up from the table, was out the
door and back in within seconds carrying a guitar. Colin was
enjoying the game-playing perpetrated by Pete and Steve, and
Joe too in absentia, and he hoped that it would bring results, but
he wasn't sure what results that Joe would be looking for. Meanwhile, he decided that he best sit back and let the professionals
create the evening's excitement.

Rico quickly grabbed a tall stool from the small band area
that sat empty in one corner of the room. His tablemates scooched over to make room for their private singer and Rico lost no
time getting to his first number.

"You know that I would be a fool.

You know that I would be a liar

If I was to say to you

Girl we couldn't get much higher.

Come on baby light my fire.

Come on baby light my fire.

Try to set the night on fire," sang Rico and then he went into
a guitar solo that left the ladies at the table for eight all at sixes
and sevens.

"...try to set the night on fire," and Rico ended his song.
Applause and a few whistles emanated from the table and from
other tables, the bar and the pool table area of Tom's Tavern. Rico
acknowledged his fans. He set his guitar in the corner behind
him and then sat in the chair that he had vacated just a few min-

314- Murder at Maple Springs

utes ago in favor of the stool.

"Rico, you are wonderful," said Opal and the other three ladies echoed her compliment and then plied him with questions about his playing, his music training and songs from his repertoire.

Enter the wings, in square cardboard dishes, delivered by Stevie. One square cardboard dish contained a veggie calzone and a small container of red sauce, the variety that is put over spaghetti. On his second pass at the table, Stevie brought a pile of napkins, a big bowl of celery and carrots and blue cheese dip and a large wooden bowl placed in the center of the table to collect the stripped chicken bones, wings and legs. Whitey delivered a tray of glasses filled with ice and two huge pitchers of water complete with lemon slices floating throughout. Whitey returned to the bar and Stevie sat and joined in the wing devouring and the conversation.

Vonny proved to be the champion, although there was no actual contest, wing eater. Colin had none. Stevie and Rico indulged in wings, but were more interested in keeping the conversation going than they were in eating. The Stone sisters enjoyed, ate not sparingly, but with great daintiness. Pearl, probably as a child she wouldn't let her dinner selections touch each other on her plate, seemed bothered by the red, sticky, chicken wing sauce that stuck to her fingers. She reverted to holding the wings with a napkin as she nibbled at them, but she soon abandoned that method and let the sauce stick where it may; fingers, lips, cheeks, William's sweatshirt.

"Stevie, you got a phone call. Take it on the phone in the kitchen," hollered Whitey from the bar. Stevie hurried into the kitchen, but was out in a minute holding the cordless telephone to his ear, but with his hand over the mouthpiece.

"Is Tad here?" he hollered. There was no response.

"Anyone know if he's showin' up tonight?" No response.

"Anyone know how to get in touch with him?" No response.

Stevie returned to the kitchen, obviously he hung up the phone, and he was back to his seat, pouring water for everyone, making a mess and laughing when the ladies sullied his waitstaff skills.

"What was that hollering message all about?" asked Ruby.

"What? Oh, just someone looking for this new guy that's begun coming in here. He, the new guy, not the guy on the phone, fancies himself a pool shark. Folks are wanting to take him on. He does well the first game or two, but then after a couple beers, he falls apart. Tad somebody. Newbie." said Stevie.

"Ruby has hot pool skills. Learned them at the Boy's and Girl's Club in Savannah and honed them at every sleep away camp and every bar she ever went into. Ain't I right sistah?" said Opal. "Don't be shy. It's nothin' to be 'shamed of."

"Yes, I have, or rather I had, hot pool skills as Opal so eloquently put it. I was a real shooter. That green felt table sucked me in many times. No more. This Tad character, is he any good, young, old, he a banger?" asked Ruby. Colin tuned right in on Ruby, up until now she hadn't been a part of the conversation.

She seemed agitated.

"What's a banger?" asked Vonny. "I thought bangers were sausages in the UK."

Ruby laughed, she was finally relaxing.

"A banger is someone just starting to play pool, a sloppy player who is just banging the balls around, hitting the rails, the balls hitting each other, no real planned interplay between the balls, the cue and the rails."

"Let's clear up this mess," said Stevie. "Wash your hands Rico. You're on in ten minutes."

There was a mad flurry of arms as the huge wooden dish of chicken bones, the pile of greasy napkins and bottles and glasses were removed from the table. Opal and Pearl and Vonny went to the ladies room to wash their hands. Vonny and Opal came back, it was a one holer. Wet Ones were passed around, Whitey wiped the table, Rico tuned his guitar. Colin got a styrofoam container to take home a huge left-over portion of his calzone.

"This Tad guy, does he live in Maple Springs?" asked Pearl. "Young? Old?"

"Don't know," answered Stevie. "He came in a few times, didn't play pool, just watched. Then he started to look for someone to play with. I think he was casing the joint, lookin' to see if there were players he could beat. He played a lot, won a few bucks and now folks are lookin' to challenge him. Don't know where he lives. Young, not thirty yet, skinny, looks ya might say scraggly. I'll point him out if he comes in."

"Wings are on Rico and the beer and pop are on the house,"

said Whitey as he set down two large pitchers, one beer and one pop, that he had effortlessly carried with one hand, and a new tray of clean glasses. Lots of 'thanks' and 'you're sweet' were passed around.

"Looks like Rico is making beautiful music, but it's not the kind that we can dance to or sing along with," said Vonny as she nudged Colin to look at Opal and Rico. Opal was holding the guitar and Rico was behind her with his arms around the two of them, the guitar and Opal that is, and he was adjusting her fingers on the neck of the instrument gently prying those fingers into place for a particular cord that he was casually teaching her. They were enjoying themselves and lo and behold, a chord was heard. Time to move on to the next cord.

"That's her style," said Pearl also looking at Rico and her sister. "I thought she'd be monkeying with his instrument even before we were served those wings." Pearl followed that statement with a loud, dirty, appropriately barroom laugh. She poured herself a glass of pop. "What you all call pop up here, in Georgia we call it coke. Any kind of pop, we call coke, small c, not the capital C like the advertised brand of soda drink. Anyway, anyone want some coke?" asked Pearl and she poured for herself, Colin and Vonny.

"I think I'll head back to the Inn," said Ruby. "It's late and I am tired and I think I might need some Tums after eatin' all those chicken-legs-n-wings."

"It's just after 8:00, you're not turning in just yet," said Pearl. "Your green felt friend is lonely over there. Come on, demonstrate for us a trick or two or show us how you can crush an opponent. Colin, I bet he has some pool skills, will play ya. Let's go."

And with that Pearl guided Ruby from behind, you might call it pushing, to the pool table and even chalked a cue for her.

"Pearl, I can't do this," said Ruby, but then she was drowned out by the sounds of the two quarters being pushed into the table's slot, thirteen balls falling from inside to a trough at one end of the table, and then the sound of Colin racking the balls and calling out, "Your break."

"One game and that is all, I'm tired and ya know I'm rusty," said Ruby.

"We need that Tad character here so you can beat his butt. Hang around till he shows up. He shows early," said Stevie who had migrated to a table next to the pool table. Vonny and Pearl joined Stevie. "Let the games begin."

Ruby was becoming flustered. "Cut the chatter, Stevie, and I am not about to hang around to beat the butt of someone I don't know or want to get to know." That said, Ruby made the break and in the process sunk two striped balls. She managed to sink two more during that first turn, two that had been expertly placed by corner pockets. Then it was Colin's turn and he showed that he too could play the game. With each solid ball that he pocketed, Vonny jumped up and ran to him and gave him a quick kiss and returned to her seat. Colin never got another turn, nor did he get another kiss after those first three. On her second turn, Ruby sunk her remaining striped balls and called and sunk the eight ball.

"Night y'all," said Ruby as she gently laid her pool cue on the table, grabbed her small purse and headed out the door that she had entered two hours earlier. Stevie, took a big swig of the beer he was nursing, went to the bar and talked to Whitey and then followed Ruby out the wide door that exited onto the porch.

"She always was a party pooper," said Pearl. "I'm not goin'. I think I'll sit at the bar and talk to Whitey. Opal and Rico are spoonin' by the popcorn machine. You two stayin?" she asked Vonny and Colin.

Opal and Rico were indeed entwined, and Vonny, Colin and Pearl teased them as they passed them on their way to the bar.

"Get a room," said Pearl.

"Hey you two, cool it," said Vonny.

Colin made clicking sounds with his lips, tongue and teeth.

"We better go," said Vonny. "I have a busy day tomorrow and you, my dear husband, have a honeydew list that has spilled over into page two."

Vonny turned to Pearl who was just getting herself settled on a bar stool and pouring herself a beer from the pitcher that she snagged as she passed their dining table for eight. "What are your plans Pearl? You and your sisters, did the sheriff say you could go?"

"I, we, wouldn't think that we would need permission to leave Maple Springs, the Inn. But then, correct me if I am wrong, the sheriff did say that we were suspects. I was plannin' on con-

tinuin' my stay at the Inn for at least one more night and I believe
that my sistahs were contemplatin' a similar plan of action. I will
tell the sheriff directly of our plans. Maybe he'll throw us in the
county jail till all this investigatin' has been accomplished. Ruby
wants to leave, but won't go until we, Opal and I, leave. For now,
I'm remainin' right here on this stool. I'm waitin' for Rico to play
the "*The Theme from Deliverance*".

After they made sure that Pearl and Opal were comfortable
with getting themselves back to the Inn, Vonny and Colin said
goodnight and headed home. Colin was feeling as though he
should be performing some deputy duties, but he had no orders.
Rico and Stevie, in actuality Pete and Steve, were "surveilling"
two of the Stone sisters and as far as Colin knew, Whitey was also
part of the sheriff's department and he was keeping an eye on
Pearl. Colin hadn't heard from Joe in a while. He was in Buffalo
with Bill Morris. What was that all about?

CHAPTER 39

As Colin and Vonny exited Tom's, they did not see Ruby and Stevie, but, in the line of duty, Colin decided to take the shortcut to the Inn that he had told the sisters about earlier. Vonny didn't care if they were walking out of their way. She loved to walk in the evening, especially in Maple Springs, and as September would soon be part of the past, she knew those after dinner walks would have to wait until spring, excepting if an Indian summer prevailed.

"Evening folks," came a deep, not too loud voice from behind a tree next to the Inn's garage. Vonny and Colin startled, and instinctively Colin got between the voice and Vonny. Before Colin could say anything, he did manage to get out a couple guttural sounds, the voice stepped out of the shadows and Colin could see that it was Steve Johnson, Stevie.

"Sorry if I startled you guys," he said. "I'm just keeping an eye on the Inn to see if Ruby is retiring for the night or is headed out for a walk as she has done before."

Colin and Vonny unstartled themselves.

"We walked this way to check on Elizabeth. William is still away. We can check on Ruby without her knowing that's what we're doing. I'll come back and report, OK?" said Colin.

"Great," said Steve, "and also, call the sheriff. He asked me to convey that message. It was him on the phone instigating the Tad activities a couple minutes ago up at Tom's. He'll fill you in on other stuff too. 'Scuse me while I slip into the shadows." And with that, Steve was gone.

Colin and Vonny went to the Inn's kitchen door, they could see Elizabeth in the kitchen, and they knocked softly as they walked in.

"Hello Vonny, Colin. Come on in. I am making muffins for breakfast. In the morning, I will do omelets to order, but I needed to get the muffin situation under control. I have two more guests besides the Stone sisters and don't forget, Beth is having her book launch here, tomorrow, in the late afternoon. The place should be jumping," said Elizabeth. Then she added, "Bill, I mean William, should be home sometime after midnight. The book launch is catered and I don't have to do much, caterers are using the kitchen, so I'll need to be on hand."

"We just wanted to check on you," said Vonny. "Sounds like you're in control. I should be so pulled together."

Colin moved close to Elizabeth. "Know where Ruby is? We are trying to keep tabs on the sisters. Two are at Tom's where there's one-on-one surveillance going on."

"Miss Ruby came in a few minutes ago," said Elizabeth. "But then I heard her go out through the outside exit door in her room. That's the only guest room with an outside door. It used to be my mother's room and I put wind chimes just outside the door. You can't miss hitting them when you use that door. Those chimes helped me to keep good track of mom. Ruby's probably gone for a flip-flop-walk in the dark."

Colin excused himself and went to look for Steve. Instead Steve found him. Startle.

"Elizabeth said that Ruby went out the outside exit in her

room," said Colin.

"Thanks Colin. Tell Elizabeth that I've borrowed a bike and call Joe," and Steve slipped into the Inn's garage and was quickly off, down the driveway on a pink, ladies, beach bicycle, with chrome fenders front and back, going like the wind.

As Colin went back to the house, he could see through the kitchen door window that Vonny and Elizabeth were seated at a small round table in a bay window at the far end of the kitchen having coffee. He reentered the Inn and asked to borrow the cordless kitchen phone that was on the wall just inside the door and then he sat outside at a picnic table not too far from the kitchen door and called Joe.

"Colin, my man, so glad you called. I told, Steve, Pete and even Whitey to have you call me. Have I got news for you. We are just getting off the Thruway in Dunkirk-Fredonia, headed home, and have I got info. I'm giving you all I know, so no questions," and Sheriff Joe Green tore through the details that would surely be helping to crack this case.

"Bill Morris called me early afternoon and said that he wanted to follow up on a feeling he had. He had picked up the Stone sisters in Buffalo, but you knew that, and the one, Ruby, didn't look like she had been traveling. He remembered that there were surveillance cameras in both the arrival and departure levels at the airport. He picks up and drops off in those areas three or four times a week and as he has to wait sometimes, he watches the cameras change position. Since he knew the day and their exact time of arrival, or within a half hour or so, he thought that we should check the tapes from those cameras and maybe see how it was that Ruby arrived at the airport. Bill was sure that she hadn't flown in. Well, to make a long story short, I called security at the airport and those guys were great and had pulled up appropriate tapes for us. So when we got there, we sat down in a lunchroom with a TV/DVD player and watched tapes for Tuesday, yesterday, during the hours of 2:00 to 4:00 in the afternoon. Ruby is on both the arrival tape and the departure tape. She's dropped off on the departure level and then she appears with her sisters on the arrival level. We even see Bill picking up all three sisters at 3:30. It's the departure tape that is most interesting. A white van pulls into view and stops at the curb. Two people get out. One is a lean, thirty-something guy with jeans, big boots, wearing two or three shirts and a generic ball cap who gets out of the driver's side. It's Ruby, in that long skirt and flip flops, that gets out of the passenger door. The guy unlocks the back door to get Ruby's bag and we can see that the Van is jammed with boxes. You can also see that the van is sitting low on its springs. Big load. Ruby gets her bag and they stand in the street behind the van talking. He's giving her orders, finger in her face, got her by the arm, giving her a scare it looks like, shakes her, a hand grabbing each shoulder. Then he kisses her, she brightens up, hugs him and she goes into the terminal and is out of sight. He lights a cigarette and gets back into the van and is soon off the screen. I think this is that Tad guy that she mentioned when she was giving her history. I think that he's still in her life. She's been lying to us, or at least not being forthcoming with real information. How's that sound for progress in this case? Don't answer, I am not through. The security guys made us DVDs of the security tapes so we have footage of Ruby, Tad, if that indeed is him, and the van. Oh, because I think that that is that Tad person, I had Pete and Steve use his name at Tom's. I heard that Ruby did react when his name was used. We are setting that Tad up for some grief from Ruby when she sees him. Ruby now thinks he's been in Tom's drinking and playing pool. He's going to deny it, but what I think it's really gonna do is have Ruby lead us to him, pin him. I'm sure it's the same van that has been in The Springs a couple times this week and maybe even Brad-the-craftsman's van."

"I gotta break in here Joe," said Colin. "I'm at the Inn now and Ruby skipped out the outside door in her room. Steve is on a bike riding around The Springs looking for her. I'll get my car and do the same."

"Bill and I will be there in about 20 minutes. Get hoppin'," said Joe before he hung up. Colin replaced the telephone and told Vonny to wait for him, he'd be right back.

Colin moved more quickly than he expected that he could. Does just the title deputy make you more physically fit? All the sheriff department men that he'd met were in good shape, Joe must be a stickler for good health when it comes to the men under his command. In spite of his age, Colin was sure that he could pass the deputy sheriff physical fitness test. It's a possibility, but there might be a need for some training first.

Colin was home, in the car and on the streets of Maple Springs in less than five minutes. He had Vonny's car. It was last in the driveway, it was quieter and she probably had more gas in it than he had in his old Prism. He was feeling good about being back serving as a deputy, but then he had a few other thoughts; what would he do if he found Ruby? Was Ruby meeting up with Tad? Did the scenario that Joe had concocted make sense? What's in that white van of Tad's? If the contents of the boxes in the van are traded out items, did that make Tad the killer? Ruby the killer? Was there ever a Brad working at the Stone's cottage? I don't even have a cell phone!

I gotta pay attention to the here and now, thought Colin. I'm looking for Ruby. Joe's on his way. Steve's out here too. Pearl and Opal are accounted for. Vonny is safe with Elizabeth. Colin drove slowly with only his running lights on. It wasn't dark yet, but that sun had the habit of slipping behind the horizon lickety-split. If you were looking at the setting sun and turned away to do something, tie a shoe, pick up a piece of litter, by the time you turned back to look at the sun, it would be gone and all you would see was a horizon glowing in reds.

Colin cruised the streets working his way away from the lake. Lakeside Promenade, Whiteside Parkway, Chautauqua Avenue, no Ruby.

After he'd been on the streets going north and south, he carefully cruised the streets going east and west, no Ruby, no white van.

There were fifteen streets in Maple Springs. One was a circle, so Colin did not count that because in order to be classified as a street, Colin felt that a piece of roadway should at least take you somewhere. So Maple Springs had only fourteen streets and Colin searched them all again; no Ruby, no white van, no Steve.

CHAPTER 40

There was something shiny on the side of the road, right where the Whiteside Parkway Bridge crossed the creek. Colin slowed down a bit, but tried to retain his casual out-for-a-ride pace and not look like a cop on the beat. He stopped before he crossed the bridge and put on his brights, got out and walked to the shine. He had to push back some bushes to get a better look. It was the beach bike that Steve had borrowed from the Inn. It had a banged up front tire, one of those old fashioned tires with the wide white wall, and the handle bars were askew. Looks like he ran into something, maybe hit a pot hole, and abandoned the bike. I hope he's okay. I doubt that someone bushwacked him. What am I doing standing out here being a possible second victim?

Colin quickly got in the car, headed over the bridge, turned onto Chautauqua Avenue and headed back to the Inn. As he approached the Inn, he saw ahead of him, down the road headed away from the Inn, a white van. Then he saw a figure walking up the driveway, it was too dark to even know if it was a man or a woman. The figure was walking quickly cloaked in a black coat and wearing a baseball cap. Probably, thought Colin, that's Ruby who just got out of the van, driven by Tad, and he is headed "home", wherever that is. She'll be easy to collect later, I better follow the van.

The van moved slowly and wound its way out of The

Springs. Colin followed, but gave the van lots of room, he knew where the roads were headed. There were only three roads into The Springs, the same three out. When the van turned left onto Route 430, Colin was right behind and he followed at a comfortable distance. Route 430 was a two lane road with "no passing" signs within constant view. The speed limit was 45mph in the summer and hadn't yet been changed back to the 55mph winter speed limit. The van went through Dewittville and Hartfield, slowed and took a right into a camp grounds up a dark, dirt road. Colin parked on the shoulder of Route 430 headed west and walked up the dirt road. He'd seen the sign often, but had never been up the road to Charlie's Campground.

It wasn't a long road, it was actually a driveway, and it was well graded and plenty wide. Bushes edged the driveway and Colin walked just off the road, being flapped by the bushes as he followed the van to the check-in cabin. The driver got out, but was pretty much in shadows because the yellow no-more-mosquito porch light didn't cover much of an area of the porch. When the driver was well inside, Colin quickly went up to the van. Was Steve in there? Tied up? What the hell am I doing here?

The back door of the van was locked. Colin tried the driver's side front door. Unlocked. He eased it open and pressed the button on the inside door panel that unlocked all the doors. He quietly, and quickly, shut that door and opened the back door, all boxes, no Steve. Colin was dying to look in a box, but they were all taped shut, he had no time, no knife to cut the tape, no guts. He shut that door too and went twenty yards back down the driveway, moved into the bushes and waited for Tad, was it indeed Tad?, to come out of the office. It only took Tad a few minutes to check in and get back into his van and then to head up a road within the campgrounds to his assigned overnight camp site.

Colin hurried to his car, now what? There was no source of light and it had gotten dark, quickly. He opened the car door and slipped in behind the wheel. He'd have to drive into Mayville and find a phone. He didn't own a cell, didn't want a cell, was too cheap to have a cell, wished that he had a cell just for this one phone call. Vonny had a cell, in fact she had two. Her employer insisted that all members of the management team be accessible, at all times. Her management cell she kept in her car so that she always had it at work. The office staff, switchboard operator and her assistant knew to use her personal cell if they needed her outside of business hours. This was her car. A couple minutes of rummaging through the door pockets and the glove compartment produced a cell phone, a charged cell phone.

Colin repositioned the car so that he could watch for arrivals and departures at Charlie's. He dialed 911,

"Chautauqua County Sheriff"s Department, what's your emergency?"

"Hello, this is Colin O'Brien and I have important information for Sheriff Green. I just spoke with him and I know he is headed to Maple Springs, but he might want to stop off at Charlie's Campground on Route 430 between Hartfield and Mayville.

I have his cell number, but thought that it best to call 911."

"Hi Colin, Deputy Carter here, Patty. I was at Tom's earlier tonight, playing pool. I know the case. What your emergency?" Colin quickly told the deputy about the van, who he thought was driving it and that he was sure that the sheriff would want to talk to the driver and examine the van's contents.

"I got cars on 430 as we speak," said Patty. "We've been in Charlie's before, usually finding pot smoking campers. Charlie's cooperative. We got this."

Colin felt compelled to warn his fellow deputy, "He could be a murderer you know."

"Thanks, Colin. Can you hang out there till someone shows?"

Colin said that he could, Patty hung up and within three minutes, three cars and five men, were on the scene. Two cars went slowly, quietly up the driveway. One car blocked the driveway.

The driver came over to Colin. "Joe is gonna be one happy sheriff. We've known this van, this guy, was around, but we didn't have the manpower to keep up a constant search. Patty got Joe on his cell, he's headed here and he said for us all to form up at the Maple Springs Inn. You go ahead. We will bring this guy, Ward I guess, there. Looks like we are in store for a family reunion."

The deputy returned to a place near his car that blocked the end of the driveway. Colin followed orders, but he did want to stay and be a part of the "take down".

CHAPTER 41

Colin parked Vonny's silver Honda next to the garage behind the Inn and walked cautiously to the kitchen door. A motion light came on, a very bright motion light. Colin thought he was at a movie premier and a Klieg light had singled him out. There'd be no sneaking into this Inn at night. He knocked on the window of the kitchen door and entered.

"Colin, I was so worried about you," it was Vonny. "Where've you been?"

Although she was worried, Vonny didn't come to him, hug him. She and Elizabeth were busy ministering to Steve. They both had tweezers and it looked like they were picking little stones out of an arm and a leg belonging to Deputy Johnson.

"I fell off that stupid bike," said Steve. "Road's a mess, and these ladies have been kind enough to tend to my wounds, earned in the line of duty I might add. They look bad, but I'm not hurting, but I think that beach bike is down for the count."

Colin moved a little closer to the threesome settled at the kitchen table, but was careful to keep from having a clear view of the deputy's wounds. Colin didn't think of himself as squeamish, but he also made it a point to avoid wounds, boo boos, abrasions, any breaks in skin or bones, sometimes raw chicken, blood and, oh yes, vomit. When the kids were little, it was always Vonny that gallantly changed those saggy, poop-filled diapers, bandaged skinned elbows and knees and cleaned up upchuck. Colin would

forever be grateful to her for her service in this area of childrais-
ing.

Colin pumped himself a cup of coffee from the carafe on
the counter near the sink and then told the threesome where he
had been, what he had been doing. He flashed Vonny's work
cell phone and thanked her for having it in the car, charged. He
then gave advance notice that a large percentage of the sheriff's
department would soon be on the premises; a sheriff, at least five
deputies and one Mr. Tad Ward were enroute.

"They might as well join the party on the sun porch; the
three Stone girls and Pete are out there," said Elizabeth. "Ruby
came back about fifteen minutes ago. She hasn't said a word. She
is beyond grumpy, you might say hostile. The girls know Pete's
not Rico, but they still like him. Opal said that she was flattered
that the sheriff used spies, that's what she called Steve and Pete,
to try to get information out of them. Then she clammed up too.
Pearl's talking, but it's all about Pearl; the heartache of being a
runner up knows no bounds. I think they all have things to tell
us. I hope Joe gets here soon and that he has some aces up his
sleeve or we could be here all night."

"Honey, we're almost done here. You go in and see if the
gang on the sun porch needs anything, will ya?" said Vonny.
Colin gave himself a quick pump of coffee and headed to the sun
porch.

Elizabeth was right. Opal was at one end of the room in
a chaise, feigning sleep. Ruby was flipping through magazines,
destructively, not looking up. Pearl and Pete sat at a card table in

the middle of the room that was covered with pictures and clippings. Pearl was talking and pointing, enjoying attention from the handsome Sergeant Gianna. She was wearing a tiara.

"For this pageant, I sang a medley of Elvis Presley songs... *Blue Suede Shoes, Hound Dog, Love me Tender*...the judges did not love me tender or otherwise, they treated me like a hound dog. Who wanted to be Miss Savannah Magnolia Queen anyway. Oh, Mr. O'Brien, won't you join us? We, actually I, was just reminiscing about the sweeter days of my youth,"

"Thank you Miss Pearl, but I just came in to see if there is anything that you all need and to tell you that Sheriff Green is on his way and he will be wanting to talk to you all. He has much to share with us." Colin stopped there. It wasn't his prerogative to give out information. Joe surely had a plan, of some sort. Colin was looking forward to watching Joe in action.

"I think we are good," said Pete. "Elizabeth brought in some crackers and cheese and bottles of juice a little while ago. I think we are set. How long do you think it will be before Joe arrives?"

"Joe and a special guest will be along very soon," said Colin. Damn, he thought, too much information. Before he could be quizzed, Colin quickly left the room.

Everything was under control in the kitchen and sun porch of the Maple Springs Inn, so Colin went into the Inn's entrance way to await the parade of sheriff's department personnel that he knew to be headed there. He was pretty sure that the Tad apprehension at Charlie's Campground would go smoothly. Joe had probably made the scene there and surely he had plans for the reunion here at the Inn. There was much information from Buffalo, Savannah, Maple Springs and Charlie's that needed to be sorted out.

Colin sat at a small writing desk in the main hall of the Inn and took a piece of Maple Springs Inn stationery from a basket of paper and envelopes that were placed there for guests to use. He made a list of things that he was sure that needed to be part of the ongoing investigation regarding a 'trade out' and a murder. He had full confidence in Sheriff Joe Green, but he also wanted to be able to help him to bring to mind any details that were a part of this, for him anyway, confusing situation:

> *Talk about the security video from the Buffalo airport...who is this guy driving the van (Tad Ward), what's in the boxes in the van?
>
> Was it Ruby and Tad who effected the trade out/murder...if not, who?
>
>> relationship...Ruby & Tad
>>
>> the campsite at Charlie's
>>
>> *Owen Adams (the big O)...
>>
>> relationship with Opal
>>
>> relationship with Pearl
>>
>> relationship with Audra Somerville.....other
>
> Scarlet and Kyle information
>
> Information from Jimmie Lee Sands in GA (Sgt.) (was there any?)
>
>> *New Information

 Coroner...Rhoe Anderson...Neil Robertson...

Chaut. Cty. Sheriff Dept.

 Bill Morris...Eileen Miller...Elizabeth (Inn)

Colin did not know the full process that Joe used to get the information that he needed to solve a case. He'd witnessed Joe's easy-going-right-to-the-point interrogating style for the last two days and he saw that Joe had great results, used many tactics, could segue with the best of them. Colin was sure that Joe could wrap up this situation, maybe even tonight. Colin folded his list, put it into his shirt pocket and went into the kitchen.

"I assume all's well in the sun porch," said Elizabeth. "We are done in here."

"Joe called me on my cell and they're in The Springs. He wants to enter the sun porch via the outside French doors," said Steve. "I told them that you and I would be at the doors. We should get in there. They can't be more than a coupla minutes away."

As Colin and Steve walked through the sun porch, they could see someone trying to come in through the French doors. They hurried forward, each took a door handle and swung the doors open energetically, each standing aside to facilitate what they thought would be the sheriff's entrance.

"Thanks guys, my timing, your timing, was great. I didn't know how I was going to handle the doors and not lose this dolly with all these books for tomorrow's launch," said Eileen as she humped the dolly up the one small step into the sun porch and walked quickly into the room.

Right behind Eileen was Sheriff Green and his band of deputies. Too small to be called a phalanx, they nonetheless moved forward with authority and quickly inhabited the room.

All of a sudden there was great commotion within the room from all corners and on the part of all the inhabitants including the newcomers (Joe, four sheriff deputies and one handcuffed man): Opal awoke and sat up; Ruby moved to a wing-backed chair that was facing more toward the windows than toward the center of the room; Pete, Pearl and the card table were quickly moved off to the side near the table of snacks; Elizabeth and Vonny entered from the hall and found seats on a love seat that was facing a similar love seat in a reading corner of the room; Eileen and her boxes of books joined Vonny and Elizabeth; Colin and Steve sat on chairs that they pulled in front of the recently closed French doors; two deputies sat on each side of the prisoner in chairs that they took from a stack of folding chairs that was by the French doors; two deputies sat by the door that exited to the hall, one opened a lap top computer and immediately began to type; Joe paced in the middle of the room. Joe was obviously securing his position as the alpha dog of this hastily assembled pack, secure in his continuation of his earlier role of questioneer, the number one law enforcer of Chautauqua County, Sheriff Joe Green.

CHAPTER 42

As Joe paced, he was sure to make eye contact with each individual, he gave a slight smile to some and his eye contact with some was actually a glare. Once settled, no one moved, no one spoke.

"You're probably wondering why I called you all together," said Joe with a smile in his voice and on his face. One could feel the room relax, a tad.

Joe, you are really something, thought Colin. We'll be out of here in an hour.

"It's only 9:15. I got seven deputies here who I don't want to pay overtime or have to give comp time and their shift ends at 11:00, so listen up good you all, ladies and gentlemen. I will try to be courteous, but I make no promises. I have a case to solve. I am tired, we all are, no more BS."

You go Joe, thought Colin. You do have a plan. We'll be out of here in forty-five minutes.

"You all know the purpose of this meeting. You all pretty much know everyone in the room. The only person that we need to introduce to the assembled is the man in the hand cuffs. This is Tad Ward," said Joe pointing to the prisoner between the book-end deputies. There was intakes of air, voicings and slight mumblings of words by the ladies in the room.

"We know who he is from the identification that we found on him when we arrested Mr. Ward at Charlie's Campgrounds.

338- Murder at Maple Springs

Ruby Stone could you positively identify this man for us?" Joe continued pointing at the prisoner.

Everyone in the room, except the prisoner, turned to look at Ruby. Most could not see her because the chair that she had chosen to sit in was not facing the center of the room. Steve Johnson who was seated nearby moved to Ruby and instantly turned her chair so that the eyes trained in her direction actually saw her. Joe waited. Everyone waited. Joe maintained his pointing pose.

Without even looking up, Ruby Stone said," Sheriff, I believe that the man you are indicating is Mr. Tad Ward."

"And Mr. Ward, can you identify for us just who it was that positively identified you," said Joe. He lowered his pointing arm and hand.

"I will not speak without the representation of a lawyer, a lawyer here beside me to insure that my rights are kept respected," said the positively identified prisoner.

"Then we will not require you to speak. You know your rights, you were Marandized shortly after our arrival at your campsite. We will talk. We will surely talk about you. I hope you will listen. If you feel the need to engage in conversation with any of us, possibly to correct an erroneous statement, please don't hesitate, just speak right up, we'd appreciate any input that you may have regarding the murder investigation that we are undertaking at this time in this lovely room. Thank you Elizabeth for allowing us to complete our investigation in this lovely room."

I heard that Joe, thought Colin, you said complete, complete our investigation. I bet Joe can wrap this up in 30 minutes.

"Eileen Miller, I must say that I am surprised to see you here, but I'd like you to define for us the term 'trade out' as it pertains to this case. Our investigating team was working under the assumption that whoever it was that traded out the Stone cottage was also the murderer of Selma Stone. I now have reason to think that that might not be the case. In any event, Eileen would you please define for us 'trade out.'" It was Joe speaking and moving in his best form.

"I'd be happy to tell you in plain terms what a 'trade out' is and how it looks at the Stone cottage. I am not crashing your party here Sheriff. I was just helping Beth Peyton get ready for tomorrow and I barged right into your meeting. I'm more 'an glad to be here. A 'trade out' it is. A 'trade out' is something that someone does when they take stuff not belonging to them and replaces the stuff with similar stuff hoping that the owner will not notice the exchangin'. At the Stone cottage, there was a small change in the 'trade out' process. The traded stuff was real valuable and the replacement stuff was hardly even near the value or the look of those stolen things. It's just plain robbery, thievery whereby the thief, it could be a he or a she, thinks the stuff is theirs, should be theirs and they even things out by getting their share the only way they know how. You told me sheriff that trade outs is almost always carried out by a family member," here Eileen paused and looked at the Stone sisters. "Who are your suspects sheriff?"

There was just a beat of time, and then Joe spoke, looking

at individuals as he named them. "Misses Pearl, Opal and Ruby Stone, and you Eileen were all at one time on a list of suspects, but after we examined the contents of the van that Mr. Ward here owns and drives, I have revised my thinking, abandoned that suspect list and at this moment, Mr. Ward is the only name on a new list."

Joe was silent, but others in the room were not.

"You found our dishes, our books, our art?" said Opal. She immediately corrected herself remembering that the Everlasting Evangelical Spirit Church was the real owners of those traded out items. "I should have phrased my thoughts in a different fashion…then you have retrieved art objects, dishes, books, etc. that are missin' from the Stone cottage. Is that correct?"

Joe nodded yes in the direction of Opal.

"Joe, that's great. That white Brad van must be the one that Ward is driving, rather was driving," said Colin.

"Right Colin. We also found inside the van magnetic signs advertising 'Brad, the craftsman', that Ward must have attached to the van doors when he was trading out," said Joe. "Remember too, by Ron Hughes' calculation, the traded out items have a value of over half of a million dollars."

"The fact that my name ever appeared on that suspect list is a caution to me. I assure you. A caution. A vexation," said Pearl, loudly and with a scowl.

Joe did not even acknowledge her statement.

"But I must add that I believe that Mr. Ward had an accomplice," said Joe quickly and loudly; Joe did not want to succumb to the voice of the rabble. "Ruby Stone, Ruby Ward, because you are the only person in the room with at least a passing acquaintance of Mr. Ward and his van, I name you as his accomplice."

Colin couldn't resist offering Joe support. "There were two people in the white Brad van at Stone's when the trading out occurred."

"What say you Miss Stone," said Joe as he moved to within a couple feet of her in her high back chair. "Should I add your name to my new list of trade out suspects?"

There was a collective intake of air and the holding of breaths as Miss Ruby mulled over in her mind the extremely short list of possible answers to Sheriff Green's direct question.

"Sheriff," began Ruby as a collective exhale permeated the sun porch. "I do know this man. At one point, several years ago, we were close, yes, I think that's the correct word, close." Ruby was sitting up straight, talking directly to Joe, fighting for a foothold on a slippery slope. "We had a parting of the ways and I have not seen or talked to him for many months, perhaps as much as a year and a half."

"Is that your final answer?" asked Joe.

Ruby did not respond verbally, but let her erect posture and solid eye contact with Joe be her affirmative answer.

"Elizabeth, is it possible to show a DVD in this room?" asked Joe.

Elizabeth spoke not a word, but went straight to what looked like an armoire against one wall. She pushed aside a trifold door that exposed a large screen television.

"Just slip the disc into the slot on the top of the television and the console will turn on and show your DVD immediately," she said.

As Elizabeth spoke, a deputy that was guarding the door to the hallway stepped forward, produced a DVD from a small leather pouch that he carried, slid the disc into the correct slot on the television and stepped out of the way, but insured that he too could see the screen. Joe moved against a wall so that he was not blocking the view of anyone in the room. There was little movement in the room as folks moved in their seats to see the television screen. The armoire and its television was perfectly situated in the room to allow for easy viewing on everyone's part.

On the screen, the setting was the departure level of the Buffalo-Niagara International Airport and a white van was coming into view. The van stopped at the curb and a man got out of the driver's side door and a woman exited the passenger's side door. They met at the rear double doors of the van. In the sun porch, Ruby Stone began to cry. All the men in the room had either seen the DVD or at least knew its content, but to the ladies in the room, there were six, this was new information thrust at them, they flinched physically and verbally.

The deputy that had input the DVD quickly pushed stop, eject and then off.

"Sheriff, your honor, neither Miss Stone nor I will be party to the wildly imagined story that you are concocting on the spot. I demand a community defense lawyer." said Tad.

"A public defender will not be available until morning.

Feel free to maintain your silence. We will proceed without your participation." said Joe as he moved from Tad to Ruby. "Miss Stone, your role of accomplice will undoubtedly be proved by fingerprints taken either in the van or on the items in the boxes in the van. From what Mr. Ward here told us in the sheriff's car on the way here, you were the mastermind of this little caper; he's tired of hanging around this place, he has a couple beers and plays a couple games of pool at Tom's, and you get all hyper on him. That's what you said, hyper, wasn't it?" Joe was back at Tad. Tad wanted to speak, needed to speak, didn't speak. Ruby too was silent, for the moment.

Not a sound in the room.

"Who in the room saw Tad hanging out at Tom's? Don't be shy, just raise your hand." Joe asked the question and then scanned the folks sitting around the room. Vonny raised her hand and Eileen and Elizabeth quickly followed suit. Steve, Pete and Colin joined the three ladies in the hand-raising gesture.

Before Joe could acknowledge the six hands in the air and thank them for their helpful but untrue contribution to the investigation, Ruby was up, loud, feet planted, glaring at Tad, almost wild. "You sleaseball, you low life. You told me, swore to me that you did not go in Tom's, you said 'the cops are lyin' to ya baby. I'm just layin' low, waiting for ya, we're off to AZ, we're a team baby.' You don't know team, you turd bird. I tried, I worked, I let you talk me into a 'trade out', you and that Big O, that big ass. Yes, sheriff, Tad is the brains behind this. I can't be the brains, I got no brains to stay with him, to let him smack me around, treat

344- Murder at Maple Springs

me like crap. To be thirty-three and to have nothin', nothin'. 'But there's a last chance' Tad said, 'all that cottage stuff' he said, 'we need it, you deserve it. Selma's dead in Italy, yer daddy won't care, he's got lots of stuff, it's yours, you're the big sister, come on baby. Selma's dead, yer daddy's in grief, he won't care.' Oh daddy, I stole from my own daddy, daddy," and Ruby fell into a ball in her chair. Joe signaled Steve Johnson and Ruby's chair was returned to its previous look-out-the-window position.

Opal and Pearl moved to join their sister. Joe's glare did not let that happen.

"So Tad," said Joe. "Any rebuttal? None? Last chance."

Tad, a sometimes man of his word, said nothing.

"So Sheriff, the trade out team has been determined. Right? You haven't explained why Ruby and Ward aren't the murder team too. Previously you did say that you had reason to think that whoever accomplished the 'trade out' was the murder- er, but now you've contradicted yourself," said Colin feeling like a straight man for Joe. "I don't get it."

"Right Colin. I best get to that. It was easy to make that trade out perp list, but making a murder perp list is not so easy. It's doubtful that our silent friend here is a murderer. He's a lot of things, but not a murder. Ruby either. If they had murdered Selma, it was later after the 'trade out'. They would have had to go back to the cottage, take the chance of being seen. If they had killed her, would they have hung around for a will reading? Re- member, Ruby knew there was a change in the ownership of the cottage, she was pretty sure that she'd get nothing. Ruby gave us some information, but kept a lot from us, wasn't honest about her time here, when she was east and there was that phoney business of flying into Buffalo and all those healthy walks she took. She was trying to keep tabs on Tad boy here while she was also trying to keep up with what was happening within the investigation here in The Springs, in the Inn. She could work at keeping a trade out secret, she could be creative with dates and places, she could easily lie, but she could never murder and try to fake her way through a murder investigation," said Joe. "Any questions?"

No one spoke. Actually, there wasn't time to formulate a question. Joe went on. "Murder. A heinous act. Selma Stone deserved no such end. How does one come to the act of murder? How can someone murder a family member, a loved one, even a stranger, and in this case, if we stick with our separation of trader outer and murderer we don't even have a murder motive. Does there have to be a motive? Could there be a murder in Maple Springs, quiet little Maple Springs on Chautauqua Lake?" Joe was on a roll. "But, just as trading out is usually completed by a family member, so too is murder."

"Now just one minute Sheriff Green," said Pearl. "It is apparent to me where you are going with this line of supposition. And just as you so cavalierly placed me on the suspect list as a trader outer, you're hell bent on placing me, actually the three of us Stone sisters, on your murderer list. 'Cause we are family? 'Cause we weren't fond of Miss Selma? 'Cause we are disappointed with our family wealth being scooped from our grasp and bestowed upon a church not of our choice? Don't you dare, sir,

346- Murder at Maple Springs

make a list, any kind of list, that includes a member of the Stone family."

"Miss Pearl, you do protest prematurely. I have no intention of placing you or your fine sisters on a list of possible murderers, but I would like to expound upon a theory, but in order to do so, I will first need your full cooperation and honest answers to several questions. Is that possible?" queried Joe.

Pearl looked at her sisters and answered yes, for them all.

Joe continued. "For two days now, here at the Maple Springs Inn, we have conducted an investigation into the murder of Selma Stone and the theft of many personal and valuable items from her home. You three sisters, important principals in the investigation, have been evasive, hardly forthcoming and not committed to the investigation. We just determined that Miss Ruby was less than truthful with information regarding air flights, travel east, visits to Maple Springs, etc. Once we knew the truth regarding her movement and the role of Mr. Ward in her life, we were able to resolve at least one portion of this case."

Joe paused, took the folding chair that was vacated by the deputy who was still standing at the DVD player ready to show more footage if it were to be required, and then Joe sat on that chair in front of Opal and Pearl.

"Ladies, think carefully, think clearly, answer honestly. Savannah, Georgia is about 850 miles from here and I am a country boy here in rural western New York, but I feel that I have at least a cursory understanding of the night life in your city. I have asked you to be honest, so I will be honest too. I charged two investigators in Savannah to go on the town so to speak and to report to me regarding the activities of your Mister Owen Adams."

Joe took from his pocket a piece of paper and scanned it for a minute. Pearl and Opal moved, it wasn't squirming, in their seats, kept eye contact with Joe, watched him read.

"At a night club named The High Life, Mr. Adams, they said he was a regular, was in close conversation with a young lady. Would you like to know her name?" asked Joe.

"In the name of all honesty, it would behoove you to pronounce that name," said Opal, probably too eagerly.

"Audra Somerville," were the only words Joe said and he said them precisely and loudly while looking directly at Opal and Pearl.

"Audra," it was a duet.

"Somerville," was a solo performance by Opal. She continued. "He was with Audra Somerville? The woman has the intellect of a pea and she hasn't the appearance to be on the arm of Owen. How did..."

"There's more," interrupted Joe. Opal became quiet. "The investigators learned that..." Joe referred again to his faux notes, "...she, Miss Audra, is a part owner of Georgia Grafix and Owen is her coworker." Joe plunged forward with more information. "It was learned that he is recently free from a job and a relationship and Ms. Somerville views Adams as a valued professional and personal friend."

That information carried great weight. No one in the room, Joe thought, except Opal, Pearl, Colin and himself was understanding the enormity of what was being said.

"The investigators saw eight other women from Adam's past, but none, save one, would speak of him. This one said that the police had to convince Mr. Adams that indeed the lady, she herself, did not want to see Adams ever again. The Police, mainly a Sergeant Jimmie Lee Sands, has a file of complaints."

"Owen Adams was in our cottage here at Maple Springs," it was Pearl talking. Sounds, intake of air, 'what?', and changes in posture followed this statement.

"Pearl, thank you for finally becoming serious about this investigation." said Joe. "That said, I have a scenario that I would like to pass by you and Opal, but I would like to hear from you first," said Joe.

Colin was sure that Joe was hoping that Pearl would drop some information that he could weave into the scenario that he was concocting and going to try to pass off as the results of actual police investigations. This should be fun Colin thought.

"He, Owen that is, was very taken with the lake, loved the cottage, he didn't want to leave," Pearl again. "It was about five months ago. We were in Syracuse, Miss Greater Syracuse USA, and as we headed home to Georgia, Route 90 west to 79 south, when we were by exit 60 I think it was, I said casually, that we were just about 16 miles from a cottage my parents owned. He wanted to see it, thought it would be fun to be there on our own, no harm done. He was my driver and he helped once we got where I was heading to consult with a pageant. We had to be very discrete. I couldn't be a contestant consultant and have a man in my room. We had to sneak around a lot. He liked it, called me Ms. Stone, snuck food from buffets. We saved a lot of money. I always requested transportation money and got the airfare from Savannah to wherever. Airfare for one always covered the expenses for driving the two of us. That arrangement worked out until he was lured away by Opal."

"I neveh cajoled Mr. Adams. He created a place for himself in my organization. It was not a regular job, he worked from home. Oh he had duties, but I didn't see a lot of him...at work. He also had family problems, had to go to Memphis multiple times to help with a failing family business. Fact is, now that I think of it, he was more of an idea man. I still maintained control of the organization. Marketing was done by Georgia Grafix, ring a bell...," Opal stopped talking, her imagination began to call the shots and she felt a loss of control.

"Ladies of Savannah, but not you Ruby, I'd like to present a scenario that is based upon (1) the information received from our investigators in Savannah, (2) from Sergeant Jimmie Lee Sands of the Savannah PD and (3) the pieces of information that you have shared with us, although I am not certain that I have a grasp on all the details," said Joe as he moved in on the two Savannah sisters, got comfortable.

Others in the room moved, sighed, checked watches, some sitters stood, one stander sat.

"This may sound like a long rambling mash up of facts and probabilities, but I think that I can break it down so that you Savannahites, and possibly others in the room, can accept the story as fact or at least as a possible truth. It's been congealing since I first heard yesterday about the existence of Owen Adams. Ready?" Joe waited for assents from Pearl and Opal.

"I am sure that we will hear this tale whether we want to or not," said a surprised Opal.

"I look upon this as another assault upon the Stone family," said Pearl.

"I will take those two answers as affirmative," said Joe and he proceeded, up, pacing, thinking, stalling before he jumped into his story.

Colin had to laugh to himself when Joe was talking about his investigators in Savannah (Kyle and Scarlet) and the former girlfriend of Adams that spoke about him (Scarlet again). The notes Joe referred to were actually the bulleted items from the e-mail Kyle had sent regarding her, and Scarlet's, prowl for Owen. Colin was sure that Joe had never contacted Sergeant Sands although it looked as though he might have to make that contact in the near future. Colin was enjoying the Sheriff Joe Show.

"I'm going to try to present this tale in some sort of chronological order, but I will probably be out of synch upon occasion. You ladies, and I include you in this Ruby, pleaded hazy when it came to details and dates about visits here to The Springs, visits to Buffalo, Pittsburgh, but my tale starts somewhere in the recent past when Opal and Pearl were both entwined with Owen Adams. Simultaneously," said Joe. He had the rapt attention of all of those in the room. Colin was beginning to think that Joe was either delusional or psychic.

"Owen had worked his way through many Savannah debutantes," started Joe. "He dated, he used, he had his way in many ways, and records say that there was some abuse, no one would press charges, few sought the help of the police, but there is a file, a collection of tales, corroborated and uncorroborated, but I digress.

"Owen had his eye on Stone money, that we know, and while he was working for you Opal, he was on the road with Pearl, or perhaps he was in Memphis being the dutiful son. He knew the disposition of the Stone money, as did all of Savannah, but he thought too that you two still had some of that family money, you had income, you were savvy businesswomen. He dated and delved into your lives and your businesses. He didn't find a lot, no real glut of discretionary money, but then there was enough to keep him attentive, enough to provide a salary and then there was often free room and board, a company car, usually rented, and he was discrete, even mysterious, was having fun, and was sure that there were funds somewhere that he could find, appropriate, if he were only patient.

"And then his patience paid off and things began to look up for him. Selma died in Italy, G.E.M. was still out of the country, there was a house full of art to be turned into a slush fund for him. Did you ladies know that he planned to move to Atlantic City and partner up with an old friend, a lady, and open a casino?"

Body language and facial expressions told Colin that the casino project was news to Opal and Pearl, but neither one said a word. But then, it was probably news to Joe too, just a creative piece of his sprawling saga of the south.

"Who told him about Selma's death in Italy?" asked Joe.

"I did," it was another Opal and Pearl duet. They looked at each other, their looks not showing anger or disdain, but understanding.

"So, I bet too that he knew about the change in the will," Joe expected another Stone sister's duet, but did not wait for it. "Adams had all the information he needed, he had his family excuse to fall back on, and he headed to Maple Springs. He has no car you say? Well he rented enough cars for you Pearl, he knew the drill. I think that we'll see the Enterprise Auto Rental records for as far away as Charleston, South Carolina, will inform us of a car rental by Adams. Georgia and South Carolina are in the same Enterprise sales district. I'm confident too that we can coordinate the time of Selma Stone's death with Adams' rental."

Joe you are amazing, thought Colin, you're not lying or entrapping, you're just running a scenario up the flag pole to see if any sister salutes.

Joe went on.

"Adams knew he had a brief window of time to head north, he knew what he'd find when he got here and he had been taught how to access the Stone cottage and to avoid the security system. He'd been carefully taught." Joe stared right at Pearl.

"When we snuck into the cottage, I never thought that I would bear any responsibility for the death of Miss Selma, poor, sweet Miss Selma," said Pearl.

Pearl, although she may have been tired, showed signs of attentiveness, she was just about ready to salute in the direction of the flagpole.

"Please finish our story hour Sheriff Green. It is late, we have had a full day, I am pummeled by information, shocking revelations, and now find myself bored by a fantastical scenario purporting to wind up this murder investigation," Opal spoke clearly and remained calm, but it was obvious that she wasn't fond of Joe's tale. "I should like to retire for the night. May I?"

"You may," said Joe, but before she could rise from her chair, Joe was back in story mode.

"I'm just guessing that Mr. Adams appreciated the art work and the other valuables in the Stone cottage. Can you verify that for us Miss Pearl?"

All eyes were on Pearl. "Owen appreciated the art work at the cottage. Although he was unfamiliar with Peterson, he knew Ansel Adams and he was especially fond of Remington statuary. He said that the cottage was like a mini-museum of Americana. I think your story, sir, is credible. I think I aided and abetted." Pearl was in full salute.

"Pearl, you have no culpability in this act of murder. Our investigations north and south of the Mason-Dixon line lead us to Adams." Joe paused, he could see Opal perched to spring from her chair. He looked at his watch, sure that everyone else in the room was acutely aware of the time, their tiredness, the strain of the day; Joe was easily beating his end-by-11:00 deadline.

"I thank you all for your patience and attention in this

pursuit of justice," said Joe. "Our judicial system demands that we take seriously our way of life when we convene to consider justice. Our county entrusts some of us to keep that justice foremost in our daily proceedings and our intense investigations. I am sure that you all see the solemnity in our proceedings."

Oh brother, thought Colin. Joe is filling up with Joe or perhaps it is a part of his scheme to garner information, put it in order and to, hopefully, paint a realistic picture that could be verified or just as easily, be trashed.

"So, can I safely say that we have a name to initiate our murder perpetrator list?" Surely this was a rhetorical question on Joe's part, but nodding heads and even a 'yes' or two spurred Joe onward. "And we have a motive and an opportunity outlined that is for me at least making perfect sense." More head nodding.

"Could we consider one last particle of information before we call it a night?" asked Joe. Everyone in the sun porch, smelling the end of the long day, silently agreed that one more topic could be considered.

Joe looked toward a deputy, the one with the airport DVD. The deputy walked to Joe and handed him a Manilla folder.

"Thanks Keven."

Then Joe spoke to the others in the room, spoke as he walked away from the Stone sisters, slowly. "I have here the coroner's report concerning the death of Selma Stone. I would like to read aloud a small portion."

"Really Sheriff Green," said Opal. No one else spoke. Most shifted in their seats.

Joe flipped through a few pages in the folder, all the time

pacing, folded pages back, they were held in the folder with a large black paper fastener. When he had exposed the page that he was to read, he stopped pacing and read aloud, clearly.

"Coroner Fourtney reported, 'There are no visible marks on the arms, face or legs. There is major force trauma to the back of the skull. There appears to have been several strokes to the head with a weapon with a flat surface (a frying pan as opposed to a baseball bat), not a sharp weapon like a shovel, a large weapon as opposed to a small weapon.' I was hoping......"

Before Joe could explain what he was hoping for, Colin was up in a flash, by Joe's side and talking rapidly.

"I got it, I know the murder weapon, is that what you're hoping for Joe? I'm sure, it just came to me, anyone else know? I know."

Joe put his face right in Colin's, a finger to Colin's lips, and said, "Don't spaz out on me Colin. Just tell us what you know, what you think you know."

All of a sudden Colin realized that he was being dorky, in front of the investigating team and all the others in the room. He looked at Vonny and got a great smile and a wave of inspiration.

"The weapon is a frying pan, even the coroner said that was the right shape, size. This morning when we saw the cottage tour video that Lula, G.E.M. and Eileen made in 2006, at one point Lula opened the oven and there was a set of cast iron skillets, a set of three nestled inside each other. But later in the day, today, when Ruby, Pearl, Opal and I went to the Stone cottage to look for family photos, I was looking for wooden spoons that G.E.M.

had made and opened the oven, course the spoons weren't there, but there were two frying pans, the biggest and the smallest. The middle sized one was gone. It was a weapon, the weapon." Colin ran out of steam.

Joe gently turned Colin and gave him a nudge in the direction of his seat next to Steve, by the French doors to the outside. Steve gave Colin an attaboy. Colin sat, sat tall, and was feeling very deputy-like. Vonny still inspired him from across the room. Attention went back to Joe. Surely he was ready to wrap up this information fest.

"With this piece of information, thanks to Colin, I believe that I can complete this evening's story hour. Now it wasn't so fantastical was it?" Joe paused and scanned the room with his eyes. He received smiles in return.

"Back to the day that Selma Stone was killed," began Joe. "It was early, Selma was still in her bathrobe when she answered the door. Adams was expecting to see G.E.M., remember that Selma was to have died in Italy, but there was Selma. And Selma, she wasn't expecting to see Adams. I assume that she had met him at some point in Savannah, but she never expected to see him at her door, not alone anyway. Even though she was surprised by Owen Adams, I'd say that Selma welcomed him. He came into the house, was probably chatting up Selma, probably noticed the newly traded items that were out and visible. The Peterson originals and the Remington statues had been right there in the living room, off the front hall. He was there to commit a down and dirty, quick robbery, but he'd been bested, others had beat him to the goods. Perhaps Selma got scared and asked him to leave, perhaps he went to the kitchen and saw the frying pan was on the stove, greasy from making Selma's breakfast, perhaps Adams got belligerent and made a threat when Selma didn't answer his questions about her supposed death in Italy, where's G.E.M.?, perhaps she told him to leave, perhaps she went to the telephone, perhaps the frying pan was put into service."

"Too many perhapses, no proof, a far out rendition on your part sheriff. I have grown weary of your story. May I go now?" said Opal.

Just then Vonny's cell, in Colin's pocket, rang. Colin, appearing embarrassed that he disturbed Joe's performance, scrambled to get it out and answered it with his hand covering his mouth and most of the telephone. He spoke for a moment.

"Joe, it's for you," Colin said as he got up from his chair and walked to Joe. "It's Sergeant Jimmie Lee Sands of the Savannah PD."

"I gotta take this. Talk amongst yourselves. I'll give you a topic: Selma Stone's murder. Discuss," said Joe with a laugh as he moved between the two deputies at the sun room's door and into the hall. Little or no talk took place in the sun room, it was as if a collective breath was being held.

Joe was back in a flash.

"Sergeant Sands has Owen Adams in custody." The deputies in the room were excited, Vonny, Elizabeth and Eileen were pleased, the Stone sisters were hard to read; they were tired, embarrassed, confused.

"Sands also has car rental paperwork from Charleston,

South Carolina, and positive identification from a clerk at the car rental office, a lady who Adams put the moves on when he was in the renting process." More movement within the room; the case is settled, everyone was relieved. "But, Adams admits renting the car and being here at the Stone's cottage, but he said that he didn't touch Selma." Joe paused for dramatic effect and then added, "He's working out a plea bargain before he names the real murderer."

He was up in a flash, like a wild man, cursing, yikes was he cursing, struggling with the handcuffs. "That sack-a-crap rebel SOB can't drag my ass into this mess. I took all that crap from Ruby's house, OK, OK, I was gonna sell it, it weren't Ruby's idea. It was big ass O's idea. Couldn't leave it to us, had to drag his ass north, make sure we got it all and then he runs into Selma, can't take being had, jerk, turd bird. Ruby, you tell him, tell this sheriff, I ain't no murderer, tell him! We never even seen Selma, she was dead in Italy."

Ruby couldn't talk over her sobs, couldn't look at anyone, just couldn't. Pearl went to her sister and sat in the chair with her, cradling and gently rocking.

"You call that sergeant back sheriff." Tad had no filter in operation. "You call that guy, tell that sergeant 'bout me, I know it all. I know other things 'bout Adams too. I ain't fallen into no plea bargain trap where Adams wins and I get stung with murderin' that ol' lady. Call him, ya gonna call him?" shouted Tad. His book-end deputies grabbed him and took him from the room, out the French doors, into a sheriff's department car and he was gone ranting all the way out.

CHAPTER 43

With Tad Ward gone, the room relaxed, people knew that they had just experienced a final chapter in the investigation of the case regarding the 'trade out' at the Stone cottage and the murder of Selma Stone. No one called for adjournment, but everyone sensed that this evening's meeting, Joe's story hour, had come to an end.

Lots of things happened within the next fifteen minutes, the day was ending and many of the attendees had final thoughts to express.

"Ladies and gentlemen, may I have your attention?" it was Elizabeth, ever the entrepreneur. "This has been most interesting, but I'd like to take a minute to remind you all about Beth Peyton's book launch to take place right here in this room tomorrow, 4:00 until 7:00 with a reading at 5:00. I promise that it will be as exciting as this meeting, a different type of excitement, but exciting nonetheless. Please join us."

"While we have everyone's attention," Joe spoke, he wasn't through just yet. "Reports, let's not forget reports. Pete, write up what happened at Tom's earlier this evening. Keven, you fill out the paperwork for the pick-up at Charlie's Campground. Colin, how about a few words on paper regarding you following Tad Ward to Charlie's. Steve, I saw you taking a few notes so you get to write a synopsis of this gathering. Give it to me rough and I will add to it and finalize." Joe paused for a minute. "I'm sorry

Miss Ruby, but we have to take you to be booked too."

Protests from all six women in the room ensued, but Ruby was to be taken away, everyone knew it was the thing to do. Elizabeth offered to call Neil Robertson and have him arrange Ruby's bail in the morning. Joe assured Pearl and Opal that he would make sure that everything would go smoothly with regard to Ruby's release. Then Joe signaled Kevin who handed Vonny a brown paper bag, lunch size, and gave her a whispered assignment. She looked in the bag and went to the place where Ruby, Pearl and Opal were seated. She gave them each a black, velvet box, tied with a silver string-like ribbon that Europeans seemed to use a lot.

Vonny made sure that the sisters opened the boxes. She showed them her necklace and there was a tear or two, hugs to be sure, a point was made. Joe sure had a knack for doing the right thing at the right time.

"One more thing before we all head out," said Joe. "We need to thank Colin for arranging the phony cell phone call from Savannah that motivated Mr. Ward to blab. It was not a real call from Savanna, folks. How did you arrange that Colin?" asked Joe.

Colin was feeling that maybe he had done the wrong thing or that he had, at least, butted in on Joe's story.

"Well, Joe, when you started talking about justice and how some of us are sworn to seek justice, I thought that you were stalling, fumbling around waiting for inspiration, maybe even divine intervention. I signaled Vonny across the room to call me on her work cell that she knew I had in my pocket and when it rang I

told you it was Sands, because I thought that he might be someone that could help you finish your story. He did, but he doesn't
even know it. It took me some time to get Vonny to call me."

"I couldn't imagine what he was trying to signal to me,"
said Vonny. "I thought he had developed a couple serious ticks.
I finally got 'telephone' and he then patted his pocket. I know he
doesn't have a cell, but earlier in the kitchen he showed me my
work cell phone and said that he had used it to call 911 about Tad
Ward at Charlie's Campground, so I slipped out my personal cell
and called him. It was all his idea."

"And a doozie of an idea it was," said Joe. "You did get me
off the hook Colin. I was stymied, right in the middle of my scenario. Now I need to call Sands and have him arrest Mr. Adams.
Great work Deputy O'Brien. So let's call it a night. I will have a
press conference, with the coroner, in the morning, 10:00, and no
one else is to talk to the press. I say that for your own good. They
hound you, misquote you. Let me take the grief. Pearl and Opal,
I will have Pete come here in the morning so that you can collect
Ruby at the jail. Any questions?"

"Sheriff," it was Opal talking as Pearl pushed her from the
perimeter of the room to the center. "My sisters and I want to say
thank you for your expeditious handling of this case and to apologize for rude remarks or what I know you know to be avoidin' of
questions and giving answers that were evasive. We...."

"No need to apologize, Miss Opal. It's been stressful for us
all and being a part of a murder investigation can be confusing
and even frightening," said Joe being Mr. Congeniality. "Every-

one, please no phone calls to friends, relatives, neighbors, north or south. Let the press conference happen. Let's see this entire process through properly."

No one argued Joe's points. The room was quickly cleared, everyone had things to do, places to go, thoughts to straighten out.

It had indeed been a long day, thought Colin, but it was only 10:30, Joe had them out of there in one hour. You're something Sheriff Joe Green.

CHAPTER 44

When Colin got home, he e-mailed Kyle and Scarlet and said that the case was wrapped up and that he would call them after noon the next day, after Joe's press conference. He said that there were a lot of details, but he had orders from Joe to keep quiet. Colin then called Bill Morris and gave him the same message verbally. Bill said Joe had sent him home earlier, wouldn't let him come to the Inn and that he'd probably go to the press conference in the morning. He hoped that Joe would mention him and his idea concerning the video tapes from the airport; "It'd be good publicity."

No sooner had Colin hung up from Bill and the telephone rang. It was Kyle.

"Hello Colin, thank you so much for e-mailing and no need to give us any details. Just knowing the investigation is wrapped up is good news enough for us. I am currently seeing a gentleman, whom I became acquainted with on the 'High Seas Single Mingle', who is a reporter here in Savannah and he works for a big news bureau of some sort and he can have a stringer from Buffalo at the press conference in the morning who can have a live television feed right to his desk at the *Savannah Morning News*. I can get all my news from him, and he gets a scoop of a sort too. Scarlet will surely be called by news outlets too. She is working with the sheriff, a lawyer up your way and a man at a funeral home in Jamestown, I believe. I daresay that we will all be inundated with information come tomorrow. You go to sleep now, and Colin, you couldn't have been a better friend to Selma and G.E.M....no wonder they loved you and Vonny as they did. Bye for now."

Colin was sure that Vonny was asleep, so he slipped off his Crocs and went into the darkened bedroom to get his pajamas. The room was light enough that he could see that Vonny was not in bed.

"I'm out here hon," said Vonny.

"Out where," said Colin as he opened the door that lead to their front porch. There in a large, white wicker rocker with floral print cushions sat Vonny in her shortie pajamas and matching robe. "I asked Joe, he said I could get the chairs now. They just can't be taken over state lines." There was a matching chair for Colin, he moved it next to Vonny's. They sat and rocked, there were a few tears too.

CHAPTER 45

Colin and Vonny were up early with Vonny off to work with a vanilla yogurt and a Tupperware container of fruit compote that Colin always had on hand; breakfast at her desk. She promised to be home by 4:00 so that she could join Colin at the B & B for the launch of *Clear Skies, Deep Water*. Colin walked her to her car, hugged and kissed her and waved until her car was out of sight.

Colin sat down at the computer, clicked onto *Word* and quickly outlined his actions as he drove around Maple Springs, finally spotted Tad Ward's van, followed him to Charlie's Campgrounds and then called 911 so that the sheriff could take Tad Ward into custody. He e-mailed the brief report to Joe as an attachment, logged off the computer and then quickly walked to the Maple Springs Inn to see if he could help Elizabeth prepare for the late afternoon festivities. As he walked up the driveway, he saw William dumping bedraggled potted plants into a wheelbarrow and stacking the clay pots in a wooden box. The porch looked barren, but Colin knew that bright orange pumpkins and orange, red, yellow and purple mums would soon fill those empty spots once occupied by planters of dusty miller, million bells, spikes and Gerber daisies and geraniums, he couldn't forget the geraniums.

"Good morning William. Long time no see," said Colin as he met William at the top of the porch stairs. William removed his work gloves and shook hands with Colin.

"Hello Colin," replied William. "Guess I missed a lot when I was gone. Elizabeth and Eileen filled me in when we had coffee earlier. Sorry that I missed the September adventures in Maple Springs. She said you saved the night with your phony phone call. Genius."

William told Colin about the plan for the day...caterers would be there soon, Eileen and Elizabeth were just completing the set-up of the sun porch, Girton's would soon be delivering mums and pumpkins for outside and vases of flowers for inside, and as soon as he set up the Inn's small public address system, his work for the day would be completed. William also told Colin that a sheriff deputy had picked up the Stone sisters that were staying at the Inn and had taken them to a bail hearing in the court at Mayville. The day was taking the shape that Colin had thought it would.

Colin felt at loose ends, but then he realized how much of his own personal life he had set aside over the last few days. When he got home, he sat at the kitchen table and consulted Vonny's list of the things that he needed to do in order to catch up with life: he collected the remainder of his inheritance of wicker and set up his front porch sure in the fact that there would be a few more weeks of summer and early fall to enjoy the gift; he went to the post office and collected four or five days of mail, it was mostly junk, he followed William's lead and dumped flower pots that, frankly, he was tired of trying to keep fresh looking; he showered and shaved and got dressed for the launch party; he wrote a group e-mail to his children giving them a synopsis of the investigation and he even had the confidence to mention his role as Deputy O'Brien. He knew they'd mock him, but dammit he had enjoyed the role and he'd done well. Several times during the morning, he had thought of Joe and hoped that the press conference was going smoothly. The *Jamestown Post-Journal*, the Buffalo TV news programs and the Buffalo newspapers would probably heavily cover the murder and its solving.

Vonny was home almost on schedule, made a quick change and they were off to the Inn arriving fashionably fifteen minutes late. The Inn looked great. Sue at Girton's Florists had dressed the Inn in just the right amount of mums, just the right colors in just the right places. The pumpkins she overdid, but still the Inn looked great.

In the Inn, trays of artistic appetizers were being butlered and a light buffet was set up in the large dining room and small tables for four were placed in the foyer, the living room and at one end of the sunporch. Cloth napkins and table coverings in gold brightened the rooms and invited. Beth Peyton, local author and terrific neighbor, "worked the room", joyous in her satisfaction that her book, a memoir, was finished, proofed, rewritten, approved, printed, bound, reviewed and would soon be bought, autographed, read, loaned and saved prominently on coffee tables all around Maple Springs at least.

It was a lovely event, with conversation and interactions so different from those that had taken place in the Inn over the last two or three days; no loud talking, no snarky repartee, no skirting issues or avoiding of truths. The attendees were more gentile and as a rule were glad to be there, not like the last crew of deputies and suspects.

The food, divine. The company, the same. At precisely 5:00, Beth, looking calm and even serene in a peasanty white dress with a pale blue tunic top almost to her knees and a narrow scarf tied in a knot like a bulky necklace of silk, asked guests to have a seat in the chairs in the sun porch. Jeff, her husband who was featured prominently in the memoir, helped guide guests along. Colin and Vonny moved quickly into the sun porch and sat in one of the upholstered love seats that was towards the back of the room. William activated the sound system and then he briefly introduced Beth, although in this case with this audience, she truly needed no introduction.

Beth greeted her quests and talked briefly about her writing process. It was a stellar moment in her life and Beth was loving every minute of it. Colin surveyed the room happy in the thought that calmness, maybe to the point of ennui, was reentering his life. He commented to Vonny on the vases of fresh flowers, gerber daisys again. Vonny shushed him, took his hand and slid closer to him.

Beth told her audience that she would like to read a selection from the first chapter of the book. William turned on a small unobtrusive reading lamp and Beth began to read:

"Even during the summers in Maple Springs, at the height of the tourist season, it is so quiet that if you walk at night after ten o'clock, you can sometimes hear people snoring through their window screens. The water gently laps the shore; it is rhythmic and soothing and lulls us to sleep. But in the winter, it is so quiet you can sometimes hear the snow fall. Not just during a storm, when the snow is hard and icy, but during those beautiful snows where the soft, fat flakes drift gently down. If I listen carefully, I can hear them land on the snow-covered ground with a tiny pat.

The summer was lovely, but somehow we needed the winter. During winter, the color of the lake is stripped of its vibrancy. The view through the windows was all whites, grays, and watery blues; gray tree trunks running to black, dark gray hills on the opposite shore, and white-grayskies. Dock stanchions and sections were stacked on the lakefront amid the scattered boatlifts, and the bare trees stood out in base-relief, in stark contrast yet enveloped by the white and the gray. We walked this muted landscape, resting our weary hearts and minds, holding still and gathering strength, waiting for our future to be revealed."

Yes, thought Colin, here comes winter to reveal my future. Maple Springs is in my future. Bring it on.

EPILOGUE

Winter in Chautauqua County can be fierce. Snow swirls, blankets, pelts, peaks, drifts, floats, can be beautiful. There's flakes, sleet, powder, slush, hail, granules. There can be snowstorms, gusts, blizzards, flurries, snow watches, zero temperatures, cold snaps, squalls. It can be cold, nippy, blustery, frigid, just plain nasty.

But winter does pass, although it seems, about early March, that it's back, full-blown, never to end. With its eventual passage comes all that growth that folks are sure will never reappear in spite of the centuries where reappearance has been a certainty: green grass, crocuses, daffodils, forsythia, phlox, dianthus (often called pinks), robins and other feathered harbingers.

For Colin and Vonny O'Brien, this winter, their first at the lake, seemed like a whole new experience, a winter from another Mother Nature. City winters of the past seemed like a punishment, a series of challenges, "Survivor" or *The Hunger Games* where everyone was forced to be a participant. Their lake winter was a sparkling white milieu of sometimes bluster and yet periods of serenity and winter beauty.

The O'Briens had survived the winter, cherished the holidays, hunkered down, read, rented a video or two, played board games, experimented with cross country skiing, beat old man winter with scarves, gloves, coats, shovels, deicers, lip balm and NyQuil.

Spring sort of snuck in, after all there was some snow in April; just enough snow so that those early, little, white flowers were still visible and provided a sparkle along the stream beds. Colin called them snowdrops as his mother had when he was a kid. And besides the arrival of various natural wonders, the summer Maple Springers began to reappear too. Of course they were preceded by little men in trucks who made ready the way for the Springers. Canvas winter porch jackets were removed, windows washed, gardens planted and mulched, awnings put in place and, most importantly, docks and boatlifts took their rightful places on the shore and jutted out into Lake Chautauqua.

During the winter, telephone calls, e-mails, articles clipped from the local newspapers and notes jotted on Christmas cards had brought all the Springers up to speed regarding what quickly became known as "the situation at the Stone cottage".

During the winter also, Colin had kept in touch with Sheriff Green, Kyle Kennedy and Scarlet Ames in Savannah and there was also contact with Lawyer Robertson, Rhoe Anderson of Anderson Associates Insurance and Jeff Carson at Lander's Funeral Home. Colin would have welcomed it, but there was no contact with Ruby, Opal or Pearl Stone.

Colin knew that he and Vonny, yearrounders and friends with G.E.M. and Selma, would be a primary source of information for those with but a cursory understanding of the elements of the situation at the Stone cottage. The O'Briens were okay with this designation and during those many winter telephone conversations, they had been able to insure that Springers had real facts, knew the real story and indeed Colin and Vonny were able to quash rumors and rein in wild conjectures and suppositions.

The specifics of the situation itself were easy to relate and Colin and Vonny did so willingly, but it was the aftermath of the investigation that the O'Briens worked to keep susinct and to add to as the investigation progressed and the judicial system took its slow course.

The O'Briens sat one evening, and made a list of specifics that they thought needed to be compiled so that they could speak definitively and answer accurately any questions poised by family, neighbors and friends.

The next morning, Colin called Sheriff Joe and told him about the investigation status list that he and Vonny had formulated and asked Joe if it was okay that they compiled the list and could they use it when talking with Maple Springers. Colin told Joe that it was his version of the steps that Joe had for spreading bad news, only this time the news was good, was part of the healing of the community and the status of the investigation needed to be told accurately and consistently validated. Joe agreed that getting the word out in an orderly manner was a good idea and he made a few suggestions and gave Colin some sheriff words to insert so that the outline would carry an air of authority. Joe reminded Colin not to talk to the press - although at this point it was pretty obvious that the local paper had tired of reporting on the situation at the Stone cottage - and Joe even graciously offered to call Colin with new information whenever it surfaced.

Colin made adjustments to the list, being sure to include

Joe's suggestions, then sent the list to Joe as an attachment to an e-mail. Colin then printed off copies for himself and Vonny to use when discussing "the situation" with Maple Springers.

THE STATUS OF THE INVESTIGATION OF THE SITUATION
(at the Stone Cottage)
Steps for Disseminating Information

A. State the Current Status of the Perpetrators (promotes calm) (start out with "you are safe" or "Maple Springs is a safe place")

1. <u>Tad Ward</u> remains in jail in the custody of the Chautauqua County Sheriffs' Department awaiting trial...authorities in cities out west want their piece of him once his New York State debt to society is paid in full...he is charged with the "trade out" at the Stone cottage (robbery, etc.). He has been reluctant to talk, except about Owen Adams.

2. <u>Owen Adams</u> was extradited from Georgia, after much legal wrangling, and he too is awaiting trial in the Chautauqua County Jail...he

is charged with the murder of Selma
Stone among other charges all stem-
ming from the same event.

(complete Section A with words of
finality and closure, for example;
"Sheriff Green is confident that the
perpetrators in custody are the only
perpetrators and he is confident in
their future conviction and incarcer-
ation.")

B. State the Current Status of
other Principals Involved (this fills
in the big picture and helps folks
know things are back to normal, that
others are healing and folks are moving on) (start with..."You'll be glad
to know..." or the like)

1. Ruby Stone was released in
the custody of her sisters and was
allowed to go to Savannah, GA. She
will return to Chautauqua County
for the Ward and Adams trials and is
expected to testify against both men/
give testimony for the prosecution. A
grand jury failed to indict her in
conjunction with the "trade out" and/
or the murder. "The long-term abusive

relationship that she suffered in affected her decision-making process-es."

In Savannah, she is in the process of securing the money that her father left her in order to start a business. No word on what type of business that would be.

2. Opal and Pearl Stone have joined forces. Pearl has dissolved her pageant and contestant consulting business. The newly created Savannah Dance and Social Arts Academy has begun to offer classes in modeling, elocution, demeanor and fashion in addition to the current dance curriculum. Looks like these two Stone sisters have "reunited". Their return to Maple Springs is doubtful.

3. Elizabeth and William White, proprietors of the Maple Springs Inn, have bought the Stone cottage (named it "The Maple Springs Cottage")...the highly valued art works belonging to the Stones, that were "traded out" and then recovered by the Sheriffs'

Department, were sold...the money
from this sale and the sale of the
cottage was claimed by the Everlasting Evangelical Spirit Church of
GA...the Whites replaced those art
works with reproductions of the sold
items as much as possible and the décor of the cottage was maintained.

    4. <u>Eileen Miller</u> began to work
full time for the Whites and main-
tains the Cottage and the Inn. Eileen will also continue to serve her
former clients with "opening" and
"closing" chores.

    (complete Section B with excite-
ment for the movement of the principals...for example, "I'd say these
folks are all well and eager to move
on.")

    C. Offer to answer questions,
note your availability and the availability of the sheriff. ("The sheriff
(or we) would welcome your questions")

Colin was pleased with the information sheet that he and
Vonny, and Sheriff Green, had assembled and he was sure that
they would be referring to the three sections as they spoke with

returning summer folk.

In less than a week all the Springers who habitually came for the whole of June, July and August would be back, ensconced for the lazy hazy days of summer on Lake Chautauqua. Colin was eager for them to arrive. He needed them to help him slip back into the carefree days of summer, to put reality into perspective. He had faced "the situation at the Stone Cottage" and he declared victory over winter, but he wanted accomplices, reinforcements, allies to embrace the summer.

There was one last meeting scheduled to finalize plans for the dedication of the Maple Springs Community Dock. G.E.M. and Selma had given the dock space on the shoreline and all the equipment (dock pieces, stanchion, lighting, furniture and awnings) for the benefit of the Maple Springs community. The planning committee had decided upon a short ceremony at the dock, the unveiling of a huge rock with "Welcome to the Lake" lasered on to one side and "A Gift from the Stone Family, lakeside residents since 1948" on the back. After the dedication ceremony, everyone would retire to the back deck of The Maple Springs Cottage (forever to be known to Springers as the Stone's Cottage) for the kick-off to the summer season, the Summer Wine Festival, again a gift of the Stones. Will and Elizabeth White would be hosting the event with assistance from the yearrounders who had met many times to plan the ceremony and the party.

The dedication and the festival were sure to bring the community together. The talking and laughing at the festival would set a pace for the summer and the reminiscences of past festivals, fourths of July, excursions, emergencies, boating adventures, picnics, fire department fund raisers, lakefront storm damage, etc. would sooth the souls of the attendees and plunge everyone into a swirl of summer activities, all guaranteed to promote R & R. Scarlet Ames and Kyle Kennedy, from Savannah, would be visiting for a week and would be present for the dedication of the community dock and the celebration of the local grape. Vonny and Colin would be their hosts. Will and Elizabeth insisted that they stay at the Maple Springs Cottage and plans for Guppy's, Tom's, the casino, etc. were in place. Bill Morris would be fetching and delivering and Joe, Neil, Rhoe, Jeff and Eileen were written on Kyle and Scarlet's metaphorical dance cards. Everyone was anxious to meet these two Savannah style southern belles. Everyone was sure that these two ladies would be more sincere, more fun and more genteel than the last visiting ladies of the south.

Acknowledgments

Writing can be a lonely process, but ultimately it is not accomplished alone. I had help getting this book to this finished state and am very grateful for that help.

Thanks Beths:

Thanks Beth Johnson for introducing me to the cozy mysteries, keeping me supplied with reading material and for encouraging me as I finessed this manuscript;

Thanks Beth Wappman for your 'down and dirty' critique of draft #1 and your helpful, cogent insights;

Thanks Beth Peyton, writer, neighbor, friend, for keeping me on task, for invaluable advice and the computer assistance I desperately needed.

Thanks:

Carrie Wolfgang, at "Novel Destination Used Book Emporium", for the encouragement and the freebee books and magazines for would-be writers;

Neil Robinson, Esq. for early legal advice, but then I "took the law into my own imagination";

Irene Terreberry, my wife, and Binnie Kurtzner, a friend, for being the first, kind readers who gave me encouragement, critique and kudos;

Debbie Basile for computer help and encouragement;

Kathy Cherry for your terrific maps that will help to draw the reader into the story and will help to give life to the wonderfulness of Maple Springs.

And thanks to Mark Pogodzinski at No Frills Buffalo for patiently guiding me through the publishing process.

I couldn't had done it without y'all.

About the Author

Robert John Terreberry (call me BOB) is a native of Niagara Falls, NY. He and his wife Irene currently live in Maple Springs, NY after residing in nearby Jamestown for 30 years. Bob served in the US Navy, is a retired Special Education teacher and spent 13 years as the Director of a Foster Grandparent Program. During the Jamestown years, Bob and Irene, were a consistent part of the theatre scene, participated in much charity fundraising and raised three children. These children are off working hard (yea, they all have great mates and health care) and are raising grandchildren for Boba and Rena (Bob and Irene) to dote on. All this and the opportunity to write a mystery series…ain't life grand?